THE CHANGE

THE
CHANGE

a novel

KIRSTEN MILLER

WILLIAM MORROW
An Imprint of HarperCollins*Publishers*

HarperCollins books may be purchased for educational, business, or sales promotional use. For information, please email the Special Markets Department at SPsales@harpercollins.com.

FIRST EDITION

Designed by Bonni Leon-Berman

Library of Congress Cataloging-in-Publication Data

Names: Miller, Kirsten, 1973- author.
Title: The change: a novel / Kirsten Miller.
Description: First edition. | New York, NY: William Morrow, [2022]
Identifiers: LCCN 2021036844 | ISBN 9780063144040 (hardback) | ISBN
  9780063144064 (ebook)
Subjects: LCGFT: Fiction.
Classification: LCC PS3613.I53984 C47 2022 | DDC 813/.6—dc23
LC record available at https://lccn.loc.gov/2021036844

ISBN 978-0-06-314404-0 (hardcover)
ISBN 978-0-06-325222-6 (international edition)

22 23 24 25 26 LSC 10 9 8 7 6 5 4 3 2 1

For Erica Waldrop,

my lifelong friend

and Inspiration,

who was always the

baddest witch around

THE CHANGE

GONE TO SEED

No one had seen the woman who lived at 256 Woodland Drive since early November. Now it was late April and the house looked abandoned. A modern masterpiece, set back from the road and surrounded by gardens, it had once been the neighborhood's biggest attraction. Real estate brokers ferrying clients contemplating a move to the suburbs had gone out of their way to drive past it. Now the gardens had grown wild and a gutter dangled from the roof. The children across the street speculated that the owner, like so many unfortunate old ladies before her, had probably been eaten by cats. Their mother assured them that couldn't have happened as she cast a worried look at the family pet.

The owner's name was Harriett Osborne, and though she wasn't new to the neighborhood, few people on Woodland Drive could claim to know her. For over a decade, she and her husband had left for work early each morning, and if they returned, it was late at night. The two would vanish completely for days at a time, but while they were gone, the house rarely seemed empty. Twice a week at nine on the dot, a small army of cleaners and gardeners descended on the property. The curtains on the tall street-facing windows were yanked open and the house's interior was revealed to all. Cars passing by often slowed or pulled over. The house developed a significant social media following after influencers christened it a monument to good taste.

When the Osbornes were profiled in the country's most prestigious shelter magazine, newsstand sales spiked in the vicinity of

Mattauk, New York. The couple had no children or dogs that would have forced them to engage with the community—and no desire to mingle with their neighbors at any of the coastal town's seafood-themed festivals. So the residents of Mattauk made do with what little they could glean from the article. Chase Osborne was the chief creative officer at a Manhattan advertising agency best known for a long-running campaign that featured a family of talking pigs. Harriett Osborne ran a rival company's new business department. They both appeared to be well-preserved specimens in their mid- to late forties. Chase had a tattoo on his neck and wore his blue suit without socks. Harriett's chunky black glasses framed intelligent eyes, and her matte red lipstick drew attention to a subtle smirk. When the attractive pair weren't off traveling the world, they split their time between their house in Mattauk and an equally stunning penthouse in Williamsburg. The Osbornes, the author of the article more than implied, were leading the kind of life readers should have been living.

Then, at some point in September, the cleaners and gardeners failed to arrive for work at the Osborne house. They were no-shows later that week as well. Once the neighbors began comparing notes, it became clear that Chase Osborne hadn't been home in a month. Not long after, on the night before Halloween, a blond woman was spotted walking up Woodland Drive in a rain-drenched velvet skirt with no coat to cover it, her feet barefoot and a pair of three-inch Acne pumps in her hands. It wasn't until she pulled out a set of keys and unlocked the front door that the witnesses realized it was Harriett Osborne.

After that, the interior of 256 Woodland remained hidden from view—and so did Harriett. She wasn't dead yet. Passersby often spotted a shadowy figure in the garden at night. When the sun was shining, she received regular visitors. The UPS man arrived every day but Sunday and deposited a mound of boxes outside her door. They would wait there for hours until no one was watching, and then somehow disappear all at once. On Tuesdays and Fridays, a young man from the grocery store would show up like clockwork at six fifteen P.M., his arms loaded with paper bags. The door would open, and he would step over the threshold, only to emerge precisely one hour later with empty hands.

IT WAS ON JUST SUCH an evening at seven fifteen that Jeremy Aversano happened to be walking a borrowed cockapoo past the Osbornes' house. He let the dog root around in the foliage while the delivery boy backed out of Harriett's drive. Just as the car reached the curb, Jeremy waved to the young man and gestured for him to stop. The window lowered and Jeremy leaned over with an avuncular smile.

"Yeah?" The delivery boy was twentysomething and movie star handsome.

"Everything okay in there?" Jeremy asked.

The young man grinned broadly, revealing an impressive assortment of teeth. "What?" He sounded both confused and amused. The vehicle reeked of pot.

"The lady inside—she doing all right?"

"You're eighty feet from her door, bro. Why don't you ask her?"

After a moment of stunned silence, Jeremy shook off his embarrassment. The kid was clearly a moron. "Forget it. Sorry to bother you."

Jeremy stepped back from the window and waited for the car to drive away. Then he looked up at the house. The sun had dipped below the horizon, but as usual, the house lights hadn't turned on. In the growing darkness, the abundant foliage felt primal and threatening. God only knew what it might be hiding. Jeremy's wife had recently filed for divorce, and their house at 261 Woodland was now on the market. An eyesore just down the street would strip thousands off their asking price. Something had to be done.

Jeremy was on the verge of marching right up to the front door and offering to mow the lady's lawn himself. But when he tugged on the cockapoo's leash, the dog resisted. Its head was still stuck in the brambles that had sprung up around the Osborne woman's lawn. Annoyed, Jeremy gave the leash a yank. The dog yelped, but refused to budge, forcing him to reel it in like a fish. When the beast's head emerged, Jeremy realized there was something clamped between its jaws. The object was fleshy, faintly gray in color, and ended in five limp fingers. The dog, whose name he could never remember, dropped its discovery at Jeremy's feet.

Later, as he was speed-walking home, Jeremy made a mental list of the neighbors who might have seen him stumbling backward into the gutter while the dog mocked him with its slobbery grin. (As it turned out, only one person had witnessed the scene. Unfortunately, that person was a twelve-year-old with a popular TikTok account, whose video of the incident would break platform records.) After the tumble, which left his Dockers stained with sludge, Jeremy had crept toward the object with his palm poised to shield his eyes. He was one hundred percent certain the dog's discovery had recently belonged to a human. Upon closer inspection, however, it appeared to be a species of mushroom. *A monstrosity*, Jeremy fumed as he cut across his own perfectly manicured lawn. If that was the kind of revolting fungus the Osborne woman was introducing to the neighborhood, the gloves would need to come off. It didn't matter *what* people whispered about her. He wasn't afraid to take her on. So as soon as he was safely inside his 1950s Cape Cod, Jeremy pulled out his phone and dialed an old friend, Brendon Baker.

UNTIL MARCH, BRENDON BAKER HAD never missed a meeting of the Mattauk Homeowners Association. His encyclopedic knowledge of the rules, and his fervor for enforcing them, had helped him rise from member to treasurer to president of the organization in record time. When he moved to Mattauk five years earlier, he'd been appalled by the town's lackadaisical approach to landscaping. In the spring, the grass on half the town's lawns had been allowed to grow far past the two-inch limit. In autumn, piles of leaves were left to molder for months. It took a single HOA gathering for Brendon to identify the problem. The board was composed of former stay-at-home moms who seemed far more interested in sourcing organic mulch for the playground or building beaches for babies than in enforcing regulations. When Brendon decided to run for a seat on the board, he went door-to-door every weekend, when he knew the husbands would be home. It was time, he convinced the men he met, for the HOA to finally get serious.

As soon as Brendon was elected president, he made good on his promise. Everyone he spoke with agreed that Mattauk had never looked better. Then, in March, complications from a hemorrhoid operation kept him home for a month. Brendon had never placed much faith in his HOA colleagues, and he knew work would pile up while he was away. But he'd never imagined that a dire situation like 256 Woodland Drive would remain unaddressed for so long.

His first day back from medical leave, Brendon walked into the HOA board meeting ten minutes late and dropped his leather messenger bag down on the table with a satisfying thump. Instead of claiming a seat, he crossed his arms over his fleshy chest and stood with his thighs pressed against the table's edge, displaying his crotch for the five women who'd been waiting. He'd done this often, even before his condition had made sitting a challenge. His fellow board members couldn't be certain he chose the posture on purpose, but all agreed it was completely revolting.

As usual, there was no chitchat. Brendon preferred to get straight to business. "Have any of you been down Woodland Drive lately?" he barked at his colleagues.

They all had. Woodland Drive was a main route to the train station. But no one in the room spoke up. They'd known this moment was coming, and they'd made a pact.

Their silence only fed Brendon's indignation. "Does anyone here know"—he glanced down at his phone and the notes he'd taken—"a woman named Harriett Osborne?"

A couple pairs of eyes inadvertently darted in the same direction.

"Celeste?" Brendon asked.

"Yes, I know her." Celeste Howard had won a seat on the board the previous fall after her youngest had started kindergarten. She was a perfect example of the kind of woman the HOA attracted, Brendon thought. Her most recent work experience was limited to changing diapers and singing nursery rhymes. He suspected that just like the rest of them, Celeste had no real interest in community management. For her, the board was a social club—and a sad attempt to justify the fancy education she'd wasted.

"Is the Osborne woman a friend of yours?" he asked.

"Harriett used to work with my husband. I can't call us friends."

Celeste considered herself more of a secret admirer. Years earlier, when Celeste and her husband had started out in the advertising business, most of their equals had been women. Then Andrew was tapped on the shoulder to become the COO's latest protégé. The higher he rose, the less estrogen there seemed to be in the atmosphere. Harriett was one of the few women who never slipped or got shoved off the ladder. She managed to hold on far longer than Celeste had. In fact, for a while, everyone had assumed Harriett would be the company's first female president.

"Last night, I received an anonymous tip from one of Harriett Osborne's neighbors," Brendon announced. As a favor, he'd promised to keep Jeremy's name out of it. Situations such as these were likely to become emotionally charged. "I have to say, I had a hard time believing what the gentleman told me. So I drove past the house, and turns out, it was true. The place is a jungle. What the hell happened to all of the gardeners?"

The question was directed at Celeste. She knew he would wait until she responded. "It seems they've stopped showing up."

"You think? And where is the husband?" Brendon asked. "My source says he hasn't been in town since last fall."

This time, Celeste refused to speak. She failed to see how Harriett's marital status had anything to do with her lawn.

"He's gone," someone else confirmed. Chase Osborne was, by all accounts, living in the couple's Brooklyn apartment with the head of his agency's production department.

Brendon nodded as if everything suddenly made sense.

"I believe Harriett might be going through a bit of a rough patch," Celeste offered. She wasn't going to give him any more than that.

THE PREVIOUS OCTOBER, CELESTE'S HUSBAND, Andrew, claimed he'd seen two security officers drag Harriett Osborne out of the advertising agency where they worked and deposit her at the curb. Rumor had it that an altercation had taken place behind the closed doors of the CEO's office. The promotion Harriett had been expecting hadn't come through, and she hadn't received the news gracefully. After hours, Andrew had peeked inside the office to confirm the stories he'd heard. The Cannes Lions and One Show pencils were back on the windowsill, but telltale gouges in the Sheetrock confirmed they had, indeed, been flung at the walls.

"I don't understand. Why would they let her go?" Celeste knew she sounded like a fan whose idol had fallen. "You always said she was excellent."

"And she is," Andrew said. "But sometimes good's not enough. The president is the face of the company. They decided to go with someone younger and fresher." Celeste was on the verge of asking the obvious follow-up question when the grin on her husband's face stopped her.

She gasped. "Oh my God, they chose you?"

"They did," he confirmed.

She had to say something. "I had no idea you were in the running!"

"Neither did I!" He seemed so thrilled that she hadn't had the heart to question their wisdom. Andrew was a decent account guy and a world-class schmoozer. But even she knew he was no Harriett Osborne.

It wasn't until after the champagne had been popped, poured, and consumed that Celeste made it back to the question she'd intended to ask.

"How old is Harriett, anyway?"

"I dunno." Andrew was already tipsy. "Forty-seven, maybe? Forty-eight?"

"You're forty-four!" Celeste briefly teetered on the edge of panic. She'd been let go from her job while pregnant with their second child. After the baby was born, Andrew had encouraged her to take time off from her career to care for the kids. The family was now dependent on his salary. "Does that mean you could be out of a job in a few more years?"

Andrew chuckled as if the suggestion were silly. "Don't worry about that, honey. It's a bit different for men." He reached out to stroke her cheek. When Celeste flinched, he must have realized he'd said the wrong thing. "It's terrible, but it's true. Now that I'm part of the leadership team, I'll be doing my best to change things."

Celeste was old enough to smell bullshit. She had recently turned forty-two.

In the six months since that moment, Andrew hadn't been home much. His days ended later. The business trips lasted longer. He always apologized. The president of an ad agency had to work harder than anyone, he told her. Celeste knew it was a lie. He was fucking someone at his office. What upset her most was that he seemed to have forgotten she'd once been in advertising, too.

AS BRENDON BAKER TURNED HIS Subaru down Woodland Drive, he had to work hard to contain his excitement. Home visits were his favorite part of the job. During the workweek, he was at the mercy of clients and committees, on an endless, hopeless quest for consensus. As the president of the homeowners association, he'd made it clear that the buck stopped with him. One of his first acts had been to fine the elderly lady on Cedar Lane who was infamous for keeping her Christmas decorations up all year round. Eventually her lien grew so large that the HOA foreclosed. After that, Brendon's word was law in Mattauk. He had the power to make people grovel if he wanted to—and he always did.

"I've changed my mind," Celeste spoke up from the passenger seat. "I don't want to go in."

"It's for your friend's sake," he reminded her. "It will be easier for Mrs. Osborne if another woman is there."

"I told you, she and I aren't friends." Celeste knew he wanted her there in case Harriett cried. "I don't even know if Harriett will remember me." It might be even worse if she did.

"How many complaints about the Osborne property did we receive while I was out sick?" Brendon inquired. It was Celeste's duty, as secretary, to keep track of them.

"A few," Celeste admitted reluctantly. She'd stopped counting at twelve.

"Those calls could be a liability for you during the next election," he said. "Things could get ugly if the Osborne woman isn't dealt with expeditiously. Word will get out that you're the one who let the situation spiral out of control, and by this time next year, you'll be back to baking muffins for the PTA."

Brendon parked along the curb in front of 256 Woodland. A line of rosebushes planted parallel to the street had grown to form an impenetrable bramble shot through with lovely red-stemmed sumac and glistening poison ivy leaves. Climbing vines scaled the house and hanging ferns of prehistoric proportions dripped over its roof, shielding the interior from view.

"How can it have gotten this bad so fast? The house looks like Grey Gardens, and it's not even May." He swiveled toward Celeste with a schadenfreude smirk. "This lady's not going to come prancing out in a leotard with a scarf on her head, is she?"

Celeste didn't dignify the question with an answer.

Brendon's sense of humor vanished when his joke flopped. "All right, let's get this over with," he ordered.

Celeste stayed put. She was calculating the distance from 256 Woodland Drive to the car she'd left parked downtown. It was almost walkable, she thought. But not quite.

"Celeste?"

She didn't want to know what had happened to Harriett. She wanted to remember Harriett as the person she'd been. She couldn't bear to see another woman brought low. Alone and abandoned. Depressed and defeated. If it could happen to Harriett, it could happen to anyone. Celeste was terrified that when the front door opened, she'd see her own future.

"Let's *go*," Brendon ordered.

And she went.

Brendon rang the doorbell and Celeste held her breath. A bee touched down on Brendon's back. Celeste watched as it walked in circles and willed it to sting.

"May I help you?"

The tall woman standing in the doorway bore little resemblance to the woman Celeste had chatted with at holiday parties. Harriett's hair hadn't been touched by a stylist in months, and its natural waves were no longer ironed out. The gray had grown in, and silvery strands mingled with blond. A smear of rich black dirt stretched from her right cheekbone to the ear. She wore an army-green mechanic's jumpsuit, its sleeves rolled up past her elbows and the zipper pulled down just enough to reveal the top of a black sports bra. Her arms looked lean and strong. One of her hands held a half-eaten apple.

"Celeste Howard," Harriet said, her smile exposing a significant gap between her two front teeth. It was such a distinguishing feature that Celeste was amazed she hadn't noticed it before. Together with eyes that seemed unusually focused and a mouth that stretched from ear to ear, the gap gave Harriett a feral, hungry look. "What a pleasure to see you."

"Harriett." Celeste hadn't expected to be remembered, and found herself at a loss for words. "You look so different."

"Yes," Harriett readily agreed. "I've really let myself go."

"That's not what I meant!" Celeste rushed to clarify.

Harriett placed a hand on the younger woman's shoulder, sending a wave of heat down Celeste's arm. "I know what you meant," she said.

Brendon stepped forward. Celeste noticed he seemed less sure of himself. Whatever he'd been expecting wasn't at all what he'd found. "We'd like to have a word with you, if you don't mind. May we come in?"

As Harriett's attention migrated slowly to the man, the smile remained on her face. "Do I know you?" she asked, her head cocked, like a cat contemplating a roach.

Brendon offered a hand, which Harriett regarded with amusement but didn't deign to touch. "My name is Brendon Baker." He let his hand drop. "I'm president of the Mattauk Homeowners Association."

"Ah," Harriett replied, as if that were enough and she didn't care to know any more. "So how have you been, Celeste? You certainly look well."

Celeste blushed. It felt like it had been ages, she realized, since anyone had given her their full attention. "I am well. And you?"

"I've been busy." Harriett took a bite of her apple and chewed leisurely before continuing. "Very busy, in fact. I've been catching up on my reading. There are so many fascinating subjects I never had time to explore. Botany, primarily, but also—"

"Excuse me, Mrs. Osborne—" Brendon cut in.

"*Ms.*," Harriett corrected him, without glancing in his direction.

"Of course. *Ms.* Osborne. We're here to talk to you about the state of your property. I'm afraid we've had multiple complaints. I'm aware you've suffered some setbacks lately, but you will need to resume maintenance of your house and lawn or we will be forced to impose fines."

Mortified, Celeste turned her gaze to the porch, where a colony of black ants was following a twisting trail up a railing. Then she heard Harriett laugh, and looked up to see that the amusement appeared genuine.

"How about that? We've only just met, and yet you know so much about me." Harriett leaned lazily against the doorframe. "How do you do it, Mr. Baker? Are you psychic? Have you hacked into my accounts? Or are you just one of those men who thinks he's an expert on women?"

Celeste had made other house calls with Brendon. She'd heard terrified owners plead with or praise him. Harriett was the first to belittle him. She must have known Brendon had the power to make her life miserable, but she wasn't going to kneel down before him.

"I apologize if my assumptions were incorrect," Brendon said flatly, his true feelings revealed by the flush creeping up past his shirt collar. "Regardless of your financial situation, something must be done about the state of your lawn."

"No." She said it firmly, without anger or urgency.

"No?" Brendon repeated, as if he weren't familiar with the word.

Harriett swept an arm toward the horizon. "This is the way it wants to be," she replied.

"Less than a year ago, this property was the pride of Mattauk." Brendon tried trading vinegar for honey. "Your gardeners were here twice a week."

"Poisoning the earth with their weed killers and pesticides. All so my former husband could feel like he'd conquered nature. Chase was so happy when you took over the HOA, Mr. Baker. He used to phone in anonymous complaints several times a week. You two would love each other. He's an uptight little prick as well. No doubt you're both compensating for the same deficiency."

For a moment, it didn't sound like an insult. It simply seemed like a statement of fact. Then Harriett let her eyes roll down to Brendon's crotch, where they lingered for a moment before returning to his reddening face.

Brendon stiffened his spine and puffed out his chest as though trying to appear larger. "You have a legal obligation to maintain this property and abide by the community's landscaping regulations."

"You're wrong, Mr. Baker." Harriett studied her apple for a spot to bite. "My house predates the homeowners association. My ex-husband voluntarily signed the agreement when the property was in his name. Now the house belongs solely to me, and I never signed anything."

"But you're still bound by—"

Harriett sighed and shook her head as if he were wasting her time. "No," she said. "I checked. For the first time in my life, I'm not bound by anything."

"We'll see," Brendon fumed. "Our lawyers will be in touch. Come along, Celeste."

Harriett sank her teeth into the apple and watched with amusement as Brendon stomped down the drive.

"'Come along, Celeste'?" she repeated as she chewed. "Why would someone like you take orders from someone like that?" Harriett made it sound like one of the great mysteries of the universe.

"I honestly don't know," Celeste admitted. Brendon got in the car, slammed the door, and turned on the engine. "I should probably go. I rode here with him."

"I think you'd be much happier if you stayed here with me." Harriett reached out and slid a hand down the slope from Celeste's shoulder to her elbow. She let it linger there for a moment, her fingers cupping the joint and her thumb pressed against the throbbing vein at the arm's crease.

Though the offer seemed clear enough, Celeste was sure she'd misheard. "But you know my husband—"

Harriett cocked her head again and grinned. "What does any of this have to do with him?"

Celeste was stunned to find herself unable to answer. Surely, she thought, it had *something* to do with Andrew. After all, she'd married for love, and that love hadn't died. She remained fond of her husband. She'd just grown to see romance for what it was—a sappy-sweet fantasy she'd entertained in her youth, like fairies or the Easter Bunny. Though she felt nostalgia for those early days, her marriage had become a financial arrangement. She remained devoted to keeping up her side of the deal. She would ensure that the children were happy and healthy. Their home would continue to run efficiently. For several wonderful years, the agreement had included exclusive access to each other's bodies. But Celeste's had come to feel like her own once again.

That's why she wasn't hurt by Andrew's affair, she realized.

That's why she'd never asked her husband who was he seeing after work—or who accompanied him on all his business trips. For a while, she'd wondered if she was afraid to have those questions answered. Now Celeste knew the truth—as long as Andrew upheld his end of the bargain, she just didn't care. Andrew was her business partner. What Harriett was offering was something quite different.

"I QUIT THE HOMEOWNERS ASSOCIATION," Celeste informed her husband later that night.

"Oh?" he replied, without looking up from his phone. Now that his salary was in the high six figures, her decisions were of little consequence. "Good for you, darling."

"I spent some time with Harriett Osborne today."

That got his attention. "With Harriett? Poor thing. How's she doing?"

"Well," Celeste said, "I think she and I are going to hang out more often."

"Doing what?" His lack of imagination had always amused her.

"Lady things," Celeste replied with a smile.

"Are you sure she's not out to—" He stopped. "I mean, do you think she might be—" He was smart enough not to give voice to his hunch—that Harriett was out to get even with him for the job she'd lost. If nothing else, she had to know that befriending his wife would unsettle him. Why else would a woman like Harriett want to spend time with Celeste?

His wife chuckled lightheartedly. "No, Andrew," she told him. "My relationship with Harriett doesn't have anything to do with you."

HOT AND BOTHERED

Holy shit." Jo Levison cackled and let her Toyota Highlander slow to a stop. "What the fuck is going on over there?"

"Come on, Jo," her husband groaned. "Language?"

"That's nothing," droned eleven-year-old Lucy from the back seat. "She says way worse when you're not around."

"Snitch!" Jo stuck out her tongue at the rearview mirror.

"She's not the only one," Art chided their daughter. "I've heard you two talking when you think you're alone. It's like listening to a couple of Hells Angels."

"Yeah, well, sometimes *fuck* is the only word that will do," Jo said. "You'd know just how appropriate it is in this case if you bothered to put down your fucking phone."

Art finished what he was typing and peered over the rim of his reading glasses. When he cracked up, Jo had no choice but to join him. His booming laugh was one of the reasons she'd fallen in love with him in the first place. He could be such a prig at times, it was a relief to know he still had a sense of humor.

"What the hell is he doing?"

Brendon Baker was out on his lawn, yanking at the stem of an enormous weed that had consumed an entire flower bed. Jo had driven past his house just the previous day and nothing had seemed amiss. She certainly hadn't noticed a giant, wicked-looking plant with toothed leaves, long white flowers, and egg-shaped seedpods covered in spikes.

"It's like something out of *Jurassic Park*," Lucy marveled.

They watched as Brendon tried to uproot the plant from a different angle. He bent over to grasp the stem at its base, exposing pasty white flesh and a fur-lined ass crack. Lucy and Jo both made retching noises.

"How would you describe the theme of this scene?" Art asked their daughter.

"The epic struggle of man against nature?"

Art turned to Jo and raised a pompous eyebrow. He'd been helping Lucy with her homework lately.

"I was going to say karmic justice," Art said, "but sure—'the epic struggle' works too."

The previous summer, the Levison family had been forced to pay a two-hundred-dollar fine when Art hadn't found the energy to mow the grass one week. At the time, Jo couldn't figure out who infuriated her most: her husband, who literally had nothing else to do, or the sadist who'd been waiting for Art to neglect one of his few remaining duties.

"Well, I say the motherfucker's getting what he deserves."

"Jo." Art gestured toward the child sitting behind them. "You really want her speaking that way?"

"I wasn't aware we were raising her to marry into the royal family," Jo said. "Lucy, darling, which of the princes do you prefer? Gorgeous George or Luscious Louie? Though if you like Cuddly Charlotte, that's lovely, too."

"Which one of them is going to be king?" Lucy asked with characteristic bluntness.

"George," Jo informed her.

"Then I'd choose George, throw him in jail on our wedding night, and take over the United Kingdom."

Jo swiveled around to give her daughter a high-five.

"You're setting a bad example." Art was serious. He never knew when to let it go.

"How exactly am I setting a bad example?" Jo felt her palms grow damp against the steering wheel. The bubbling pocket of heat beneath her sternum began to spread through her body. "I'm raising my daughter to be strong and speak her mind."

"You're raising *our* daughter to get kicked out of sixth grade."

Jo wheeled around toward him, ready to retaliate.

"Fuck the sixth grade," said Lucy. "Didn't we just decide that I'm gonna be queen?"

The car went silent. Then all three howled with laughter. Thirty feet away, Brendon Baker paused his labors and glanced over his shoulder. Lucy ducked below the window and the Levison family laughed even louder as Jo hit the gas and sped away.

LATER THAT EVENING, JO THOUGHT through the exchange as she stood in the kitchen with her second glass of red wine, waiting for a pot of water to boil. She and Art had narrowly avoided a confrontation, but others were sure to follow. Even when Jo knew one was coming, it still blindsided her. She always walked away feeling like she'd been T-boned at an intersection, and it wasn't always clear who'd run the red light. Since she'd become the family's sole breadwinner, the arguments had become an everyday occurrence. Art felt powerless, so he criticized Jo to drag her down to his level. It was all so pathetically transparent, and the unfairness made Jo want to rip him to shreds. She'd taken on the burden of supporting the family only to find herself tending to his fragile ego as well. She loved Art too much to point that out. She just wished he'd get a fucking job.

Jo heard Lucy whoop and glanced over at her husband and daughter. Lucy was on her feet, pumping her fists triumphantly over the Scrabble board while Art bowed down before her. He was an excellent father—warm, attentive, and eager to teach—just as her own father had been. Jo wanted that for her daughter, even if it meant carrying more of the family load. When her business had taken off, Art had resigned from his editing job to pursue his dream of being a playwright. She'd gone along with the plan, assuming he would be taking on more of the housework and childcare duties. Instead, she came home to a filthy house, a hungry child, and a husband who sometimes forgot to shower for days.

When the fights first began, Art swore he'd try harder. Home-making just didn't come naturally to him, he said. Dinners were burned. Bills went unpaid. Lucy was often forgotten at school. And slowly, chore by chore, Jo resumed doing it all. In the meantime, Art's plays weren't being produced. His agent dropped him. And thanks to a crippling case of writer's block, he hadn't typed a single word in months. Jo didn't want to add to his worries. She prayed to whatever gods might be listening that Art would get his big break and they could go back to having a functioning partnership— before her rage detonated and destroyed them both.

At two o'clock in the morning, Jo woke up drenched in sweat, just as she had almost every night for over a year. She climbed out of bed, stripped out of her T-shirt, and left her yoga pants in a heap by the side of the bed. Bare-chested and wearing only her underwear, she walked out onto the master bedroom's balcony and stood spread-eagled in the chilly late-spring air. Jo could have sworn she saw steam rising from her muscular limbs. She no longer questioned what was possible. Her body had become a constant source of amazement, even pride. She didn't duck back inside when a faint glow lit the trees at the edge of her lawn. It grew brighter until a car's headlights appeared. A slight swivel of his neck, and the driver would see Jo standing there, her naked chest exposed to the elements. But it felt too good to go in. And she'd already given up giving a shit.

As soon her temperature dropped to the normal range for a human, Jo returned to the bedroom and sat cross-legged on the floor.

She sensed every atom in her body pulsating. Her nerves buzzed, her synapses crackled, and loaded blood cells raced through her vessels. She'd never be able to sleep right away. Jo closed her eyes and laid her hands in her lap, palms facing up. She visualized the energy coursing through her body's passageways, traveling up and out through the crown of her head, then cascading around her in a shower of silvery sparks. It was all part of Jo's regular meditation routine. But for the first time, she experienced a strange sensation in the palms of her hands. She could feel the presence of a fiery ball hovering just above them. Had her eyes been open, she would have seen the bathroom light flicker.

When she climbed back into bed, Art rolled over and threw an arm across her waist. "Everything okay, naked lady?"

"Yeah." She hadn't planned to say any more, but it all came out at once. "I was meditating, and it felt like I generated a ball of fire in my hands. I swear to God, Art, I could literally feel it."

"Hmmm," Art mumbled sleepily. "That's great, honey. But can I be honest with you?"

"Sure," she said warily.

"That's the dumbest superpower I've ever heard of."

Jo couldn't stop laughing while he kissed her, and she didn't stop until his pants were off and he was inside her. That was one thing about their relationship that kept getting better.

FOR YEARS, THE ONLY GYM in Mattauk had been a meat market for the recently divorced and soon to be single, where the women wore thousand-dollar outfits and meticulous contouring while middle-aged men pumped and preened for the mirrors. Jo had driven to a dingy old gym in a neighboring town to avoid the scene. Dressed in ten-dollar Old Navy sweatpants and an army surplus tank top, she would climb on a bike and ride until the rage burned off. There was nothing pretty about it. Back then, she was still managing a hotel in Manhattan. On top of her long hours, she spent an hour at the gym every day after work. Art bitched and moaned a few times until she explained that her workouts had probably saved his life. The more time she spent at the gym, the less likely he was to end up buried in the backyard he never bothered to mow.

As the months passed, Jo began to spot more of her neighbors at the run-down gym. Every one of them was a woman her age. Their choice of equipment varied. Some stuck to the treadmill; others showed an unsettling devotion to a particular elliptical. While they worked out, Jo watched their lips form silent curses and their fists punch the air. She saw them walk in wearing prim professional attire and later head for the showers with crimson faces and hair plastered to the sides of their heads. And Jo realized her fellow women had all driven miles out of their way for the same reason she had. They were blowing off steam before they exploded.

Jo saw an opportunity, and for the first time in her life, she leaped on it before anyone else could snatch it away.

She called her gym Furious Fitness. It took up two stories of an old five-and-dime on Mattauk's main street and accepted only women as members. Jo hired the two hottest male trainers from the meat market gym to offer private sessions, but her other employees were all female. Even though Art wasn't allowed in the building during business hours, he had been supportive of the enterprise from the very beginning. She waited until the gym was a success to confess that she'd liquidated her 401(k). Fortunately, it didn't take long to get the business up and running. Jo knew how to give her clients exactly what they were after—and it wasn't exercise. Almost all of them wanted things to punch, pound, and kick. Even in the dead of winter, her air-conditioning bill was often higher than the rent. The energy released in that one little building could have powered most of Mattauk—or, as Jo sometimes fantasized, burned the whole fucking town down.

JO WAS AT THE FRONT desk when the latest newcomer walked in. She could spot the newbies a mile away. They were almost always in their mid- to late forties, and they all arrived looking lost. No wonder, Jo thought. For decades, they'd been dutifully following the map the world laid out for them. School led to work. Dating led to marriage and then to motherhood. But now those milestones were behind them, and they'd entered uncharted territory. Somewhere in the distance lay the final destination, but that was decades away, and a featureless wasteland seemed to stretch in between. These women, who'd done everything that had ever been asked of them, now felt forsaken. Just when they were reaching the height of their powers, they felt like life had led them astray.

The newcomer approached the counter, where Jo was helping another client. She was wholesome-looking and pretty, with shoulder-length black curls and a large, lovely butt. She wore leggings and a silky pink shirt that would never survive in the wash.

"I'll be with you in just a minute," Jo told her, assuming the woman was there for a membership. She usually took newbies under her wing for their first visit. "Have a look around if you like. If I take too long, just go ahead and hop on a machine and knock yourself out."

"Okay." The woman smiled shyly, revealing a sweet set of dimples just before she backed away.

Jo kept watch out of the corner of her eye as the woman made her way around the ground floor. She saw her pause at the base of the stairs, glance anxiously toward the second floor, and then retreat to a treadmill near the entrance. She climbed on and stood with a finger hovering a few inches from the screen.

"Just start walking and the machine will guide you through setup," Jo called out.

Thank you, the woman mouthed gratefully, as though she'd been spared from great embarrassment. Jo watched until she was walking at a steady clip, then turned her attention back to her other client. By the time she made it over to the newbie, the woman was walking with a limp.

"What happened?" Jo reached over to the control panel and brought the treadmill to a halt. "Did you get hurt? Can I help?"

"Oh no, it's nothing." The woman smiled through her agony. "Just a cramp in my calf. Not much you can do."

Jo knew who she was dealing with. The sweet-tempered stoic was a common type. They'd pass out from pain before they dared complain. "Mind if I try?" Jo asked. "I've been told I have magic hands."

The woman stared at Jo with such intensity that Jo wondered if she was attempting to read her mind. "Okay," she finally said, and sat down at the end of the machine.

Jo gripped the woman's calf between her hands and let her palms grow hot.

The woman's eyes widened. "You weren't joking. How do you do that?"

Jo winked at her. "I channel my hot flashes. Dunno about you, but when I get one, I swear I could poach an egg in my fist."

The woman laughed. "I was spared the hot flashes. I got the weight gain instead. Believe it or not, I used to be an itty-bitty thing."

"Didn't we all," Jo said. "Don't know about you, but I like taking up more space. I'm Jo Levison, by the way."

"Nessa James," the woman replied, grimacing as Jo honed in on the source of her pain.

"You get cramps like this often, Nessa?"

"I've never worked out before," Nessa confessed.

Jo never laughed at anything her clients told her. She knew that for many of them, Furious Fitness was one of the few places where they were always taken seriously. "Well, that explains it. Why'd you decide to start today?"

"I didn't. I mean, not really. I get these impulses sometimes, and today I ended up here." Nessa threw up her hands as if to suggest she was quirky, not crazy. "I'm glad I did, though. Last time I saw the doctor, he told me I needed to get more exercise because he said I'm—" She cleared her throat to make room for the word that came next. "Overweight."

Jo often wondered if some of the doctors around Mattauk had chosen the profession so they'd have an excuse to humiliate women. She counseled her clients not to go through menopause with a male doctor, who was more likely to see it as a condition to be treated than an evolution to be embraced. "Yeah, well, that's his opinion," she said. "You ever gotten any complaints?"

Nessa giggled like a girl. "Nope."

"Then fuck that asshole." The words slipped out, and Jo glanced up nervously. "Sorry about the language."

"Why?" Nessa asked. "I look like some kind of prude to you?"

"No," Jo said. "But you do strike me as the upstanding, church-going type."

Nessa had never gotten so much as a speeding ticket, and she could be found sitting in the third pew of the town's Baptist church every Sunday. "I've read the Bible a few times," Nessa admitted. "I wouldn't say I'm an expert when it comes to scripture, but as far as I know, Jesus never had a problem with the word *fuck*."

This time, Jo had to laugh. "Was that the first time you've said it out loud?" she asked on a hunch.

Nessa grinned. "Not exactly." But it wasn't something she said on a regular basis.

Jo leaned toward her conspiratorially. "Felt good to get it out, didn't it?" she stage-whispered, then sat back on her haunches. "What do you say you and I add some good old-fashioned cussing to our workout routine?"

"You're a trainer?" Nessa asked. "I thought you owned this place."

"I do, but training gives me an excuse to work out. I wouldn't have started a gym if I didn't need one more than anyone else." That may have been true, but Jo hadn't accepted a client in over a year. And Nessa was a newbie. Even a less experienced trainer would have a great deal to teach her. But there was something about Nessa's presence that soothed Jo. For the five minutes they'd been chatting, she'd felt remarkably calm. There was no one in sight that she wanted to kill.

She stopped kneading Nessa's calf. "That better now?"

Nessa looked down at her calf as if she'd almost forgotten it was there. "It is. You're amazing."

"Take it easy for the rest of the day." Jo stood up and offered Nessa a hand. "Then how about you and I get started tomorrow at five?"

"That sounds good." Nessa seemed surprised that the conversation was over. "But before you go, I gotta be honest with you. I didn't come here for the exercise. I think I'm here to see you."

"Me?" Jo asked, just as a man brushed past her with the gym's assistant manager trailing behind him.

"Sir, sir!" the assistant manager called out, but the man kept on going. Despite the sign on the front door that made it clear that Furious Fitness was a women-only environment, they would still get the occasional male visitor. It was hard for some men to understand there were places in the world where they weren't wanted.

"Excuse me," Jo told Nessa. "I'll be right back."

She caught up to her employee and gave her a sign that she'd take over from there. Then she stood her ground and waited. Most of the men who made their way into Furious were there to leer. This one appeared to be on a mission. His head swiveled from side to side on his thick neck as though he were searching for someone. He wasn't a giant, but he was powerfully built. He looked like a man whose muscles might be his meal ticket.

Jo watched as he hit the back wall of the ground floor and came marching out again toward the stairs to the second floor.

"May I help you?"

The man would have stormed right past if Jo hadn't blocked the way with a hand held out in front of her. His momentum came to a halt when he made contact with her palm. He glanced down at her hand in surprise before meeting her eyes. Jo held his gaze without blinking until he looked away. She felt the energy streaming down the arteries of her arm toward her fingers. The gym went silent, aside from the pop music piped over the speakers. Her clients had paused their workouts to watch. Their faces glowed, their eyes sparkled, and the corners of their mouths twitched with glee. They wanted to see the man taken down. Jo wished she felt as confident as her clients. She'd only used her power twice before—both times by accident. She still wasn't convinced that either incident had been more than a fluke.

"I'm sure my colleague informed you this gym is for women only," Jo said.

"I did!" the furious assistant manager confirmed. "I told him five times!"

"I'm looking for someone," the man said, his eyes now everywhere in the room but her face. He wanted her to know their conversation was beneath him.

"Who?" Jo demanded. Whoever it was, Jo would want to warn her.

The man didn't see any need to respond. She was nothing to him but a momentary inconvenience. He'd barged into her business, ignoring Jo's signs and insulting her employee. They were just women, after all, and he owed them nothing, least of all his respect.

"I'm afraid you'll have to go," Jo informed the man, hoping he'd leave without a fight.

"I'll finish looking," he told her. "*Then* I'll go."

A blast of red-hot rage shot through her veins and left her cells boiling. "I'm sorry. Maybe you didn't understand. By *leave*, I mean get the fuck out of here. *Now.*"

"Step out of the way," the man ordered. "This doesn't concern you."

Jo glanced back at Nessa, who already had her phone to her ear.

"I hope you're dialing an ambulance," another client called out from a treadmill, "'cause if that motherfucker touches Jo, he's going to need one."

Before Jo could turn back around, he came at her with his shoulder dropped slightly, as though breaking down a door. The force sent Jo stumbling back a few steps. Then she surged forward, her body acting of its own volition. She smashed the heel of her hand into his face, grabbed his arm, and effortlessly flipped him over her back. He landed faceup on the floor, his head pinned to the mat by the heel of Jo's Nike trainer on his neck. Blood gushed from his nose and ran in rivulets down the sides of his face. Rage and fear coursed through Jo's body. Every part of her vibrated with energy. The muscles of her raised thigh shook with it. She could destroy him. And she wanted to. When she pressed down harder with her sneaker, the release felt almost orgasmic.

The women watching were riveted. They'd all been in her place at one time or another. They wanted her to kill him, too.

"Don't." Nessa's soft, soothing voice washed over her. "Not now."

Just then, Jo sensed new eyes on her. She glanced up, past Nessa's worried face, and found a woman standing frozen on the staircase. Rosamund was one of the gym's warm-weather clients. Jo couldn't recall ever seeing her in the winter. In late spring and summer, Rosamund showed up every afternoon at four o'clock and pounded the treadmill for ninety minutes straight. She'd exchanged fewer than two dozen words with Jo—or anyone else at the gym, as far as Jo could tell. When she ran, Rosamund didn't wear headphones or watch TV. She kept her eyes focused on an imaginary spot in the distance, and only the alarm on her smartwatch would bring her to a stop.

Now she locked eyes with Jo. Her fingers were latched onto the staircase railing so tightly that her knuckles were white. There was little doubt she was the one being hunted. Jo nodded and her client bolted down the stairs, out the door, and into the evening. Flashing red lights swirled on the ceiling as a police car pulled up in front of the gym.

Two officers entered. One was an old hand named Tony Perretta who'd gone to high school with Jo and whose youngest son was classmates with Lucy. At his side was a lanky kid named Jones who looked far too green for his uniform. Perretta escorted the intruder outside while Jones stayed indoors and nervously scribbled notes as Jo offered her account of the incident. She kept an eye on Perretta in the parking lot, where his conversation with the suspect quickly evolved from professional to practically chummy. A few minutes later, the older cop returned to the gym, leaving the man leaning casually against the side of his car, dabbing at his bloody schnoz with a Kleenex.

"What the hell are you doing!" Jo demanded. "That asshole

barged into my business and attacked me and you're leaving him out there on his own?"

"Jones, go outside and keep an eye on our guy while I have a word with Ms. Levison," Perretta ordered the younger man. Then he gestured for Jo to join him away from her clients and employees.

"He shoved me, Tony," Jo argued once they were on their own. "I know the law, goddammit. That's assault."

When Perretta replied in a low voice, Jo knew he was going to piss her off. Men always lowered their voices when they tried to talk sense into you. "He claims you were blocking the exit and he was just trying to get past you."

"And you're taking his word for it? Did you bother to ask any of the fifty women who witnessed what happened? Would you like a look at the security tapes? Who is this guy, anyway, Tony? One of your fucking poker buddies?"

The cop raised his eyebrows to let her know she was pushing it. "His name's Chertov, and I've never spoken to the guy before in my life. I've made it pretty clear that he'll be in deep shit if he ever comes back here. Though considering the ass-kicking you gave him, it seems pretty unlikely he'll try. I don't think you need to be concerned for your safety, Jo."

"He was hunting for one of my clients. What are you going to do to protect her?"

"You're talking about Rosamund Harding?" Perretta asked, and Jo nodded. "Then there's no need to protect her. Chertov works for her husband."

"I don't give a damn who pays the thug's salary. She bolted out the door when she saw him. She obviously didn't want him to find her."

Perretta sighed wearily and leaned in closer. "Look, I'll arrest Chertov if you ask me to. But he'll be out in less than an hour—and you'll be starting something you might not be able to finish. Take my word for it, Jo, you don't want this to go any further."

"Why not?"

"Your client's husband is Spencer Harding," the cop said.

"So?" Jo demanded. "Is that name supposed to mean something? Who is he?"

"You know that empty lot down on Ocean Avenue—the one where the Italian restaurant used to be?"

"Yeah," Jo said, bemused by the sudden turn the conversation had taken.

"Five years ago, the man who ran it was out for a jog with his dog. A passing car swerved and hit the dog. It could have been an accident, but the driver kept going—didn't even bother to stop. As you can imagine, the dog's owner was pissed as hell, so he did some detective work and found a surveillance camera that had caught the whole thing. He got the car's license plate and filed suit against the owner. The case was settled for a few thousand dollars, and the guy figured everything was over and done with. Then, the same day he received the settlement check, he got word that the building that housed his restaurant had been sold to an anonymous buyer, and he had two days to vacate the premises. The same night the restaurant closed for good, the building was bulldozed. It's been an empty lot for the last five years."

"Let me guess. The car that hit the man's dog was owned by Spencer Harding?"

"That's right, and Chertov is his bodyguard."

"His bodyguard?" Jo scoffed. "Who the hell is this guy—some kind of mobster?"

"No," Perretta said. "Just a man with enough money to always get his way."

DAYS LATER, JO WAS STILL infuriated. Even the smoothie in her hand and Nessa's presence couldn't cool her down.

"What was I supposed to do?" she asked as they drove along the winding road through Nessa's neighborhood. "Lose everything I've built over the last three years just to make a point?"

The two women had become fast friends, despite the fact that they had nothing in common. Less than a week had passed since they'd met, and they'd already developed a routine. Each afternoon, Nessa would walk down to the gym, they'd work out for an hour, then grab Purple Haze smoothies before Jo drove Nessa home.

"You called the Harding guy's wife," Nessa said. "You warned her."

"Yeah." Rosamund Harding had politely thanked Jo for calling and assured her it was all a misunderstanding. But she hadn't been back to the gym since. "Maybe I'm just paranoid. I looked up Spencer Harding. He's an art dealer, for God's sake, not some kind of supervillain. But why is he sending some thug to hunt down his wife? It's like the start of a *Newsnight* episode. This kind of shit is how women end up getting hurt. I shouldn't have let the bodyguard get away with it."

"Well, he didn't get away with it *completely*," Nessa pointed out. "You did kick his ass."

Jo gasped. "Nessa," she said. "Did you just say *ass*?"

"I did," Nessa responded proudly, like a kid holding out a straight-A report card.

"Sweetheart, that is some motherfucking *excellent* progress."

"Awww, thanks, baby," Nessa cooed. "I owe it all to you."

Jo turned her eyes back to the road and whistled. "Would you look at that." She slowed the car down to appreciate the sight of Brendon Baker's yard. A week had passed since she'd spotted Brendon doing battle with the giant plant in his lawn. Now no trace remained of his perfect green carpet of grass. Weeds bursting with spiny seedpods or shiny black berries now competed for every square inch of space. Poison ivy climbed the trees, and thick green stalks shot out of the earth, exploding into umbrellas of little white blooms ten feet off the ground. "Those giant flowers weren't here the last time I drove by. I like them. They add a certain Seussian touch."

"You haven't spent much time in the country, have you? That's hogweed," Nessa informed her. "Brush up against it, and it'll scar you for life. The rest of those plants are dangerous, too. Nightshade. Jimson weed. Hemlock. The guy who mows my lawn told me all the landscapers think Baker's been cursed. That's one of the reasons he can't pay anyone to come clear it out."

"One of the reasons?" Jo was loving it. "What are the others?"

"Well, look at it! No one wants to mess with a thing of beauty. The tyrant of the HOA gets kicked to the curb for failing to obey his own rules? That's some first-class poetic justice right there," Nessa said. "Serves him right for harassing that woman."

"Harriett Osborne," Jo said.

The name, said out loud, seemed to cast a spell of its own. "You ever meet her?" Nessa asked.

"A long time ago. If I thought she'd remember me, I'd go knock on her door and shake her damn hand. Getting Brendon Baker kicked off the HOA board was the best thing that's happened to Mattauk in years."

"He's still telling anyone who'll listen that she's responsible for destroying his lawn." Nessa looked over at Jo. "What do you think?"

"I think if you're gonna go around saying shit like that, you better have proof. There have to be a thousand security cameras between here and her house. As far as I know, not a single one of them got a picture of Harriett Osborne," Jo said. Then she smirked. "Though I'm not sure that means she's innocent. Have you seen her property lately?"

"She lives half a mile from me. I walk past it every night," Nessa said.

"Harriett's got quite a green thumb."

"That's the other reason nobody wants to help clean up Brendon's yard. They say the Osborne lady has powers. Nobody wants to get in her way."

"Do *you* think she has powers?" Jo asked carefully, feeling her friend out. She'd considered telling Nessa about the ball of fire, but she hadn't quite worked up the nerve.

"Seems pretty obvious to me," Nessa said. "Brendon Baker messed with the wrong bitch."

THE QUIET LIFE

The moment Nessa entered her house and shut the front door behind her, the silence surrounded her. As always, she stood still in the foyer, closed her eyes, and listened. It was still there. When she'd first heard it weeks ago, the sound had been so faint that Nessa needed days to identify it. Now it was louder—the crash of waves. For a while, she'd held out hope that it might just be the ocean. She asked the neighbors if they heard it too. They politely reminded her that the nearest beach was more than three miles away.

Yesterday, Nessa had heard something new—a whisper that seemed to roll in with the waves. *Here,* a girl said. Over three decades had passed since Nessa's ears had picked up anything like it. Still, she knew it was a message, and she knew what it meant. Someone was lost and wanted to be found.

Her grandmother Dolores called it the gift. Before Nessa was born, Dolores had started a tradition that no one in the family dared abandon. Every time one of Dolores's granddaughters turned twelve, the girl was required to spend a summer with her in South Carolina. Despite their protests, granddaughters had been shipped down from all over the country. Nessa's cousin Melinda, whose parents were both in the army, had been flown in from Japan. Nessa was the sixth girl to go. Before she boarded the train, she'd met her grandmother only twice.

That was the year she learned what she'd inherited. One night, she'd woken to hear a woman moaning. It wasn't her grandmother, and the two of them were alone in the house. She knew the sound came from far away, somewhere in the swampy wilderness beyond town. But the moan held such misery and pain, there was no thought of ignoring it. A woman out there in the darkness needed help. When Nessa went to get her grandmother, she found Dolores in the living room slipping into her sandals.

"You hear that?" her grandmother asked the twelve-year-old girl.

Nessa nodded, not sure if it was a good thing.

"Should have known. It's always the quiet ones," her grandmother said. "Go on, then. Get your shoes."

The air outside was so thick, they might as well have been swimming. They could see the whole universe in the sky above. They hadn't taken a flashlight. Neither one of them had ever been afraid of the dark. Mosquitoes buzzed around but only seemed to bite Nessa. She swatted them away and never once thought about turning back. Her grandmother was a serious, hardworking woman who'd never been prone to fits of fancy. Wherever she was going was important, and she wouldn't have let Nessa come unless her presence was necessary.

They followed the sound down one road, then another. Her grandmother seemed to hear it more clearly. She walked with a limp—a leg broken in her youth hadn't been set properly—but she moved quickly, even when the asphalt turned to gravel and the gravel to dirt. They were miles from town, with only a single forlorn house far away in the distance, when Nessa's grandmother turned off the road and into the swamp.

They waded through waist-deep water that Nessa knew for a fact harbored snakes and gators. But her grandmother charged forward without fear and Nessa stayed by her side. They found the woman floating facedown on a clump of swamp grass. Dolores gently rolled the body over and brushed the wet hair from her face. She had been beaten too badly to identify. Her tangerine dress was torn straight down the front. Its tattered edges rippled with the water.

Nessa spotted a young woman wearing a ruffled orange dress perched in a tree a few feet away, looking down at the body. Dolores saw her too and sighed.

"Dear God. It's Loretta's daughter." She bowed her head and said a silent prayer. "You can go now, baby, I'll tell your mama where you are," she called out, and the girl in the tree disappeared.

"She's dead." Nessa was horrified. "We didn't reach her in time."

"She was dead when she called to us," her grandmother told her. "She wanted to be found. She would have stayed here until someone stumbled across her. I'll go see her family tonight. Let them know where she is."

"Someone did this to her. Shouldn't we call the police?" Nessa asked.

Her grandmother gave Nessa the same look Nessa had been getting from people since she'd traveled down south—a mix of sorrow and surprise, with a hint of envy. The world she came from wasn't perfect; far from it. But it was still so very different from theirs. "No, baby. That's why she wanted us to come. Men like that won't care about a poor girl like her."

"Still." Nessa couldn't just let it go. "Whoever did this has got to be punished."

"That's not our job. There are other women who see to that."

"Who?" Nessa demanded.

"'Round here, it's my friend Miss Ella."

Miss Ella was an old white lady who lived in a fishing shack that her granddaddy had built on an island in the middle of the swamp. You needed a boat to reach her, and given the gator population, it wouldn't have been smart to leave your gun at home, either. But none of that kept a steady stream of visitors from knocking on her door—and anyone with the guts to visit was always welcomed.

She was the only one around who knew where to dig up the plants that could soothe a fever or how to grind the roots that would set an enemy's insides ablaze. Nessa had met her once already, outside the church where Nessa's grandmother claimed a spot in the second pew every Wednesday and Sunday. Miss Ella had given the girl a good looking over.

"This grandbaby's special," she'd told Nessa's grandmother before heading off toward the swamp. Miss Ella had no time for church—and wouldn't have been welcomed inside if she had.

Now, at last, Nessa knew what the older woman had meant.

"Is what we do hoodoo?" Nessa asked as they made their way toward the home of the dead woman's mother. She'd heard talk of islands off the coast where rootworkers and conjure men lived.

"Hoodoo belongs to the people down here. But there are women all over the world who can do what you and I do. They've got different names for it in other countries, but we all share the gift."

"The gift?"

"The dead call to us," Nessa's grandmother explained. "In our family, there's always been a woman in every generation who can hear them. I heard my first haint when I was your age. My auntie told me what to do if it happened. So I went out looking, and I found a body washed ashore by the river. Her name was Belinda. Her lover had held her head underwater after she told him she was with child. After Belinda, I didn't find another girl for thirty-five years."

"How many haints have called out to you?" Nessa asked.

"Fourteen," her grandmother said.

"Now they'll call to me too?"

"Not just yet, Nessa," her grandmother told her. "If a girl's got the gift, it makes itself known before her bleeding begins. Then the haints go quiet so you can start your own family. They won't call out to you again till you're older and you know what to do."

"How much older?" Nessa asked.

"It's different for all of us," her grandmother said. "But one day your life will grow quiet, and that's when you'll be able to hear them again. Like my auntie used to say, the gift arrives after the curse ends."

THE DEAD HADN'T GONE AWAY completely. Nessa had always sensed they were there. Occasionally, she would pick up snippets like static on the radio. Once, when she was in college, she'd passed an accident on the highway and seen a young girl standing outside a mangled vehicle watching EMTs working feverishly to extract her body from the wreckage. The girl looked over her shoulder at Nessa as she drove by, but never uttered a word.

When Nessa began working as a nurse in Queens, she saw the dead more often. She'd walk by a hospital room where a patient had passed and see them standing at their own bedside. They always seemed resigned to their fate. Most of the ghosts didn't even acknowledge her. They knew where they were and had no need of her gift.

One night, she'd stopped to pay her respects to a patient who'd died shortly before Nessa had started her shift. She had cared for the comatose Jane Doe for over a week, changing her bandages and cleaning her drug-ravaged body, knowing it was unlikely the woman would ever wake up. When Nessa reached the room, she found a figure standing at the bedside, hat in hand. It wasn't the patient but a police officer named Jonathan. He was the one who'd discovered the woman eight days earlier. She was a sex worker in the neighborhood he patrolled. A client had beaten her senseless and shoved her, half naked, from a moving car. Nessa watched from the doorway as the policeman prayed over the woman's body. He took his time and did it right. Whether he knew it or not, his prayers were the only ones aside from Nessa's that the poor woman would likely receive.

They were married six months later, and the fifteen years Nessa spent with Jonathan were the best of her life. Then, shortly after their twin girls turned ten, she'd woken up in the night to find Jonathan standing by her bedside with a face full of sorrow. He should have been working late, interviewing an informant in an ongoing case. When she saw him there, she knew he had come to say goodbye.

It was Nessa's frantic call that led to Jonathan's body being discovered. Another detective, a man named Franklin Rees, later told Nessa that Jonathan might have been alive at the time of her call. That thought had weighed on her mind for nine long years. She'd been powerless to save the person she loved most in the world.

After Jonathan's death, Nessa and her daughters had moved out of the city to live with her parents. Both former schoolteachers from Brooklyn, they'd met on a beach near Mattauk as teenagers and retired to the island fifty years later. Nessa took a job at a clinic where no one had cause to pass away, and for years, she didn't hear from the dead. She thought maybe she'd lost the ability, but her mother thought not. Nessa still had the gift. Her life was just too loud to make use of it. Then the girls left for college at Barnard. A year later, after her mother was diagnosed with cancer, Nessa quit her job. Her parents had helped her raise her daughters, and the time had come to help them die. Her mother went quickly and her father followed shortly after. The house that had once been home to a boisterous family was now silent. If Jonathan had been there with her, it would have been different. Without him, the loneliness started to pull her under.

Nessa threw herself into redecorating the home her parents had left her, but those efforts only made her feel more cut off from the past. She'd left most of her friends back in the city, and without a job, she had no way to meet new people. Back in her grade-school days, the village just west of Mattauk had still been known as the Oak Bluffs of New York—a vacation haven that had welcomed Black families like Nessa's for over a century. Most of that formerly vibrant community was now buried beneath condos and hotels. The ladies who lined the pews of the church Nessa attended were in their seventies and eighties. Once they were gone, Mattauk and its surroundings would be Wonder Bread white.

Out on the island without friends or family to anchor her, Nessa felt adrift. Her days were featureless, her destination unknown. She tried therapy until she couldn't find the energy to drive herself to her appointments. She stopped getting dressed in the morning. She let the sink fill with dishes. When her groceries were delivered, she paid no mind to the handsome deliveryman. Aside from her girls, the only person she spoke to was Jonathan. Finally, she decided she might as well join him. Her girls would always have each other. All she was doing by hanging around was eating through their inheritance.

The night she swallowed too many sleeping pills, her grandmother came to her in a dream. "What the hell are you doing, Nessa? You were chosen for a reason," the old woman scolded. "You've got thirty good years left. You need to stay put and use them. Jonathan will wait for as long as it takes."

Nessa had woken up at four in the afternoon the next day, her mouth parched and her head pounding. She took her first shower in over a week and never considered suicide again.

TEN MINUTES AFTER JO DROPPED her off, Nessa was out the door once more. She let her feet guide her, and just as they had the day she met Jo, they turned her away from the beach. Nessa had a hunch *where* they were taking her, but the *why* was a mystery. She'd always assumed she'd know just what to do when the gift came back. Wisdom and maturity were supposed to go hand in hand. Nessa had turned forty-eight in February, and she still didn't have a clue.

The homes she walked past were all dark. A dog howled and a second responded. Security lights switched on as she passed and off as soon as she was gone. There were no cars on the road. Nessa knew it was dangerous for a woman to be out so late on her own, but she wasn't worried. Something had told her to leave her pepper spray and penknife behind. That night, no harm would come her way.

Nessa's destination appeared on a slight rise ahead of her. The moon hovered just above the jungle that had overtaken the infamous Osborne home. Leaves of every size and description glowed with its silvery light. A dense border of brambles repelled all intruders and shielded the garden from prying eyes. Nessa walked toward the property line and stopped at the thorny barricade. For the life of her, she couldn't seem to find a way through.

"Hello," said a woman from somewhere on the other side of the brambles. "Are you here to see me?"

"I think so," Nessa replied. "Is this a bad time?"

"No, not at all," the woman assured her, as if nothing were out of the ordinary. Her voice made Nessa think of rich dirt and golden honey. "I'm just doing a bit of gardening."

"You usually garden this late?" Nessa asked.

"Some plants prefer moonlight. Some people do, too."

It made perfect sense to her. "My grandmother was like that," Nessa said. "She never did own a flashlight." When lightbulbs in her house would burn out, she wouldn't bother to replace them for weeks at a time.

"And you? You don't strike me as someone who's afraid of the dark." Harriett sounded as if she might be grinning.

"No," Nessa told her. "Never have been."

"Nor have I. Would you like me to show you my garden?"

"Yes, please." Nessa felt a rush of childlike excitement, as though she'd been invited to tour a magical world.

"Then come on through. Just step over the brambles. I know they look bloodthirsty, but I swear they won't bite."

Since the night she and her grandmother had found the dead woman, Nessa had always felt the cool calm of the graveyard. When she'd encountered Jo, she had been drawn to her warmth. Together, they balanced each other out. This woman was different—far more powerful and less controlled. She pulled Nessa toward her, and though Nessa was neither scared nor reluctant, she also knew there was no point in resisting. Some forces in life are so strong that the only thing you can do is submit.

As Nessa passed through the briars, not a single thorn scratched her, and when she emerged on the other side, she knew she'd found someone she'd needed to meet. Harriett was tall, her hair woven through with silvery strands that caught the moonlight. Despite the chill in the air, she'd removed her clothes. She stood naked before Nessa, her skin sprinkled with the soil of her garden. Magnificent flora sprouted from the earth all around her. Burdock, poppies, henbane, angel's trumpet. Hanging from her arm was a basket filled with pale gray fungi that resembled the delicate hands of young girls.

"I've never seen mushrooms like those before," Nessa said, figuring it wouldn't be proper to acknowledge the woman's nudity.

Harriett glanced down at them. "No, I suspect not," she replied. "They aren't native to this part of the world."

"What are you going to do with them? They're poisonous, I'd imagine."

Harriett picked one up by the stem and twirled it between her fingers. "It depends how you define poisonous. There's a very fine line between what cures and what kills. Come," she said. "I don't have many visitors. This will be fun for me. Let me show you around."

Harriett led Nessa along a path that wound through the garden. Raised beds radiated in a spiral around a giant mound in the center of what had once been the lawn. Nessa wondered if it might be some sort of ritual altar.

"That's where I perform the human sacrifices," Harriett said, as though she'd been reading Nessa's mind.

Nessa gulped comically and Harriett laughed.

"Kidding," she said. "It's a compost pile. Here in my garden, looks are deceiving. You must judge what you see with something other than your eyes." She stopped by a patch of unimpressive waist-high weeds with toothed leaves. "These, for example, are stinging nettles. The leaves and stems are bristling with thousands of microscopic needles. When you brush against them, they deliver chemicals that cause a painful rash. Yet nettles are one of the most medicinally useful plants in the world. You can use them to treat everything from arthritis to diabetes." She moved on to a shrub from which plump orange fruit dripped like teardrops. "This is an iboga plant from West Africa. Its extracts are used in other parts of the world to treat opioid addition. They're illegal here in the United States." Last, she pointed to a regal plant on the other side of the path, the top of its tall stem crowded with delicate purple flowers. "And that is a species of aconite, also known as monkshood or wolfsbane. Every part of it is highly toxic. Touching it will turn your fingers numb. Eat even the smallest bit, and you'll suffocate on your own vomit. Growing beside it is holy basil, which has been used as a medicine for two millennia."

Nessa looked around. There had to be thousands of different species planted in Harriett's garden. "What do you plan to do with all of this?" she asked.

Harriett pondered the question as though it had never occurred to her. "Make things for those who have need of them, I suppose."

"Or use them to punish men like Brendon Baker?" Nessa asked.

Harriett's smile spread across her face, revealing a rather large gap between her two front teeth. "Perhaps," she said.

"He deserved what he got. He's not a good man."

Harriett shrugged. "Good, bad—they're mostly meaningless concepts. Baker is a pest," she said. "I should have done worse. I guess I always still could."

Nessa sensed the opportunity to get to the reason for her visit. "I met a woman like you when I was little."

"You don't say?" Harriett's smile gave nothing away. "What kind of woman would that be?" She seemed to be daring Nessa to call her a witch. Nessa knew she needed to choose her words carefully.

"Her name was Miss Ella. She lived near my family down in South Carolina. My grandmother told me she'd worked as a librarian for thirty-five years. Then one day, Miss Ella left her husband and moved out of town and into her grandfather's old shack in the middle of the swamp. The only things she took with her were her books. She taught herself how to make nature do her bidding. They said she could heal or kill depending on which mood struck her. An uncle of mine swore he'd once spied on Miss Ella talking to snakes."

"I've never tried talking to a snake before," Harriett said. The idea seemed to appeal to her.

"The point is, Miss Ella and my grandmother worked together sometimes. On projects, you might say. I was hoping you and I might do the same."

"You have a project for me?" Harriett asked.

"There's a dead girl down by the ocean who needs our help. She's been calling to me, and she won't be found unless I go look for her." Nessa stopped and sighed. She'd never told anyone outside her family about the gift. She hadn't even been able to confess to Jo. "I'm sorry. Does this all sound crazy?"

Nessa waited for Harriett's reply. The woman had absorbed the information with no sign of incredulousness. Nessa had anticipated some healthy skepticism. But maybe it all seemed perfectly normal to a witch who preferred to do her gardening in the nude.

"If the dead girl's been calling to you, why haven't you gone to her?"

Nessa had wondered the same thing. She gave Harriett the only answer she'd found. "The gift wanted me to find you first. I think the situation might end up being dangerous. I was sent to another woman before you—one with powerful energy. I think she'll be able to protect us."

"So you'll find the body. She'll make use of her powerful energy. And what will I do?" Harriett asked.

"You'll punish whoever's responsible for killing the girl."

Harriett nodded as if that was all very acceptable. "When can we start?" she asked.

"First thing tomorrow morning," Nessa said.

JOSEPHINE LEVISON'S
THIRTY-YEAR WAR

Jo ran five miles every morning, regardless of the weather. She took a different route each day, and over the course of a month, she'd travel most of the roads in town. Only when the ground was covered in snow would she resort to a treadmill. She needed the run to remind her of what she could do. And she wanted Mattauk to see what she'd become.

She'd grown up in town, the daughter of the town's optometrist. Back then, Mattauk's loops, squares, and cul-de-sacs had felt like a maze—one Jo was seldom allowed to explore. Her childhood memories all seemed to take place in the same cramped corner on which the old family home sat. That was the one intersection in town Jo did her best to avoid. The moment the brick Tudor came into view, the air would grow close and her claustrophobia would kick in. Jo waited eighteen years to get out of that house, watching silently, teeth gritted, as her three older brothers escaped one by one. Back then, she would have thrown herself into the sound if she'd known she would one day return to Mattauk to spawn.

Jo wondered if any of her neighbors still thought of her as the girl she'd been—the quiet redhead with the prissy, overbearing mother. The girl whose mom chose her clothes and wrote notes to excuse her from gym class. The girl the kids in ninth grade had called Carrie.

Like being the smelly kid or the kid with home-cut hair, it wasn't the kind of thing you ever really lived down. Jo had carried the humiliation with her for thirty-three years. It was finally something she felt like she owned.

THE FIRST TIME A KID in high school called her Carrie, she hadn't understood. It seemed perfectly plausible that the boy who'd whispered it had simply forgotten her name. Jo had never called attention to herself. She'd discovered early on that if you stayed still and silent, people often forgot you were there. With a mother like hers, that seemed the right strategy; every movement called attention to a flaw to be fixed. Eventually, Jo was certain, she'd follow her brothers to freedom. Until then, she did her best to fly under the radar.

And then one day, everyone in school was staring straight at her.

"Carrie?" she asked a girl who'd muttered the name as they stood side by side at the bathroom sink.

"Like the book," the girl explained with a roll of her eyes, as though everyone else in the ninth grade had read it. The revelation meant nothing to Jo. She skulked through the rest of the school day, and when the last bell rang, she bolted across Mattauk to the public library, pulled a copy of *Carrie* off the shelves, and sprinted all the way home without stopping. It was a five-mile trip, all told, but Jo was through her front door before her mother ever suspected a thing.

She locked herself in her bedroom that evening, ignoring her mother's demands to open the door, and read the scene that told her what it all meant. Sixteen-year-old Carrie, kept innocent by her freakish mother, is convinced that she's dying when she gets her first period. Jo reread the chapter twice, her entire body burning with shame. She knew what had happened. Brownnosing Ellen Goodwin had sold her out for a few glorious days in the spotlight.

It wasn't until years later that Jo read the rest of *Carrie*. She wondered what would have happened if she hadn't put the book down back in high school. She suspected things might have turned out differently for her—and *very* differently for Ellen Goodwin.

ELLEN HAD BEEN SITTING IN front of her two days earlier when Jo felt the first trickle halfway through algebra class. She instantly knew what it was. Her mother had kept her out of the health classes the other kids attended—not to leave Jo innocent of the ways of the world, but so she could explain it all to her daughter in her own flowery words.

Jo still cringed when she recalled her mother leaning forward and clutching Jo's hands as if imparting a secret. "Soon you'll be getting your period," she'd announced in a hushed, honeyed tone. "It's a very special day in every girl's life. It's the day you become a woman."

Jo recoiled in horror. She had no interest whatsoever in joining any club to which her mother belonged. When she saw her mom's lipstick-slathered smile start to flicker, she did her best to hide her feelings. It wasn't easy. Because there was more. So much more. Over the course of an hour, the woman who had trained Jo to sit up straight, cross her legs daintily at the ankle, and comport herself like a lady informed her (in much more elegant terms) that blood would gush from her vagina once a month and would continue to do so until Jo married a man she "loved very much," at which point he would use his penis to fill her vagina with his "seed." Then, for nine months, she would grow into a ravenous, monstrous, "glowing" version of herself until a "gorgeous little baby" popped out of her and the gushing commenced once more. Even more terrifying, Jo's mother made it clear that the whole process might be set into action if Jo were ever to let down her guard. "Boys who can't help themselves" would do their best to get past her defenses, and girls who weren't careful ended up with babies they couldn't feed, diseases that couldn't be cured, and lives that were wrecked beyond repair.

At the end of the talk, Jo promptly burst into tears.

"Oh my goodness, Josephine, what's the matter?" Her mother had read several advice books and couldn't understand how it had gone so wrong. "These are things all of us go through."

"No," Jo insisted, her fists clenched in her lap. "Not me." None of her secret escape plans had involved tending to leaking privates five days every month. And never in her worst nightmares had she imagined a life spent defending a hole she barely knew existed against wanton boys, oozing pustules, and squalling infants.

"Yes, you," her mother informed her. "There's no way to avoid it. It's just part of being a woman."

"We'll see about that," Jo said.

The three years that followed were filled with dread as Jo waited for her mother's prophesy to come to pass. Though she never joined in, she eavesdropped on other girls talking, and by the beginning of ninth grade, she knew most of them had been visited by the curse, as they called it. Jo prayed the curse would just pass her by—the way her aunt Aimee had never grown molars. Instead, it waited just long enough for her guard to come down. Then it struck when she least expected it—right in the middle of algebra class— forever ruining her best pair of Forenza jeans.

She remained in her chair after the other kids filed out of the classroom—until she and Ellen Goodwin were the only two left. Jo was only vaguely aware of Ellen hovering over Ms. Abram's desk. Her brain could no longer process the barrage of stimuli. She felt feverish and light-headed. Her entire nervous system was buzzing, overloaded by fear.

Later, Jo recalled the concerned look on Ms. Abram's face when the teacher was suddenly standing over her chair—and the crimson smear left behind on the wood when the teacher and Ellen coaxed Jo out of her chair. Then the scene changed, as if in a time lapse, and she found herself crying in the principal's office with Ms. Abram's shawl wrapped around her waist. The men who passed by did their best to ignore her. The ladies at the front desk smiled and attempted to lift her spirits.

"It happens to all of us at one time or another," one of the school secretaries whispered. "There's nothing to be ashamed of."

"Then why are you whispering?" Jo hissed back. The secretary had despised her from that moment forward.

Back at home, Jo sat in the bathroom with the kit her mother had prepared for her, a white wooden basket with a pink satin bow that had been hidden under the sink behind the toilet paper packages, waiting for that very moment. Inside were six bulky sanitary napkins, a frilly bag in which to stuff them, and a little bottle of Midol. Jo dumped it all out on the floor and sobbed. She'd never felt so betrayed. And over the two weeks that everyone called her Carrie, she didn't blame Ellen Goodwin or her mother or even God. Instead, she focused her wrath on the body she hadn't been able to train or control.

THE WAR THAT BEGAN IN ninth grade lasted for thirty-three years. Throughout those decades, Jo lived under constant siege. She kept a secret calendar designed to help her anticipate her period's monthly arrival, only to be ambushed several days in advance. She devised ingenious methods for smuggling bulky pads to the school bathroom—and disguising the lumps beneath her clothes. She crafted cunning excuses for keeping her shorts on at the beach and took to wearing sweaters around her waist. Later, she scouted for hiding places for the Tampax her mother refused to buy—and hoarded quarters to procure the tampons from public restrooms.

The hardest part, though, was keeping her private war secret. No one could know what was happening. Certainly not her father or brothers—or, God forbid, the boys at school. But even females couldn't be welcomed as allies. Other women showed no signs of struggling. It seemed inconceivable that all of them—all the teachers and waitresses and teenagers and store clerks and cleaning ladies whose paths she crossed every day—were suffering the same way she was. There was clearly something fucked up about Jo.

She expected to claim one small victory once she left Mattauk and her mother behind for college. Tampons, at least, would no longer be contraband. Ads told Jo that a carefree life of horseback riding and snowy-white hot pants awaited her. Then Jo lost her virginity and a new front in the war opened up. The stakes only grew higher. The fear of humiliation had kept her on her toes in high school. Now there were STDs and pregnancy to avoid. She'd wake up, heart pounding, from dreams in which she was forced to confess her sins to her mother. The nightmares didn't prevent her from having sex, but they certainly made the afterglow less delightful. She now spent the first five days of her cycle battling her period—and the last five praying for it to come.

Then she was with Art and in the working world—no longer at risk of teenage motherhood and able to choose and pay for her own birth control. Yet her body refused to cede control. Her first boss paid more attention to her ass than he did to her work. Her second boss asked if she'd sit on his face—and called her a humorless cunt when she reported him to HR. Guests at the hotels where she worked grabbed, groped, and fondled her. She watched men kiss their mistresses in the lobby, only to return the next week with their wives. On more than one occasion, while wearing a suit and button-down shirt, she was mistaken for an escort. No matter what Jo accomplished, her body—and those of the women around her—made her question what was truly valued.

That all ended when she got pregnant. The moment she began to show, the spotlight shut off and Jo disappeared. She'd dreaded pregnancy her entire life, only to find it was the respite she'd been waiting for. While her body was preoccupied and men turned their attention elsewhere, she managed a feat that her colleagues had long thought impossible.

A month before she announced her pregnancy, she was made staff manager at the hotel where she'd been working for two years. The promotion came as a surprise to Jo. Though she knew her performance had been exemplary, she'd struggled to catch senior management's eye. Six hours after her new title was made public, a colleague informed her that it was considered as a dead-end position within the hospitality company that owned the hotel. Jo had convinced herself that was just jealous gossip when she received a phone call from a reporter at the *New York Times*. Was she aware, the reporter asked, that turnover among the hotel's female workers was three times that of its male employees? Jo said she had seen nothing to suggest that was true and referred the reporter to the chief communications officer of the organization. The company's C-suite knew all about the problem, the reporter informed her, and the problem was hardly unique to the New York location. Staff managers seemed to make convenient scapegoats whenever stockholders or the media took notice. Where did she imagine her predecessor had gone? If Jo cared to discuss the issue in the future, the reporter said, she would gladly make herself available.

That night, Jo went through the HR files and realized it was true. Fifteen women had quit in the previous year alone. Thirteen had signed NDAs and were sent home with several months' pay in their pockets. Two had filed suit against the hotel for failing to protect them from known sexual predators. The blunt reports of harassment and assault turned Jo's stomach. A room-service waitress had been held hostage in a bathroom for hours. A member of the cleaning staff had barely escaped being raped by a guest. Jo made careful copies of all the files. She wanted it to stop, and if it didn't, she'd use them. The previous managers valued the guests and considered employees expendable. The women Jo worked with were worth something to her.

The next day, Jo introduced a handful of new policies. Going forward, the cleaning staff would work in teams of three. No woman would ever enter a guest's room on her own. Room service to male guests would be delivered by men. Female employees would see to the women guests. Guests who harassed waitresses in the hotel's restaurants and bars would be flagged and served by male staff—the buffer, the better. Those who managed to do it twice would be banned.

It seemed so obvious, and too easy. Surely, Jo thought, similar policies had failed in the past. But in the six months after Jo put her plan into motion, no female staff members resigned. No hush money was paid and no new lawsuits were filed. When she first found out she was pregnant, she'd worried about being laid off following maternity leave. It happened, she'd noticed, more often than not. Instead, she was welcomed back with a promotion. The policies she'd introduced in New York had saved the corporation so much money that they were being instituted around the world. Within two years, Jo was general manager of the Manhattan hotel.

Jo's body did not welcome this development. After a yearlong truce, it returned to battle with a vengeance. The periods that had long been unpredictable trickles of blood were now torrents. For three days in a row, Jo would pass multiple clots the size of plums, each filled with enough blood to overwhelm an ultra-size tampon and a mattress-thick pad. Her gynecologist assured her she wasn't dying. It was a common problem—a common problem, Jo noted out loud, for which no gynecologists had bothered to find a solution. She wondered how other women managed to survive in workplaces without hundreds of toilets. At least once a month, Jo found herself slipping into an empty guest room with just seconds to spare before her body released a horror movie's worth of gore. She knew the day would come when she wouldn't make it on time, so she kept a change of clothes tucked behind some files in her bottom desk drawer. When anemia drained her will to live every month, she swallowed iron supplements and devoured chopped liver to get through the day. She learned the location of every public bathroom between work and home. She discovered it was possible—though uncomfortable—to wear two tampons at once. She looked forward to cold weather, when a winter coat would hide anything that might leak through her pants.

She thought she was a champ for managing to hold it together. Then the hot flashes began. That was when Jo finally started to crack. She was thirty-nine—far too young for menopause. When her gynecologist told her no one really knew what caused them, she almost exploded. Her blood pressure skyrocketed. She lost liters of pit sweat every day.

"I can't live like this anymore," she said.

"Try exercise," she was told.

Those two flippant words from a doctor who was staring straight at her vagina when he uttered them were the only advice that ever made a real difference.

Jo was forty the first time she set foot in a gym. She stepped on a treadmill and began to run the rage off. Five miles later, she almost felt human. When she hit ten, she knew something was happening. Her body, which had long held her back, had finally freed her. Over the next three years, she grew stronger than she'd ever thought possible. Jo sensed the power building within her, but she had no idea what she could do with it. Until Lourdes.

Three years to the day after Jo was made manager, the young woman showed up in her office shortly before eleven A.M., her uniform disheveled and her face drained of color. She was new—only three days on the job. Jo had hesitated to hire her. She'd felt terrible about it, but Lourdes was too pretty, with a figure that—even in a uniform—was certain to draw unwanted attention. Jo had gone through the short interview fully expecting to turn her down. Then the young woman had asked if she could work mornings. In the evenings, she went to school.

"What are you studying?" Jo had asked casually.

"Hotel management," Lourdes said. "Someday, I'd like to have a job like yours."

Jo hired her on the spot. The limits of her own influence were becoming clear. She'd need an army of women to change things in the industry. "Come in at eight," she'd said. "You can spend your first two hours of every shift helping me. If that works out, I'll find the money to employ you in my office full-time."

Now the same young woman was standing before her, looking like her soul had spilled out. All that were left of the top three buttons of her uniform were a few dangling threads. She clutched the rest of her shirt together in her fist.

"Lourdes." Jo ran to her and searched for injuries. "What happened?"

Lourdes opened her mouth but couldn't speak.

"Where's the rest of your team?"

The young woman shook her head. Somehow, she'd ended up on her own.

"Call 911," Jo ordered the executive trainee who'd been embedded in her office. "Tell them we've had a sexual assault. Have them send an ambulance and the police."

"What room was she in?" the trainee asked. Handpicked by the C-suite, he considered himself Jo's superior in everything but title. "Was it a VIP suite?" The corporation had guidelines to follow in such situations, and Jo had tossed them out the window.

"Just do it," she ordered.

She found Lourdes's cart on the thirty-ninth floor, outside the hotel's second-best suite. She used her pass to let herself in. A man in his fifties, naked beneath an open hotel robe, greeted her in the suite's living room. His limp red penis protruded from a tuft of salt-and-pepper hair.

He looked her up and down. "Where's the coffee?" he demanded in an international accent that rang of cash.

"I'm not room service," she informed him. "I'm the hotel manager, and I've called the police."

"Oh really?" He seemed intrigued and amused. "For what?" He closed his robe and tightened its belt, then sat down on the edge of the bed, and crossed his legs.

Jo's pulse was accelerating, and she could feel the heat beginning to build. She wanted to murder him, and she was worried she would. "You attacked the woman who came to clean your room."

"The girl's a hysteric." He dismissed the charge with an almost dainty wave of his hand. "I didn't leave a mark on her."

"You had your penis out when I got here."

"I wasn't expecting you!" The man laughed. "Ask your boss," he added, as if that would clear everything up. "He knows I am a very pious man who would never do such things. And it is not very hospitable of you to burst into my room and accuse me."

The tenor of his voice changed as he switched from defense to offense. The guest was someone important, Jo remembered. She'd taken the reservation from the CEO's office herself. She couldn't recall who he was. Mafioso, dictator, mogul, or Nobel Prize winner. It made no difference. He was a VIP. And the rules were different where VIPs were concerned.

"Your face," the man said, adopting a tone of concern. "It is very red. I'm afraid that you are not well. Perhaps you realize that you have made a mistake?"

The heat that had begun in Jo's chest had crept up her neck and laid claim to her head. Beads of sweat formed along her hairline. She desperately wanted to rip off her suit jacket, but she knew doing so would expose the sweat stains spreading under the arms of her silk shirt.

There was a knock at the door. The police, she assumed, before she realized that the NYPD couldn't have made it to the hotel so quickly. The door opened before she could make a move toward it. Hotel security had arrived, led by the trainee. The relief she felt lasted less than a second.

"Jo, can you come with us for a moment?" the trainee inquired.

Something was up. "Where's Lourdes?" Jo demanded.

"She's totally fine," the trainee cooed. "It was all a big misunderstanding."

"The police will decide that," Jo said.

"We don't need the police. Like I said, it was all a misunderstanding. Lourdes is with HR right now, figuring out her next steps."

Three men in their forties and fifties would be pressuring a twenty-two-year-old woman to take a payout in exchange for an NDA. "I want to see her first."

The trainee had the chutzpah to smile at her. "I've already spoken with senior management. That won't be possible."

She knew then what she should have known all along. He'd been hired to keep an eye on her. "You fucking traitor," Jo spat.

"Say what you like, but we need to leave this room. I'm very sorry for the inconvenience, sir," the trainee told the guest.

"Don't apologize." The man stood up from the bed and laid an avuncular hand on the young man's shoulder. "These poor women—they are at the mercy of their hormones. You and I are lucky to be men. I can only imagine what their suffering must be like."

Jo later told Art that something inside her had ignited—a powder keg that had been filling for a very long time. The force of the explosion propelled her across the room before she knew what was happening. With one hand, she grabbed hold of the VIP's throat and slammed him into the wall. Her free arm reared back and sent her fist flying toward the man's face. In the last millisecond, it veered to the left and hit the wall less than an inch from his ear. When her arm finally came to a stop, it was wrist-deep in the drywall. It was clear that the impact would have killed the man in her grip. Miraculously, Jo felt no pain at all.

When security dragged her backward, her heels fell off. She didn't fight. She watched as the man slid down the wall to the floor, where a puddle of urine was growing. Around his neck was a second degree burn in the shape of her hand.

Forty-five minutes later, Jo was standing shell-shocked in front of a departures board at Grand Central Terminal, clutching the few personal belongings she'd been allowed to take from her desk. There hadn't been an opportunity to change her tampon before she left the hotel. She suddenly sensed how heavy it had grown inside her, and all at once, she felt it slip, and knew the dam inside her had given way. As hundreds of commuters and tourists wove around her, Jo felt the warmth overwhelm the backup pad she'd stuck to her underwear that morning and begin to soak through her pants. The closest bathroom was across the main hall and down the stairs to the dining concourse. She knew she wouldn't make it.

"I give up," she told the universe. She'd lost the war. It had been inevitable. There was nothing she could have done to avoid this moment.

The epiphany came as the blood flowed freely down her legs. She should never have attempted to fight it.

How many years—how much energy—had she lost trying to control something that could not be controlled? How long had she feared being outed as female? How much frustration had she endured, inhabiting a world that wasn't designed for her kind? How long had she prayed to be seen and accepted as more than a body? How hard had she tried to fix things that simply refused to be fixed?

So much fury had built up inside Jo. But at last she'd identified the true enemy. She'd been waging war with herself since she was fourteen years old. But the problem wasn't her body. The problem was the companies that sold shitty sanitary pads. Otherwise reasonable adults who believed tampons stole a girl's virginity. Doctors who didn't bother to solve common problems. Birth control that could kill you. Boys who were told that they couldn't control themselves. A society that couldn't handle the fact that roughly half of all humans menstruate at some point in their lives.

The real problem was the hotel where women were being assaulted, the corporation that owned it, and the men who ran it. In a filing cabinet in her home office was a folder filled with everything Jo needed to burn the place to the ground. And in her contacts was the phone number of the reporter at the *Times* who'd called after Jo's promotion.

Out of courtesy, Jo sat on a plastic bag on the train ride home. She didn't bother to hide the stain on her pants.

"Ma'am, are you okay?" the female conductor whispered. "Can I get you something?"

"You don't have to whisper," Jo told her. "This shit happens to all of us."

The following morning, Jo sent the hotel's HR files to the *New York Times*. Then she went for a run. For the first time in decades, Jo's body felt like it was finally hers. She not only owned it, she fucking *loved* it. It carried her all the way across town without getting winded. On the way, she made a point of running past Ellen Goodwin's house, just as she would at least once a week for the next five years.

THE GIRL IN BLUE

This is a joke, right?" Jo asked, a half smile on her face as she wiped the sweat from her hairline and fanned her belly with the bottom of her tank top. She'd just come back from her morning run, and as usual, she was sopping wet.

Nessa gestured toward her car in Jo's driveway. Sitting on the passenger side was a woman with wild hair.

Jo gasped. "Holy shit. Is that who I think it is?"

"Mmm-hmmm," Nessa replied.

"I figured she'd gone to seed. She looks amazing." Jo stepped back and lowered her voice even further. "So lemme see if I have this straight. You hear dead people?"

"Yes," Nessa confirmed. She didn't know if it was the right moment to confess that she could often see them, too.

"And you, me, and Harriett goddamn Osborne are going to go look for a corpse that's been calling to you from beyond the grave?"

"That's right." Nessa was getting a bit nervous.

Jo nodded thoughtfully. "Well," she finally said, "beats the hell out of everything else I had planned for the day. If I can get someone to teach my Spin class, I'm good. Gotta take a shower and drop the kid off at school first, though. That okay with you?"

Nessa was so relieved, she would have agreed to anything. "Take your shower. We'll give Lucy a ride when you're done."

Jo peeked around the corner at Harriett and laughed. "Oh man. My kid's gonna *love* this."

"WHO'S THE LADY SITTING IN Nessa's car?" Lucy asked as they walked down the path to the driveway.

"A very special guest," Jo whispered. "I'd hate to ruin the surprise."

She opened a door to the back seat and let Lucy scramble in first before her.

"Hi there. I'm Jo Levison." She thrust a hand between the front seats. "And this is my daughter, Lucy."

"Harriett Osborne." The woman took Jo's hand, but didn't let go. Instead, she turned it over, examined both sides, and traced Jo's life line with her index finger. "Fascinating," she said. "How long have you been like this?"

"Been like what?" Lucy asked, craning her neck for a look at her mother's hand.

"A few years," Jo said.

"It will get stronger," Harriett predicted. "You'll have great power, but it won't last forever. Don't wait to make use of it."

"How do you know all of that?" Jo asked.

Harriett shrugged. "Does it matter? We both know it's true."

"Hold on a sec," Lucy interrupted. As an only child, she'd spent too much time in the company of adults to be properly intimidated by them. "Did you just say your name is Harriett Osborne?"

"I did," Harriett confirmed. Then she turned back to Jo. "Someday she'll be one of us, too."

"*The* Harriett Osborne?" Lucy asked skeptically. Kids at school whispered about her at recess. One of the boys who lived across the street from Harriett claimed to have seen her dead body, half eaten by cats.

"Will you believe me if I pull up my pant legs and show you all the cat bites on my shins?"

Lucy's eyes nearly popped out of her head.

"She's pulling your leg, baby," Jo assured her. "I think."

"I am," Harriett confirmed with a wide, toothy smile that managed to be both attractive and unsettling. "When animals eat a person, they don't go for the legs first. They generally eat the nose, lips, and anus. Apparently, those are the tastiest bits."

Nessa grimaced as she checked the rearview mirror to see the child's reaction. Her own daughters would have been horrified at that age. Jordan and Breanna were wonderful girls, and tough as nails in their own right, but they avoided death like regular humans. Nessa had known early on that neither of them had inherited the gift. Sure enough, they'd found out a couple of years back that it had passed to her niece, Sage, instead. On the morning of her twelfth birthday party, the girl had discovered a woman's body floating facedown in a pool in suburban Atlanta. The woman's husband was arrested for murder before Sage had taken her first bite of birthday cake.

Lucy was peering up at her mother. She didn't appear bothered at all. "Do you think the anus thing would make a good science fair experiment?"

"Where would we get a corpse?" her mom asked.

"Maybe Nessa knows," Harriett quipped.

In the driver's seat, Nessa cleared her throat, uncomfortable.

"Do you really know where to get a dead body?" the girl asked.

"Lucy," Jo laughed nervously, "Harriett was kidding again."

The woman in the passenger seat smiled slyly and left it at that.

Traffic slowed as they approached Lucy's elementary school. The sidewalks were filled with parents and children who lived close enough to walk. One of the moms caught sight of Harriett first and stopped dead in her tracks. Several kids plowed into her. Soon an entire line of pedestrians had turned to face the road. When Harriett greeted the crowd with a royal wave, most of the adults seemed embarrassed. The kids went wild and waved back.

Nessa giggled. "You're famous, Harriett."

"So it seems," Harriett replied.

"OMG, I'm going to be the most popular girl in school today." Lucy was beaming as Nessa pulled up to the drop-off point.

Harriett turned around and gave her a wink. "Tell your classmates they're welcome to visit me anytime. I've always adored children. They're absolutely *delicious*."

FOR AS LONG AS ANYONE could remember, there had never been anything along Danskammer Beach but sand and scrub. A thin barrier island just off the main island's south shore, it disappeared beneath waves during any strong storm. The stretch of ocean it faced was no good for swimming, and the lonely five-mile road that ran beside the beach was often closed for repairs.

At the far end of the island, just outside Mattauk city limits, the road passed over a bridge before swerving inland away from the sea. On the far side of the bridge, a tall steel gate blocked the sole entrance to a long, narrow stretch of land that jutted out into the water. The only people allowed access were the owners of the mansions in a community known as Culling Pointe. Before Memorial Day, the Pointe was a ghost town. Even during the summer, it was easy to forget anyone was out there. Occasionally one would spot a perfectly groomed woman browsing the shops in Mattauk. But for the most part, the millionaires and billionaires kept to themselves—and kept Mattauk's full-time residents out of Culling Pointe.

They were halfway along Danskammer Beach Road when Nessa suddenly steered the car onto the shoulder. "The voice just got a lot louder. We should stop and look."

"I jog down here all the time," Jo said. "Kind of creepy to think I might have been running right past someone's dead body."

Nessa parked and the three women climbed out. A hundred yards of impenetrable scrub separated the highway from the beach. Stunted by salt water and gnarled by wind, the trees hunched closely together, their leaves whispering to each other in the breeze. Nessa hurried along the side of the road, listening for the girl's voice over the crashing of the waves. Harriett and Jo trailed behind.

"You really think Nessa can hear the dead?" Jo asked Harriett. She'd come along for the adventure. She was still on the fence when it came to Nessa's psychic powers.

"No reason not to believe her," Harriett replied. "She seems perfectly sane, and I don't think she's capable of lying." She didn't seem to have anything more to say about the matter, and they walked in silence for a minute or more.

"You probably don't remember, but you and I met once," Jo said. "Years ago. At the grocery store."

"Yes, I remember. You backed into my car."

Jo felt herself blush. "It was right after Lucy was born, and I was a total disaster. I remember I was still bleeding like a stuck pig and I had baby vomit down the front of my shirt, and you got out in this amazing dress, looking like someone in a magazine, and you told me you'd take care of everything. I was so relieved my insurance premiums weren't going to skyrocket. I had no idea you were actually going to send someone out to my house to repair the taillight I'd broken."

"Don't make it out like I gave you a kidney," Harriett said. "I only made a call."

"Harriett—I was the one who backed into *your* car, and you sent someone out to my house to fix *my* taillight. He didn't even take any money when he was done. He said you'd already paid him. Why did you do that?"

"Who knows," Harriett said with a shrug, as though her motives were a mystery even to her. "Why wouldn't I? You seemed like you had other things to worry about." As far as Jo could tell, Harriett wasn't being modest. She truly didn't think her behavior had been remarkable. It had, however, made a huge difference to Jo. She'd thought about it several times a week for the past ten years.

"I like what you've done with your garden," Jo said.

"Thank you," Harriett replied happily. "I'd be glad to give you a tour sometime."

"I like what you did to Brendon Baker's lawn, too. The mother-fucker deserved it."

"Yes," Harriett readily agreed, "the motherfucker certainly did."

"When did you discover your . . ." Jo hesitated. ". . . ability?"

"My divorce attorney helped me see it. But I suspect I had it long before that," Harriett mused, as though it were something she'd often pondered. "I wish it hadn't taken so long for me to realize it was there. I feel like I spent the first twenty years of my life try-ing to figure shit out. The second twenty, I wasted on the wrong people—my husband, the assholes I worked with. Then I reached this stage of my life, and all of that fell away. For the first time in my life, I was alone. And for the first time in my life, I knew what the hell I was doing. And you?" She turned to Jo and picked up one of her hands. "When did you discover you could generate this kind of energy?"

"I punched a hole through a wall," Jo said. "I was managing a hotel in Manhattan and a woman on one of my cleaning teams was assaulted. So I went up to confront the guy, and he's sitting there in a robe with his dick hanging out. I swear to God, it felt like I exploded. Before I knew it, I had the asshole up against the wall with my right hand and I'd put my left hand straight through the Sheetrock next to his face."

"I hope he was more respectful to women after that," Harriett replied.

"Doubt it. But I did make him piss himself, which was fun," Jo said. "The hotel tried to cover up the incident. So I turned over a bunch of documents to the *New York Times*."

"So that was you? How wonderful!" Harriett lit up with glee. "I remember reading that story in the paper. It was very impressive how you shut the place down—so neat and professional, like one of those building demolitions they used to show on the evening news."

"Yes, and just like those implosions, the cockroaches all made it out alive," Jo said.

"For now," Harriett said. "Look." She pointed ahead of them, and both women immediately broke into a jog. Up ahead, Nessa had come to a stop.

"I think the girl's down there," Nessa said once they caught up with her. She was fixated on a nondescript section of scrubland. The voice had grown louder and more insistent, as though its owner knew they'd come for her at last.

Jo looked for a way into the thicket, where brambles and branches were woven together as tight as a net. "Anyone bring a machete?"

"Now, now. There's no need for violence." Harriett took the lead, slipping effortlessly into the foliage. Jo and Nessa followed, certain at first that she'd tamed nature with her magical powers. Instead, Harriett had spotted a slim trail that hadn't been in regular use for some time. Inside the scrubland, the vegetation closed in all around them. Nessa glanced back and realized she could no longer see the road. The sound of waves slamming into the beach told her the ocean lay straight ahead. When she turned her eyes upward, she saw swatches of sky. Otherwise, there was nothing to guide them. They'd entered alien territory. It felt like the kind of secret world you might've stumbled upon when you were little. But this one was bad. At least one person had entered the thicket and never left.

Jo paused on the trail and wrinkled her nose with disgust. "Do you smell that?" she asked. "Is that what I think it is?"

"Yes," Harriett confirmed without stopping. "It's death."

Nessa pulled the collar of her T-shirt up over her face, but the sickly sweet smell stayed in her nose. She'd been preparing herself for the sight of a body, but the stench took her by surprise. The girl down south hadn't been dead long enough to reek. This poor thing had been waiting for quite some time. That morning, Nessa had woken up at the crack of dawn and prayed on her knees that the voice she'd heard was a hallucination—the product of a malfunctioning, middle-aged brain. The putrid odor of death had just stripped that last hope away.

While the other women forged ahead, something held Nessa back.

"*Here.*" It felt as if someone was whispering in her ear. Nessa turned her head and saw the girl standing just off the path, a few feet away.

Nessa let go of her T-shirt and the collar slipped down. The dead girl was a baby. Seventeen, maybe, eighteen at most. Her own daughters' age. She was dressed for a party in a pale blue dress that clung to her thin body. A tiny quilted leather purse dangled from her shoulder. The girl's black curls were styled in twists. Someone had spent nine long months making this beautiful creature. Whoever her parents were, she must have brought them great joy. And then some demon had killed her and dumped her here, wearing her prettiest dress, on the side of a desolate highway.

"Where are you, baby?" Nessa did her best not to cry. Her grandmother had warned her that her heart was too soft and she would have to work hard to stay strong. Nessa's job was to find the girls so their families could mourn.

"*Here,*" the girl said without moving her lips. She pointed at a black plastic mass that lay slumped against a tree twenty feet off the trail. Nessa forged her way through the dense foliage. Poison ivy brushed her exposed ankles and branches snared her hair. The stench grew overpowering as Nessa got closer to the garbage bag.

The second most important part of the job was to bear witness to the wounds. You have to look at the truth, Nessa's grandmother had told her, no matter how awful. The ghosts need someone to know what happened before they can move on. Nessa stared down at the black trash bag. She wasn't supposed to cry, but she couldn't help it. Some other mother's baby was wrapped up in that plastic. It was only by the grace of God that it wasn't one of Nessa's own girls.

"Dear Lord, give me strength," she whispered. She knew she'd have to open the bag, but there was nothing on earth she wanted to do less.

"You found her," Harriett said. She and Jo had appeared at Nessa's side.

"I can't believe this is happening." It hadn't seemed real to Jo until that moment. "We have to call the police."

"Not yet," Nessa told them. "I need to see what was done to her."

"Oh my God, *why*?" Jo cried. "So you can be completely fucked up for the rest of your life?" She had no idea what Nessa had seen during her years working at the hospital. She didn't know yet what Nessa knew—that God needed some people to look at things the rest of the world couldn't face.

"I need to see her so she can go and be at peace knowing there's someone who will never forget."

Nessa squatted down beside the trash bag. The red plastic cinch string had been tied in a fancy bow. She took several pictures before she used a twig to pull the bow loose and open the mouth of the bag. Nessa heard Jo vomiting behind her, but refused to turn away. Curled up inside was a rotting corpse. If not for the girl's hair, Nessa wouldn't have recognized her. Her smooth, lovely skin was now a mottled green, and there was no trace left of her pretty blue dress. Naked and broken, she'd been used up and thrown away.

Nessa rose and returned to the spot where she'd left the ghost standing on the side of the trail. She reached for the girl's hand, and while she couldn't quite grasp it, she could feel its presence. "You can go now," she told the girl. "I promise you, I will find your family, and my friends and I will punish the person responsible."

Back in South Carolina, the dead girl had vanished as soon as Nessa's grandmother had spoken to her. This one remained. She wasn't ready to leave.

"*There*," she told Nessa. She lifted one of her long, bare arms and pointed down the trail toward the ocean.

"Baby, I told you, I found your body," Nessa assured her. "You don't need to be here anymore."

"*There*," the girl repeated, her arm still raised.

"Nessa? What's going on?" Jo asked carefully. "Who are you speaking to?"

"I'm talking to the girl's ghost," Nessa told her.

"What?" Jo spun around. "Holy shit. You can *see* her? Where is she?"

Nessa gestured with her chin. It didn't seem polite to point. "They're supposed to leave when you find them, but this girl is hanging around. She wants us to go farther down the path. Should we?" She half hoped one of her friends would say no.

"Of course," Harriett replied. "She brought us here. We have to find what she wants us to find."

That was easy for Harriett to say, Nessa thought miserably as the three of them continued down the narrow path toward the ocean. When the branches drew back and daylight appeared, Nessa breathed a sigh of relief. There were no other girls in the thicket. Then she stepped out onto the beach and realized she, Harriett, and Jo were far from alone.

"Please tell me you see them," Nessa begged her companions.

"Who?" Jo asked, then managed to grab hold of her before Nessa fell to her knees.

There were two more ghosts standing in the water. The waves crashed over and into them, but they stood unmoving, like pillars sunk deep into the sand. One girl was white and wore a black dress. The other girl, who appeared to have Asian ancestry, was clothed in a red hoodie. The only thing all three dead girls shared in common was their youth. None of them looked older than eighteen.

"Where are you?" Nessa called out to the girls. Their bodies had to be somewhere nearby. The girl standing closest had pale, freckled skin and long red hair. She pointed out across the ocean.

"How can I find you?"

To that, neither girl had an answer.

"Nessa? What do you see?" Harriett asked, but Nessa was too overwhelmed to answer.

They were dead, their bodies resting on the ocean floor. How could two young women have died without anyone knowing? Where were their mothers? Why had no one come looking?

"Nessa?" It was Jo. "Tell us."

"Somebody's been killing girls," Nessa said, her knees giving out once again. This time, Jo couldn't hold her, and Nessa collapsed onto the sand and cried.

"WHAT WERE YOU LADIES DOING out here this morning, anyway?" the police officer demanded. He was new to the area, and Nessa didn't care for his tone. She'd accomplished more than enough in life to deserve some respect.

"Enjoying the public land that our federal tax dollars maintain," Harriett said.

"We were heading down to the beach," Nessa added. "I needed to go to the bathroom, so I stepped off the trail. That's when I found her."

"Was the trash bag closed when you found it?" the officer asked.

"Yes," Nessa confirmed.

"And you took it upon yourself to open it up?"

"I didn't know what was inside of it." Nessa's hackles were up. "Someone could have cleaned out their freezer and tossed the bag into the thicket. I didn't want to call 911 to have y'all clean up a bunch of rancid garbage."

"You contaminated the crime scene."

"No I did not!" Nessa shot back.

"If she says she didn't, she didn't," said a voice from behind her. "Nessa James is a nurse practitioner with a Ph.D. Her husband was a detective for the NYPD. She knows what she's talking about."

Nessa spun around to see a fiftysomething man in a navy suit. He stood just under six feet, though his perfect posture made him appear much taller. He'd thickened a bit since she'd seen him last, but in a way that made him seem sturdy, and the gray in his close-cropped hair added to the gravitas he'd always possessed. He wore glasses now, but the dark eyes dancing behind them were the same.

"My apologies, ma'am," Nessa heard the younger cop say. He did a poor impression of sorry, but at least the words had been said.

"You can go now," the older man dismissed him.

"Hello, Franklin," Nessa said as the other cop slunk away.

"Nessa." He didn't seem at all surprised to see her in such surroundings. "I was wondering if you were still here after all these years. I always figured we might meet again someday."

She'd known it, too. "What are you doing all the way out on the island?"

"Moved here about six months ago. Couldn't bear to stay in the city after Aiesha died."

Nessa reached out and laid a hand on his arm. "I'm so sorry to hear that she's gone." Nessa had met his wife once, long ago, at her own husband's funeral. Aiesha had kept Nessa's girls entertained that day with stories about her childhood in Kenya. If Nessa had stayed in the city, they might have been friends.

"Death comes for all of us. Aiesha was sick for a year. She had time to get ready. The poor girl you found this morning—" He looked past Nessa to where Jo and Harriett were watching the crime scene team assemble by the side of the road. "Those the two ladies who were with you?"

"Jo! Harriett!" Nessa called out and waved them both over. "Franklin Rees, this is Jo Levison and Harriett Osborne."

"Ms. Levison, Ms. Osborne," he said, shaking their hands. "I'm a detective with the Mattauk PD. I used to work with Nessa's husband back in the day. I'll be covering this case going forward."

Nessa noticed Harriett giving Franklin an appreciative once-over. Given the circumstances, it couldn't have been less appropriate. But Nessa wasn't blind, either. Franklin looked good.

"What can you tell us about the girl we found, Detective Rees?" Jo wasted no time.

"Not much at the moment," Franklin said. "She appears to have been out here for quite a while."

"Given the weather, I'd say no more than two weeks, give or take a day," Harriett said.

"How did you reach that conclusion?" Franklin asked. There was no challenge in the question. He sounded genuinely curious.

"I noticed the blowfly larvae had stopped feeding and the house-flies had arrived."

"Oh my God." Jo looked queasy.

Franklin nodded respectfully. "Well, we'll find out if your hypothesis is correct when we get the lab results back."

"It's correct," Harriett assured him.

"Has anyone reported a girl missing in the past two weeks?" Jo asked.

"No one locally," Franklin said. "But we'll certainly check all the databases."

"When you locate her family, I'd like to speak with her mother," Nessa told him. On that night back in South Carolina, she'd waited in the hall of the dead girl's house while her grandmother spoke with the family. When her grandmother emerged, she'd looked much older and frailer than she had going in. That was the part of the job that would kill her, she told Nessa. But it was also the most important.

"If we locate the mother, I'll pass along your request." Franklin was trying to let her down easy, as though she were innocent of the ways of this world. "But don't get your hopes up. We find Jane Does like this from time to time. Most are sex workers with drug problems and many have fled abusive homes. Even when we manage to ID the victims, their families often don't want to be involved."

Nessa looked past Franklin. The girl had come to stand behind him. She was listening to everything he said. She wasn't going to go away. Not this one.

"This girl was loved," Nessa informed him. "And not that it makes a difference where these things are concerned, but she wasn't an addict. When she died, she was strong and healthy."

Franklin studied Nessa's face. "What makes you so sure?" he asked quietly, as if he knew he was entering dangerous territory.

The night Jonathan died, Franklin was the officer who'd answered Nessa's frantic phone call. Few other cops would have given a wife's intuition a second thought. But Franklin had listened—and he'd taken her seriously enough to check on Jonathan. He'd been just a few minutes too late. When someone had to call Nessa back with the news, Franklin had stepped forward. The connection they'd forged during those calls would last the rest of their lives.

Later, at her husband's funeral, Franklin had come to stand beside Nessa at the coffin.

"You knew something was going to happen," he'd said.

"Yes," she told him, never taking her eyes off her husband's face. "And it made no fucking difference." It was one of the few times that she'd ever said the word *fuck*.

"It will make a difference someday," he told her. He wasn't repelled by her grief or intimidated by her rage. "God doesn't give gifts like yours for no reason."

For a few years following the funeral, they'd stayed in touch. Then one day an email went unanswered, and the next was never sent. As fond as she was of Franklin, his voice always reminded her of the worst day of her life. But now, standing on the side of the road with a dead girl's body fifty feet away, she no longer felt the urge to flee.

"Nessa, what more can you tell me?" Franklin pressed her.

She turned her eyes away from him and watched as a photographer and a forensics technician were swallowed up by the scrubland along Danskammer Beach. "I'm still not sure what I know." It wasn't a lie, she tried to tell herself, but it certainly wasn't the truth.

BY THE TIME THE THREE women were free to go, the sun was well on its journey toward the ocean on the opposite side of the continent. They'd spent almost an entire day at the beach. Back in the car, the three of them were lost in their thoughts—or so Nessa assumed. Then, just as the car's wheels rolled over the town line, Harriett broke the silence.

"That man Franklin wants to sleep with you, Nessa," she said.

"Excuse me?" Nessa couldn't believe what she'd heard. "I thought you were contemplating the meaning of life back there, and instead you're thinking about sex? Have you forgotten where we spent the afternoon?"

"It's perfectly normal to think of life in the presence of death," Harriett replied. "I don't know if you were paying attention, but your friend's not bad-looking."

"If you say so," Nessa replied. "I hadn't thought much about it." Not really. Not until that very moment.

"You should have sex with him," Harriett encouraged her. "You may find the experience much more pleasurable now than when you were younger. There's certainly a lot less to worry about. I try to have sex whenever possible."

Jo, who'd felt hopelessly shell-shocked by the morning's discovery, burst out laughing in the passenger seat.

"What?" Nessa nearly swerved off the road. "Harriett, I'm married!"

Jo's laughter trailed off, and a pall fell over the car. Whether Nessa could see him or not, it was clear that Jonathan's ghost never stopped haunting her. Suddenly, they could all feel his presence. He was there with them now.

"Do you think having sex with a living man will make you love your dead husband any less?" Harriett wasn't afraid to tackle the subject head-on.

"No," Nessa pouted. "It just wouldn't be right."

"Why not?" Harriett probed. "Sex is natural. It's a bodily function."

"I'm too old for that bodily function," Nessa said.

"Oh really?" Harriett snickered like a dirty-minded schoolgirl. "Who told you that?"

"No one had to *tell* me." Nessa was getting annoyed. "Some things you just know."

"You *know* because that's what women our age have been trained to think," Harriett said.

"What the hell are you talking about?" Nessa demanded. "No one's been training me."

"Then you'll do whatever you want," Harriett said. "And you won't give a shit what anyone says."

"Damn straight I won't," Nessa told her.

"You'll have sex with Franklin Rees if you feel like it," Harriett said.

"Hell yes I will!" Nessa told her.

"Good," Harriett said with a lighthearted shrug. "'Cause that's all I'm asking."

"Good," Nessa repeated, suddenly aware of the one-eighty the conversation had taken. "Can we talk about something else now? Like blowfly larvae or serial killers?"

THE PURIFICATION OF
HARRIETT OSBORNE

The office of the ad agency where Harriett had worked featured
a central staircase that connected the company's three floors.
It was a gorgeous staircase, designed by a brand-name archi-
tect, with clear glass steps that made it look as if one were climbing
through air. Though it was far less convenient, women in the office
often opted to take the elevator instead. The staircase, which had
been featured in countless design magazines, was also known for
its spectacular up-the-skirt views. This, it was explained to Harriett when she first pointed it out, was a feature, not a flaw.

She happened to be wearing a skirt the day she returned from
vacation. She hadn't mentioned where she was going, but everyone in the office assumed she'd traveled somewhere exotic. That's
what rich women did when their marriages ended. They set off
on spirit quests or death-defying adventures. They climbed Mount
Everest. They ate, prayed, and loved. Now Harriett had returned,
with the lean limbs and bronzed skin of an Aegean goddess. The
huntress stalking a stag, perhaps, or an enchantress surrounded by
swine. No one would have guessed that Harriett had acquired the
tan while walking naked among the plants in her own backyard.

The skirt was a failed attempt to get back in the swing of things.
She hadn't worn clothes in two weeks, and she hadn't missed them
at all. That morning, she'd stood in her massive walk-in closet, looking around at all her beautiful things. Once Harriett had thought of

them as her prizes. Win a new account, get a YSL Le Smoking. Convince a creative team to accept her ideas as theirs, collect a bracelet from Hermès. Shake a handsy client without pissing anyone off, take home a badass Rag & Bone leather jacket. Now she realized none of her belongings spoke to her any longer. She wasn't sure if they ever really had. The skirt she chose to wear was vintage Tom Ford–era Gucci. For the life of her, she couldn't recall why she'd bought it.

The skirt was the reason she was the last of her colleagues to walk through the door of the new creative director's office. She'd been informed of his hiring at the beginning of the month, but he'd arrived while she was on vacation, and she had yet to meet him in person. She entered the room to find him already holding court. Chris Whitman was Scottish, like Max, the agency's CEO. He and Max had worked together back in London, and now Max had brought his protégé to New York at enormous expense. The agency had been on a winning streak for two years, and after they'd doubled their billings, their holding company, which had previously squeezed every spare cent from them, decided it was best to let Max do as he liked. They and the press attributed the agency's success to Max's swashbuckling leadership. He was tall, dark, and rugged. No matter the setting, he wore the same uniform of black T-shirt and jeans. He fit the ad world's picture of a renegade genius. The fact that the agency's winning streak hadn't begun until Harriett was brought on as new business director was deemed a coincidence. When Max decided he needed a "partner in crime," it never occurred to anyone but Harriett that he might already have one.

Harriett took Chris's measure from the doorway. He was attractive but short. Max liked to have good-looking people around him, but he was careful not to hire anyone taller or more talented. Chris didn't share the CEO's height or bombastic personality, but their egos appeared to be a perfect match. Like his boss, Chris seemed

perfectly at home in New York with a group of American syco-
phants hanging on his every accented syllable.

There were four men in the room, all a few years younger than
Harriett. When she appeared in the office, they glanced up with
unease. Her presence always altered the energy of the room—like a
teacher returning from a bathroom break or someone's mom showing up at a keg party.

Chris paused in the middle of the tale he was telling and turned
to Harriett. "So how long will he be?" he asked.

Movement on the couch caught Harriett's eye. Andrew Howard,
the head account guy, was squirming. "How long will *who* be?"
she asked.

"Max," the CD replied with a touch of exasperation, as though
trying to make sense to a sweet but dim-witted child.

"Why would I know when Max will get here?" Harriett kept
her voice cool and pleasant.

The creative director looked around at the men gathered in his
office. Suddenly, none of them wanted to meet his eye.

"Who do you think I am?" Harriett asked. She knew. She just
wanted to hear him say it. He thought she was an admin. If she'd
played along, he might have asked her to bring him a cup of coffee.

Three months earlier, their exchange would have shaken Harriett's confidence. What about her appearance made him mistake her
for support staff? Did she lack gravitas? Did she look unsuited for
her job?

The head of client services leaped to his rescue. "Chris, this is
Harriett Osborne, head of our new business department. She's been
on vacation for the past few weeks."

"Oh, of course!" Chris made a beeline for her, hand outstretched,
no trace of shame or contrition anywhere on his face. He seemed to
have no clue he'd committed a faux pas. "What an honor to finally
meet you in person. I hear you were married to Chase Osborne.

He does the Little Pigs ads. I'm a huge fan of his. The man is a genius."

"I'm sure Chase would agree with you," Harriett replied. "I'd pass on your kind words, but I don't see him much anymore. He's too busy fucking the head of his production department."

The men in the room appeared to stop breathing. They all knew it. They would have filled Chris in the moment she left the room. But none of them expected her to beat them to the punch. Harriett grinned broadly. For years, veneers had disguised the natural gap between her two front teeth. During her vacation, she'd decided to get rid of them. Now they were all staring at the gap, struggling to remember if it had been there all along. It was fun, she thought, to keep them wondering.

"I believe we're all here to talk new business." Harriett took a seat in one of the office's white leather chairs that no woman would have chosen. "And I'm the new business director. We don't need Max for this, so let's start. Who's running the meeting?"

"I am." Andrew Howard slid forward on the couch. He was a smarmy little asshole, Harriett thought. He couldn't have cared less about the quality of the work, but he possessed a remarkable homing instinct for steak houses, golf courses, and strip clubs. Max liked him because he kept the clients happy—and happy clients didn't call Max. "While you were out, we were invited to take part in two pitches. First up is Pura-Tea. It's a new line of sparkling teas from Coke. They want to bring women over thirty back with the promise of great taste and health benefits. They're pretty confident in the strategy, and they're keen to see work. Chris and his teams have a few things to show us."

"Anyone actually try the product?" Harriett asked.

"Yeah," said the strategist. "It underdelivers on taste, so we've focused on health benefits."

"Are there any real health benefits?" Harriett asked.

"No sugar, great hydration, and loaded with antioxidants."

"What the fuck *are* antioxidants?" Harriett joked. "Anyone know?"

Andrew snorted and shrugged. The others in the room shook their heads.

"So basically we're selling shitty carbonated water with a few vitamins thrown in."

"That's why they need advertising," Chris chimed in. "Shitty carbonated water won't sell itself. We're going to convince these women it's what they've been missing all their lives."

Harriett spun around to face him. "So brilliant," she gushed. Men in advertising loved to explain how it all worked. "Max said you were a genius. I can't wait to see what you've got. Is that it?" She pointed to a tall stack of foam boards lying facedown on Chris's desk. The message was clear. She wasn't interested in a lecture on advertising.

The smile he gave her wasn't terribly warm or friendly. She made sure the smile she offered in return was pure light and joy.

"Yeah, so I have four ideas to show you this morning." Chris grabbed the first board off the stack on his desk and turned it over to reveal an illustrated frame from a video ad. A very young woman in a very small bathing suit lay by a glistening blue pool surrounded by forest, a bottle of Pura-Tea on the rocks beside her.

"Fuck, this isn't the spot I wanted to start with. Andrew, can you rearrange these like I asked?"

As Andrew leaped from the sofa like a well-trained puppy, Harriett pointed at the image of the bikini-clad girl.

"You said they're going after women over thirty. How old is the woman in the picture supposed to be?" Harriett inquired. "The illustration makes her look sixteen."

"It's meant to be an aspirational image of our female audience," Chris explained. "Fit, gorgeous, and healthy."

It was funny, Harriett thought. Twenty-five years in advertising, and the aspirational female had never changed. It was always whoever the art director wanted to screw. And, equally serendipitously, she could only be found in places the creative team wanted to travel.

"Women over thirty don't aspire to be sixteen," Harriett said. "We can be fit, gorgeous, and healthy at any age. Plus, once we hit thirty, a lot of us can afford a fuck-ton of overpriced iced tea."

"Let's not get hung up on the casting right now," Chris said, handing the boards to Andrew. "Just imagine our heroines the way you'd like to see them."

"As badass bitches who keep the world running and never get their due?" Harriett asked.

Chris glared at her. "Sure," he said. "Why not."

"Great!" Harriett said. "I love it already."

Andrew passed a set of rearranged boards back to Chris, who plucked several off the top of the pile and held the first up for his guests to see. Fortunately, the ad he'd chosen to start with didn't feature a half-clad teenager, but rather a plain wooden door.

"So," Chris said, looking down at the board. "We open with the camera locked on the door of an apartment. The door's a bit scuffed and the paint's peeling in places. It's clearly the kind of apartment you had in your twenties." He moved on to the second board. "Then we see a young man strut down the hall with a bottle of wine in one hand. He knocks at the door, and a pretty girl opens up and drags him inside. The next time the door opens, he's coming out. There's no wine bottle in his hand, and his clothes and hair are rumpled. He's obviously spent the night."

He let the board drop, revealing another illustration of the original door.

"We watch as the door gets dingier and more scuffed, marking the passage of time. As we're watching, a different guy shows up and knocks at the door. The door opens, and the same girl throws her arms around him and pulls him inside. He, too, leaves after spending the night."

Chris was smiling as though he couldn't wait to get to a punch line.

"So we see the same thing happen a couple more times. It's always a different guy and the same girl. Each time she waves goodbye the next morning, she seems a little less satisfied. The last time, she stays at the door, looking a bit miserable. There's a bottle of Pura-Tea in her hand. The camera moves in close as she lifts it to her lips. We see her skin sparkle as the purifying antioxidants work their magic. When the camera pulls back again, she's framed not by a doorway but a wedding arch, and we see she's wearing a flowing white bridal gown. One hand is holding her new husband's hand. The other is still clutching the bottle of Pura-Tea. The tagline appears: 'Pura-*Fide*.'"

Chris burst into laughter, and the rest of them instantly followed suit.

Harriett leaned forward in her chair to study the last board. It was truly remarkable. If she hadn't known better, she would have sworn the whole thing had been crafted by an alien species. *They live alongside us,* she thought. *Some work with us. Some fuck us. And some do both. And yet they seem to know absolutely nothing about us.*

"What is it?" asked Andrew, sensing trouble.

Harriett sat back and wove her fingers together. "I don't think I get it," she said.

"What don't you get?" Chris asked.

"The whole thing," Harriett told him. "So this chick sleeps with lots of guys, and it makes her sad. Then she drinks a tea. It purifies her, and suddenly a man wants to marry her."

"That's it!" Chris seemed relieved. "You got it!"

"So sleeping around made her dirty?"

He cleared his throat. "It's meant to be tongue in cheek. We're just riffing on society's hang-ups."

"Ah," Harriett said. "I see. You're playing off the common misconception that women who like to fuck are whores, and men won't marry whores. Perhaps the girl in the ad should be douching with Pura-Tea instead of drinking it? I mean, you'd want ladies to purify their real dirty bits, would you not? How much tea would they need to buy for each guy they've fucked?"

The four men in the room stared at her.

"I think you may be taking this a little too personally," Andrew finally said.

Harriett grinned. "You're married. How did you make sure Celeste was pure before you slid a ring on that finger?"

Andrew blanched. "Can we *not* bring Celeste into this?"

"Now who's taking it personally?" Harriett laughed. Not at her joke, but his chutzpah—acting as if she were besmirching his wife while everyone in the agency knew he was screwing a junior copywriter. "Show the ad to Celeste. See what she makes of it."

"Celeste has retired from advertising."

"As I recall, Celeste *was retired* from advertising," Harriett corrected him. "Who's the target audience for this campaign, again? May I see the brief?" She read the target section, though she needn't have bothered. "They call them the Mindful Moms. Affluent, health-conscious women age thirty-plus. They love yoga, drink herbal teas, and champion social causes . . . Holy shit, that sounds just like Celeste, does it not?"

In fact, it sounded like every woman in Mattauk. From the viewpoint of giant corporations, they were all the same person. They were all Mindful Moms.

"By the way," Harriett added, "how old's the girl in this spot? She looks a little young for a Mindful Mom. Where's she hiding her kids while she's banging everyone in the neighborhood?"

"Max loves this script," Chris interjected. "He thinks it's fucking brilliant." The way the words came out, it was perfectly clear that he intended them to be the end of the conversation. Harriett had no intention of stopping.

"Max is a fifty five-year-old Scottish male. I'd much rather hear what Andrew's wife, Celeste, has to say. Presumably, she's the one who'll be buying this shitty carbonated water."

"I don't give a fuck who the ads are for," Chris sneered. "Max thinks this spot could win awards, and that's why he brought me here. To win awards. You're here to sell the work I tell you will win those awards."

Harriett almost admired him for saying out loud what they were all thinking.

"*I'm* here to sell work that *you* tell me is good?"

"I think I'm the best arbiter of what's good and what isn't. How many Gold Lions have *you* won?" Chris asked.

Thirteen was the answer. Her ideas, her lines, her scripts had gone on to win thirteen Gold Lions at Cannes. But her name wasn't on a single one of those trophies. And unless your name was on the trophy, and the trophy was displayed on a window ledge in your office, you were a loser just like everyone else. That was one of many mistakes Harriett had made over the years. She'd let men take credit for her work assuming they would be grateful and her contributions acknowledged. But selective amnesia was endemic in the advertising community. Most of the men she'd helped didn't even remember. The rest saw her generosity as a sign of weakness.

"I've brought in seventeen new accounts since I came to this agency two years ago," Harriett told him. "I'd like to make Pura-Tea the latest. We can discuss this script later with Max. Let's see what else you've got."

Harriett knew it was going to get ugly. And she couldn't wait.

SOMEWHERE IN THE MISSION STATEMENT of every ad agency in New York was a nod to their respect for the "consumer." It had always seemed to Harriett that a good way to show real respect might be to give them a label that didn't call to mind brain-dead omnivores. At all five agencies where Harriett had worked over the course of her career, she'd made it clear that these faceless "consumers" were flesh-and-blood women. Around the world, she would tell whoever would listen, women purchase or directly influence the purchase of 80 percent of all goods—and the women dropping serious change are usually over thirty-five. Whenever a man questioned this, she'd ask him when he last bought toilet paper. What brand was it? How much did it cost? Nine times out of ten, they couldn't answer.

When Max had hired her as new business director, Harriett's first step had been to put together a presentation on that very subject. Max hadn't been in favor of showing it. He worried the agency would develop a reputation for specializing in women's brands. Eventually, it became apparent that Harriett's "lady deck," as Max called it, drew clients in. People whose jobs actually depended on selling things bought what Harriett was offering. She became the bait that the agency dangled in front of them until the papers were signed. Then Harriett handed the new clients over to an organization that employed a grand total of six women over thirty-five. Two were administrative assistants. One was the office manager. One ran the agency's feminine hygiene account. Another was a midlevel art director. The sixth was the head of the new business department.

Outside the new business department, the agency was one hundred percent devoted to making great advertising. When he'd taken over the flailing organization, Max had made it clear that that was all that mattered. "It's all about the work," he would say. Every year, he sat on award-show juries along with other creative rock stars. His fellow judges were almost always men, almost always in their forties and fifties, and almost exclusively white. This cabal of rich white dudes was responsible for deciding what was "good advertising." No other opinions mattered. Their stamp of approval could lead to prize money, industry-wide adulation, and seven-figure salaries. When a creative team sat down to develop a new campaign, these men were invariably their true target audience. Assignments that weren't deemed to have award-show potential were quickly shunted off to junior, less favored, often more female creative teams.

Harriett had spent her first years in advertising on one of those teams. That was back in the mid-nineties, a time she now recognized as a golden age in advertising, when television ads were often treated as short films and award-winning work could open the door to a career in screenwriting or directing. That was the dream—one Harriett could never have pursued directly. She'd gone to school with kids whose parents subsidized their careers in film or publishing. Harriett needed a job that would pay the bills.

That's how she ended up writing tampon copy. Not for television ads, of course. Those were handled by a more senior team. Harriett's first job was writing Q&A–style advertorials that would run in magazines aimed at teen girls. The ads encouraged readers to write in with their own questions, which would be answered in future issues. *Will everyone know?* the girls asked. *Will I still be a virgin? What should I do if the worst happens?*

Harriett had once wondered the same things herself, and for a while she was pleased to offer answers. No one ever needed to know it was that time of the month, she'd tell her readers. The brand's new line of compact tampons could be easily concealed in a pocket or the palm of a hand. They would leave your virginity intact—and were designed to be so absorbent that the worst *wouldn't* happen. She considered it a testament to her talent that she'd managed to write about tampons for months without ever using the words *menstruation, period, vagina,* or *blood.* At some point, she realized she'd been answering questions about periods for over a year. She'd invented new euphemisms. She'd devised new forms of camouflage. Still, the questions kept coming. Terrified, ashamed, miserable girls were scribbling their most mortifying questions on pieces of lined notebook paper and mailing them to a faceless corporation. That's when Harriett realized she wasn't providing solutions. She was part of the problem.

Then one day, she was handed a new question to answer. *Why is this happening to me?* asked Jennifer, age 13, Pittsburgh. The despair was so palpable that Harriett promptly burst into tears. *You are NOT alone,* she wrote back. *It's happening to me, too. It's happening to every girl you know. It's happening to the actress on television and the lady across the street. It is happening, has happened, or will happen to most women on earth, and it's time we all stopped working so hard to hide it.*

Harriett couldn't stop writing to Jennifer, age 13, Pittsburgh. By the end of the week, she had a series of ads that she called the "Half the World" campaign. The executions spoke about menstruation as if dealing with your period was just as mundane as brushing your teeth. They used all the words Harriett had been trained to avoid. When fluid was shown, it was red, not blue. And most important, they encouraged girls to talk to each other and share what they knew.

Harriett took the campaign to her agency's creative director. She'd set up a time to present to him alone, but when she reached his office, she found the new business director and a senior copy-writer lounging on the couch.

The new business director, a closeted gay man named Nelson with a gentle soul and an old-fashioned fondness for three-martini lunches, winked at Harriett and nudged the copywriter. "Let's leave," he said. "Harriett's here to knock his socks off."

"No. Stay," the creative director ordered flippantly, much to Harriett's dismay. "She needs to get used to presenting to more than one person."

So Harriett presented her "Half the World" campaign to three men, two of whom looked thoroughly disgusted by it.

"Did it ever occur to you that there might be a reason we use blue fluid instead of red?" the creative director asked when she was done. "No guy wants to think about what that shit really is or what hole it comes from," he informed her.

"But these ads aren't *for* guys," Harriett had responded.

"*We're* guys," he responded. "So are most of the people who sell these tampons. Know your audience, Harriett."

Her face was still burning an hour later when Nelson knocked on the side of her cube.

"Come work for me," he said. "I need a right hand."

"But I want to write," she told him.

"I loved the honesty of what you wrote. That's why I'm going to be equally honest with you. Do you know what happens to women creatives here?" he asked her. "Until you're thirty-five, you'll spend your time slaving away on shitty assignments and fending off men who want to fuck you."

"And after thirty-five?" Harriett asked, thinking she might be able to stick it out.

"There are no women over thirty-five in the creative department," he said. "Come with me. You'll work on all the best business and see your ideas come to life. I'll even throw in a good title and a raise." He cupped a hand around his mouth and glanced theatrically in both directions. "And you won't need to worry about me trying to fuck you."

THE NEXT SIX YEARS WERE the best of Harriett's career. Together, she and Nelson made a formidable team. He did the schmoozing. Harriett did most of the thinking. Because she brought in the business, she knew every account in the agency. When an idea popped into her head, she would give it to a creative team who could make something out of it. She had a talent for convincing them they'd come up with it first. That was how she met Chase. He was one of two copywriters assigned to a pitch she was leading. The other guy was a prick, so Harriett slipped Chase an idea she'd been working on. She inserted it into a conversation, repeating it twice to make sure he caught hold of it. After that, Chase always talked through his work with her. When they were alone, he called her his good luck charm.

Harriett did well in advertising. At forty-eight, she was still employed, with a mid-six-figure salary. People whispered that she'd be the next president of the agency, though she never encouraged such idle chatter. Chase, though, was a phenomenon, racking up awards and pulling in millions each year. Harriett couldn't quite pinpoint when he'd stopped thanking her in his acceptance speeches. Most likely around the same time he began an affair.

When Chase left her, Harriett had had every right to be furious, and she was. But she also felt oddly restored. She took three weeks off as an experiment. In twenty-five years, she'd never taken such a long vacation. She spent the time in her garden, ignoring the emails that continued to accumulate in her inbox. For the first time in ages, she shared none of herself. Only when her magic began to return did she realize just how much she'd given away.

IT WAS ALMOST SIX WHEN Harriett was called into Max's office. When she arrived, he gave her a hug.

"How are you, my dear?" he asked. "How was vacation? You're looking tanned and rested."

Harriett knew his game. Pretend nothing's happened and shoot the shit for ten minutes until tempers cooled. She'd fallen for it so many times.

Two years earlier, she'd accepted Max's job offer, hoping to replicate the work relationship she'd once had with Nelson. What Max lacked in talent, he more than made up for in charisma. Max was the kind of man who made other guys feel like they belonged to an exclusive club. Harriett wasn't invited, of course, but that was fine with her. While Max and the clients fluffed each other's egos, she could get good work done. When she'd arrived at the agency, it was hemorrhaging accounts. The two of them together had saved it. But Max still believed he was running a one-man show.

"What's up, Max? I want to get home, and I know you didn't call me in here to discuss my tan."

"Chris came to see me earlier. He says you don't like the Pura-Tea work."

"It sounds like you're asking for my honest opinion. Is that what you really want?"

"Of course," he insisted.

"I saw four executions. Three left no impression. The fourth was one of the most offensively sexist spots I've ever seen. And I once pitched a beer brand from Brazil."

"The Pura-Fide execution?" he asked, as though he couldn't quite believe it. "I thought it was funny—and you have to admit that the structure is clever. I showed it to my wife. She laughed her ass off at the reveal."

That was a lie. She knew his wife. The woman hadn't laughed in years.

"Your daughter is how old? Seventeen?"

His megawatt smile dimmed considerably. "Come on, Harriett."

"Seriously, Max. I grew up watching stuff that taught me that women who enjoyed sex were whores. That we should try to be who men wanted us to be—not who we really were. It fucked me up. It fucked up a lot of the women I know. Is that what you want for your kid?"

"So this is personal."

"Of course it's personal. Everything is personal. Anyone who tells you it isn't is trying to screw you over."

"Well, Chris is worried that you and he may not be able to work together. You're going to need to smooth things over. Let this one go, Harriett."

How many things had she let go? How much of herself had she already given away?

"Why me?"

"Because you're wrong."

"I'm a woman in the target audience. I'm also a woman with twenty-five years of advertising experience who hasn't lost a single new business pitch in two years. And you're telling me that I'm wrong about this?"

"Yes," he said. "You don't know what younger people find funny."

It was a low blow, but she'd been expecting it. "If you say so. But I won't present that ad to a client."

"The way things are going, you won't have to."

Harriett's laugh seemed to throw him. "You haven't won a piece of new business without me," she said. "You need a win now to justify bringing your boy in from London. I've heard you're paying him five times my salary. Won't look good if he falls flat on his face the first time out. You sure you want to risk it?"

"You know, you're not as good as you think," Max said.

No," Harriett agreed. She'd known he'd get mean. She'd been waiting for it. "I'm better."

His lip curled into a snarl, and Harriett glimpsed the fear that lay beneath his contempt. "You may not believe this, but there's a reason I'm CEO of this agency and you're not."

Harriett laughed again. She saw how it infuriated him and laughed even harder. "Oh, I believe it. There is a reason, but it has nothing to do with talent."

"Chris Whitman is worth a dozen of you."

"You're afraid of me," Harriett observed. It was hard to believe it had taken her so long to see it. "That's why you have to keep me in my place."

"I'm *afraid* of you?"

"Yes, you're afraid of me because I'm better than you are. And if you give one talented woman the power she deserves, another will follow. Then another. And together they'll show that their way is better. Then your whole fake fucking world will come tumbling down."

Harriett picked up a One Show pencil and tossed it to him. "You wouldn't have this if it weren't for me."

Max caught the golden pencil and promptly hurled it at the wall, where it left a satisfying gash in the drywall.

Next Harriett tossed a Silver Lion, followed by a Webby. "Or these."

They hit the wall as well.

"I made all of this happen. Without me, they'd have put you out to pasture a long time ago."

"Fuck you, cunt," he snarled.

The door opened and two security guards appeared just as Max was prepared to hurl another Lion. "You better walk me out," she advised them. "If this asshole does anything to me, I'll own the whole place."

That evening, she kicked off her shoes on the train and didn't bother to slip them back on when they reached the Mattauk stop. As Harriett strolled home from the train station barefoot in the rain, she knew the neighbors were peeping at her through the blinds, and she didn't give a rat's ass. She felt totally free for the first time in her life.

MONTHS LATER, HARRIETT RECEIVED AN invitation in the mail. Her presence was requested at the unveiling of a new exhibition in Central Park. The image on the front showed the park's famous Shakespeare statue transformed into Eleanor Roosevelt.

OF THE TWENTY-NINE STATUES IN CENTRAL PARK,
ONLY ONE IS A WOMAN.
THIS YEAR, FOR INTERNATIONAL WOMEN'S DAY,
WE WILL BE RIGHTING THAT WRONG.
JOIN MANHATTAN FINANCIAL ADVISORS IN CELEBRATING
WOMEN'S CONTRIBUTIONS TO THE WORLD.

Beneath was a handwritten note from Max.

YOU WERE THE INSPIRATION. PLEASE COME BACK.

Harriett sent her regrets, along with a bouquet of flowers handpicked from her garden.

THE TWINS

Nessa parked her car in her drive and sat staring straight ahead at her white colonial. It took a minute to find the strength to get out. Then she unlocked her front door, closed it behind her, and stood quietly in the foyer of the house she'd inherited.

She'd had plenty of bad days in recent years, but it had been a while since one had felt quite so unrelenting. First the dead girls at Danskammer Beach, then Franklin's appearance, and finally Harriett's bizarre insistence that she sleep with a man she hadn't seen in ages. If this was how things were going to be, Nessa wasn't sure she wanted to stick around for thirty more years.

Her gaze swept the foyer as she listened to the crash of waves on a distant beach. In the grief-filled months following her parents' funerals, her daughters had begged her to see a therapist. Nessa had turned first to interior decorating instead. She'd spent weeks shopping for the room's antique table and porcelain lamp. She'd splurged on the wallpaper with its hand-painted cherry blossoms so visitors would see something beautiful when they entered her home. It had never occurred to her that the loveliest corner of her house would one day be the best spot to hear the dead.

After her parents died and her daughters left for school, there were times when the silence had almost driven her mad. Now the once quiet house was filled by the sound of the ocean, and Nessa was terrified of what she might hear next. She turned on the television as she passed through the living room and into the kitchen.

Rooting through the fridge, she found a bottle of white wine that a friend had brought months earlier. She uncorked it and poured herself a glass. Sitting at the kitchen table, she put her phone faceup in front of her. Then she dialed the last number she'd called.

"Hey, Mama." Breanna sounded worried. "Everything all right?" She was the elder of Nessa's twins, the first daughter of a first daughter, and she'd always had a touch of the sight. Even as an infant, she'd been so in tune with her mother's moods that Nessa hadn't been sure whether the child was reading, causing, or predicting them.

"Yes, baby." Nessa kept her voice even while the tears trickled down her face. They weren't tears of sadness, but rather of gratitude. Her children were safe. For years, the twins had been Nessa's sole source of solace. They'd stayed close by her side after their father died. Neither one of them would leave her for more than a few minutes at a time. "Where's your sister? She okay?"

"Jordan's fine, Mama. She's at the library."

"Good, good." Nessa paused to blow her nose. "So tell me what's been going on. How's life?"

She wanted to hear her daughter talk about normal things. Boys and books and the Korean soap operas both girls loved.

"'*How's life?*' You're really worrying me now, Mama."

There was no point in pretending nothing was up. Breanna could see straight through her. "Okay, fine. I was calling to let you both know not to get upset if you spot me on the news this evening."

"Oh my God, Mom!"

"No, no, no. Don't jump to conclusions. Nothing happened to me. I just—" Nessa took in a breath. "I found a dead girl today."

Breanna went quiet. Her next words were a whisper. "Who was it?"

Nessa had never hidden anything from her daughters. They knew all about the family legacy. She'd sat them both down at the age of ten and told them every story she could recall about their great-grandmother Dolores and Miss Ella. When Nessa confessed that she, too, had the gift, Breanna had sobbed for hours.

"I don't know who it was yet," Nessa admitted. "Just someone who needed to be found."

"So it's started?"

"I suppose so." Nessa suddenly felt exhausted.

"Was it horrible? You can tell me."

Nessa could imagine her daughter cringing on the other end of the line. Breanna didn't want to hear the details. Like other normal people, she preferred to avoid the subject of death. But Nessa knew her daughter would listen if she needed her to.

"Yes, it was horrible," Nessa confirmed. "She was just a young girl. They killed her and dumped her by the highway like a piece of trash."

They. The word had slipped right out of her mouth. She'd always assumed there was a single killer. But the truth was, she didn't know that for sure.

"Oh my God, Mama, that's awful," Breanna moaned. "Do you need us to come home to be with you?"

"No!" Nessa wasn't going to say so, but the last thing she wanted was her two girls in town with people going around killing women their age.

"I wish the gift had gone to someone else. You sure you don't need our help?"

"I've got help," Nessa told her.

Breanna knew what that meant. "You're saying you found a witch like Miss Ella?"

"I found two. A protector and a punisher."

"In *Mattauk*? Hold up. Jordan just came in." Breanna put the phone down, but Nessa could hear her talking to her sister in the background. "Mama found a dead girl today." Then she heard a thump and a thud as the phone changed hands.

"Where'd you find her?" That was Jordan—just like her father the cop. Loving and warm, but always straight to business.

"In some scrubland between the beach and the road."

"Which beach? Which road?"

"Danskammer."

Jordan's next question followed so quickly, it took Nessa by surprise. "Was she redheaded?"

"No," Nessa said, thinking only of the girl in blue. "Why?"

"Hey, Breanna." Nessa heard her daughter put the phone down. "Mama found the girl out by Danskammer Beach," Jordan told her sister.

"You're kidding!" Breanna responded in the background.

"You remember Mandy Welsh?" Jordan asked her mom.

"No," Nessa said. "Don't think so. Should I?" There were vast stretches of time when Nessa had been oblivious to everything but her daughters, her parents, and her patients.

"She was the girl who went missing when Breanna and I were juniors in high school."

That rang an unpleasant bell. "Remind me?" Nessa said, sitting up a bit straighter.

"They say she left her house one evening and never came back. The last place she was seen was Danskammer Beach. The cops claimed she ran away. But no one at school believed them. Mandy wasn't the type."

Nessa shivered. "You said someone saw her? Who was it?"

"Someone out fishing on the beach. They said they saw Mandy walking past all alone, wearing a fancy outfit. She didn't even have a suitcase. And no one gets dressed up to run away."

"Why do you think she was out by Danskammer Beach?" Nessa asked.

"No clue," Jordan said. "But it was sometime in April, so she definitely wasn't out for a swim."

"What did Mandy Welsh look like?" Nessa felt dread rising inside her.

"White girl with red hair and freckles. When we were little, she looked just like that girl from the books."

"Anne of Green Gables!" Breanna called out in the background.

"Hold on a minute, baby—" Nessa got up and cracked open the laptop she'd left sitting on the kitchen counter. She typed in the girl's name. The first image that popped up was a missing person poster. Nessa's heart sank. "I saw her ghost today, too," she said. "She was standing on the beach not far from where we found the other girl."

For a moment, all Nessa could hear was Jordan's breathing. "Oh my God. Does that mean Mandy's dead?" Jordan finally asked.

"I think so," Nessa said. "I didn't find her body. It must be somewhere out in the ocean."

"Mom." Jordan was using her no-nonsense voice. "This isn't what Great-grandma used to do—finding women whose husbands beat them to death. There's more than one dead girl this time. This sounds like a serial killer. You're out of your league. Did you tell the police you saw a redhead, too?"

"What was I supposed to say without a body to back me up? What do you think they'd do if I told them I see dead people?"

"Mom. Someone killed two girls."

Nessa didn't have the heart to tell her there had been a third girl on the beach.

"Franklin Rees is the detective on the case," she said. "I'll give him a call."

"Franklin Rees?" Jordan repeated cautiously. "The guy who found Daddy? *He's* the detective on the case?"

"Yeah," Nessa said with a sigh. "He works out here now."

"You're joking." Jordan sounded frightened. "Mama, this is getting way too weird." She put the phone down. "Remember Franklin Rees?" she asked her sister. "Mama says he works for Mattauk PD."

Breanna grabbed the phone away. "Is he still handsome?" she wanted to know.

"Oh, Lord, Breanna, you too?" Her mother sighed.

"Sounds like he's still handsome," Breanna informed her sister as she handed the phone back.

Jordan wasn't amused. "I don't care if he's Idris damned Elba. Just promise me you'll tell him about Mandy Welsh."

"I promise," Nessa said with a groan.

SHE DOWNED A SECOND GLASS of wine before she looked up Franklin's number. She'd hoped the alcohol would relax her. Instead, her heart pounded faster.

"Nessa," Franklin said when he answered. "We go years without talking, now I get to hear your voice twice in one day. Everything okay?"

"I've had two glasses of wine and I'm a little bit tipsy," Nessa confessed. She wasn't sure what was happening to her. First she'd taken up cursing, and now she'd started drinking alone. There was no telling what she'd end up doing next.

"I've found a few bodies in my day," he responded. "Sometimes a drink or two is the only thing that helps."

Nessa's spine stiffened. She hadn't meant to get personal. "What's the latest on my girl?" she asked.

Franklin sighed. "Fentanyl overdose," he said. "There were signs she'd had intercourse shortly before she died. Odds are, she was a sex worker who took one pill too many while she was out with a client. When she died, he didn't know what to do, so he dumped her body on the side of the road. It happens around here—a lot more often than any of us like to think."

"How often?" Nessa asked.

"A few times a year," Franklin said.

"In *Mattauk*?"

"The general vicinity."

The statistic was hard to swallow. "Then why haven't I heard about it?" Nessa demanded.

"Because the deaths of drug-addicted sex workers rarely make the news," Franklin said. "That's not how I'd like it, but that's how it is. You're a nurse, Nessa. You know I'm right."

She did. Nurses know better than anyone just how dark the world gets. "Okay, but that's not what happened to my girl," Nessa said. "She was clean."

"The test showed high levels of fentanyl in her system."

"Then someone drugged her," Nessa shot back.

Franklin stayed quiet for a beat too long. "You want to tell me how you could know that, Nessa?"

She came right out with it. "I saw her."

"You *saw* her?"

Nessa had planned to tell him everything, but at the last moment, she lost her nerve. She'd held on to her secrets for thirty-five years. She wasn't ready to reveal them all at once. "I saw her in a dream," Nessa lied. "That's how I knew where to look for the body. She's been calling to me. She's been waiting for me to find her."

This time, the pause that followed was so long, Nessa felt the need to fill in the silence.

"The girl I saw looked seventeen or eighteen but could have been younger. She died wearing a pale blue dress and black heels, and she had a little quilted black leather handbag. Her hair was in twists and it looked like it had just been done. She was dressed like she was on her way to a party."

"There was a bag like the one you described underneath the body," Franklin said. "It was empty but the label said 'Ofelia.' That mean anything to you?"

"Ofelia? Never heard of it."

"Me neither. But according to Google, it's a popular Caribbean retail chain. We're checking the files for missing girls who might have family there. Right now, it's our best lead, unless you can give me something else."

She could. "The girl wasn't alone in my dream. There was another young woman down there—a Mattauk girl who disappeared two years ago. Whoever killed her must have dumped her body in the ocean. She was my daughters' age. They went to the same school. I believe her name was Mandy Welsh."

"You're telling me that in your dream, this girl Mandy Welsh was dead too? Are you sure, Nessa?"

"No, I'm not sure!" Nessa snipped. "I'm new to all of this. All I'm asking is that you go take a look. Will you do that or not?"

She expected pushback, but he offered none. "I will," he said.

"Good," Nessa huffed. The combination of wine and emotion was making her head swim. "Now if you don't mind, I'm going to get off the phone and go to bed."

"Thank you," Franklin said. "Thank you for trusting me with your dream."

She paused, taken aback by his words. "You're welcome," she said, though she didn't feel like she deserved his thanks. She should have told him more. "Don't make me regret it."

An hour later, she passed out with her head on the dining-room table and the empty wine bottle in front of her.

HURLING BEGONIAS

After Nessa dropped her off at home, Jo walked through the door to find Lucy playing Zelda on the giant television her father had purchased for video games. Whenever Jo popped home from work during the day, that was usually where she found Art.

"I'm sorry I'm late." Jo kissed Lucy on the crown of her head. "You must be starving, poor thing. I brought you a sandwich from the deli on Main Street."

"Thanks," Lucy said, without looking up. "I'll take it to school for lunch tomorrow. Dad and I made beef ravioli from scratch."

"You did?" Jo marveled. "Was it edible? How's your belly feeling?"

"It feels fine. The pasta was yummy. Hey—can you take me to visit Harriett sometime?" she asked.

"We'll see. Where is Dad?" Jo asked.

"Bedroom," Lucy told her, still without looking away from the screen.

Upstairs, Jo made as much noise as possible as she walked down the hall. She'd learned it was best to give her husband fair warning. Still, she found Art on the bed with the computer on his lap. He closed the top as she entered.

"Maybe wait until the kid's in bed?" Jo didn't give a shit if Art watched a dirty video now and then, but she couldn't disguise her disgust at what she'd come to see as a massive waste of time.

Video games and porn consumed so many hours of her husband's day, it was a minor miracle he managed to feed himself or their daughter.

"For your information, I was working." Art sounded indignant. Who knew, maybe this time it was true. "Where have you been? Lucy said you were hanging around with Harriett Osborne. So what's the story? She really a witch?"

"Yes." Jo glanced down at the clock on her phone. She'd timed the trip home perfectly. "Turn on the local news."

"You mean on the television?" It was as though she'd asked him to tune the wireless to *News of the World*.

Harriett snatched the remote off the bedside table and switched the TV to channel 4. The news had started, and they were playing footage taped earlier that day. Two burly EMTs emerged from a thicket at the edge of Danskammer Beach Road, lugging a blue plastic body bag. Several yards away, Nessa was talking to her detective friend while Harriett listened in. Jo saw herself standing apart from her friends, her eyes fixed on the body bag. A car drove between the crime scene and the cameras. By the time it had passed, the EMTs were loading the dead girl onto a stretcher, but Jo hadn't moved an inch.

"Oh my God, Jo. Did you murder someone?"

"What the hell?" When she saw Art's face, she could have sworn he was serious. "No! We found a dead body."

When the news hit him, his eyes went wide. "You did?"

"You really thought I might have killed someone?"

"One has to consider all possibilities." It was clearly a half-hearted attempt at humor. "You do have a nasty temper. But yes, of course I was kidding. What the hell happened? Where did you and your friends find a body?"

Jo wanted to tell him everything. It didn't feel right to hide important details from Art. But she, Nessa, and Harriett had agreed to stick to the official story. "We were walking down to Danskammer Beach, and Nessa stepped off the trail to pee and found a black trash bag with a body inside."

"Jesus Christ. Who was it?"

It was such a simple question, and one Jo had anticipated. Yet she stood there, unable to answer. The day had been such a blur that she hadn't had time to absorb the horrible truth. "It was a girl." It wasn't until she heard her own cracked voice that she realized she was crying.

"Come here." Art set the computer aside, took Jo's arm, and pulled her down beside him on the bed.

"It was a girl," Jo wailed into his shoulder. "Seventeen, maybe. Just a little girl, a few years older than Lucy. Naked and used up and thrown away by the side of the road."

He held her tighter. "Oh, Jo, I'm so sorry."

"Who would do something like that?" She'd listened to hundreds of crime podcasts. She knew there were people who hunted women, but she'd always imagined them as comic book villains or bogeymen, whose victims had only been nameless bodies.

"I can't even imagine," Art replied, and she knew it was true. Art Levison, for all his flaws, had never willfully harmed another human being in his life.

She rested her head on her husband's chest. When they were younger, they had spent hours lying with their limbs entwined. Jo tried to count the years that had passed since she'd last sought comfort from Art. The warmth of his body and weight of his arms were so calming. The scent that had once driven her mad now soothed her. Her eyes felt heavy, and she might have fallen asleep if she hadn't spotted Lucy peeking into the room.

"Do you need something?" Jo asked.

"Nope," Lucy said. "Just making sure you haven't killed each other."

"Then your work here is done," Art said. "Please resume whatever you were doing before you felt the urge to play detective."

When Jo began to sit up, he resisted. After a two-second struggle, he set her free. "Where are *you* going?"

Jo wiped her eyes. "I should pop by the gym for a few minutes," she told her husband as Lucy bounded back down to the living room.

"Can't it wait? You've had a rough day. Are you sure you have to go now?"

"Yeah." She rose from the bed and looked down at her husband. "I need to check in with Heather. She's only been assistant manager for three weeks, and this is the first time I've left her on her own."

"If that's what you need." Art gave in and reached for the computer beside him. When he opened it, Jo caught a glimpse of a Word document on the screen.

"What's that?" she asked.

"Just something I've been working on. Be careful, will you? Sounds like there could be a killer out there."

IT WAS SEVEN THIRTY WHEN Jo slipped behind the wheel of her car, and Furious Fitness closed at nine. Heather had texted her throughout the day, assuring Jo that everything was running smoothly. But Jo had never missed a full day of work before, and she wasn't about to start.

She was idling at a traffic light on Main Street, across from the Mattauk police station, when someone lurched across the road in front of her car. The woman's bottle-blond hair was slipping out of a loose bun on the top of her head, and she looked ready for bed in a spaghetti-strap top and a pair of men's boxer shorts. There was little doubt she was drunk.

Jo watched with growing concern as the woman stomped into

the center of one of the police station's flower beds, pulled up a plant, roots and all, and hurled it at the building's windows. Jo rolled down her window in time to hear the plant hit with a loud thud and a satisfying spray of dirt.

"You fucking motherfucker!" the woman screamed as she uprooted a small bush. "I told you! I told you someone killed my baby!"

Jo gasped when the door opened and an officer appeared, his service revolver drawn. He lowered the firearm when he recognized the attacker. "Mrs. Welsh? Put the begonia down!"

The woman lobbed the plant at his head. Her aim was surprisingly good, but he ducked just in time. "I fucking told Rocca someone killed her and you fuckers did nothing. Now some other girl is dead. You fucking useless pieces of shit! This is on you!"

Jo steered her car into the station's parking lot and hopped out. Her gut was telling her the woman was the mother of one of the girls Nessa had seen on the beach.

"Mrs. Welsh!" A second policeman with a gun ran outside. Someone was going to get shot.

"Fuck you! Go ahead and shoot me, you spineless piece of shit. What the fuck do I have to live for, anyway?"

The woman reached down for a large rock, and Jo knew the time had come to intervene. She sprinted toward the flower bed and grabbed the woman by the wrist.

"Don't," she heard herself tell the drunk woman. "Not now."

Jo's iron grip seemed to convince the woman that a struggle wasn't worth it. She dropped the rock, and Jo released her. The woman teetered for a moment, then fell backward onto her butt. "Who the fuck are you?" she demanded.

"My name is Jo Levison." She held out a hand and pulled the woman up to her feet. Mulch from the flower beds remained stuck to the woman's boxer shorts.

"I've seen you before," the woman said. "You were on the news."

"I was," Jo said. "I was one of the people who found the girl today."

"My girl is out there, too." The woman's jaw was clenched tightly enough to break all her teeth. The stench of alcohol wafted from her skin. "And these worthless motherfuckers won't even look!"

"I'll help find her," Jo told the woman.

The woman's face went slack with surprise. She didn't know what to make of Jo's offer. "You will?"

One of the police officers was inching toward them as though they were terrorists with bombs strapped to their chests rather than two civilians armed with nothing more than begonias. "Mrs. Welsh," he said. "You need to come with me. I'm going to have to book you for destruction of government property."

"Oh, come on," Jo said. "She threw a couple of plants. What property did she destroy?"

"There's a crack in one of the windows."

"I'll have it fixed," Jo said. "I own Furious Fitness. I'll send my repairperson over to take a look tomorrow. Whatever it costs, I'll pay the bill. Now save yourself some paperwork and let me take this lady home. As soon as we're gone, you can go back to looking at naked ladies on your phone."

It had just been a shot in the dark, but the look on his face told her she hadn't missed the mark.

"Why are you helping me, rich lady?" the woman whispered as Jo led her away.

"What makes you think I'm rich?" Jo asked.

The woman responded with a drunken titter. "If you weren't rich, that cop would have shot your ass. Where you from, anyways?"

"Here," Jo said.

"Me too! How'd you end up looking like one of those bitches who show up every summer?"

"I don't know. I guess I just got lucky." It was the only explanation Jo could offer.

Once she'd been loaded into the car, Mrs. Welsh promptly passed out. Jo tried calling Nessa. The phone went straight to voice mail, and when she drove past Nessa's house, the lights were all off. She couldn't haul the woman back to her own home, so she continued down Woodland Drive and pulled up in front of the town's most infamous residence.

Harriett answered the door in a sheer linen muumuu that did nothing to conceal the naked body underneath. "Long time no see," she said.

Jo tried not to stare. "Hey, yeah, I'm sorry to bother you. I was on my way to my gym and I ran into a woman throwing plants at the police station." She knew how crazy it sounded, but she kept on going. "I think she's the mother of one of the girls Nessa saw. She's drunk off her ass and looks seriously ill. She needs our help."

"Of course. Darling?" Harriett called back to someone. "Would you mind pulling on some pants and giving me a hand for a moment?"

Jo watched in astonishment as the sexiest man who'd ever worked at a Mattauk grocery store appeared buck naked in Harriett's living room with a pair of old jeans in his hand. Jo averted her eyes until he'd managed to put them on.

"What can I do for you?" he asked Harriett.

"There's a drunk woman in my friend's car. Will you please bring her into the house?"

"Sure thing," he said, flashing the ladies his movie-star smile.

They both watched him walk out to the drive, bare-chested and shoeless. "You're my hero, Harriett," Jo said. "But for the record, I could have brought her inside."

"I know," said Harriett. "It's just that Eric likes feeling useful. And it was about time he got dressed and went home, anyway. Come in and make yourself comfortable."

When Jo looked around, she could hardly believe she was in-doors. The walls of the house had been transformed into vertical gardens, and trees bearing unusual fruit grew out of containers. Jo examined the herbs sprouting from the hanging planter affixed to the nearest wall, but couldn't identify a single one of them. Books bristling with scraps of paper marking important pages were stacked high on the Eames coffee table and rose like columns from the floor beside the Knoll sofa. On top of the piles closest to her were *Working Conjure: A Guide to Hoodoo Folk Magic, Cleansing Rites of Curanderismo,* and *Shen Nong Ben Cao Jing.* Squirrels were building a massive nest in the living room fireplace, and a flock of little green parakeets chased each other around the high ceilings.

Harriett's gentleman caller reappeared with a limp Ms. Welsh cradled in his arms.

"Just put her on the sofa, please," Harriett told him.

When the woman was laid out like Sleeping Beauty, Harriett handed the man his shirt and shoes, then leaned down to examine the new arrival. She pried open one of Ms. Welsh's eyes, examined her fingernails, and sniffed at the breath leaking out of her lungs.

"Jo, would you mind popping into the hall linen closet and grabbing a spare blanket for our guest?"

Jo did as she was asked. On her way back to the living room, she stopped to wait while Harriett finished saying a very warm good-bye to her gentleman friend.

As soon as she heard the door close, Jo headed for the sofa and spread the blanket over the sleeping woman. Harriett had slipped on a pair of glasses and taken a place behind a wooden counter that had once served as a bar but appeared to have been transformed into a workbench. There were still liquor-filled bottles lining the shelf behind her, but stuffed inside them were leaves, roots, and various other ingredients Jo wasn't certain she wanted to identify.

Glass jars with cork stoppers held dried mushrooms, a rainbow of berries, and something that upon closer inspection appeared to be shriveled caterpillars.

"I hope it's not rude to say so, but your boyfriend is smoking hot," Jo remarked casually.

Harriett smirked as she plucked dried buds from a branch and dropped them into a marble mortar, followed by a handful of fresh green leaves. "I'm long past the boyfriend stage," she said. "I don't need to own anyone. And I certainly don't want anyone to think they own me. Eric and I just enjoy one another's company. At least twice a week."

"Twice a week? Damn, Harriett. I can't even *remember* what it's like to have sex twice a week."

"I have sex with *Eric* twice a week. He's not the only one." Harriett seemed to relish the shock on Jo's face. "I'm making up for lost time. I didn't have enough sex before I got married," she explained. "My family was conservative, and everyone made it seem like such a big deal. My grandmother had me convinced I'd catch AIDS, get knocked up, and be branded the town whore if I dropped my trousers. For years I was too worried about going to hell to realize how much I liked fucking. I'm not worried about anything anymore."

Harriett added a handful of seedpods to the mortar and ground its contents into a mush, which she spooned into a glass. Then she added a splash of pale green liquid from one of the liquor bottles, poured some Evian on top, and stirred.

"What are you making?" Jo asked.

"An antidote for the alcohol sloshing around in our guest's system, along with a few other things that will help her feel better. What she really needs is a month of good meals and a lot of rest. Her system is on the verge of collapse," Harriett said. "There are clear signs of heavy drinking, and the color of her tongue indicates she's severely malnourished. Her troubles must have started long before her daughter's disappearance. This woman's life has not been easy. She's too young to be so ill."

"Young? How old do you think she is?" Jo asked quietly.

Harriett glanced up and took another look at the woman laid out on the sofa. "Late thirties," she replied.

"No." Jo couldn't believe it. That would make her much younger than both of them.

"Nothing ages a person like poverty and misery," Harriett said. "Despite what all the ads claim, it's not skin cream that helps some women keep their glow. The only true youth serum has two ingredients—luck and money."

Harriett finished mixing the strange herbal cocktail and held it up to the light for inspection. Seemingly satisfied with the result, she came out from behind the bar and took a seat on the edge of the sofa. Ms. Welsh's eyes fluttered open as Harriett gently lifted her head.

"Drink," Harriett ordered as she poured a thin trickle into the woman's mouth. The patient swallowed and grimaced at the taste. A few seconds later, she sat upright, took the glass from Harriett's hands, and guzzled the rest of its contents, twin streams of green liquid running down either side of her chin.

She sat back and wiped her mouth with the palm of her hand. "That was disgusting. What the hell did you just give me?"

"Just a little something I made. I assume it worked?"

"You could get rich selling that stuff."

"Why would I trade a creation as pure as this for something as filthy as money?" Harriett laughed.

The woman looked at Harriett as if she might be insane. Then her eyes widened. "Fucking hell! You're the witch, aren't you?" She cringed and recoiled when she realized what she'd said. "Sorry,

sorry, sorry. I didn't mean to piss you off. That's just what people at work call you."

Harriett's smile broadened, exposing the gap between her teeth. "That doesn't offend me. 'Witch' is the label society slaps on women it can't understand or control. But feel free to call me Harriett. And you are?"

"Amber Welsh."

Jo stepped forward. "I'm Jo Levison. I found you outside the police station. I brought you here."

The memory appeared to make Amber wince. "Thank you," she said. "I'm sure I'd be sleeping on the floor of a cell right now if it wasn't for you. Wouldn't be the first time. But I swear to God, I'm not like that anymore. I've been mostly sober for three whole months. Been talking to my sponsor every day. Then someone texted me a video about the body they found, and I lost it."

"I think you have a good reason to be angry at the cops," Jo said. "It sounded like something happened to your daughter."

Amber pulled in a long, shaky breath as she nodded. "Mandy disappeared two years ago around this time of year. When I went to the Mattauk police, they said girls like her run away all the time. I told them they didn't know my daughter. She was responsible. Always had dinner ready when I got home from work. Helped with the little ones. After their dad got sent away, I don't know what I would've done without her. To be honest, I don't know how I manage now." Amber bowed her head. "Maybe she wasn't an honor student or prom queen, but Mandy was a good kid. I told them that. The night she didn't come home, I went straight to the cops and told them that something had happened to my girl. But they didn't listen. They've had it in for my family for years now. They know I've been in trouble and they know her dad went to jail for meth, and they figured that was all they needed to know about

Mandy. They said it would be a waste of resources to send someone out to look for her."

"Those bastards." Jo's fists were clenched and throbbing. "Why do they get to decide who's worthwhile and who's not?"

"What do *you* think happened to Mandy?" Harriett asked.

Amber wiped her tears away with the edge of the blanket. "Somebody killed her, of course. Just like that girl they found down by the beach today. That's where Mandy was last seen. Walking down the road that runs next to Danskammer Beach."

"She was walking by herself? Where do you think she was going?"

"Well, there's only one place she could have been going, isn't there? The Pointe. She was wearing a dress we bought for her grandmother's funeral. I think she might have been going to see someone about a job. But you know what? The cops never bothered to ask a single fucking person out there if they'd seen her."

"The Pointe is a long way for a girl her age to walk. What kind of job would she have been interviewing for?" Jo asked.

"I don't know. House cleaner, maybe? She was good with kids, too. Maybe she was going to be somebody's nanny."

"She didn't tell you?"

"I was going through a rough patch back then." Amber watched as her toes dug into the soft, spongey soles of her flip-flops. "Truth is, she might have told me, and I might just not remember. But when I realized she was missing, I went straight to the cops. If they'd gone out to look for her the same night, they could have found her." Amber kept her gaze directed at the floor. There was such horror and grief on her face that Jo had to look away. She couldn't bear to imagine what the woman might be seeing. If it had been her kid, Jo would have thrown more than plants at the police station's windows. Amber had gone to the cops because she'd lost the most precious thing she had—and they couldn't even be bothered to look for it. They'd assigned a price to Mandy Welsh's life and decided a girl like her wasn't worth their time.

"We'll find Mandy," Jo promised.

Amber shook her head hopelessly. "She's dead."

"We know," Jo said. There was no point in pretending it might not be true. "But we'll bring her back to you so she can rest in peace. Then we'll take care of the person who killed her—and make sure he never hurts anyone ever again."

Amber shook her head as though the thought were ridiculous and Jo was cruel to even suggest it. "How are you gonna do that?"

"We were the ones who found the girl by Danskammer Beach today," Harriett told her. "Our friend heard her calling."

Amber blinked. "I'm sorry," she said flatly. "*What*?"

"Our friend Nessa has a gift," Jo explained. "When the dead are lost, they call out to her so she can find them."

Amber rose slowly from her seat as if she'd spotted a snake slithering toward her across the floor. "You ladies are sweet and I appreciate your help, but I know the cops here, and they aren't going to listen to a witch and a lady ninja and some woman who talks to dead people." When she was on her feet, she headed straight for the door. "Thanks for everything you've done tonight, but I really need to get home to my kids. My thirteen-year-old is not the babysitter his sister was."

"Harriett gave you a drink that sobered you up in about ten seconds flat. Would you have believed that was possible?" Jo asked.

Amber paused at the door.

"I can do more than that," Harriett added. "It will take a lot more than a single drink, but I can restore your health. All you have to do is pay me a few more visits. How long has it been since you haven't felt broken?"

Long enough for her to take the offer seriously, apparently. "And what would I need to do in return?"

Jo hoped Harriett knew it wasn't a good moment for a joke about selling her soul to Satan.

"You just have to talk to our friend tomorrow," Harriett said. "Tell her what you told us about Mandy—and anything else you remember between now and then."

"That's it?" Amber asked.

"That, and you let me give you a ride back to your car," Jo said. "It's getting late, and someone in Mattauk's been killing women."

"Car?" Amber asked. "My car hasn't been running. I walked into town. And in case you haven't noticed, somebody's *always* killing women."

AMBER'S HOUSE WAS A SINGLE-WIDE trailer parked on a bald patch of sandy dirt. Broken toys lay scattered around the building and a run-down Corolla with three wheels and no license plate sat parked in front. The trailer's rusted screen door looked as though it had been kicked in multiple times, and a broken window was patched up with duct tape. Jo had always known there were people around Mattauk who weren't well off. But she couldn't have imagined this kind of poverty existing a few miles away from her middle-class subdivision or the mansions on Culling Pointe. Mattauk hid its poor people well. Or maybe, Jo realized to her chagrin, she'd never really bothered to look.

Jo had wondered what kind of job would have driven a sixteen-year-old girl to walk five miles down a deserted road in her best dress. Now she knew—and she could have kicked herself for being so dense. A girl who lived in a place like this would have walked five miles for any job that would pay her. Whatever the salary, the money was desperately needed.

A potbellied little boy wearing a pair of basketball shorts stood on the other side of the screen door. The light from a television flickered on the wall behind him. He watched, one hand digging into a bag of Cheetos, as the car pulled up. When the headlights went out and he saw his mom in the passenger seat, he darted out of sight.

"That's Dustin," Amber said.

"He's cute," Jo said. "How old is he?"

"Seven." Amber sighed. "Damn it. He was in bed when I left. His brother shouldn't have let him out. I bet all three of them have been up the whole time. Mandy would have—" She stopped and stared through the windshield, her eyes focused on nothing in particular.

"I'm sorry," Jo said. "If there's anything I can do . . ." She wished she knew how to offer help without offending Amber's pride.

Amber turned to her. "You kept me out of jail tonight. That's the best thing anyone's done for me in a really long time. And if your friend can find Mandy's body, that might just help more than anything else. I can't go anywhere until I know there's no chance at all that she's coming home again."

"What time do you get off work tomorrow?" Jo asked.

"My shift at the Stop & Shop ends at seven," Amber said.

"Okay," Jo said. "My friend Nessa and I will pick you up after work."

WHY AMBER CRAIG
TURNED TO ARSON

er sophomore year in high school, Amber Craig, reporter for the *Mattauk High Herald*, was sent to interview the area's oldest resident, who'd recently turned 102. The woman lived in what had once been the guesthouse of a gilded-era mansion that her family had erected more than a century earlier. When Amber rang the bell, she expected the door to be answered by a nurse or a housekeeper. Standing there instead was the woman herself, as alert and high-strung as a rat terrier. They spent the better part of an hour chatting about Mattauk over the decades before Amber got to the clichéd question her journalism teacher had insisted she ask.

"So what's the secret to a good, long life?"

The woman leaned forward as if she'd been waiting for that very question. "You must do whatever you can to rid yourself of bad luck."

Amber chuckled politely, imagining it was some kind of old-person joke.

"If it finds you, it will stick to you." The old lady was dead serious, Amber realized, and she believed her advice was urgently needed. "Should that happen, you must not be afraid. You'll need to fight back with all your strength. Do whatever is necessary to free yourself quickly, or else you will never escape."

Amber sat there with her mouth wide-open, unable to muster a response.

"I am telling you this because you are a sweet, smart, pretty girl.

I was like you once," the woman informed her. "Bad luck waits for women like us around every corner. When it found me, I dealt with it expeditiously. And that is the only reason we are here talking today." Then she smiled, as though it were a relief to have unburdened herself of such weighty knowledge. "Now, would you care for some more apple strudel, my dear?"

Six months later, it was this advice that led Amber to set her softball coach's beloved boat on fire.

AMBER'S FATHER HAD ALWAYS WANTED a boy. Everyone knew it. He didn't complain, nor did he do anything to hide his disdain for the feminine creature he and his wife had produced. A lobster fisherman, he spent long days offshore. His wife worked full-time as a receptionist at a clinic in town. Every night, she came home to a second shift of cooking, cleaning, and childcare. Amber was expected to help her mom with the housework, while her father sat drinking beer and watching any baseball game that happened to be on TV. After her chores were done, Amber would often sit beside him, cheering for whichever team he seemed to prefer. Unless she was handing him a fresh Budweiser, her father didn't seem to know she was there.

Looking back on that time, Amber couldn't recall ever feeling deprived. Her family wasn't rich, but she had everything she needed. She ate three balanced meals every day. She had clean clothes to lay out at the bottom of her bed every evening. She made good grades and won awards at school. She had plenty of friends and could name no enemies. Then she joined the softball team.

It was only a lark. The guidance counselor had suggested a sport would look good on her college applications. Amber never expected to excel at anything physical. She was as surprised as anyone when she hit a home run her first time at bat. When the coach put her on the mound, she only gave up one hit. She saw him watching from the dugout, arms crossed. As usual, his face gave nothing away. It was the astonishment of the girl sitting beside him that told Amber everything. Jamie Roberts had been the team's best pitcher for the previous two seasons, and she'd just been blown away. Amber couldn't help but notice the girl looked thrilled.

"Keep pitching like that, and you'll have a full ride to any college you like," the coach told Amber after practice.

Until then, Amber had kept her hopes modest and her ambition in check. Her father wasn't a lawyer. Her mom wasn't a doctor. There was no college fund sitting in a bank account with her name on it. Now the coach of the island's best softball team was saying her options might soon be limitless. And John Rocca wasn't the sort to lie. At thirty, he was already a decorated police officer and a deacon at St. Francis. His prim, pretty wife and three little boys attended every softball game. Though Rocca was ten years younger than her father, he was the kind of man her dad held in high esteem.

"That girl of yours is a phenomenon," Rocca informed Amber's father the day of her pitching debut.

Over twenty years later, Amber could still see the pride on her dad's face. Until she was sent to juvie, he never missed one of her games.

EVERYTHING WAS GOING WELL. AMBER didn't want to jinx it. So when it all started, she tried her best to brush it off. Rocca's appearance in the locker room when she was getting out of the shower was an accident, as was the way his hand often landed a little too high on her thigh. She wrote off all the lingering hugs as evidence of his affectionate nature. It had to be her imagination that he always seemed to find excuses to touch her. The other explanation just didn't make sense. There was no way a handsome, happily married police officer would be making the moves on a gawky fifteen-year-old. Rather than make a fuss or complain, she always managed to squirm away.

Jamie, the pitcher who'd been sitting beside Rocca the day Amber tried out for the team, quit two weeks into the season. She was a senior, and she wanted to enjoy her last year in high school. At least that's what she told the other girls on the team. But whenever Amber saw her, Jamie never seemed to be having much fun. She sat on her own at lunch and walked home alone every afternoon. Amber caught her staring whenever they passed in the hall. Then one day, the girl reached out a hand, grabbed hold of Amber's sweater, and yanked her over to the side.

"You been out on his boat yet?" Jamie asked, her voice low and serious.

"No," Amber said. There was no question Jamie meant Rocca. Other than softball, the boat was all he talked about.

"He'll ask you soon," Jamie said. "Don't go."

"What do you mean?" Amber asked.

"Are you dumb?" Jamie demanded. "Just don't go, okay? And don't tell anyone that I said so."

It seemed so preposterous. Why would Rocca invite her out on his boat all alone? What would his wife say? What about her parents? They would never agree to something like that.

TWO WEEKS LATER, ROCCA STOPPED her family as they walked to their car after another winning game.

"This Monday is the beginning of spring break," he said. "You folks want to come out on my boat to celebrate our perfect season?"

Her parents couldn't, of course. They both had to work.

"Then would you mind if my family and I take Amber out for an hour or two? She's been working hard. She deserves to have some fun. What do you think? Would that be all right?"

Her parents thought she was lucky—and said so. Amber wasn't so sure. She could still see Jamie's face in her mind. What should she have said? What magic words might have freed her? Twenty years later, she still didn't know.

That Monday, she walked the three blocks to the marina where Rocca's boat was moored. As she drew closer, he appeared alone on deck.

"Where's everyone else?" she asked as dread rose inside her.

"The boys came down with something last night," Rocca said. "Juliet had to stay home to watch them. Don't worry. It'll be more fun without them, anyway."

For the first twenty minutes, everything seemed perfectly normal, and Amber almost relaxed. Once they were out on the ocean, with only the tip of Culling Pointe in sight, Rocca brought the boat to a stop and stepped away from the wheel. He'd slipped his penis out of his pants. And Amber realized there was nowhere to go.

He let her keep her virginity. He'd save it for another boat ride. From that day forward, oral sex always made her seasick.

Going to the police didn't seem like an option. Quitting the team would mean giving up on her future. But she couldn't go back out on the boat. Then a solution occurred to her—a way to rid herself of the bad luck once and for all. The night after the boat ride, she snuck out of her house at two in the morning and walked the three blocks to the marina, clutching the gas can her father used to fill the family lawn mower. She poured the gasoline out on the deck of the boat, lit a kitchen match, and tossed it over the rail. She'd never set anything on fire, of course. She had no idea the explosion would be powerful enough to singe her eyebrows and wake the neighbors.

AMBER COULDN'T PROVE WHAT ROCCA had done, and Jamie refused to talk. But two witnesses had seen Amber sprinting out of the marina that night, and the police found her father's plastic gas can floating in the sound. It was more than enough to send Amber to a juvenile detention facility for the remainder of her high school years.

The lobsters around Mattauk had been dying in droves, and countless businesses had been dragged under. One afternoon when Amber was in the second year of her incarceration, her father jumped over the side of his boat and swam out to sea. Unable to pay the mortgage after her husband's suicide, Amber's mother lost the house later that year. Six months after that, she moved in with an abusive boyfriend, who knocked out her front teeth and introduced her to meth. The old woman Amber had interviewed died a few weeks before Amber was released from jail. Amber likely never would have known if a shocking discovery inside the woman's house hadn't made the news. Two bodies were found in the basement—both men. One was the old lady's uncle, who'd vanished when she was fourteen. The second was the woman's first husband, who'd supposedly run off the year she turned thirty.

TWO DECADES AFTER THE FIRE, Amber still fantasized about what might have been. She'd decided long ago that if she could do it all over again, there was only one thing she'd change. She would still go out on the boat with Rocca. But as soon as they were far enough from shore, she would push the motherfucker over the side.

She'd had her chance, and she'd missed it. There was nothing she could do now. The bad luck had found her, and now it stuck like glue.

THEY WALK AMONG US

t was late when Jo finally made it back home. No one was up, but her family had left the living room light on for her. Lucy's schoolwork was spread out on the coffee table, with a half-empty glass of milk and a bowl of Goldfish cracker crumbs serving as paperweights. The handmade throw Jo had purchased from a boutique in Brooklyn had literally been tied in a knot, and the giant television was paused on a scene from *Bob's Burgers*. Jo had no trouble reconstructing the evening's events. At some point well past nine, Art had yelled down to Lucy that she should have been asleep a long time ago. Lucy ignored him until he made an angry appearance at the top of the stairs. Threats were issued, but never seen through. Teeth may have been brushed—though probably not. Lucy definitely pouted and asked when Mom would be back. Art would have kissed her forehead and said he didn't know. *You'll see Mom in the morning,* he'd have told their daughter, as if there were nothing more certain. As if mothers and daughters always came home.

Jo rode a wave of panic all the way up the stairs. She rushed past the dimly lit room where her husband was snoring and threw open the door at the end of the hall. A girl in striped pajamas lay curled up on the mattress, the bedsheets and blankets all kicked to the floor. Awake, Lucy played the role of a miniature adult. She sassed her mother and cursed like a sailor when her father wasn't around. Only when Lucy was sleeping could Jo see how small she still was—and how easy it would be for someone to hurt her.

Jo lay down beside her daughter and pulled Lucy into her arms. Their world always seemed so safe and predictable. But the truth was, they'd just gotten lucky so far. Jo cried for Mandy Welsh and the mother who hadn't been able to protect her. And though she didn't often pray, Jo begged any god that might be listening to grant her the power to keep her own child safe.

SHE WOKE THE NEXT MORNING with her arms still wrapped around Lucy. The covers had been lovingly tucked around both of them, and she could smell oatmeal cooking. Jo peeked in the bathroom mirror and rubbed away the mascara smudges under her eyes before heading downstairs.

Art was at the stove, stirring frozen blueberries into a pot of bubbling oatmeal. She didn't interrupt him. She wanted to watch. There was something so comforting about seeing him there in his bare feet and boxers, his hair still sleep-tousled and a streak of blueberry juice on his shirt. But she'd barely come to a stop when Art turned straight toward her, as if he'd felt her presence. "You going to be okay?" he asked.

"I don't have a choice," she said.

"Why don't you take the day off?" he suggested.

"I'm not going to the gym today."

"Really?" He sounded surprised. "I mean, *great*. I think that's wise. We can do something nice, just the two of us. Maybe . . ." His words trailed off when he noticed Jo's pained expression.

"I need to find out who murdered that girl."

Art closed his eyes and shook his head as if he should have known it was too good to be true. "Jo, the police—"

"No one's going to stop them from doing their thing," Jo said. "I'll just do mine, too."

"But *why*?" Art asked. "Why do you have to do *anything*?"

"Because I saw a girl's body rotting inside of a trash bag. And I swear to God, Art, I will never get that picture out of my head. I hope someone would do the same thing for me if it was my daughter who'd been killed."

"*Our* daughter," Art corrected her as he always did. She braced herself for the argument to come, but her husband simply nodded. "Okay. I get it."

"You don't think I'm crazy? You won't try to stop me?"

Art's smile seemed hopeless. "Would you let me?"

Jo closed the gap between them and wrapped her arms around him. "Nope," she said with her head on his chest.

"For the record, I do think you're nuts," Art said as he planted a kiss in her hair. "But that's always been part of your charm. Just promise me you won't get yourself hurt."

"I'll try. Right now I'm going to go out for a run. Gotta stay fit if I'm going to fight all the bad guys. I'll be back in time to take Lucy to school."

JO JOGGED DOWN DANSKAMMER BEACH Road, expecting to find it deserted as usual. She knew she wouldn't encounter the spirits Nessa had seen, but she wanted Mandy and the other girls to know she was there. They would not be forgotten. She hadn't told Art exactly where she was headed, of course. He would have warned her against it, and he'd have had a good point. Whoever had murdered the girl and dumped her body in the scrub might return for a visit. A woman running along an empty highway in the early morning would make an irresistible target. The killer could be lurking out there right now, waiting for another victim to wander into his trap. Jo hoped so. She fantasized about what she would do to the asshole if she found him—and wondered if she'd grown powerful enough to rip him limb from limb.

A truck sped past with two men in the cab. It swerved to the center of the road to avoid her, but didn't slow. Another car drove by a minute later, ferrying a group of young women with their windows rolled down. More vehicles followed, one after another, all headed away from town. Jo couldn't imagine where they all might be going. Even on summer weekends, Danskammer Beach didn't attract many swimmers or sunbathers. The road was out of the way for anyone not bound for the Pointe.

Then a gleam in the distance caught her eye. As she drew closer, she could make out the hood of a car with the morning sun bouncing off it. The vehicles that had passed her were there, too, parked along both sides of the road. People milled about at the edge of the scrubland. Jo picked up speed, her feet slamming against the pavement. Another body must have been found. She sprinted toward a middle-aged couple standing with their backs to the ocean. She'd almost reached them when she saw the man lift a phone and smile. It was too late to stop. She arrived just as the selfie was snapped. The two of them greeted her with startled expressions.

"What's going on?" Jo panted.

"They found a body here yesterday," the woman explained, looking over her husband's shoulder as he inspected the photo they'd taken.

"Let's try it one more time," he said, putting his arm around his wife and holding the phone aloft once again.

"Why are you taking photos?"

"Friend of mine's an EMT." The woman kept the smile on her face and her eyes on the camera. "Said it looked like the work of a serial killer. This beach is going to be famous."

"For God's sake, stop talking," her husband ordered.

Jo left them to their photo shoot and wove her way through the others who'd gathered to gawk. A few hearty souls were inspecting the edge of the scrubland, searching for a way into the thicket.

None of them spotted the entrance to the path, which now seemed clear as day to Jo.

"You were here yesterday when they found the body." A young man had sidled up beside her. His clothing appeared slightly disheveled. There were bags under his eyes and the scruff on his chin was quickly turning into a beard. He looked as though he might have slept in his car. "I saw you on the news. You were one of the women who found the body."

Jo ignored him. It would be safer for the kid if he just went away.

"Jo Levison, am I right?"

She was itching to punch someone, and he'd just become the likeliest target. "Who the hell are you?"

"My name's Josh Gibbon," he continued, undaunted. "I host a top-rated true crime podcast. Maybe you've heard of it? It's called *They Walk Among Us.*"

Jo had heard of it, all right. She'd been a regular listener when the podcast launched. At first it had been a scrappy one-man show. By the time she stopped listening, *They Walk Among Us* was sponsored by insurance companies, home security systems, and men's underwear manufacturers. Serial killers and dead girls were a lucrative business.

"I know, I know." His smile seemed a little too slick. "The name of the podcast's a bit over the top. But I assure you, we're a very serious show. We analyze unsolved homicides, looking for similarities. We've managed to alert authorities to the existence of five serial killers at work in the northeastern United States. One of our guys was captured two months ago. Have you heard of the Head Hunter? We even gave him his name."

"Because killers need catchy names?" Jo sneered. "What's next, collectible cards?"

Josh shook his head. "We're not trying to glorify serial killers."

He'd had his response ready. "We want to get people to listen so we can bring attention to the crimes."

"And what were the Head Hunter's crimes?" Jo asked.

"He murdered ten women—maybe more. He'd pick them up outside of shelters, drug them, dismember them, and leave their heads around Providence, Rhode Island. He was a very bad guy, and thanks to us, he's off the streets now. I drove out here from Brooklyn this morning because it sounds like there may be a predator at work on the island. If I'm right and you were one of the people who found the body, I'd love to ask you a few questions." He was already pulling his phone out of his pocket.

"The ten women the Head Hunter butchered. What were their names?"

Josh's face reddened, but he didn't hesitate. "You got me. I guess I'm better at giving names than I am at remembering them."

"But I bet you could tell me where all the heads were found, couldn't you? You probably have a whole file filled with pictures."

This time, the answer didn't just slip off his tongue. "I assure you that all the victims were named on the podcast," Josh said.

"Then maybe you should go back and listen to it." Jo could feel her arms throbbing with energy. "I need to finish my run."

She sped past the gawkers, eager to leave them all in her dust. Fueled by fury, she could have kept going forever, but the gate to Culling Pointe appeared before her, its tall metal slats reaching up toward the sky. While there was nothing but sand and scrub on Jo's side of the fence, the drive that stretched out in front of her was lushly landscaped. The Pointe's beachfront mansions remained hidden from view. It occurred to Jo that she'd never actually seen them up close. There were plenty of pictures to be found online, and anyone with a boat could admire them from offshore. But Culling Pointe's gate had never once opened to let Jo through. The chop of a helicopter drew her eyes to the sky. She watched the craft descend from the clouds and fly alongside her, its landing skids almost skimming the waves. Then it passed over the Pointe and vanished out of sight.

Watching Jo run toward the gate were two uniformed men in an air-conditioned guardhouse. As she got closer, one of them stepped outside to meet her at the gate. It seemed unnecessary. She wasn't able to burst through iron. *Yet.*

But he didn't try to shoo her away. Instead, he reached through the gate's slats and handed her a bottle of water.

"You run all the way from town?" he asked as she opened the bottle and gulped down its contents.

"Thanks," she panted. "And yeah, I did."

"All those vultures still down by the beach?"

"Yep," she said.

The guard shook his head, his lip curled with disgust. "I saw them on my drive in, just waiting around for the sun to come up. What kind of people take selfies at the site of a body drop?"

"Assholes," she said. The guard laughed, giving Jo the green light to keep going. "You guys see anything weird down here over the past few weeks?"

The guard held up a finger, then gestured to the earpiece he wore. He was receiving a message. "Sorry, ma'am," he said when he'd finished listening. "Would you mind stepping to the side for a moment? I've just been informed that a resident is arriving."

While the gate opened, Jo watched a black speck in the distance rapidly grow into an enormous black SUV. By the time it arrived, the gate was wide-open. The vehicle came to a brief stop while the guard checked the driver's ID. The back window was down, and Jo saw Rosamund Harding sitting inside. Jo lifted a hand in greeting, but Rosamund stared straight through her. It wasn't a snub—Jo was sure of it. Rosamund's eyes looked flat and glassy. A second later, the SUV sped away, and the gate closed.

"Thanks," the guard said.

"The lady in the back seat," Jo said. "She's a client of mine. I've been a bit worried about her. Does she live out here?"

"I'm sorry, ma'am." The guard looked back over his shoulder at his colleague. "I'm not at liberty to discuss any of our residents."

That was all she was going to get from him. The guard didn't give a damn about Rosamund Harding. His job was to protect Culling Pointe.

"Thanks for the water," Jo said. Then she turned her back and ran for town.

CULLING POINTE

Jo made it home with barely enough time to jump in the shower. She pulled on some clean gear and grabbed her keys. Lucy was already waiting for her in the car.

"Hey, I've got a question for you," Jo said as she slid into the driver's seat. "What would you do if someone you didn't know offered you a ride?"

Lucy gave her mother the stink eye. "Do you think I'm dumb?"

"Okay, fine." Jo tried again. "Imagine your dad forgets to pick you up from school and someone offers to drive you home. Let's say it's someone you know, but not very well."

Lucy appeared thoroughly unimpressed by the latest scenario. "I have a phone, Mom. I'd just call you to come pick me up."

"What if a man tried to drag you into his car?"

"Then I'd scream my head off and kick him in the balls and bite and punch and make the pervert wish he'd picked some other kid." Lucy sounded like she'd enjoy nothing more.

"Good," Jo said, though the conversation had done nothing to settle her nerves. The dead girls down by the beach must have had similar chats with their mothers. "But there's one more thing I want you to do if anyone ever tries to hurt you. I want you to look them right in the eyes and tell them 'If you mess with me, my mother will fucking kill you.' Make sure you use the word 'fucking,' and try to look crazy when you say it."

"Sure. I can do that." Lucy seemed confident.

The traffic in front of Lucy's school was worse than usual, and there were fewer kids walking alone. The line of cars came to a stop. "Show me," Jo ordered.

Lucy lowered her chin and looked up at her mother with a hideous grin. "If you mess with me, my mommy's going to fucking kill you. She's going to rip your intestines out of your butt and shove them into your eye sockets and out through your mouth."

"Yeah." Jo nodded with genuine admiration. "If that doesn't do the trick, I don't know what will. Did you come up with that last part by yourself?"

"Yep!" The adorable eleven-year-old Lucy was back. "Pretty good, right?"

"Absolutely terrifying," Jo commended the girl. The line of cars surged forward until they reached the drop-off point. "But seriously, Lucy, be careful. I can't lose you. And I don't really want to kill anyone. So please stay safe, okay?"

"Okay, Mama." Lucy leaned over and planted a kiss on her mother's cheek. And then she was out, the car door was slammed, and Jo's most precious possession was skipping away from her across the schoolyard. It wasn't until the SUV behind her honked that Jo finally stepped on the gas.

Her unease only intensified when she pulled up in front of Nessa's prim two-story white colonial ten minutes later. Though she knew her friend to be an early riser, there were no signs of life inside. Jo felt the first flicker of panic as she hurried down the flagstone path to the front door. She should have checked on Nessa the previous night when her call went straight to voice mail. After all, there was a killer in town, and as anyone who watched shows like *Dateline* or *Newsnight* would know, Nessa's picture-perfect house, with its jolly red door and white picket fence, was the ideal setting for a gruesome murder.

Jo rang the bell six times and tried the door handle. She'd started pounding with her fists in frustration when Nessa answered the door, still in the outfit she'd worn the previous day. The sunlight hit her face, and she recoiled with a hiss like a vampire.

Jo grabbed hold of the doorframe. Relief had weakened her knees. "Oh my God, I thought you were dead."

"I wish," Nessa said. "What time is it?"

"Eight forty-five," Jo informed her. Then she leaned toward the woman and sniffed. "You smell like a winery. Did you throw a party after I dropped you off?"

"Don't you go smelling me," Nessa scolded her. "I saw three dead people yesterday. I needed to take the edge off."

Jo gave her a hug. "How many bottles did you go through, you lush?" she whispered in Nessa's ear.

Nessa pushed her back. "Just one," she said with a wince. "But apparently that was one too many."

"Aww. Poor thing. Thank goodness I know where to fix you up," Jo told her. "Don't bother putting on fresh clothes. Just hop in the car."

"Take me to the hospital," Nessa ordered as she shuffled toward the driveway. "If I'm unconscious when we get there, tell them to give me oxygen and hook me up to a saline drip."

"Trust me," Jo told her. "We're going somewhere much better than the hospital."

Nessa strapped on her seat belt and closed her eyes for the ride. She'd barely settled in before the car stopped again.

Nessa opened a single eye. She could see Harriett's jungle pushing against the property line as if eager to claim more territory. "*This* is where you brought me?" she asked.

"Trust me." Jo helped Nessa out of the car and escorted her to the house, holding on to Nessa's elbow as if she were ninety years old.

Jo had just lifted her knuckles to knock when the door opened and Harriett emerged from a fragrant fog of pot smoke like a magician appearing onstage. She was wearing what appeared to be a blue linen shawl with a hole cut for her head and a vintage YSL belt to cinch the waist. A pale cloud followed her outside and drifted up into the atmosphere.

"Jesus, Harriett." Jo fanned the smoke away from her face. "It's not even nine."

"Did you come to tell me the time?" Harriett replied with her gap-toothed smile. "I know this might surprise you, but I do own a clock."

"Oh yeah? Where is it?" Jo challenged her.

"I have no idea. Perhaps in one of the drawers."

"Have you been smoking marijuana?" Nessa asked. She spun around to confront Jo. "Is that what you think's gonna fix my hang-over?"

Jo rolled her eyes. "Nobody's gonna make you do drugs, prin-cess," she assured Nessa. "Brought you another patient," she told Harriett as she pushed Nessa into the house. "Unless you're too stoned to cure anyone else."

"I was stoned when you brought me the last patient," Harriett noted. "I didn't kill her, did I?"

"What patient?" Nessa asked suspiciously. "Who are you talking about? What have you two been doing?"

"Sit down," Jo ordered. "We'll fill you in when you're cured."

Harriett put on her glasses and took her place behind the work-bench. Jo did her best to keep Nessa distracted while Harriett tossed an assortment of leaves, roots, and something that looked like it might be alive into a blender. The liquid she poured into a champagne flute was a thick, murky brown.

"What's in this?" Nessa asked when Harriett handed her the cure.

"Just a few things from my garden," Harriett replied casually.

"You didn't put one of those nasty mushrooms in there, did you?" Nessa asked.

Harriett grinned. "I'm trying to cure your hangover, not send you to the moon. Drink it. I promise it will make you feel better."

Nessa took a timid sip and wrinkled her nose. "It tastes like poop." Her eyes widened. "Don't tell me there's poop in this."

"Okay." Harriett pushed her glasses on top of her head. "I won't tell you that."

"I hope that's one of your jokes." Nessa stuck a finger in the drink. It was coated in brown when she pulled it back out. "Harriett! This looks like a rectal exam!" Then she stopped, her face frozen in confusion. Jo later swore she watched the veins in Nessa's bloodshot eyes fade until they disappeared altogether.

"Yes, but how do you feel?" Harriett asked.

"Good enough not to care what's in it." Nessa pinched her nose and chugged the rest. She banged the flute down on the coffee table and sat back with her lips puckered in disgust.

"Just so you know, all of my potions are one hundred percent feces-free," Harriett informed her.

Nessa's eyes rolled up toward heaven. "Thank you, Jesus," she muttered. "I promise I'm going to lead a clean, healthy life from now on." Then she brought her gaze back down to earth. "So. Y'all ready to tell me what you've been doing without me?"

"We may have identified one of the girls you saw on the beach." Jo took out her phone and pulled up a picture of Amber Welsh's pale, redheaded daughter "Does she look familiar?"

Nessa glanced up in astonishment. "That's Mandy Welsh."

It was Jo's turn to be surprised. "You know her?"

"No, but my daughters did. They were in the same grade at school. And yeah, she was there at the beach yesterday. How did *you* find out about her? My girls said the police have everyone convinced that Mandy ran away."

"They didn't do a very good job of convincing Mandy's mother," Jo said. "I met her last night. She saw a news report about the dead girl and went on a bender. When I found her, she was drunk as a skunk and throwing plants at the police station's windows. I brought her back here and Harriett sobered her up. She told us her daughter disappeared along Danskammer Beach Road and the cops never bothered to search for her."

"You met Mandy's mother? Why didn't you call me?" Nessa pouted.

"I *did*, but you didn't answer. I even drove past your house, and your lights were all out. If I'd known you were in there tying one on, I would have knocked. But I figured you needed your rest. We told Mandy's mother you'd want to talk to her this evening. She works at the Stop & Shop. We can pick her up right after her shift."

Nessa wasn't completely sold on the strategy. "That feels backward to me. Usually you find the body and *then* talk to the family. What if I'm wrong and it's not Mandy out there?"

"Do you think there's a chance of that?" Harriett asked.

"No," Nessa admitted. "But shouldn't we wait a few days to talk to the woman? I called Franklin last night and told him I thought Mandy Welsh's body was out there in the ocean. He promised me he'd have a look."

"Did he tell you how long it might take to find her?" Jo asked. "It's a pretty big ocean."

The previous night, with her common sense clouded by two glasses of wine, Nessa had assumed the police would be out there first thing in the morning. Now she realized just how ridiculous that was.

"If it was your daughter, would you want to wait another day to know?" Jo asked.

If it was one of her babies, Nessa thought, she would have already gone mad with grief and pulled her hair out with worry. Even the notion was too much to bear. She bit her lip to keep it from quivering. Fat tears rolled off her chin and left blotches on her blouse.

"What is it?" Jo asked softly.

"Some evil asshole is going around killing girls, and I'm the one who gets to tell their mamas. What did I do to deserve this?"

"You're the light that holds back the darkness," Harriett said. "Women like you have always existed. Without you, the world would be thrown out of balance."

Jo and Nessa turned their eyes to Harriett, who'd returned to her workbench, where she was filling a little glass bottle with a syrupy black liquid.

"What?" she asked when she looked up to find her friends staring at her. "I've been doing a lot of reading."

"If I'm the light, what are you guys?" Nessa said with a sniffle.

"I'm the punishment that fits the crime." Harriett returned to her work. "Jo is the rage that burns everything down. Nessa will have to talk to the dead girls' mothers. But we'll all have our parts to play."

Silence followed. Then Jo giggled nervously. "Harriett is so fucking stoned," she said.

Harriett grinned. "Nessa knows what I'm saying."

She did. She'd heard something like it before—the day she'd asked her grandmother if she ever wished she hadn't been born with the gift.

You don't waste your time wishing when you got a job to do, the old woman had told her. *Our work is important. We keep the scales balanced.*

"Harriett's right." Nessa wiped her face and pulled herself together. "We need to get down to business. Anything else I need to know?"

"I jogged down to Danskammer Beach this morning," Jo said. "There were cars parked along the highway and a crowd of people hanging around the crime scene snapping selfies."

"Selfies?" Harriett looked up over her glasses.

"What in God's name?" Nessa sounded mortified. "Why?"

"I guess word got out that there could be a new serial killer and all the ghouls are thrilled. Some kid actually stopped me and said he'd seen me on the news yesterday. Asked if he could interview me for his true crime podcast. I was standing a few feet from where we found that poor girl's body, and this little asshole is looking to make a buck off the story."

"Did you punch him?" Nessa said, making it clear she would have approved.

"No. Thing is, I know his show," Jo admitted. "I'm embarrassed to say I used to listen to it all the time. Art made me stop after I slept with the lights on for a month."

"Shows like that aren't my thing, but I don't blame you for listening," Nessa said. "You gotta know what monsters are after you if you plan to avoid them."

"It makes sense to listen if you're a woman. But it doesn't explain why serial killer stories are just as popular with men," Harriett said. "Think about it—straight guys are almost never the victims. They don't have to worry about anyone chopping them into bits. So what's the appeal?"

"It's pure entertainment for them," Jo said. Dead women's bodies fertilized a whole industry. Books, movies, shows, podcasts. "They all turn the murderers into supervillains with comic book names. It's all about the killers—not the women they kill. There was one guy in Providence—they called him the Head Hunter because he cut off women's heads. The podcast kid I met today could probably have rattled off every place in Rhode Island where the guy hid a head, but he couldn't name a single one of the victims. The women are just props in the killer's story."

"You keep talking about a serial killer," Harriett said. "Are we sure it was one person who murdered these girls?"

Nessa was curious to hear Jo's answer. The same thought had occurred to her.

"What other explanation could there be?" Jo asked.

"It's too early to draw any conclusions," Nessa said. "I have to go back to Danskammer Beach. I didn't get a good look at the third girl. I need to be able to sketch them all."

"Do you think it's smart to be sketching dead girls with half the town down there snapping selfies?" Jo asked.

"We'll travel by water," Harriett announced as though it had long been decided. "I have a friend with a boat. What time do you two want to leave?"

THAT AFTERNOON, CELESTE WATCHED FROM the prow of her boat as the three women made their way down the dock, with Harriett in the lead. Even in a plain white shirt tucked into a pair of old jeans, Harriett looked like a visitor from another realm. The two women walking side by side behind Harriett couldn't have appeared more different. One was pretty and plump, with a wide smile punctuated by two girlish dimples. Her manicure suggested she wasn't a fan of manual labor, and her fancy silk blouse wasn't made for sailing. Her companion was a compact little redhead with ripped limbs, a tight ponytail, and an outfit that suggested she might drop and do thirty at any moment. Yet the fact that the two women belonged together was perfectly clear. They were a matching pair.

There was a time when Celeste might have been jealous to see Harriett in the company of interesting women. In her youth, she'd demanded everything from her lovers. Every ounce of affection. Every second of spare time. Now her desire to possess had dwindled, and she knew trying to own someone like Harriett would be pointless. What Harriett gave freely was much more precious than anything Celeste might try to take.

Her affair with Harriett had changed her relationship with Andrew, though not in the ways she'd imagined. They were still happy together. And they were just as happy apart. For the first time in her life, Celeste wasn't afraid to be on her own. Her time with Harriett had taught her a great deal. Harriett had a six-year head start on Celeste. She'd made it to the top of the hill they'd been climbing, and she knew what lay on the other side. Celeste had watched other women cower or crumble once they reached the summit. Harriett had grown powerful instead. Celeste didn't know for sure what had happened. Harriett claimed she'd simply decided to see the world with her own two eyes. Whatever that meant, it was what Celeste wanted. And she could tell the two women with Harriett had made up their minds as well.

Harriett greeted Celeste with a kiss on the mouth that left Celeste weak in the knees. She could feel Harriett's hand on the small of her back, pulling her closer. Neither of them cared who was watching—though Celeste worried Harriett might try to drag her belowdecks. She snuck a glance at Harriett's friends, who were doing their best to appear nonchalant.

"Hello." She gently pushed Harriett back. "I'm Celeste."

"My apologies," Harriett said. "Celeste, I'd like you to meet my friends Jo and Nessa. Ladies, this is Celeste."

"Nice boat," Jo said awkwardly, struggling to hide her amusement.

"Thanks," Celeste replied. "It was my husband's forty-fifth birthday present to himself. From what he tells me, it's something all big shots need, even the ones who vomit at the sight of the ocean."

Celeste saw Nessa's eyes pop at the word *husband*. Harriett noticed, too, and gave her friend a wink.

"Her husband, Andrew, and I used to work together," she said. "Now he has the job I deserved, and I have sex with his wife. I think I got the better deal, don't you?"

Nessa was getting used to Harriett teasing her. "Couldn't tell you," she replied coolly. "I've never worked in advertising."

Jo let loose a cackle. "Nice one," she said, and with that, the ice was officially broken.

"So you guys ready to set sail?" Celeste asked. "Harriett says you want to go out by Danskammer Beach to whale watch? I warned her you might not see many whales this time of year."

Celeste felt an arm wrap around her waist. "And I promised Celeste that she wouldn't go home disappointed," Harriett said. "I called ahead and told the whales we were coming."

IT HADN'T OCCURRED TO NESSA to take the whale comment seriously. She assumed Harriett was kidding around to entertain the pretty lady whose blue-striped sailing shirt and pearl earrings made her look like Jackie Kennedy. Yet just as Danskammer Beach was coming into view, Nessa saw a massive slab of dark gray flesh break the surface on the starboard side of the boat, and a spray of water shot ten feet into the air.

"Goodness!" she yelped, feeling the tingle of spray on her bare skin. "What is that?" If something so big could appear unannounced, who knew what else might be lurking beneath the waves.

"It's a whale," Harriett said with a knowing smirk. "A female humpback."

"You guys got lucky!" Celeste shouted from the wheel. Harriett lifted an eyebrow and her smirk spread into a grin.

"You really can talk to whales?" Nessa asked.

"You said your grandmother's friend Miss Ella spoke to snakes. I thought I might have a go at chatting with a whale. I've spoken to this one, but I can't confirm she's listening. She's the strong, silent type. I yammer away, but she never talks back."

The whale swam alongside the boat as if escorting them to their destination. As they got closer to Danskammer Beach, Nessa felt her body go cold. The two girls were down there, their faces staring up at her from the murky water.

She laid a hand on Harriett's arm. "Would you ask Celeste to stop here?" Nessa asked. "And keep her busy for a little while, if you would." They hadn't discussed the importance of being discreet; it went without saying that no one needed to know they were looking for ghosts, not whales.

"Not a problem." Harriett made her way to Celeste at the other end of the boat.

With the engine off, the boat bobbed up and down on the waves. The whale cavorted around the vessel, launching herself upward, twisting high in the air, and sending a burst of water into the sky when she slammed down on the surface.

"She's putting on a show." Jo took a seat next to Nessa. "It's like she's covering for us."

"Yeah." Nessa pulled a sketch pad and pencil out of her handbag. She wasn't feeling chatty.

"Can you see the girls?" Jo asked quietly.

Nessa glanced up, her face grim. "Yes," she said. "It looks like their bodies were dropped in the same place. If so, I don't think it can be a coincidence. The same man must have killed them both."

They floated just below the surface, their long hair undulating in the ocean's currents. Mandy Welsh's pale face shone like the moon. She had frank, honest eyes the color of moss. The rest of her body, clad in a billowing black dress, blended in with the depths below. With so many photos online, Nessa didn't need to sketch Mandy. Her subject was the Asian girl in the red hoodie with long black hair and lips parted as if she wished to speak. She looked even younger than Mandy, Nessa thought. She couldn't have been more than sixteen. *Don't you dare cry, Nessa,* she heard her grandmother chide her.

"You're good at that," Jo said. "I didn't know you were an artist."

"I'm not," Nessa told her as she sketched the outline of the girl in the hoodie. "I haven't opened a sketchbook in years."

THE LAST MORNING OF NESSA'S summer in South Carolina, her grandmother had slid an envelope full of cash across the breakfast table. She'd never had much to spare, so Nessa knew it was meant for something important.

"When you get home, find somebody who can teach you to draw," she'd said. "You don't need to be Leonardo da Vinci. But you need to be able to sketch a face so people know who they're looking at."

Nessa had never shown any promise as an artist, but she didn't dare say so.

"You won't always know the people who call to you," her grandmother told her. "And sometimes the bodies are too messed up to identify on their own. You'll need a picture of the ghost to figure out who they are."

Nessa's grandmother got up from the table and returned with a scrapbook, which she opened to a pencil-drawn portrait of a girl. Her eyebrows were plucked to thin black arcs over round, heavily lined eyes. She'd tried her best to conceal her youth, but plump cheeks and a mischievous smile betrayed her. It may not have been a perfect portrait, but it made a lasting impact. One look, and Nessa knew just who the girl had been—and how much her family had lost.

Nessa flipped through the scrapbook, past portraits of other dead women. She shook her head sadly. She wasn't up to the task. "I don't think I can do this. Why can't I describe them and have someone else make the drawings?" she asked.

"Because they're more than just pictures," her grandmother said. "They're a contract. When you draw a ghost, a bit of their soul gets transferred to the paper—where it's mixed with a little bit of your own. The dead will trust you when they know you've got something at stake. If they believe you'll keep looking, they'll be able to rest."

"What if I can't find their people?" Nessa had asked.

"Then you'll lose that little piece of yourself that you put down on paper. So make sure your pictures are good."

WHILE WAVES ROCKED THE BOAT, Nessa finished her sketch of the unidentified girl. Whatever details hadn't made it onto the paper were still in her head. As soon as she was home, she would transform the sketch into a portrait. She was too exhausted to polish it right away. Too much of her own soul had gone down on the paper. She handed the book to Jo, who'd stayed by her side the entire time. She watched as Jo studied the page.

"She doesn't look anything like Mandy Welsh—or the girl we found yesterday," Jo noted. "Aren't serial killers supposed to have a type?"

"I think it's safe to say that the killer likes young girls," Nessa pointed out.

"True," Jo said. "He also owns his own boat, and knows that the water out here is deep. A fisherman, maybe?"

"Maybe," Nessa offered wearily.

Jo gave her friend's shoulder a squeeze. "Okay, we can talk about all of this later." She passed the sketchbook back to Nessa. "But before we go, do a quick drawing of the whale," she said. "So we can show our captain what you've been up to."

While Nessa sketched, the only sounds were the whistling of the wind and the chattering of the women at the other end of the boat. As she finished her drawing, a third noise arose—a faint buzzing that was growing louder. Jo searched the sky, but the glare from the sun made it hard to determine the source. Then a flying object swooped down from above and traveled along the length of the boat before shooting back up into the clear blue sky.

"What the hell?" Jo hopped to her feet and made her way toward the captain's wheel. "Was that a UFO?"

Harriett met her halfway. "It was a drone," she said. "We have an admirer. Is there a chance its camera captured anything it shouldn't have?"

"Just this." Nessa had joined them, her sketchbook closed and a sketch of the whale in her hand. She presented the drawing to Celeste. "I drew this for you. To thank you for bringing us out here today."

"It's lovely!" Celeste said. "But are you sure you're okay? You don't look very well."

"I'll be fine," Nessa told her. "I think the drone really rattled me. Where'd it come from?"

"Looked like it came from Culling Pointe," Celeste said.

"Do you think it was spying on us?" Jo asked.

"Seems unlikely," Celeste said, "but if you guys want to take a look, I can steer the boat that way."

"Will we get in trouble if we head over there?" Nessa asked.

"I don't see how," Celeste said. "Nobody owns the ocean."

THE MANSIONS THAT LINED THE Pointe's pristine beaches grew larger as the boat sped toward them. Some were classic shingle style, others starkly modern, but all were empty palaces. The kings who'd built them didn't rule countries. They ran pharmaceutical companies or data-mining operations disguised as social media. Millions of subjects paid them tribute each month, but few people even knew their names.

"I read a book about the history of this area," Harriett said.

"Did you know there's a story behind the name Culling Pointe?" She looked over at the others, who all shook their heads. "Back in the sixteen hundreds, the English attempted to start a colony here. They massacred most of the island's native people and built a fort where Mattauk sits. Then one day a couple of colonists were hunting in the woods when they spotted a pair of deer walking around on their hind legs. The people who'd lived on the island for centuries could have told them that wasn't unusual. The animals had learned how to reach fruit that grew in the trees. But the Europeans believed the deer were possessed by Satan. So they killed all the creatures and dumped their carcasses in the ocean. When they finished, they blamed the local midwife for inviting the devil to town and hanged her as a witch. She had her revenge the following winter when all but two of the colonists starved to death."

"People were barbaric back in those days," Celeste said.

"We haven't changed," Harriett said. "We just smell a bit better."

"Have you been out to the Pointe?" Jo asked.

"As a matter of fact, I used to go once every summer," Harriett said. "My ex-husband does the advertising for Little Pigs BBQ. The CEO of the company is a man named Jackson Dunn. He has a house on the Pointe, and he invites all his favorite toadies out for a big bash every Memorial Day."

"I've heard about that party," Celeste said. "Andrew says people would kill for an invite."

"I wouldn't be surprised if someone already has," Harriett said. "Jackson's neighbors are all billionaires and CEOs. If you're looking for clients or investors, that's where you want to be. A lot of deals get made at that party. That's how they recruit for their club."

"I always knew there were plenty of rich folks around here, but billionaires? Five miles away from my little white house?" Nessa couldn't quite believe it.

"The Pointe may be five miles away by map, but it's really a parallel universe," Harriett said. "It doesn't belong to our world. The people who live there look normal, but they're not like the rest of us. They hand off all of life's unpleasantness to others, and everything they want magically appears. After a while, it changes them. More than anything, it changes how they see *us*."

"Look over there. I think that's our drone pilot." Celeste was pointing at a tiny man standing at the end of a dock.

Jo checked him out through a pair of binoculars that Celeste kept in the boat's cockpit. She guessed he might be in his mid-fifties. He was wearing a pair of old khakis and a denim shirt rolled up to his elbows. He must have seen they were heading his way because he offered a friendly wave. Jo passed the binoculars to Nessa and didn't wave back.

"He seems normal," she said. "Kind of cute in a rumpled way."

"He reminds me of my high school math teacher," Nessa added.

As they drew closer, their assessment didn't change. He looked like the sort of man who owned several tweed jackets and knew how to pick a good cheese.

"Hello there!" he called out. "So sorry for dive-bombing you back there. I just got this drone and I'm still getting used to the controls. I thought I'd have more time to practice. The whales don't usually arrive in these waters until later in the season."

"You were whale watching?" Jo asked.

"Yeah, my girlfriend and I are just out for the day. She's organizing a party for one of the residents, and I thought I'd try out my new drone. I had no idea I'd get lucky. How'd you know the whales would be out there today?"

Nessa hugged her sketchbook to her chest. He thought they'd been whale watching, too.

"I didn't," Celeste said. "I told them it was too early for whales, but they proved me wrong."

"We got lucky," Jo said.

"Did we?" Harriett asked with a grin.

THAT EVENING, THE SUN WAS heading toward the horizon when Jo turned onto Woodland Drive. She glanced at the clock on the dashboard, which read 6:33, and goosed the gas. She and Nessa needed to drop off Harriett and get to the Stop & Shop by seven to meet Amber Welsh.

As they approached Harriett's house, Jo brought the car to a crawl again.

"There's a hobo sitting on your front porch," Nessa said.

"Really?" For a moment, Harriett was curious. The moment didn't last long. "That's just Chase," she said, disappointed.

"Chase?" Nessa asked.

"My ex-husband."

"Holy shit," Jo said. "We were just talking about him. Did you—"

"Summon him? No. I have a feeling he's here about a fungus. I meant to mail him the treatment a few months ago. I must have forgotten. Silly me."

"Are you going to be okay?" Jo asked. "Do you need backup?"

"Backup?" Harriett laughed. "If it came to combat, who would you put your money on—the hobo or me?"

"Don't murder him," Nessa said in response. "The three of us have too much work to do."

"I have no intention of killing him," Harriett assured her. "That urge passed a long time ago."

She slipped out of the back seat and made her way up the drive. The salt air and wind had blown her hair into a terrifying tangle of silver and gold that made her appear impossibly tall, Nessa thought, like the statue of a goddess come to life.

Chase rose to greet her, and Harriett drank in his surprise. In the months since they'd seen each other, he seemed to have shriveled while she had grown. Chase's beard had gone bushy and his pants looked like he'd slept in them more than once. Still, she experienced a pang, like a spasm in an organ that had been removed or a cramp in a phantom limb. It faded quickly, and she knew that was the last pain of its kind she would feel. A woman much like her had once loved a man who looked like him. Neither of those people existed anymore.

"I like what you've done with the place," he lied awkwardly. Honesty had never been Chase's strong suit.

"I don't need you to flatter me," Harriett replied. "I'm very content with my surroundings."

"You know, if you didn't like the landscaping, you could have just said so."

"I did say so," Harriett told him, without an ounce of bitterness in her voice. "Come inside, and you can have what you came for."

She stepped past him and twisted the knob on the front door.

"You don't keep it locked?" he asked. "Someone could come in and take everything."

Harriett grinned. He'd always been a bit slow. "Everyone in Mattauk knows better than that," she said, stepping through the open door. "And just in case you get any ideas, so should you. Come in."

Chase caught a glimpse of the interior and groaned. "Oh my God," he said as he followed her inside. "I paid a fortune for those chairs. What's growing on them?"

"*We* paid a fortune for those chairs," Harriett corrected him as she stepped behind her workbench and searched through the cabinet where they'd once kept the booze. "And it's moss. Here you go." She handed Chase a jar filled with rancid-looking goop. "Rub this on the affected areas. The rash should be gone by morning. Tell Bianca it's for external use only if she still intends to have children."

"Thank you." Chase set the jar down on the counter. "We managed to get rid of the fungal infection on our own. It took a couple of months and eight visits to a tropical medicine specialist, but it's finally gone."

"Then why are you here?" Harriett asked. "I haven't seen you in ages. Don't pretend this is a social visit."

Chase's chest swelled as he drew in a long breath. "I need you to remove the curse."

Harriett found the idea amusing. "I don't do curses, Chase. Fungi, yes. Rashes, sure. Infestations, absolutely. But curses, no."

He took a step forward, his fingers woven together as if in prayer. "Harriett, I'm desperate," he said. "If you want me to beg you, I will. I'll give you the apartment in Brooklyn. You can have the Mercedes. I'll do anything you want."

"Well, you certainly sound serious." Harriett was enjoying the conversation. "What's the nature of this curse you're under?"

"I haven't had a good idea in forever," he said as if he was certain she already knew the answer. "My instincts are totally shot. The agency has lost three accounts. We haven't won a single new business pitch in ten months. Little Pigs is talking about putting the account in review. And if we lose that business, I'm out. They've already told me. I've been working sixteen-hour days and sleeping in the office. I need you to tell me what I can do to fix things. Please, Harriett."

"Do you remember when you were pitching the Little Pigs account?" Harriett asked. "Remember the brilliant line that won the business?"

"Of course. And that's all I need, H—to come up with a few more great ideas like that one."

"But you won't," Harriett informed him. "And not because you're cursed."

"Then why?"

"Because it was my idea," she said. "I gave it to you."

Chase bristled, clearly offended she'd even suggest such a thing. "No, you didn't," he argued. "I remember being in the office that night. I had every team in the agency crammed into the main conference room."

"Yes. And you called me in tears because it was three in the morning and none of them had come up with anything good. So I told you I'd think about it and send you something."

"No," he insisted. "That's not how I remember it."

"For fuck's sake, Chase. I still have the email I wrote you," Harriett told him. "I let you have the idea. I even let you think it was yours. Same with the vodka and deodorant campaigns that won you all those awards. I stood next to you and listened to people hail you as a creative genius, and I never once corrected them or let your secret slip. But deep inside, I always wondered what kind of person could take credit for something that wasn't theirs. Now I know. It's a person like you."

Chase looked like a seven-year-old who'd just spotted Santa slipping out of his costume. "If that's really what happened, why didn't you call me on it?"

"I didn't think I needed to. You see, Chase, I thought we were partners. You know, two people working together toward a common goal. But that's not how you saw it. You convinced yourself that you were the one who made it all happen. It was your charm and brilliance and good looks that bought this house and the cars and that lovely suit you've destroyed. Now you're here to ask me to remove a curse, because it's easier for you to believe I've bewitched you than it is to accept the fact that I made you a far better copywriter than you ever would have been on your own."

"You're right." Chase nodded. He wasn't going to put up a fight. "I was an idiot. I should never have let things end the way they did. I'm sorry."

She laughed—at his blatant attempt to manipulate her, and at the fact that she might once have bought it. The illusions of her youth had been removed with no anesthesia. She hadn't expected to survive the experience. But she had. And now she was completely invulnerable.

"You don't need to be sorry. It was time," Harriett said. "I have no regrets."

"Harriett," he pleaded. "You have to help me."

"No," she said, "I don't. You can have what you need. But this time, you'll have to pay a fair price for it."

"I'll give you anything."

"Anything?" she asked. He seemed so eager.

"What do you want?"

"Your firstborn child," Harriett said.

Chase blanched. "I don't know," he said. "I'd have to talk to Bianca."

Harriett couldn't keep a straight face.

"So you were kidding?" Chase exhaled.

Harriett howled with laughter. "I never wanted a baby when we were married. Why the hell would I want one now? I want you to take me and my friends to Jackson Dunn's Memorial Day party."

He wasn't quite buying it. "That's all you want?"

"That's it," Harriett said. "I assure you there is nothing else I could possibly want from you. I wouldn't even fuck you these days. Frankly, I find you rather repugnant."

She hadn't intended to be cruel. Those were just facts.

"You know, you've really changed." Chase sounded wounded. "You used to be sweet."

"That was before you set fire to our marriage and tried to steal my house." Harriett walked to the door and held it open for him. "I thought it all would destroy me, but it didn't. It just turned me into something new. And now that we've made our little deal, you should get out of my house. My friends will be coming back soon."

"SO THIS LADY DOESN'T HAVE a car?" Nessa asked. The Stop & Shop where Amber Welsh worked was off a six-lane highway. The sixteen-wheelers racing by were streaks of red and white light.

Jo thought of the rusty Corolla parked in front of Amber's trailer. "She has one, but it's not running at the moment."

"I don't understand." Nessa looked around. There were no sidewalks, and the shoulder on the highway was little more than two feet wide. "How does she get here?"

Jo had been wondering the same thing herself. "I have a feeling she walks," she said.

"You're kidding. She's going to end up getting killed on that road."

Jo checked the time on the dashboard. It was 7:16, and she and Nessa had been parked in front of the Stop & Shop for half an hour.

"Where is she?" A bad feeling had settled over her. "I'm gonna go in and check on her—make sure she hasn't gotten cold feet."

Inside the store, a fluorescent light flickered as yacht rock played over the store's sound system. Jo headed for the nearest cashier, a woman with a massive bosom and the imperious air of middle management. She was ringing items up for an elderly couple who seemed eager to get home with a shopping bag filled with unusually phallic vegetables.

"Pardon me," Jo said. "I'm looking for Amber Welsh."

"Well, when you find her, you can tell her she's fired," the woman snipped without lifting her eyes from the scanner. Her name tag identified her as Linda Setzer, Manager. "I know she has problems, and she's got my sympathy. But I just can't run a store this way."

"I'm sorry, what way?" Jo asked. "I don't know what you're talking about."

The woman finally looked up at her. "Amber was a no-show today. I couldn't get anyone else to cover, so I've been manning the cash register since noon."

"Shit." Jo muttered. She knew what would come next. Every true crime podcast started much the same way—with a woman not showing up for a shift.

"Tell me about it," the manager said. "You ever worked a till? My legs are numb from standing all day and my back is spasming. I'm going to be crippled for the rest of the week."

"I'm sorry," Jo said, and the manager shrugged. "So you haven't heard from Amber at all today?"

"Nope," she said as she began to fill a paper bag with the elderly couple's assorted vegetables. "And at this point, I am no longer interested in hearing from her."

Jo hurried out and hopped back into the car. Whatever had happened to Amber, she knew it couldn't be good.

"Where are we going?" Nessa asked as Jo peeled out of the parking lot.

"Amber's house."

The first time Jo had visited the trailer, she'd had Amber to guide her. Finding the entrance wasn't as easy the second time. When she reached the end of the bumpy dirt drive, it seemed she'd made a mistake. The site was empty. There was no rusting trailer. No broken-down car. No potbellied little boy. Only dirt, rubble, and trash.

"I must have taken a wrong turn," Jo said. As she steered the car around, the headlights hit a patch of scrub and she saw something gleam beneath it. She stopped the car and got out to investigate. Parked under the bush was a little metal truck with no wheels. A boy had written his name on the hood in crooked capital letters. *DUSTIN*.

"Holy shit." The truth slammed into Jo and spun her around. Amber and her family were gone. Aside from the toy truck, there was no sign they'd ever been there. At some point in the past twenty-four hours, they'd disappeared.

THE CHIEF

Fluorescent lighting gave the police station interior the ambiance of the *Alien Autopsy* set. Nessa tried not to imagine the origins of the gruesome stains on the chairs she and Jo had been offered.

"An entire family vanishes from the face of the planet in less than twenty-four hours, and you're telling us we shouldn't be worried?" They'd agreed it was best to let Nessa do the talking, but even she was having trouble staying diplomatic.

According to the sign on his desk, the man sitting across from them was Chief of Police John Rocca. The shelves on the wall behind him were lined with framed commendations and softball trophies. Franklin stood off to the side, listening silently with his arms crossed over his chest. Franklin had lived in the area for six months, while Rocca knew everyone in town.

"It's unusual, Mrs. James," Rocca agreed. "But so are the Welshes."

Nessa glanced over at Jo and saw her friend's fists clench. The moment Franklin had brought them in to speak to the chief of police, she'd known the conversation would go nowhere. Rocca was in his early fifties, with the robust physique of a triathlete and the personality of a barbell. He had to hear them out, but he wasn't going to pretend to give a damn that the Welshes were missing.

"Amber has three little boys, Chief Rocca," Nessa said. "They've disappeared, too."

Rocca's eyelids closed and reopened in a slow, lizardlike blink. "How well do you know Amber Welsh?"

Nessa let Jo answer. "I met her a few days ago," Jo reluctantly offered.

"Well, I've known her most of her life. She's been in trouble since she was arrested for arson when she was fifteen years old. The man she married, Declan Welsh, is currently in prison for running a meth lab out of a White Castle. Between the two of them, they know quite a few people who could help the whole family disappear overnight. Trailers are called trailers for a reason. They often come with wheels."

"Amber couldn't find anyone to drive her into town when her car broke down, but we're supposed to believe she knew people who could move her trailer with just a few hours' notice?" Jo argued.

"You're welcome to believe what you like, Mrs. Levison. All I'm saying is, the Welshes could have called in a favor from a friend."

Jo turned her attention to Nessa. "I don't buy it. Last night Amber told me she was going to stay right there in that spot until she was one hundred percent certain that her daughter wasn't coming home. If it was my daughter, I'd do the same thing, wouldn't you?"

"Oh yes," Nessa readily agreed.

"Maybe she woke up to reality and realized there was no point in staying," Rocca said.

Nessa wasn't sure how to interpret that statement, and the chief's expression wasn't much help. His eyes moved to the left and locked on Jo.

"Now, Mrs. Levison, since you're here, why don't we take care of a little business. I was informed that you intended to pay for the damage to the department's front window. One of my officers stopped by your place of business this afternoon, but you were out at the time. Detective Rees, would you mind picking up a copy of the bill from the front desk when you show these two ladies to the door?"

It was clear they'd been dismissed.

"Thank you for your time." Nessa forced the words out as she rose from her chair.

Jo said nothing until they'd left the building. In the parking lot, she picked up a chunk of rock.

"Since I'm going to pay for a whole new window, what do you say I widen that crack in the old one?"

"She's joking," Nessa assured Franklin, who'd walked them out.

"No, I'm not," Jo said.

"I know you're both frustrated," Franklin said. "But he's right about the Welshes. The odds are good they'll turn up again soon."

"What if he's wrong, Franklin?" Nessa demanded, surprised to hear him taking Rocca's side. "Someone around here has been killing girls, and now a family with three little kids has disappeared. What if something happened to them? Could you live with yourself?"

Franklin lowered his voice. "I said Rocca was right. I didn't say I was going to do nothing. I'll see what I can find out about Amber and the kids."

"And what about Mandy? You told me you'd look for her body."

"Yes, and I did some research. The water off Danskammer Beach is deep. We'd need to bring in divers and special equipment to do a proper search. Right now I don't have any concrete evidence that there are bodies out there, and Rocca's not going to sign off on an expensive search because someone has a hunch."

"It's more than a hunch," Nessa argued.

"Telling him my friend Nessa dreams about ghosts is not going to help the situation. But don't worry. I haven't given up yet."

"*Dreams?*" Jo blurted out. Nessa shot her a look.

"Amber Welsh thought Mandy was interviewing for a job out at Culling Pointe, and her body was dumped in the water off Danskammer Beach Road," Nessa said. "The girl we found was left nearby in the scrub. There are houses on the Pointe with a view of the entire coastline. Maybe someone there saw something suspicious."

Franklin shook his head. "We can't just go knocking on doors on the Pointe."

"Why not?" Jo demanded. "You're a detective investigating a murder, and they're citizens just like the rest of us."

"In theory, yes. But that's not how things operate in the real world. I've made discreet inquiries regarding our Jane Doe, and we've run background checks on the staff at Culling Pointe to see if anyone out there has a criminal history, but we will not be going door-to-door asking billionaires a bunch of questions."

"There could be a serial killer around here, and the police are making 'discreet inquiries'?" Nessa scoffed.

They'd reached Jo's car. Franklin stopped Nessa before she could reach the passenger side. "What makes you think there's a serial killer?"

"Two girls have been murdered—" Nessa started to say.

"We have one body at the moment, and it belongs to a girl who died of a fentanyl overdose. We have no proof she was murdered—and no evidence that she and Mandy Welsh are connected in any way. Or do we?" Franklin paused for the answer. "Nessa?"

Nessa hadn't told him about the third girl, and she wasn't ready to reveal the true nature of her gift. An uncomfortable minute ticked past as the three of them remained frozen, engaged in a silent standoff. When it became clear that Nessa's lips were going to stay sealed, Jo sighed and unlocked her car.

Franklin shook his head and opened Nessa's door for her. "There's no reason to hold back," he said quietly. "You know you can trust me."

Nessa climbed into the passenger seat of Jo's Highlander and looked back at him. He bore no resemblance to her late husband, but his manner called Jonathan to mind. Back in the city, the two men hadn't known each other well. But Jonathan had considered Franklin one of the good guys—and he'd made it clear that good guys were few and far between.

"I'll be in touch," Nessa told him. Franklin nodded and closed the door.

"What the fuck?" Jo said as she turned out of the parking lot. "You haven't told him you can see these girls, have you?"

"No," Nessa admitted.

"Why the hell not?" Jo asked.

"It just doesn't feel right," Nessa replied sullenly.

"You don't trust him?"

"Of course I do!"

"Well, then how's he supposed to help us if you're keeping things from him?" Jo demanded. "Two girls could be a weird coincidence. Three dead girls in the same spot is a totally different story."

"I *know*," Nessa growled back. "And I'll tell him as soon as I'm ready."

Jo leaned over and put a hand on Nessa's arm. "Aww. Look at us. We're having our first fight!"

Nessa tried not to laugh, but a giggle slipped out before she could catch it. "I'm serious, dammit," she said in her serious voice.

"Me too, sweetheart," Jo said, giving Nessa's arm a light squeeze. "You better tell Franklin everything soon, or I'll fucking do it."

PICKET FENCES

B e careful what you let others have," Nessa's mother had advised her the day she graduated from nursing school. "Everyone you help's gonna want a piece of you. Give what you can, but you'll be worthless to all of them unless you stay whole." It wasn't until Nessa took her first hospital job that she truly understood what her mother had meant. By the end of the first week, she'd vomited six times and shed buckets of tears. She could feel the work chipping away at her soul.

In order to save it, Nessa built a wall around her world. Her private life was her refuge from the demands of the doctors, the suffering of her patients, and the needs of their relatives—a place she could leave them all behind. For years, the only people allowed inside were Nessa's family. She thought of her world as a house filled with memories. Some were always kept on display. Others, like her gift, were stored safely away until she had use for them.

Now her world had welcomed two new inhabitants, and a third was knocking. Nessa knew Jo was right—she had to open the door and let Franklin in. He was there for a reason, and he needed to know how her gift really worked. But she'd never expected to invite another man inside her private world. As crazy as it sounded, it felt like cheating.

WHEN SHE GOT HOME FROM the police station shortly after ten, Nessa showered and headed for bed. She lay there for an hour until she knew for a fact that sleep wouldn't be coming. No matter how hard she tried, she couldn't shake the feeling that she hadn't done all she could for the dead. Dressed in her silky pink nightgown and robe, she went out to her car and sat in the front seat with the keys in her hand. The street was empty and all the houses were dark. The world should have been silent—but it wasn't. The waves were still crashing in the distance, and now a chorus of female voices had joined them. Nessa couldn't say how many were calling, but she knew it had to be more than three.

"I'm sorry," she whispered as she slipped the key into the ignition. "I'll try to do better."

The car's engine drowned out the voices, but Nessa knew they were still there. She drove slowly through the empty streets of Mattauk, looking at the town through the eyes of a stranger. It wasn't hard. She'd never truly belonged. The storefronts were all charming, the restaurants homey, and the businesses cleverly named. If asked, she could have drawn every building from memory. But Nessa was overcome by the uncanny sense that there was so much she'd never seen. She remembered when her parents had first decided to move out of the city. Nessa had warned them things had changed on the island. She and Jonathan had driven out one summer with the twins. All that was left of the community she remembered were a few little cabins down by the shore.

But her parents hadn't been dissuaded from following their dream. The home they'd bought hadn't come with a white picket fence, so they'd promptly built one of their own. They'd come to the island to find what they'd been promised—and to claim their reward for lives of good deeds and hard work. But while they hadn't been snubbed in Mattauk, they'd never felt entirely welcome, either. They knew their neighbors referred to them not by their address or the landscaping or the color of their house. They were the Black family. Nessa had sensed her parents' relief when she'd moved to the island with her kids after Jonathan's death. It let them ignore what had become increasingly clear—Mattauk was no longer the place they remembered. So they'd doted on their grandchildren and tried their best not to look too hard.

Nessa wondered what they would have said if they'd known there was a monster lurking in the shadows of their storybook town. Someone was murdering girls. Not the girls who lived in the big, tasteful houses. Not the girls whose parents were lawyers or doctors or investment bankers. He was taking poor girls—the kind who lived in trailers that could be hitched to a truck and carted off. He was stealing them, using them, and throwing them away because the world considered them trash. Would that have come as a surprise to her parents? Or had they known, deep inside, that that's how things worked—even in pretty little places like Mattauk.

Nessa passed the courthouse and the police department, where Franklin's car still sat outside. She was headed for the far edge of town, beyond the hospital and medical offices, to a seventies-era building she'd never set foot in and had always done her best to avoid.

The county morgue's front desk was empty, but just as Nessa had expected, there was someone standing in the parking lot outside. The outline of a figure was all Nessa could make out in the dark, but she knew who it was. She threw on her turn signal and pulled the car into the lot. The girl in the blue dress focused her unblinking stare straight at Nessa's headlights, as though she'd been waiting for her ride to arrive. Inside the morgue, her cold, naked body had been lying on a sliding steel drawer inside a refrigerated cabinet for two days. Nessa stopped beside the girl and got out of the car. She walked over to the passenger side and opened the door. The girl in the blue dress climbed in.

On the way home, Nessa stole peeks at her passenger, but the girl never looked back. Her eyes remained focused on the road in front of them. Nessa wondered what it was like to be trapped between this world and the next. Whatever discomfort the girl felt, she seemed determined to endure it. She wasn't going to disappear until she knew her people would find her. Her connection to them was the source of great power.

Nessa's phone pinged as she pulled into her driveway and parked the car. A text had arrived from Jo, with her first good news in days: Harriett had finagled invitations to a party on Culling Pointe. They would have a chance to speak to the rich people Mattauk's cops refused to bother. At least it was something, Nessa thought, as she walked around to the other side of the car.

She opened the passenger-side door and motioned for the dead girl to get out. Then Nessa guided her guest through her house to the couch in the living room. When the girl took a seat, Nessa saw that she'd been taught to sit with her back straight, her knees together, and her ankles crossed. She kept her little black bag in her lap with her hands folded over it. For the first time, Nessa noticed a gold chain, so thin it was almost invisible, hanging around the girl's neck. A pendant was hidden beneath the dress's demure neckline. Nessa assumed that a cross lay near the girl's heart.

The girl's eyes followed Nessa as though she were waiting for something to happen.

Nessa sat down across from her guest and flipped open her sketch pad. "I'm trying," she said, hoping that counted for something. "I'm new to all this, and it's a lot harder than I thought it would be."

The girl sat there, polite but persistent. She reminded Nessa of the girl she'd once been.

"Your mama must be losing her mind," Nessa said. "Until we find her, you should stay here with me."

The ghost's brown eyes stayed locked on Nessa as Nessa began to sketch the contours of her face. She seemed curious.

"Don't get your hopes up about the portrait," Nessa warned her.

"I'm not the world's best artist, but let's see if I can do you some justice."

When she was finished, she showed the girl what she'd drawn. It was an excellent likeness, Nessa thought—better than the ones she'd sketched from memory. It would make it much easier for the girl's family to be found. The ghost said nothing, but by the way her gaze lingered on the page, Nessa knew she recognized herself. When Nessa showed the girl sketches she'd made of the other two victims, her eyes went blank. It was clear she'd never seen them before.

At five o'clock in the morning, Nessa arranged her drawings on the dining-room table and closed her sketch pad. Just as dawn broke, she finally fell asleep.

SHE WOKE AT NOON KNOWING exactly what she needed to do. As soon as she'd showered and her makeup was on, she grabbed her phone and dialed Franklin's number. When he picked up, she heard noises in the background and knew without asking that he was at lunch. "I'm sorry to bother you, but would you mind stopping by when you have a chance?" she said. "I have something to show you."

He didn't ask what it was. He didn't put her off or tell her he'd come when he could. "I'll be there in five," he said.

She waited at the window for him to arrive. When Franklin pulled into the drive, she felt glad to see him—and that felt wrong. Her pulse quickened when the car door opened and his form rose to full height. Since the day she'd met Jonathan, other men's charms had always bounced right off her. Now there was a chink in her armor. Nessa didn't know where it was, but she knew she was vulnerable. That didn't keep her from rushing to greet him.

"You okay?" Franklin asked as he walked up the flagstone path to her door.

She wasn't sure she should answer that question. "Come in," she said instead.

Nessa ushered Franklin through the house to the dining room, where she'd spread out the portraits of the three dead girls on the table.

"What are these?" he asked.

Nessa placed a finger on the portrait of the girl in the blue dress. "This is the girl I found in the trash bag by Danskammer Beach." She slid her finger over to the next two drawings. "I saw these girls there, too. They were standing in the water. I went back to sketch them yesterday."

"So there were three girls, not two?" Franklin asked.

Nessa nodded.

"That certainly changes things. This Mandy Welsh?" Franklin asked, tapping the portrait of a pale girl with light hair and freckles.

"Yes," Nessa said. "I don't know who the third girl is. But her body is right next to Mandy's in the water off Danskammer Beach."

"And you saw them all in your dream?"

"It wasn't a dream. They were there the day we found the first girl. What I saw—what I drew—were the three girls' ghosts."

"Ghosts," Franklin repeated, and she nodded. It didn't seem to be going as well as she'd hoped.

Feeling exposed, she fought the urge to flee. "You think I'm crazy, don't you?"

Franklin responded with a snort. "You may be able to see ghosts, Nessa, but you're terrible at reading minds."

NESSA ALWAYS REMEMBERED FALLING IN love with her husband as a one-two punch. The first blow had come out of the blue the night she'd found the handsome young police officer praying over her dead patient's body. That blow had knocked her over, but she'd gotten up and shaken herself off. If the Lord had seen fit to separate the two of them then, she could have gone on. The second punch arrived a few weeks later, when Nessa finally worked up the nerve to tell him about her gift. She'd agonized over the decision for days. Jonathan was a cop. He would want evidence, and she had none to provide. But she knew she couldn't keep something hidden from the man she was coming to love. By the time she sat down to tell him, she'd worked out the answers to every question he might ask. She had photos of her grandmother and the scrapbook she'd inherited, which included her grandmother's sketches pasted next to news clippings about the bodies she'd found. In the end, Nessa hadn't needed them.

After she told him, Jonathan just sat there. "Okay," he said.

"That's it?" she asked. "'Okay'? Don't you have any questions?"

"I have lots, but we can get to them later," he told her. "None of this changes anything. I knew you were special the day I met you."

That was the moment Nessa knew she was down for the count.

"YOU BELIEVE ME ABOUT THE ghosts?" Nessa asked, and Franklin nodded.

He pulled in a long breath in a way that told her he had his own story to share, and took a seat on the edge of the table. "When I was a kid back in Brooklyn, I had to cross the Gowanus Canal every day to get to school. One morning I was walking over the Carroll Street Bridge, and I saw a woman standing in the middle, looking down at the water. I could tell from her face that something was wrong. I was about to pass by when she grabbed me by the shirt and hauled me over to the railing. She pointed down at the canal and asked me if I could see *her*. I looked and looked, and there was nobody there. But the woman on the bridge was insisting. She was almost hysterical. She kept saying, 'There's a dead girl down there in the water!' I told her I couldn't see a thing, and she started describing a girl like she was standing right there in front of her. Black hair. Yellow eyes. A birthmark shaped like Florida on her shoulder. I was thirteen years old, and the woman scared the hell out of me. So I ran. Later that day, as I was walking home from school, they were hauling a body out of the canal. It turned out to be a girl from my school. Her name was Linda Cavatelli, and she had black hair, yellow eyes, and a birthmark shaped like Florida on her shoulder."

"You think the woman on the bridge could see the dead?"

"That's what my mother said when I told her. She didn't even seem surprised. She said she once had an auntie who was always seeing ghosts. Then she told me that if I'd been born female, I might have been able to see them, too. The ability usually runs in families, but boys never got it. I was annoyed as hell when I heard that. Wasn't long afterward that I decided to become a cop. I figured if I couldn't see dead people, the least I could do was help find out who killed them."

"Seeing them isn't as great as it sounds," Nessa told him.

"Don't I know it," Franklin told her. "I haven't come across any ghosts, but I have seen my share of the dead. I don't suppose I'll ever get used to it."

Nessa turned back to the portraits lined up on the table. "It's my job to find these girls' families so their spirits can rest in peace. I need your help."

Franklin picked up the sketch of the girl in the blue dress. "I'll go back to the station now and post your drawing of our Jane Doe on the database. That's all I can do for the moment."

"What about the other girls?" Nessa asked.

"It's unlikely their bodies would have lasted very long at the bottom of the sound," Franklin said. "But I promised you I'd look, and I keep my promises. I found a fisherman with a sonar-equipped boat. He just updated to all the latest tech. If there are remains down there, we should be able to spot them."

Nessa leaned forward and kissed him. When she pulled back, his eyes were wide with surprise.

"Sorry," she said, horrified by her own behavior. "I shouldn't have done that. I have a responsibility to these girls. I have to stay focused and I can't—"

Franklin held up a hand. "It's okay, Nessa," he said. "But for the record, as soon as all this is over, you are more than welcome to do that again."

TWO WEEKS LATER, NO BODIES had been found. The girl in the blue dress was still sitting on Nessa's couch, and the last thing on Nessa's mind was kissing Franklin.

ON TOP OF THE WORLD

Jo stared at the mirror. She couldn't remember the last time she'd worn anything that wasn't at least 70 percent spandex— or let her hair down from its perma-ponytail. The black halter sundress Harriett had pulled from her closet showcased Jo's toned arms and complemented the wavy red hair that cascaded over her shoulders.

"I look hot," Jo told the mirror.

"I'd fuck you," Harriett agreed.

"You fuck everyone," Jo said.

"Not true," Harriett corrected her. "I'm actually quite discerning."

"You got anything that would make me look that good?" Nessa asked.

"Yes," Harriett said, calling Nessa's bluff. "Have you decided to come?"

Nessa snorted miserably. Even if she'd been curious to see Culling Pointe, she couldn't bear to be close to Danskammer Beach. While the girl in blue sat on the sofa in Nessa's living room, the other two girls were still out there, drifting beneath the waves. Every day, Nessa's guilt grew heavier, and the proof of her incompetence had become too hard to ignore. Weeks had gone by since they found the girl in the scrub, and yet little progress had been made in the case. The portrait Nessa had drawn had been picked up by websites and newspapers around the state, and she'd posted it on every missing persons site she could find. Still, no one had come forward to claim the body. Meanwhile, the medical examiner had officially ruled the girl's death an accidental overdose. It was starting to seem as though the cops' theory was right—and Nessa's instincts were wrong. The gift should have passed to one of her cousins. She didn't know how to use it.

Jo told her she had to be patient. Harriett remained unperturbed, but Nessa suspected that had less to do with her confidence in Nessa than with the copious amounts of marijuana she smoked. It was Franklin whose faith she feared losing most. He'd taken a risk on Nessa, and she hadn't delivered. A couple of days after Nessa had shared her secret, the two of them had gone out on the water. As promised, Franklin had wrangled a local fisherman with a sonar-equipped boat to help them search for evidence of the two missing girls. Nessa had guided them to the spot off Danskammer Beach where she'd seen the girls staring up at her from the water, their long hair fanned out around them.

"There's something down there. Could that be fish?" Franklin had kept his eyes on the sonar screen while Nessa watched the water.

"Nope, it's not fish," the fisherman told them. "That's debris on the floor."

Her heart thumping, Nessa had hurried to Franklin's side. Far below them on the ocean floor, hundreds of strange shapes lay scattered about.

"Are those—" Nessa stopped herself.

"I don't know what you're looking for, but I can tell you what you've found," the fisherman said. He tapped one of the shapes with his index finger. "See the straight sides and ninety-degree corners? Those are lobster traps."

"There aren't any lobsters out here," Nessa had argued.

"Not anymore there aren't," the man agreed. "They all died in ninety-nine. Pesticides killed them. That's why there are so many abandoned traps down there. It's a junkyard. They call it ghost fishing. Those traps never stop killing."

Nessa stared at the screen. She was still sure the girls were down there.

"I'm guessing you weren't looking for lobster traps. You're looking for somebody, aren't you?" the fisherman asked.

Their silence seemed to be answer enough.

"Body wouldn't hold together long in the water," he said. "You might find a bone or two. The rest would be fish food pretty quickly." It was the same thing Franklin had said.

"Even if it were in a trash bag?" Nessa asked.

"A dead body releases gases. They'd turn a trash bag into a giant balloon. A body in a trash bag would have washed ashore."

She should have known that the bodies might no longer be where they were originally dumped. That revelation was followed the next day by the news that what was left of Amber Welsh's trailer had been located in a town in New Hampshire. Someone had donated it to the local fire department for a controlled-burn exercise. The name of the donor turned out to be an alias, and whatever clues might have been inside the trailer had been destroyed in the fire. Franklin had paid a personal visit to Amber's husband, who was doing time at Sing Sing. Not only had he not arranged for the trailer to be carted away, he seemed to have no idea his wife and children were missing. He hadn't heard from any of them in over a year.

That was three days ago. Nessa had been sleeping on Harriett's sofa since then. The experience, she'd discovered to her discomfort, shared a great deal in common with camping. The squirrels in the fireplace chittered away in the evenings and fireflies turned the nighttime ceiling into a starry sky. Nessa despised camping. But as much as she longed for her own bed, she couldn't face the guest on her couch, and she knew the girl in blue would never follow her to Harriett's house.

Jo plopped down on the sofa next to Nessa. "Come with us to the Pointe," she pleaded. Jo couldn't hear the voices. All she could see was that her friend desperately needed to get out of the house. "Free food, free booze, and we can rank all the plastic surgery. Why won't you join us?"

"Because for people like me, there are two hells," Nessa said. "One where there's fire and brimstone and another filled with rich white people. And I don't want you beating up the first person who asks me to get them a drink."

"Now I might have to beat up all the fancy fuckers just because," Jo told her.

"That's my job. I'm the punisher," Harriett reminded her. "And while I'm out there, I plan to settle a score of my own." She patted the pockets of her olive-green flight suit, which Jo now noticed were bulging.

"What the hell do you have in there?" Jo asked as the doorbell rang. She wondered just how far Harriett was willing to go.

"It's a surprise." Harriett wiggled her eyebrows. "Are you ready?"

CHASE OSBORNE WAS LEANING AGAINST the side of his silver Mercedes, dressed in a blue blazer, white polo shirt, and madras shorts. He gave his ex-wife a once-over as she emerged from the house.

"That's what you're wearing?" he asked incredulously "You look like Amelia Earhart."

"And you look like a douchebag," Harriett told him. "But I assume that's what you were going for, so bravo—you really knocked it out of the park. Chase, meet my friend Jo."

"Hello." Jo shook his hand.

Chase recoiled from her touch and wiped his hand on his pants. "Are you ill?" he asked. "You feel feverish. I don't want to be rude, but—"

"Then don't be," Harriett said, putting an end to it. "Anything you catch today will come from having your nose wedged in a billionaire's ass."

Jo watched the exchange with growing amusement. She'd assumed nothing could penetrate Harriett's celestial stoner vibe. But it seemed there was one person left who was determined, at least temporarily, to drag the goddess back down to earth.

"Is this what it's going to be like all afternoon?" Chase asked.

"No," Harriett told him. "Because you're going to remember how grateful you are that I saved your career."

DRIVING DOWN DANSKAMMER BEACH ROAD, they passed an uninterrupted line of luxury vehicles parked along the shoulder and left the Mercedes with a valet at the Culling Pointe gate. As they strolled up to the guard post, Jo was fully prepared to be turned away. Chase was the only one with a real invitation. Even in her flight suit, Harriett could pass for a member of the upper class, but Jo was certain the guards would recognize her as an impostor. She felt a rush of relief when their entire party was waved through without trouble. A fleet of idling golf carts waited to ferry guests to their destination. The three of them climbed into the cart at the front of the line.

"Welcome to the Pointe!" The young man at the wheel flashed a pearly white smile that suggested he'd never been denied healthy meals or expensive orthodontia. "We'll be at the house in less than ten minutes."

Soon the cart took a turn and the first mansions appeared. A single road ran all the way from the gate to the tip of the Pointe, and homes lined the beaches on either side. A flock of rowdy children on bikes rode beside them for a few minutes before they disappeared down one of the mansion's drives.

Everything looked a little too perfect, and Jo found the effect uncanny. There was no gum stuck to the sidewalks or patches of brown grass marring the lawns. The architecture was tasteful. The pools were turquoise and the tennis courts made of clay. It must have taken hundreds of people to rake all the yards and clean all the pools. Where were they hidden? And where were the maintenance vehicles? Jo wondered if the Pointe's workers traveled around via underground passages like the ones beneath Disney World. Then the billionaires who lived there could pretend their world was always this way, and the sight of the sweating, aching humans who made it all possible wouldn't ruin the illusion.

"It's too beautiful," Jo said out loud. She didn't add that it was also creepy as fuck.

"Thank you," said the kid at the wheel. "We feel very blessed to live here." He was one of them.

"I suppose God chose this life for you?" Harriett asked.

Jo saw Chase's spine straighten, but the kid didn't get it. He hadn't caught sight of Harriett's smirk.

"Yes, ma'am," he replied with flawless manners and zero irony. "My name is Archie. I'm one of Jackson Dunn's sons."

Chase instantly shot forward and leaned over the seat that separated them. "I thought I recognized you! I'm Chase Osborne. I do all the advertising for Little Pigs BBQ."

"I remember, Mr. Osborne," Archie said. "I'm a big fan of your work. My father says I owe my trust fund to you. I've got first dibs on marketing when my brothers and I join the company. Maybe someday I'll end up working with you."

"Call me Chase. If you're ever interested in seeing how the sausage gets made, just ring me up."

Harriett snorted with amusement to hear Chase shamelessly sucking up to his future boss.

"I'd love to," the boy told him, "but I probably have a few more years of school left. I guess you could say I'm taking my time."

"We offer amazing summer internships." Chase may have been a mediocre copywriter, but he was a first-class snake oil salesman. "College students from all over the country apply."

The kid's big blue eyes appeared in the rearview mirror. "I'm not sure I'd be any competition for them. I don't have much of a CV yet."

"No worries," Chase assured him. "I'm good at spotting raw talent. There's a place for you if you want it. You can even work your own hours."

"Thank you, Chase," Archie said. "I appreciate the opportunity."

"You totally deserve it," Harriett added, aiming a wink at Jo.

Chase elbowed her angrily, but the kid hadn't been listening. He'd pulled the cart up in front of an elegant house made mostly of glass. The structure's walls framed the ocean like a piece of art. Jo could see all the way through to the beach. They said their goodbyes to Archie and got out of the cart.

"Howdy there!" A red-faced man in a cowboy hat clapped a hand on Chase's shoulder. The man's Hawaiian shirt was decorated with red hibiscus flowers and little pink pigs. Only a single button was fastened, as though he'd grown bored while getting dressed. "Did y'all meet my boy Archie?"

Jo would never have made the connection between father and son. In a single generation, the family appeared to have skipped several rungs on the evolutionary ladder.

"I certainly did," Chase confirmed. "Sounds like he's interested in the ad world."

"That right? Must have dropped the poor fucker on his head once too often when he was little." A pause followed before Jackson howled at his own joke. "Chase, my friend, I'm so glad you could make it. Lemme tell you, son, I just can't get over that new campaign of yours. Goddamned brilliant. Really pulled a rabbit out of the hat with that one. And Harriett, I sure am happy you're back again this year. Couldn't let a genius like this one slip away, could you?"

Chase grimaced nervously as he awaited her answer.

"Yes, well, as you know, he grovels so sweetly," Harriett said, and the man hooted with glee. "Have you heard I left the advertising business?"

Jo glanced over at her friend. It seemed out of character for Harriett to share personal details with a Neanderthal like Jackson Dunn.

"I believe I did hear something about that." Jackson's interest was waning. "What are you doing with yourself these days?"

"I'm a horticulturalist. I specialize in invasive plant species." Just as Harriett seemed prepared to go on, she stopped abruptly and smacked her forehead. "And apparently I've been spending so much time with weeds that I've forgotten how to deal with humans. Jackson, I'd like you to meet my friend Jo."

"Pleasure to meet you, Jo." Jackson put a hot, sticky hand on her arm while his eyes took a tour of her figure. "You ever been out to the Pointe before?"

"I haven't." Jo stared at the fingers pressed into her flesh. In the three years since she'd left the corporate world, she hadn't had to let a strange man touch her. She'd almost forgotten the hugs and the pats and the kisses that had once been part of her job. Now the thought disgusted her. She wanted nothing more than to peel Jackson Dunn's hand off her arm. "Thank you for letting me tag along. This is a real treat."

"Well, we're lucky to have you." Then he leaned in close enough that Jo could smell the alcohol on his breath. "No party ever has enough redheads, if you ask me."

Jo felt the energy surging through her limbs. The man was one second away from finding himself flat on his ass when his grip suddenly released. A pair of buzzing insects shot through the air between them like bullets. Jackson yelped and stumbled backward, his glass slipping from his fingers and shattering on the ground. Jo watched with immense satisfaction as he danced around the lawn, waving his cowboy hat frantically in the air as two angry bees flew in circles around his head. Then, just as quickly as they had arrived, the bees were gone.

Jackson returned to the group humbled and panting. "Sorry about all that excitement. I'm allergic," he said. "Nearly died once when I was a kid."

"Yes," Harriett said flatly. "I seem to recall hearing that."

"Come on, let's get you folks inside and pour you some drinks." Jackson ushered them to the front door and up a flight of stairs to a vast, empty living room. Its glass doors opened onto a deck with a pool that looked out over the ocean. Jo was certain they were on the top floor of the house, yet there was a set of stairs leading upward.

"Now, if you ladies will excuse us for a moment, I want to introduce Chase to a few of the boys. All the fun is down by the water. I suggest you two grab a couple of cocktails, strip down to your bikinis, and start soaking up sun."

He put a hand on Chase's back and guided him toward the stairs. Before the two men disappeared, Jackson leaned over the banister. His confidence was back in full force. "Next time I see you two, you'd better be red as lobsters and drunk as skunks!"

"He groped me once," Harriett said, once the men were gone. "Pushed me up against a wall and fondled my crotch. I got him off me, and I never said anything. I didn't want to jeopardize Chase's account."

"You're fucking kidding me." Jo fantasized about sprinting up the stairs, shoving Jackson Dunn against a wall and grabbing *his* goods. She wanted to see his gasping mouth and panicked eyes. Would he whimper, she wondered, or shout for help? For a moment, the desire to find out was almost too hard to resist.

"That was the old me, of course," Harriett said. "I'm much less forgiving now."

"You just give me the word and I'll beat him to a pulp." Jo's body was buzzing with energy. "Doesn't he know cowboys are supposed to live by a code?"

"The Cowboy Code was a marketing gimmick. Anyway, Jackson's not a cowboy. He grew up in Pittsburgh. His real name is Joe Sharts and his father was a CPA."

"Really? Sharts?" Jo snickered. "How'd you hear that?"

"Everyone knows," Harriett said. "They just pretend his bullshit is a charming eccentricity."

"They don't care that the cowboy thing is all an act?"

Harriett held out her long arms and performed a slow twirl. "Darling, everything here is just an act," Harriett told her. "Jackson's not a cowboy, and this isn't really a party."

"What do you mean?" Jo asked. It was starting to seem rather sinister.

"This is where Chase has found his last five clients. He's meeting the next ones as we speak. Who do you think *the boys* are?"

Jo couldn't see what lay at the top of the stairs. "Where did they go? What's up there?"

"The roof deck," Harriett told her. "No one admits it, but it's men only. I've never been invited, and I've never seen another female guest go up there."

"You're saying women aren't allowed?" Jo asked.

"Of course we're *allowed*," Harriett replied. "Women are allowed everywhere these days. Golf courses, nudie bars, the Racquet and Tennis Club. It would be scandalous if we weren't *allowed*. So instead, we're just not *invited*."

The fact that this wasn't news to Jo made it no less shocking.

"The truth of it is, I don't think most of them really question our intelligence or abilities—though they don't mind us believing they do," Harriett continued. "We're just turds in the punchbowl. We spoil their party. They don't want us hanging around."

It was true, Jo knew. Every word of it. Over the years, she'd trained several smarmy young men who'd gone on to become high-ranking executives. At the time, Jo had assumed it was her fault she'd never risen any higher. The men they'd promoted weren't juggling a job and motherhood. They never had to scramble when the day care was closed or the babysitter called in sick. So Jo had watched as men who weren't as smart or diligent or trustworthy as she was worked their way past her toward the company's C-suite. And she did her best to be satisfied with rising profits, stellar reviews, and performance awards. The day after she was fired for assaulting a VIP—who had turned out to be the CEO's golf buddy— Jo had dumped those awards out onto her lawn and set the pile on fire. But still, even after the success of Furious Fitness, she'd wondered if she'd ever really had what it takes to succeed in corporate America.

Now all those nagging doubts had gone up in flames. The truth was, she'd never had a chance. Jo felt her entire body throbbing with rage. She thought of all the late nights she'd worked on presentations she'd been certain would make a difference. She remembered how, despite her name tag, she'd been repeatedly mistaken for a desk clerk by big shots from the corporate office. She imagined the tens of thousands of dollars she'd wasted on her hair and makeup, hoping that would somehow make them all see her. Most painful of all, she mourned the time she could have spent with her daughter. She'd tried so hard to prove she was good enough. And now, with a few simple sentences, Harriett had explained it so plainly. Jo had been good enough all along. They'd made her feel like a failure, when the truth was, they just hadn't wanted her around. There was nothing she could have done.

Jo had stopped in the middle of the massive living room. Harriett was already at the glass doors that led out to the beach. "That anger's like rocket fuel," she told Jo. "Either it pushes you forward or it burns you alive."

Jo got moving. She joined Harriett at the doors, and the two of them stepped out into the sunlight. When they reached the edge of the deck, they could finally see all the women and children. From the deck, a wooden walkway over the dunes ended at the stairs to the house's dock. Beside them, the beach sloped down to the water's edge. Rows of white chaises stretched out beneath blue-and-white-striped umbrellas. Most of the women were gathered in pools of shade, their hair tucked under dramatic straw hats that made them look like characters in *The Great Gatsby* and their eyes hidden behind big, dark glasses. They sipped brightly colored concoctions and chatted in small groups of three or four. Their children frolicked in the surf while a squad of lifeguards in *Baywatch*-red tank suits watched over them.

"They seem like regular human beings." Jo wasn't sure what she'd been expecting.

Harriett leaned toward Jo's ear as if whispering a secret. "Because they are," she said. "These are guests. Let's see if we can spot a few of the residents."

Jo heard a burst of laughter above their heads. With a hand raised to shield her eyes from the sun, she looked up to see several men with glasses in their hands on the roof deck, leaning drunkenly over the railing.

"I really wish they wouldn't ogle the lifeguards like that." The unfamiliar voice oozed with frustration. It clearly wasn't the first time its owner had observed such behavior, and it certainly would not be the last. "It's hard enough to get young women to visit the Pointe these days."

A woman had come out of the house to stand beside them. Pixieish and petite, she wore a simple white T-shirt and a pair of black shorts. Her black bob was pinned away from her face with a butterfly clip. Her brow unknitted when she saw Jo was listening, and a mischievous smile replaced her frown. "Hi, I'm Claude," she said.

"I'm Jo. This is Harriett. Are you here for the party?"

"You could say that." Claude's laugh made Jo want to laugh along, though she had no idea what was funny. "I organized it."

"You did a great job." Jo knew how much work must have gone into planning an event of this size. "It looks just like the beach scene from *To Catch a Thief.*"

"That was my inspiration!" Claude exclaimed with delight. "You're the first to notice. Jackson only cares if the booze is cold and the ladies are half naked." Her fingers flew to her lips and she grimaced at her indiscretion. "Sorry. I shouldn't have said that. He's probably a friend of yours."

"Nope," Jo assured her. "We're just here to drink his cold booze."

"So you work for Jackson?" Harriett seemed to have caught a whiff of something. "Do you spend a lot of time on the Pointe?"

"I spend my summers here," Claude confirmed. "But I try to avoid Jackson as much as possible. I come out to stay with my partner and wait for his fancy friends to throw business my way. I arranged to have the entire cast of the *Frozen* musical flown in next week for an eight-year-old's birthday."

"Wow. That couldn't have been easy," Jo said.

"You wouldn't believe. The negotiations were brutal. A couple of the women had heard about that murder down by Danskammer Beach. I had to hire a dozen extra security guards, which was totally unnecessary. The president himself couldn't get through the Culling Pointe gate without a written invitation."

Jo had been wondering how she and Harriett would turn the conversation to murder. She felt grateful that the woman had done their work for them.

"Were you out here on the Pointe when the body was found?" Harriett inquired.

Claude nodded grimly. "Yeah, it was my first day getting things together for the party. What a tragedy. Have they found the guy who did it yet? I've been so busy I haven't been able to keep up with the news."

"They'd have to search for the killer in order to find him," Harriett said. "The cops don't seem to think it's worth their time."

"I wish I could say I'm shocked," Claude responded grimly. "My partner has a charity that builds schools for kids all over the world. In a lot of the places we travel, women are nothing but baby machines. Girls disappear all the time, and no one ever bothers to look. We like to think that things are different here. But they're not. Not really."

"Your partner runs a charity?" Jo asked.

"That's how we met. I planned an event for him years ago. To be honest, I think he fell in love with my food. The man never met an amuse-bouche he didn't like. That's him right there."

Claude pointed down toward the ocean where a middle-aged man with curly gray hair was horsing around with a group of kids. They were all lined up at the water's edge, trying to leap over the waves as they arrived onshore.

"Isn't that the guy we saw standing on the dock the day we were out on the boat?" Jo asked Harriett.

"Looks like him," Harriett replied.

"Were there whales around that day?" Claude asked.

"Yeah," Jo said.

Claude laughed. "Then it was him. Leonard's always out there looking for whales. If I can get his attention, I'll introduce you."

Claude waved from the deck until she caught the man's eye. He returned the gesture and left the kids playing in the surf. As he walked up to greet them, he grabbed a striped towel from one of the chaises and draped it around his neck.

"Well, hello there!" He was already on his way up the stairs when he recognized them. "If it isn't my fellow whale watchers. I see you've met my better half. I'm Leonard."

"Harriett." She held out a hand. "And Jo."

"Are you two enjoying the party? Claude really outdid herself this year." He put his arm around the woman and planted a playful kiss on the top of her head. "I wonder what Jackson will think when he gets the bill."

"I imagine he'll think it's an excellent write-off," Jo said. "All you have to do is invite a few business contacts to your party, and the government picks up part of the tab."

Leonard's impish grin suggested he knew his way around the tax code.

"Claude!" They all looked up to see Jackson Dunn leaning over the roof deck railing. "Can you come up for a sec?"

Claude gave him a thumbs-up and rolled her eyes as soon as he'd vanished from view. "Doesn't matter how much cash Jackson spends," she said. "He always makes sure he gets his money's worth. If you'll excuse me, I must earn my pay." She gave Leonard a peck on the cheek and hurried off.

"That woman's a miracle worker," Leonard marveled. "She could re-create Paradise if you were willing to pay. I don't know what we'd do without her."

"Claude told us you have a house on the Pointe," Harriett said. "Why aren't you up on the roof with your neighbors helping Jackson justify his deductions?"

A young woman in a black dress appeared on the deck with a thick green beverage, which she handed to Leonard. "My afternoon smoothie," he explained. "I don't drink anymore. And I have no time for all the glad-handing going on upstairs. I spent thirty years making money for other people. Now I'd rather just hang out with dogs and kids."

"And whales," Jo added.

Leonard's face lit up at the mention of whales. "Can you believe the show that female put on the other day? I've been coming to the Pointe for twenty years, and I've never seen anything like it. I wonder what got into her."

Jo had to restrain herself from glancing over at Harriett. "You do a lot of whale watching?"

"Whenever I can." Leonard wiped away a green smoothie mustache. "They're such magnificent creatures. At some point in the future, when our own species is more evolved, we'll look back and be very ashamed of what we've done to the whales."

"While you've been out looking for whales, have you noticed the crowds down by Danskammer Beach lately?" Harriett asked.

Leonard shook his head with disgust. "The vultures haven't gone away since the body was found. I'm afraid that sort of behavior doesn't say much for our species, either."

"Neither does dumping the bodies of dead teenage girls in the scrub," Harriett said.

"This is true," Leonard agreed solemnly.

"Did you happen to see anything unusual in the weeks before the girl was found?" Jo asked.

"No one spends much time on the Pointe before May. I'll fly in for a weekend here and there, but I usually spend the spring in the Caribbean." Leonard stopped, and his impish smile returned. "So are you two going all Cagney and Lacey? Think you have a shot at solving the case?"

"Nope, just curious," Jo said. "I've always been fascinated by serial killers."

"Serial killers?" Leonard appeared to have lost his sense of humor. "I thought they said the young woman died of a drug overdose. What makes you think her death was the work of a serial killer?"

Harriett waved away the idea with a dismissive flip of her hand. "Don't listen to her. That's just what the ladies in town are saying. You know ladies   always looking for an excuse to get our panties in a twist."

Leonard laughed. "Well, I certainly hope that's all there is to it. I'd hate to think there's a serial killer on the prowl in the area."

"Isn't that what Culling Pointe's gate is for?" Harriett asked. "To keep bad guys out?"

"Yes, I suppose so." The thought seemed to lift Leonard's mood again. Shrieks of excitement came from the beach below. Something had washed up on the sand, and the children were calling for Leonard to come down.

"I think you're being paged," Jo said.

Leonard offered a theatrical sigh. "The work of a retiree is never done. Enjoy the party, ladies!"

Jo scanned the crowd as Leonard jogged back to the water. "So what should we do now? If everyone down on the beach is a guest, they won't know anything about the murder."

"How about a walk?" Harriett replied. "I'd love a look at the local flora—and the south side of the Pointe should offer a good view of Danskammer Beach. And who knows? Maybe we'll even meet a few locals."

Jo kept her eyes peeled as they strolled along the water's edge past the sunbathers and children. Once they'd rounded the tip of the point, the shrieks and shouts of the kids died away. A long, empty beach stretched ahead of them and the only sound was the rhythmic lapping of waves. The first mansion they passed was set back from the sand. A traditional beauty, it featured a wraparound porch that looked out over the scrub. The chaise longues at its pool sat empty and the sand on the beach appeared undisturbed.

"Where is everyone?" Jo asked.

"Watching," Harriett replied. "There's a man with a pair of binoculars pointed at us right now."

"Shit!" Jo didn't dare turn to look.

"Don't be nervous." Harriett's soothing tone was half hypnotist, half Jedi knight. "We're not trespassing. The key to getting away with anything is convincing yourself that you've done nothing wrong. We left the party so we could have a private conversation, nothing more."

They passed over the property line and the scenery abruptly changed. A starkly modern house, its exterior walls clad in black-stained cedar, hovered over the dunes. The island's native vegetation had been shorn and a perfect green carpet of grass laid out in its place. A long concrete planter ran along the lot line to the beach. Corralled inside were hundreds of green stalks rising four feet high, each crowded with pale yellow flowers. The transition from one property to the next was so abrupt, it was hard to imagine their owners could have anything in common.

"Interesting landscaping," Harriett mused, but Jo wasn't listening. Her attention had been drawn to a woman in a white bathing suit sitting alone on the deck that stretched out over the lawn, her blond hair wafting in the wind and her mirrored glasses reflecting the sun. A bowl of brightly colored fruit and a carafe of water rested on a table beside her. She was so still that Jo assumed she was sleeping. In the house behind her, a painting loomed over the living room furniture. In it, a young woman in her underwear stared out at the ocean. Her eyes seemed to warily follow her viewer as if watching to see what their next move would be. A white medical mask hid the rest of her face, and an old-fashioned nurse's cap was pinned in place atop a sixties-style bouffant.

Jo focused again on the blond sunbather, recognition dawning. "I know that woman," she said. "Her name is Rosamund Harding."

"You know Rosamund Harding?" Harriett asked, eyebrow raised. "You run in some interesting circles."

"She's a client, not a friend," Jo said. "Do you know her? Is she someone important?"

"Rosamund Harding used to be one of the world's best divers. She was expected to win gold at the London Olympics. Then an injury ended her career and she married Spencer Harding, the art dealer, instead."

"I've never met Spencer Harding, but I know he's an asshole," Jo said.

"That's a logical assumption," Harriett replied. "He collects Richard Prince."

"What?" Jo asked.

"The creepy nurse art." Harriett pointed at the house. "It's a Richard Prince."

"Yikes." Jo grimaced. "It's like he painted all his icky little schoolboy fantasies."

"Which is why his paintings are so popular with former icky little schoolboys," Harriett said. "So what else do you know about Harding?"

"He sent a bodyguard to my gym a few weeks ago looking for Rosamund, and she definitely didn't want him to find her. I called her afterward, and she acted like it was no big deal, but she hasn't been back to the gym since."

"So Spencer fetishizes nurses and sends thugs after his wife. Sounds like poor Rosamund lost the marriage lottery."

"No joke," Jo said. "I'm going to go talk to her. Make sure she's okay."

Behind her glasses, Rosamund must have been watching them. When they stepped off the sand and onto the lawn, it was as if they'd tripped an invisible wire. Rosamund sat up and plucked an apple from the fruit bowl on the table. She kept her head bent as she whittled away at the apple's skin with a paring knife.

"What is she doing?" Jo muttered. "Is she trying to pretend she doesn't see us?"

They were almost to the deck when Rosamund suddenly stood and tossed the whole apple onto the grass as though it were trash. It landed a few feet from Jo. When she looked back up, Rosamund was hurrying inside the house.

"Okay, that was weird," Jo said.

Harriett walked over and picked up the apple. Then she held it out for Jo to see. Etched into the apple's skin was a word. *FAITH.*

Jo took a step forward and reached out for the apple. Harriett casually raised it to her mouth and took a bite.

"What did you do that for?" Jo demanded.

Harriett gestured with her chin at a man hustling across the lawn toward them. On the Pointe, his dark blue suit instantly identified him as a worker, not a resident.

"Shit," Jo groaned.

Harriett swallowed. "Another friend of yours?" she asked.

"That's the bodyguard I was talking about. He isn't going to be happy to see me. I had to kick his ass when he showed up at my gym a few weeks ago."

"Hmmm," Harriett said. "Looks like you may need to do it again." The man had picked up speed and was now jogging straight for them. "But look at all the effort he's making. Let's see what he wants first, shall we?"

The sight of the two women patiently waiting for him seemed to confuse Chertov, and he slowed to a brisk walk. His face was flushed when he reached them.

"Well, it's about time. We've been looking all over for a waiter." Harriett took another bite of the apple. "I'd love a banana daiquiri, and my friend here would like a piña colada."

Chertov ignored Harriett. "You're trespassing on private property," he told Jo. "How did you get through the gate?"

"I walked, just like everyone else," Jo said.

"Well, it's time to go." He reached a hand out toward her. "Mr. Harding knows you're here, and he wants a word with you."

Jo glanced down at the man's hand, and it paused in midair. "Didn't you learn your lesson the other day?"

The hand that had been traveling toward her changed course and disappeared under the man's jacket. When it emerged, it was holding a gun. "Start walking," he ordered.

"Fuck you." The whole scene struck Jo as ridiculous, and she refused to play along.

"It's okay, Jo," Harriett said. "I'd like to have a word with Mr. Harding, too, wouldn't you? If nothing else, we should try to convince him to buy better art."

RESIDENTS STEPPED OUT ON THEIR decks to watch as Harriett and Jo were marched back toward the Dunn mansion. Apparently, the people of Culling Pointe weren't accustomed to having trespassers nabbed on their land. As Jo and Harriett approached the party, the guests all stopped to look. Only the children didn't seem to care.

"There you are!" called a voice behind them. "I've been looking all over for you two. What's going on here?"

"You know these women?" Chertov barked.

"Of course!" Claude exclaimed, as if Harriett and Jo were the guests of honor. "They're here for the party. They're both friends of Leonard."

That little lie seemed to give the bodyguard pause. "They were trespassing on private property. Mr. Harding wants to see them."

"What? *Why*?" Claude asked with a confused smile, as though nothing he'd said made any sense to her.

"It's okay," Harriett assured her. "We're looking forward to meeting Mr. Harding, too."

"Still, there's no need for that." Claude pointed daintily at the gun. "I'll take the ladies up to meet Spencer right now."

When Chertov hesitated, Claude pulled out her cell phone. "Would you like to check with the boss?" she asked. "I can ring him up, if you like."

When the bodyguard seemed uncertain, Claude began to dial.

"Fine," he barked. "Just tell Mr. Harding I delivered them."

"Of course," Claude replied, her voice saccharine sweet.

"Thanks," Jo told her as the bodyguard stomped away.

"I am so terribly sorry," Claude told them. "Some of the security people here are drunk with power. Is there anything I can do to make up for that? A couple of really strong drinks, maybe? A massage from a hot young lifeguard?"

"We'd like to meet Spencer Harding. And have a look upstairs," Harriett announced, pointing up at the roof deck.

Claude appeared mystified, but laughed nonetheless. "Spencer's a creep and there are houses with much better views, if that's your thing."

"It's not," Harriett said. "I've been to Jackson Dunn's Memorial Day party every summer for the past five years, and I've never once been invited up to the roof deck. I'd like to see what's there."

Claude's slim smile conveyed more respect than amusement. "I wish I could take you," she said. "But I can't afford to get canned at the moment. Let's grab Leonard and ask him to escort us. He can do whatever he wants around here. Though I promise, unless you like wrinkled old men, you really haven't been missing much."

She called out to Leonard, who was still cavorting in the surf with the guests' children. When he heard Claude, he ran toward her, grabbing a shirt and a towel off a lounge chair as he passed.

"Sorry to bug you, sweetheart," Claude said.

"You never bug me," he told her, planting a kiss on her lips. "What's up?"

"The ladies would like to see the roof and meet Spencer Harding," Claude told him. "Would you mind escorting us?"

Leonard grimaced as he toweled his hair dry. "You wanna go up to the roof, let's all go up to the roof. But why in the hell do you want to meet Harding? The man's got the personality of a pit viper."

"Told you," Claude said.

"We're worried about his wife," Harriett replied.

"Oh? You know Rosamund?" Leonard asked.

"She's a client of mine," Jo said.

"Ah. Lovely girl. Way too good for that schmuck."

"Yes, we agree," Jo said.

"Well, come on, then." Leonard led the way into the Dunn house. "But if he bites your head off, don't say I didn't warn you."

When the four of them emerged on the roof, Jo briefly wondered what all the fuss was about. Fifty middle-aged men mingled in groups of five or six. Most wore shorts and sandals. Aside from the watches on their wrists, few ostentatious signs of wealth were visible. It looked like a corporate retreat. Then, as Jo began to focus in on the faces, an uncanny feeling settled over her. She knew almost all of them, despite the fact that she'd never met any of them. Most were celebrities, but none were actors or entertainers. Tabloid paparazzi would have walked right past them. The moves they made were dutifully chronicled not by tabloids, but by reporters from the *Wall Street Journal* and the *New York Times*. These were men who ran the world.

None of the men on the roof stopped talking or stared when Claude, Jo, and Harriett made their way through the crowd. There were other women on the roof, after all. Two swimsuited lifeguards were mingling with a group of men. As Jo passed, she picked up a snippet about private swim lessons. But the atmosphere changed after their arrival. Spines straightened. The laughter sounded a little less raucous and the conversations a bit more polite.

"Hang out here with Claude for a sec and let me see if I can find Harding for you," Leonard said.

Harriett sauntered over to the railing on the side of the deck that looked over the Pointe. She'd taken her hands out of her pockets and Jo could see that she had something clenched in her fists. "I always wondered what secret things happened here on the roof, but I didn't want to get in the way. So I hung out downstairs with all the other women. I met doctors. And judges. And Oscar-winning actresses." She looked back over her shoulder, and her eyes landed on Claude. "Do you know what we all talked about?"

"What?" Claude went to stand beside Harriett.

"We talked about what was going on up here on the roof."

"Is it everything you were expecting?" Claude asked.

"Oh yes." The grin spreading across Harriett's face worried Jo.

"Harriett?" It was Chase's voice.

Jo spied him making his way across the roof, wearing a constipated smirk that he was trying to pass off as a smile. Harriett didn't bother to look.

"What are you doing up here?" he whispered angrily when he reached them.

Claude turned around to face him. "Leonard brought them," she said.

Chase reared backward, the drink in his hand sloshing over the rim of its glass. "My apologies. I'm their escort," he responded. "Chase Osborne."

"A pleasure," Claude said unconvincingly.

"Would you mind if I had a word with my wife for a moment?"

"*Ex*-wife," Harriett corrected him, without turning around.

"Of course. I'll just find out what's keeping Leonard and Spencer." Claude set off across the roof, but Jo didn't bother to move.

"What the hell, Harriett," Jo heard Chase whisper. "We had a deal. We said we'd stay out of each other's business."

"And now I've let you down," Harriett said. "How inconsiderate of me. Don't worry, I'll be out of your hair in a moment."

Jo glanced over at Harriett just in time to see her open her hands and toss a thousand tiny seeds off the balcony and into the air. The two women watched as they floated down and settled on the land below.

"What was that? What the hell are you up to?" Chase bent over the railing to look.

"Fuck off, would you?" Harriett told him. The breeze from the ocean was already carrying the seeds inland.

Jo pulled Harriett to the side, away from Chase. "You told Jackson you're working as a horticulturalist," she whispered. "Whatever you just did, he's going to know it was you."

When Harriett looked at her, Jo saw something cold in her friend's eyes. "That's why I told him. So when the time comes, he'll know."

"Jo, Harriett. Leonard sent someone over to say hello." Claude was back. At her side was a handsome man in a blue shirt and white jeans. His skin was a shade Jo would have called "Private Island Patina," and though his face was unlined, his hair had turned gunmetal gray. The man's pale eyes refused to settle on anyone. His expression remained blank, but his eyes conveyed his annoyance. He didn't seem to care much for Claude, and he had no desire to speak to either Jo or Harriett.

"Mr. Harding, I'd like you to meet Leonard's new friends, Jo Levison and Harriett Osborne."

"Hello, Mr. Harding." Harriett turned around and leaned her back against the railing. "We just had the pleasure of spending some time with your bodyguard."

"What a beautiful home you have," Jo added. "And what a lovely, terrified wife."

Spencer Harding's jaw clenched and he swallowed whatever words had risen to his lips. His eyes remained focused on Harriett. He seemed unaware that Jo existed. "My sincere apologies for my employee's behavior," he said flatly. "I'm afraid my wife has been ill recently, and we're all very protective of her these days. But it sounds as if my director of security stepped over the line. I'll ensure there are no more mistakes of this sort."

"To be honest, I'm much more concerned about your wife, Mr. Harding," Harriett continued. "I hear she hasn't been to the gym in weeks. It seems a little unusual for a former Olympian to neglect her physical fitness routine, don't you think?"

Spencer Harding's spine stiffened noticeably. "My wife suffered a painful injury that ended her athletic career," he said. "I'm afraid she's had trouble with addiction in the recent past, and she's now under a doctor's care. As soon as she returns to good health, I'm confident Rosamund will resume her regular schedule. Until then, we must keep an eye on her—and be wary of any unexpected visitors."

"And what kind of drugs was she addicted to?" Jo asked. "Oxy-Contin? Fentanyl?"

Spencer Harding glared down at Jo. "What is this?" he growled.

Jo shrugged. "I'm just worried about Rosamund," she said.

"We're big fans," Harriett told him. "If something ever happened to Rosamund, I'd be very, very unhappy." The threat, while politely delivered, was nonetheless clear.

"So would I," Jo said. "And your bodyguard knows what I'm like when I'm upset."

Spencer Harding blinked. "Thank you for your concern, ladies," he droned. "I'm afraid I really must get back to the conversation I left. Again, my deepest apologies for my man's appalling behavior. I do hope you'll enjoy the rest of the party." He turned to Claude. "Tell Leonard he has strange taste in friends."

They watched him walk away. Claude waited until he was just out of earshot. "I hate that conceited asshole."

"Gee, I wonder why?" Jo joked.

"You didn't tell me you saw Rosamund," Claude said. "She hasn't been outside in days. I know she's dealing with some issues, but I worry about her being stuck in a house with that scumbag."

"If she ever wants to get rid of him, she'll find everything she needs in the planters in her front yard," Harriett said.

Claude's eyes narrowed. "What do you mean?" she asked.

"The flowers are Korean aconite. Some call them wolfsbane. Their poison has been saving women from assholes for thousands of years."

Jo glanced nervously at Harriett. "She's kidding."

"No, I'm not," Harriett said. "Ask Rosamund to google aconite, would you?"

JO AND HARRIETT SAT SIDE by side in the back seat of Chase's car. They'd both held their tongues while another of Jackson Dunn's sons drove them back to the gate. But the moment the car doors slammed shut, Jo couldn't hold back any longer.

"Why did you—" she started to ask before Chase slid into the driver's seat and shut the door.

"What the hell?" he said, interrupting Jo's thought. "Am I supposed to be your chauffeur now? Why are you both in the back seat?"

"We have things to talk about," Jo snipped.

"You going to tell me what happened back there at Jackson's house?" Chase demanded.

Harriett rolled her eyes as she turned to face him. "No," she said. "And don't ask again." Then she returned her attention to Jo. "What were you saying?"

"Why did you say that about"—she put her lips to Harriett's ear and whispered—"*getting rid of Spencer*?"

Harriett pulled away and shrugged. "Why not? Someone's going to have to do it eventually, don't you agree? It might as well be Rosamund. She has a bumper crop of yellow wolfsbane growing right in her front yard."

Jo took in a breath. It was pointless trying to talk sense to Harriett. "You probably blew Claude's mind."

"I doubt it," Harriett replied. "Seems to me like she's considered killing him a few times herself."

"I can't see her going that far," Jo said. "Besides, I'm sure she's used to taking shit from the Culling Pointe set."

"Wait—are you two serious?" They looked up to see Chase's laughing eyes in the rearview mirror.

"Your games are boring," Harriett told him.

"I'm not playing games. You really don't know who Claude Marchand is?"

"The woman who plans Jackson Dunn's parties," Jo said.

Chase's laugh was that of a man cursed by fate. "I spent all afternoon schmoozing my ass off and getting nowhere, and you two end up best friends with Claude and you don't even know who she is?"

"This is getting tiresome," Harriett said with an exaggerated yawn. "Enlighten us or shut up, would you?"

"She's Antoine Marchand's daughter."

Harriett's curiosity was sufficiently piqued. "Is she really?"

"And Leonard Shaw's girlfriend," Chase added.

"Yeah?" Jo said. "So what?"

"Leonard's the king of Culling Pointe."

"A retired finance dude I've never heard of is the king of Culling Pointe?" Jo scoffed.

"He's the one who started the whole community. He built the first house here back in the nineties."

"Are you sure we're talking about the same guy?" Jo couldn't quite wrap her head around it. "The cuddly little mensch with all the hair on his chest?"

"That *mensch* is one of the richest men in the world," Chase said. "And now you two appear to be besties with his longtime girl-friend."

"Maybe we'll put in a good word for you the next time we see her," Harriett told him. Then she laughed. "Oh, who am I kidding? No fucking way."

"Claude invited you back?" Chase winced as if the idea caused him physical pain.

"Not exactly," Harriett said. "But Culling Pointe may soon be in need of my services."

Jo felt her smile fade as she remembered the handfuls of tiny seeds Harriett had tossed from Jackson Dunn's roof deck.

"Your *services*?" Chase sneered. "I've heard you're popular around Mattauk. Are you getting paid for your services these days?"

"You know, it's a shame you're so insecure, Chase," Harriett replied. "Your penis really isn't *that* small."

CLAUDE MARCHAND
PLAYS HER HAND

Claude stood with a champagne flute in her hand, waiting for the toast to begin. To her right, the crowd parted, and she saw the young man making his way across the room toward her. He was lovely, she thought. His height, posture, and gait spoke of generations of good breeding.

He found an empty spot a few feet away from her. A moment or two passed before he casually turned her way. He didn't want to try too hard. "Have you had a chance to view the collection?" he asked, smiling down at her. Even in heels she was almost a foot shorter than he was. Men always felt bigger standing next to her.

"Oh yes. It's the reason I'm here. I'm Claude." She saw no flicker of recognition in his eyes. He was genuinely interested. "I study art," she added.

"Owen," he said. "Where do you study?"

"Yale," she replied. "I'm just down for the weekend. What did you think of the paintings? It's in vogue these days to dismiss Singer Sargent as a brownnosing society portraitist."

"I've always been a big fan of his," Owen said. "In fact, that's my great-great-grandmother right there." He tilted his champagne glass at the portrait of a regal older woman whose corset-stiffened form was draped in pearls. "Of course, he was very prolific. I'm sure your grandmother is around here as well."

Claude blushed prettily. "No, I don't think so." He thought she was one of them. He'd find out the truth soon enough. "So you're descended from Lady Wilcott, then. I read somewhere that she was found in a storage facility that hadn't been opened in decades. She must be glad to have finally found a good home."

"Perhaps. It's a shame, though." Owen let his voice drop. "That she and the rest of these beautiful people will spend the next few decades staring back at that."

Claude followed his eyes to the spot where their host stood chatting with a small group of guests. He was easily the largest man in the room, with a belly that cleared a broad path for the rest of him. The thatch of thick black hair on his head had been temporarily tamed, but his jowls were tinted by tomorrow's beard. The party had started only an hour earlier, and there was already a stain on his shirt. Pâté, Claude guessed. There was a matching splotch on his chin, where the food had first hit when it tumbled from his mouth.

"I must get the name of his tailor," Owen said. "If they can fit a gorilla for a tuxedo, they should be able to work wonders for me."

Claude hid her frown with a sip of champagne. "Do you know him?" she asked.

"My father invests with him," the young man said. "He says he's brilliant. Grew up in France in the years after the war. He told my father he ate rats to survive. Apparently, he has no formal education to speak of, and yet—" He gestured at the grand ballroom with his free hand.

"And they say the American dream is dead," Claude quipped.

"Yes, only in America could a rat-eating French peasant corner the market on nineteenth-century portraits of American aristocracy. Funny, I would have taken him for a Koons or Hirst man. And this house. It's magnificent. I assumed he'd married someone with taste, but my father told me he's single."

"I believe his wife passed away many years ago," Claude offered.

"I wonder who she was," Owen mused. "It must have been hard crawling into bed with that every night."

"Not if you're another rat-eating French peasant," Claude replied and Owen laughed heartily as their host took his place at the front of the room. "I can't wait to hear what this one has to say."

"Good evening," their host said. "Thank you all very much for coming tonight. I am a man of numbers, not words, so rather than bore you all with a terrible speech in a thick French accent, allow me to introduce you to the person who made this all possible, my charming and talented daughter, Claude Marchand."

"Will you excuse me?" Claude asked Owen, whose horror was just beginning to register on his face. "Daddy needs me. What did you say your last name is?"

The young man cleared his throat. "Van Bergen."

"Nice to meet you, Owen Van Bergen. I'll have someone pass along the name of my father's tailor."

LATER THAT NIGHT, AFTER THE guests had gone, Claude cuddled up next to her father on the sofa in his study. The two often ignored the rest of the house when they were alone. With the lights off and a blaze in the fireplace, the study reminded them both of the little house in Brittany in which Claude had been born. They'd been happy there, the two of them, just as they were happy in the mansion her father had purchased when Claude was thirteen. As long as they had each other, Claude figured, they could be content just about anywhere. From time to time, Claude felt a pang of remorse that she'd never gotten to know her mother, who'd died during childbirth. But her father had always done everything he could to compensate for the loss. No father could have loved a child any more.

"You hired the perfect caterer, my dear." Her father patted her on the knee as he praised her. "The food was delicious."

"I can see from your shirt how much you enjoyed the pâté," she teased.

He pulled his shirt out to take a look and sighed at the sight of the pink smear. "Your father is a pig. I don't know how you acquired your gift for all this," he told his daughter.

"Anyone could do it," she said, dismissing his praise. "All it takes is money."

"No." Her father was adamant. "You cannot buy taste. It is a rare gift. One we both know I don't share. You make me look presentable, and for that I am grateful."

"Grateful enough to grant my fondest wish?" she asked, keeping her tone light.

"Of course. Whatever you want, it is yours," he replied.

"I want to come work with you at the hedge fund. I want to learn everything about your business and join you after I graduate."

He frowned. It wasn't the first time the subject had been raised, and they both knew it would not be the last. "No," he said. "Money is filthy. A beautiful girl should keep her hands clean."

She'd known what his answer would be, yet it still stung to hear it.

Claude's father took her hand and squeezed it. "I'll always take care of you," he promised.

She didn't doubt it. That wasn't the point. "You don't think I'm capable of taking care of myself?"

"It has nothing to do with your abilities, Claude. Trust is the key to my business. I do not hire women because men only trust other men with their money. I wish it were not true, but it is. I would not lie to you."

"So things would be different if I'd been born a boy?"

"Yes, they would." He turned to face her, his eyes moist beneath thick, black brows. "No boy could do what you can do, Claude. I can hire people to work for my fund, no problem. But I could never hire anyone to do your job. You are my ambassador, my translator, my guide. I don't speak the language these people speak. I don't understand their ridiculous world. But you do. You know how to make them happy. Two more investors signed on this evening—because of the party you threw. You are as important to the business as I am."

"You mean that?"

"Absolutely. Now, if you want to help the business even more, you can do your father a big favor and marry someone impressive. That way I can bring him into the fund and put his name beside ours on the door."

"You really want to marry me off to some snob with a fancy name?" Claude jested. "What is this? The nineteenth century?"

"The game is the same as it's always been," her father told her, and she knew he was serious. "You've been dealt a good hand. You can either throw your cards in the air and walk away—or you can let me teach you how to play to win."

He paused for a moment to contemplate his glass of scotch.

"To be honest, you are lucky that I am letting you choose your own husband."

Claude pulled a throw pillow from behind her back and walloped him on the side of the head. They were both laughing so hard that a member of the staff poked their head through the door.

"No one's being murdered. We are just having fun," her father told the concerned servant. Her father was always kind to the help. When Claude was away, he even took his meals with them.

"The people who were here tonight look down on us," Claude said, grabbing the glass of champagne she'd left sitting on the side table. "It doesn't matter what we do. They always will."

"Let them underestimate us," her father said with a shrug. "That's how we'll win."

Claude nodded thoughtfully and finished her champagne. "How do you like the name Van Bergen?"

"I have a client named Van Bergen. He's the fanciest of them all. I used to think he shit rose blossoms. Now I know better."

"Oh really?" She arched an eyebrow. "What exactly do you know?"

"Ask around and you'll find out," her father said. "It's not something a girl should hear from her father."

"Okay, but you still haven't answered my question. How would you like the name Van Bergen for your door?"

Her father scowled. "That bastard. Did he proposition you? These old men think they can have anyone they want."

"Calm down! Van Bergen has a son. I met him here tonight."

Her father relaxed, releasing his breath in a whoosh. "And you liked him?"

"He was very handsome," Claude said. "Though he said some mean things about you. I don't know if I could ever forgive him for that."

"Forgive him," her father counseled.

"Why should I?"

"He'll make excellent insurance. If anything were to happen to me, you would have your own fortune and a different name."

"What could happen to you?" She was suddenly serious.

Her father patted her knee. "Nothing, my darling. Don't worry your pretty head."

TWO YEARS LATER, CLAUDE WAS engaged. The discussion she'd had with her father that night was forgotten. She'd long since forgiven Owen for his snobbery, and she loved her life among the Van Bergens. Owen's father got her a job with the best art gallery in Chelsea—and his mother drew invites to every gala in town.

Claude heard the whispers about the senior Van Bergen, of course, but they weren't that different from the things she'd heard about other Wall Street titans—including her father. She didn't blame the gossips. Rumors were their way of keeping billionaires human.

Claude was at work at the gallery one afternoon when a grim-faced intern beckoned her into a conference room. The local news channel was playing on the monitor. From the pedestrian walkway of the Brooklyn Bridge, an enormous man had crawled out onto one of the beams above six lanes of cars. A tourist's camera captured the action as bystanders screamed. When the man reached the end of the beam, he stood, wobbled, and jumped. A different camera captured the fall—and the impact when Claude's father slammed into the water.

She later learned that her father had been buying a cup of coffee at the deli downstairs from his office on Maiden Lane when he got word from a member of the cleaning staff that the Feds were raiding his business. While his employees were being herded into a conference room, her father had simply slipped out onto the street. A dozen security cameras captured his trek to the East Side of Manhattan, where he joined a crowd of sightseers walking across the Brooklyn Bridge.

He jumped because he knew what the Feds would discover. There were no investments. His hedge fund was a Ponzi scheme. Every dime had been funneled into paintings and palaces. He must have realized he'd get caught eventually. That's why he'd wanted her to have insurance, Claude realized. Then he'd died while the check was still in the mail.

Owen called off the wedding while Claude was waiting to be interrogated. The gallery fired her by email. Her mansion on Seventy-Fourth Street was seized that very evening. The Singer Sargents were packed up and loaded into the back of an unmarked government van. Within twenty-four hours, Claude had been stripped of everything she owned. Desperate, she went to see Owen's father, prepared to grovel for a loan. His proposal made it clear how far she'd fallen—and how accurate all the rumors had been.

Heartbroken and humiliated, she slinked away with a thin envelope of cash. Until the authorities could be convinced of her innocence, she hid from the paparazzi in a motel room near a freeway in Queens. For the first time in her life, she knew exhaustion and hunger. The self-loathing felt worse. She despised herself for being so gullible. Her father had told her they were playing a game—and made himself out to be a master. But he'd never once told her how high the stakes were—and she'd had no idea he was cheating. Still, she loved him. When she cried, she cried not for Owen, but for him.

Claude was finally allowed to leave New York on the Saturday that would have been her wedding day. She hopped on an Amtrak and hopped off in Philadelphia. She couldn't afford to go any farther. She never planned to go back to the city.

Six weeks later, she was on a break from her job at a midprice bridal boutique when she received the call.

"Is this Claude Marchand?" It was a woman's voice.

"I have no comment," Claude informed her.

"Oh no!" the woman cried before Claude could hang up. "I'm not a reporter. My name is Jennifer. My husband invented Chit-Chat?" She paused. Claude gave her nothing. "I got your number from a friend at the gallery you worked at. I would be grateful if you could give me a moment of your time."

"Yes?" Claude asked. She didn't want to be rude, but her break was almost over.

"I hope this doesn't sound horribly crude," she said, and Claude knew it would. "I purchased a rug from the Sotheby's auction."

The auction in which the contents of the Marchand house had been sold. She paused nervously, as if expecting Claude to explode.

"It's a seventeenth-century Aubusson. My understanding is you're the one who originally purchased it?"

"That is correct."

"Would you be interested in helping me locate a few more in the same style?"

"I'm not an interior decorator," Claude said.

"No, no, of course not!" the woman rushed to say. "But your consulting skills could do me a world of good."

Claude said nothing. She was pondering the possibility.

"The truth is, I have no idea what I'm doing," the woman confessed, her voice cracking. "I grew up in a split-level ranch in Cleveland. My favorite food is tuna casserole. I don't know an Aubusson from a West Elm. I desperately need guidance. These people are so awful to me. I just don't know how to be rich."

"I'll help you." If her time in Philadelphia had taught Claude anything, it was that being rich was the one thing at which she excelled.

"Really?" the woman squealed. "Fantastic! Name your price. Whatever it is, I'll pay it."

"We can discuss compensation later," Claude said. "I have a condition you must agree to first. You and your husband must never allow anyone with the last name Van Bergen into your home."

"That shouldn't be a problem," the woman said. "I have no idea who the Van Bergens are."

"You will," Claude told her. "I was engaged to Owen Van Bergen. I can confirm that everything they say about his father is true."

"Oh my God. What do they say?" Jennifer took the bait.

"I can't bear to repeat it. Just ask around."

"I certainly will!" the woman replied, as though Claude had just done her a favor.

It was a conversation she'd have with all her clients from that moment on. For a few years, her efforts appeared to have little effect. Then a cocky finance guy from Brooklyn hired her for a charity event.

"Owen fucked you over, did he?" the client asked bluntly. Fifteen years her senior, he reminded Claude a great deal of her father. He was an outsider, too.

"He did," she admitted. She felt safe with him.

"In that case, I'll enjoy making him suffer," Leonard told her.

She thought he was showing off. But that day marked the end of the Van Bergen family's three centuries of excellent luck. Much to Claude's glee, the elder Van Bergen soon found himself juggling multiple scandals—financial mismanagement, tax evasion, and the sexual assault of his former receptionist. The younger Van Bergen, unwelcome in all his former Manhattan haunts, was rumored to be living in Nova Scotia. Claude, meanwhile, flourished. With Leonard as her partner, she wielded real power. But she swore she'd never again take her position for granted. A woman had to be ready to look out for herself.

THE SPARK

Back at Harriett's house, Nessa had spent the entire day on the sofa. As soon as Harriett and Jo drove off toward the Pointe, the voices had begun growing louder. They'd reached a crescendo around two and remained almost deafening for most of the afternoon. When her headache became bearable once more, Nessa knew her friends were on their way back. Soon the dead were just a dull din in the background.

The front door swung open and Harriett appeared. "Honey, I'm home!" she called. "Oh, there you are, darling. Tell me you didn't spend the whole day on your back."

"Where's Jo?" Nessa asked.

"Chase drove her home so she could see Lucy before bedtime. She'll come by in the morning." Harriett's eyes landed on something in the room and her lip curled with disgust. "What are those?"

Nessa followed Harriett's gaze to a glass vase overflowing with perfect white lilies.

"Oh, those came about thirty minutes ago. From one of your admirers?" Nessa had been dying to peek at the card, but good manners had prevailed.

"No one who admires me sends me dead things." Harriett approached the bouquet as though she were sidling up to a corpse and plucked a card out from between the stems. Her eyes remained on the card much longer than necessary.

"Well?" Nessa asked.

The card skimmed through the air and landed faceup in Nessa's lap. *So lovely to meet you,* it read in tight, slanted script.

"The flowers are from Spencer Harding," Harriett said.

"The art dealer? The jerk who's married to Jo's client?" Nessa didn't get it. "Why would he send you flowers?"

"We met him at the party."

"You must have made a real impression," Nessa teased.

"Indeed." Harriett smiled at a thought she didn't choose to share. "The flowers are Mr. Harding's clever way of telling me he knows where I live. I hope he pays me a visit soon. I'd love to give him a tour of my garden." Harriett pinned the card to the wall behind her workbench and grabbed the vase. "Be right back. These need to go to the compost heap." A few minutes later, she returned in a cloud of pot smoke, a blunt wedged between two fingers. Her left hand clutched a bottle of champagne.

"Are we celebrating?" Nessa asked.

"Every day is a celebration," Harriett responded. "Grab a glass and get comfortable. I've got a story to tell you."

Harriett kicked off her sandals and spread herself out on the couch with a forearm tucked under her head. She left enough room for Nessa at the far end, where the cloud of pot smoke was thinner. Nessa never partook, but she'd come to appreciate the pleasant buzz of a light contact high. By the time Harriett had finished the story of the day's events, Nessa had set down her champagne and moved out of the smoke to a nearby chair. She needed a clear mind to process the tale.

"You said our whale watcher's name is Leonard Shaw?" Nessa typed his name into Google and scrolled through the results. "Well, how about that? He's all over the internet." Nessa held her phone up for Harriett to see.

Harriett took a long drag on her blunt while she squinted at the screen. "Yep. That's Lenny. Who's the funny-looking guy he's with?"

"The president of MIT." Nessa scrolled down. "And here's a picture of Leonard with the president of Harvard."

Harriett exhaled smoke in Nessa's direction. "Lenny sure has a lot of smart friends."

Nessa waved the cloud away with her free hand and kept scrolling with the other. "Here's a picture of him with the Clintons. And another with Donald Trump. I'm telling you, Harriett. Your friend Leonard might be the most popular man on earth." She paused to scan a newspaper article. "And I think I just figured out why everyone loves him. According to the *Times,* Leonard has promised to give away ten billion dollars before he dies. The man's a saint."

"A saint would give away money anonymously," Harriett responded. "People who announce their intentions in the *Times* are out to make friends. Tell the world you plan to give away ten billion dollars and you'll have a very hard time finding enemies."

"Is that a bad thing?" Nessa asked.

"No," Harriett admitted. "It's an interesting thing."

"You wanna know what's funny, though?" Nessa looked back down and scrolled through all the articles she'd found. "I can't figure out what Leonard used to do for a living."

"He didn't *do* anything," Harriett said. "He was in finance. He just moved money around. Speaking of which, you remember Antoine Marchand?"

Nessa began to type. "Antoine with an e?"

"Do you really not recognize the name?" Harriett asked. "He ran one of the biggest Ponzi schemes of the nineties. Madoff stole his thunder a decade later, but Marchand was the OG."

"I was in nursing school in the nineties. I didn't have time for the news."

"Must have been a nursing school on Mars if you missed the Marchand story. He jumped off the Brooklyn Bridge. A crew filming a movie caught it all on camera. The video was one of the internet's first viral sensations."

"I remember a man jumping off the bridge, but why are we talking about him *now*?"

"Antoine Marchand is our new BFF Claude's dad."

"So her father committed suicide?" Nessa asked. "How sad."

"He stole hundreds of millions of dollars," Harriett said. "If I recall correctly, poor Claude had been kept in the dark, and she ended up broke after he died. I imagine that must have screwed with her head a bit. Now look up Spencer Harding, and you'll get a sense of our cast of characters."

Nessa spent a few minutes perusing the results. "There are plenty of articles about paintings he's sold, but there's not much online about Harding himself. Lot of stuff about his wife, though. She hasn't been seen in public much since they married, and people aren't happy about it. Do you think she's really addicted to painkillers?"

"I think an addiction to painkillers is an excellent excuse for keeping your wife under house arrest."

Nessa glanced up. "You know the girl in blue died of a fentanyl overdose," she said. "That's a painkiller."

"That fact hasn't escaped me," Harriett said.

"So Spencer Harding keeps his wife under surveillance, has his bodyguard threaten anyone who gets close to her, and sends you flowers to show he knows where you live? Sounds like he might be our guy."

"Maybe, maybe not," Harriett said. "Either way, he's a threat to our kind, and he needs to be dealt with. I'm rooting for his wife to save me the trouble and kill him herself."

Nessa hadn't been listening. "Is he this good-looking in real life?" She handed her phone to Harriett.

The photo was an old one, and the man on the screen had black hair trimmed with gray. His eyes, which stared straight out at the camera, were unusually light. He wore a beautifully cut navy suit and a hostile expression. He seemed to resent having his photo taken.

"Yes, he's handsome." Harriett took another drag off her blunt. "But your friend the cop is hotter. It's more fun screwing people with souls. Speaking of Franklin, we should tell him to come over so we can give him the 411."

Nessa reached for her phone, and Harriett sat up to hand it back. "I sent Franklin a text thirty minutes ago," Nessa said, scrolling through her messages. "I don't know why he hasn't gotten back to me."

"Relax." Harriett spread her long body out on the sofa again. "He will."

Nessa sensed what would come next and suddenly wished Jo hadn't gone home. When they were alone, Harriett could make Nessa spill beans she'd rather keep in their can.

Harriett took another puff off her joint. "You like him. Admit it. When are you planning to get some?"

"What?" Nessa felt her face burning. "Never!"

"Why not?" Harriett seemed to enjoy torturing her. "You kissed him, didn't you?"

Just the thought of Franklin's lips touching hers gave Nessa a jolt. "Can we just talk about Spencer Harding and Ponzi schemes?"

"I've told you everything that I know for the time being. So why don't we take this opportunity to have a chat about your sex life? I don't think you're embarrassed. We've both lived too long for that."

Nessa thought it over. "You're right. I'm not embarrassed," she concluded. "I guess I'd say I'm confused. I always thought women disappeared when they reached our age."

"Disappeared?" Harriett coughed the word out and took another toke.

"You know, to men," Nessa said. "I spent my whole nursing career getting my ass grabbed by dirty old bastards in hospital gowns. There were quite a few days when I wished I could disappear. It's a relief not having to deal with that anymore."

Harriett tilted her head back and released a smoke ring like the Caterpillar in *Alice in Wonderland*. "If you want to be invisible now, you can be," she said. "But why would you want to hide from handsome Franklin Rees?"

Nessa shrugged. "I don't know what he's interested in, anyway. I'm nowhere near as attractive as I used to be."

Harriett's head rolled back down and her gaze fell on Nessa. "By *attractive*, you mean young and thin?"

"What else would I mean?"

"When someone calls you attractive, it means you draw people to you," Harriett said. "You think a tiny waist and wrinkle-free skin are the only things that can do that?"

"Yes, I know. I have a lovely personality."

"I'm not joking. Do you know how beautiful it is to be alive? Do you have any idea how few people really are? You've got a spark. And even now, after everything you've been through, it's as strong as ever. That's what keeps Franklin fluttering around you like a lovesick moth."

"You're high, Harriett."

"True," she said. "I am indeed very stoned. But I was also in advertising for twenty-five years. Ad people like me are the ones who convinced women that being attractive was all about rosy cheeks and red lips. You know why? Because we could sell lipstick and bronzer and Botox and juice plans. There was no way to make money off the kind of allure that I'm talking about. So we sold a version of attractiveness you could buy instead. And over time, people forgot there was any other type. But some of us don't need all the crap at Sephora to draw others to us. And like it or not, you are one of those people, my friend."

"So you think that's what Franklin sees in me? My spark?"

"You're fucking hot, Nessa. Just like Jo. Just like me. And unlike Jo and me, you have that gorgeous big ass."

"Thank you," Nessa giggled.

"How long has it been?" Harriett asked.

Nessa didn't want to say. After Jonathan died, she'd packed that part of herself away. Throughout her marriage, she'd never fantasized about anyone else. The truth was, she'd never even looked at another man in that way. Nessa felt Harriett's eyes on her, and she worried how it would sound if she said that out loud. She didn't expect Harriett to believe her. But for the fifteen years they were together, Nessa had been completely faithful to Jonathan in body, mind, and soul. Since his death, nothing had changed. Once she passed forty-five, she assumed nothing ever would.

"It's time," Harriett told her.

At that moment, Nessa's phone rang. She looked down and saw Franklin's name on the caller ID. "Did you do that?" she marveled.

"You ladies have *drastically* overestimated my powers." Harriett rolled her eyes. "You even bought that whale bullshit a few weeks ago."

"You didn't talk to the whale?" Nessa looked crestfallen.

"Sure I did. But before that, I read the Mattauk newspaper and saw that whales had been spotted just off the Pointe."

"Damn you," Nessa said as she prepared to answer the call. "I was really impressed."

"Oh, I have plenty of skills that would impress the hell out of you," Harriett assured her. "Sending telepathic messages to detectives just isn't one of them. Now answer the phone."

"Franklin." Nessa's heart picked up speed. She turned her head away from Harriett so the other woman couldn't see the grin on her face.

"I called as soon as I could." Franklin sounded exhausted. "There's been some movement in the case. A woman who says she's our Jane Doe's mother has come forward."

Nessa leaped out of her chair. "Are you serious?"

"She saw the portrait we posted online and believes it may be her daughter, who disappeared a few weeks ago. I'm sending a car to pick up the woman in the city tomorrow so she can identify the body. If it turns out to be her daughter, she says she'd like to meet with the person who found her."

"I'll be ready," Nessa said breathlessly. "Doesn't matter what time."

"I'm just warning you, Nessa, even if this is the lady we're looking for, she might not say what you've been hoping to hear."

"Doesn't matter. If she's the mother, bring her to my house."

"Are you sure, Nessa?" Franklin pressed her. "This sort of thing is the worst part of my job. I don't know why you'd want to share it."

"I'll be waiting for you tomorrow morning." Nessa hung up the phone and looked down at Harriett, who was launching another perfect smoke ring into the air. "Franklin says they may have found the girl's mother."

Harriett lifted an eyebrow. "Two big leads in one day," she said. "What are the odds?"

AT ELEVEN THE NEXT MORNING, the doorbell rang. On Nessa's front porch, a skeletal woman stood by Franklin's side. Nessa had been watching them since they pulled up in the drive. The woman shared the dead girl's prominent cheekbones and their noses bore a resemblance to each other. But the eyes were different. The girl's eyes had been spared whatever horrors the older woman's had seen.

Now that she was close, Nessa could tell the woman had been beautiful once. It was evident not only in her face, but in the way she held herself—hunched and self-conscious, as though she'd been robbed of her only treasure.

"Thank you for finding my baby." The woman on her doorstep threw her arms around Nessa and burst into tears. Nessa held her as she cried, wondering how it was possible that a human body could function with so little flesh. They stood there on the threshold, the woman clinging to Nessa like a life preserver, until Franklin cleared his throat behind them.

"Come inside," Nessa told the woman. "I just made coffee. Would you like some?"

"Yes, thank you." She pulled a Kleenex out of a packet that Franklin offered and wiped away the mascara under her eyes.

"Detective Rees, go make yourself comfortable in the living room and we'll bring you a cup," Nessa told him once they were all three inside. She gently took her guest's arm and guided her toward the kitchen. "I'm Nessa James, in case the detective didn't tell you."

"Laverne Green."

"You hungry, Ms. Green?" Nessa asked. "I made some butter rolls this morning, and if you don't have some, I'm gonna end up eating the whole batch—and those calories would look a lot better on you than on me."

"I'd love some," the woman said hungrily.

In the kitchen, Nessa gathered dishes and silverware. The woman watched her. She didn't seem to know what to do with herself.

"The detective says you drew the picture that was online."

"Yes," Nessa said. "I tried my best. I hope it did her justice."

The woman retrieved an envelope from her pocketbook and pulled out a Polaroid, leaving several more stacked inside. "Her name was Venus," she said. "After the goddess—not the tennis star."

The girl's hair was styled differently, but it was unmistakably her. She was wearing a ruffled red dress in a style that seemed better suited to another decade.

"You chose the right name for her. She was a beauty. May I see the other pictures?" Nessa asked.

"Of course." The woman passed her the whole envelope.

The photos showed the girl posing in front of the same mirror in different outfits. Something in one of them caught Nessa's eye. It was the chain the girl had been wearing when she died. The pendant at the bottom wasn't a cross as Nessa had imagined. It was a coiled snake crafted from gold.

"That's a beautiful crucifix she's wearing," Nessa said. If the woman was the girl's real mother, she would know the pendant wasn't a cross.

"Thank you." Laverne wiped away a tear. "It was a gift from her grandfather."

Nessa slipped the picture into the center of the pile and handed the photos back to the woman.

"Venus seemed to love the camera," Nessa said. "And it sure loved her back."

"She wanted to be a model," the woman said. "Like her mama was back in the day. I know I don't look like much now, but I was on the cover of magazines when I was that age."

Nessa looked up to find Laverne staring at her. "I believe it," she said.

"Then Venus's daddy left me when she was a baby. Said I'd gotten fat. Everything went to hell from there. And now this— "

Back in her nursing days, Nessa had seen far too many parents lose children. Some wailed in anguish, while death struck others silent. Nessa knew grief came in countless varieties. But in her experience, this wasn't one of them. "I'm so sorry," she said.

Laverne's gaze only intensified. Nessa returned to her work, but she could still feel it.

"I just wish I could have taken better care of her. When she ran away three months ago, it wasn't exactly a surprise. Venus had been making her own money and I told her she needed to start paying rent, but she wanted to spend it on drugs. After that, she just picked up and left."

"How was she making her own money?" Nessa asked.

Laverne stared down at the butter rolls on the counter. "Men," she said, leaving it at that. "I told her how dangerous it was. I told her she'd end up dead. But you know girls. I was the same way."

It was time. Nessa had loaded a tray with the coffee cups and dishes. "Would you mind carrying that plate of butter rolls for me?" she asked.

They took everything to the living room, where Franklin was waiting in a chair.

"Have a seat on the sofa," Nessa told her guest. She chose the chair next to Franklin's for herself.

Nessa watched as the woman sat down beside the girl in blue, whose name, Nessa was almost positive, was not Venus Green. The ghost's head slowly swiveled to get a look at the woman. Then it turned back to face Nessa. Nothing had changed.

An hour later, when her guests had gone, Nessa used a pencil to pick up the coffee cup that Laverne Green had used. She carefully placed it inside a plastic bag.

"THAT WASN'T HER MOTHER," NESSA told Franklin when he phoned later that evening.

"She brought a birth certificate and photos and a folder full of documents," Franklin said.

"Doesn't matter," Nessa insisted. "I kept the woman's coffee cup. You need to test her DNA against the girl's."

"Nessa." Franklin sounded like he was going to talk sense to her.

"There is no way I can justify that. Laverne Green had all the right paperwork. What makes you think she's not the girl's mother?"

"The whole time that woman was in my living room, she was sitting right next to the girl she claimed was her daughter. The girl didn't recognize her."

"Hold on a second," Franklin said. "Are you telling me that girl's ghost is inside your house?"

"Do I sound like I'm messing with you?"

Franklin took a moment to absorb the news. "Nessa, there is no way I can justify doing a DNA test. I believe what you're saying, but as far as the department is concerned, the girl is Venus Green."

"Fine," Nessa huffed. "I'll do my own test. She left her DNA all over my cup."

"You'll need the girl's DNA, too," Franklin said. "How are you going to get that?"

"I'll ask for a few strands of her hair when I have her buried."

"When *you* have her buried?" Franklin sounded confused.

"Now that the girl's body has been identified, it will be released from the morgue. Is Laverne Green planning to take it?"

Franklin pulled in a deep breath. "She said she doesn't have the money for a funeral. The county will have to bury the body."

"Mmmhmmm." Nessa's hunch had been confirmed. "I knew there was no way in hell that woman was going to pay for a funeral for a girl she doesn't know. Tell the county they can save the tax-payer dollars. I will take care of that baby."

LAVERNE DOUGLASS GETS
WHAT SHE'S OWED

Anthony walked in at one in the morning, smelling like another woman. She wasn't asleep. Sleep wasn't an option. She hadn't made it to the grocery store and there was no food left in the house. It made her suffer if she didn't feed it every few hours.

She was sick when he opened the door. Still, she didn't yell. She'd learned better. Those powers didn't work on him anymore.

"The baby's hungry," she told him.

"Then feed it." He walked past her. "You're its mama."

"Why are you like this?" she asked.

"What did you expect after you let yourself go?"

She made to stomp out, and he didn't stop her. "Go on, then," he said. "Run home to your daddy. But if you do, don't bother coming back."

Back then, a pregnant lady walking down the street at three A.M. was a murder waiting to happen. The Lord hadn't paid Laverne much mind in a while, but he must have been smiling down on her that night. She made it to her aunt's house just as the sun came up. Across the street at her parents' house, the light in the kitchen was already on. Her father was getting ready for his shift at the hospital. But she didn't dare knock. He'd made it perfectly clear how he felt about her coming home. Theirs was a good family, and she didn't belong.

Her aunt tsked when she told her what had happened. "Bastard," she said. There were moments when it was possible to see that she'd once been as beautiful as her niece. Those moments were now fewer and farther between.

"What happened to Auntie?" Laverne once asked her mother.

"She fell for the trap that snares pretty women," her mother answered. The look on her plain face said there was a lesson to be learned. "She was sure her beauty would last forever. So she didn't bother looking for other sources of strength. And when her beauty faded, as it always does, your auntie found out she had nothing left."

Laverne had never believed her mother's tale, until now.

Across the street, the light came on in her sister's bedroom. Janelle was five years younger and went to Hunter College in Manhattan. The subway ride to the Upper East Side could take two full hours. Soon, she'd be heading out the door, wearing her mom jeans and basic sneakers.

Anthony thought Janelle was ugly. She wasn't ugly. She just wasn't a swan like Laverne. From the time she was five, Laverne's beauty had had the power to stop people in their tracks. At nine, she was on her first catalog cover. At twelve, she was cast in her first commercial. By sixteen, she'd lost count of her suitors. Men of all ages found themselves tongue-tied in her presence. She was twenty-three when Anthony spent weeks wooing her with gifts and jewelry.

When Laverne got pregnant, they married. But instead of binding him to her, the baby had broken the spell.

"Maybe I'll have an abortion," she heard herself mutter as she watched Janelle leave for school. She'd come to hate the thing growing inside her.

"Too late for that, sweetie," her aunt said. "But in a few months, you can get alimony and child support."

LAVERNE DIDN'T GO OUTSIDE AFTER that. She didn't want anyone in the old neighborhood to see what had become of her. Her parents gave Laverne's auntie enough money to feed her, but they never once knocked at the door.

Then one night, seven months in, she woke up in a pool of blood. By the time she got to the hospital, the baby had died inside her. The doctor gave her a lecture. Said she'd had preeclampsia, and it was a miracle she'd survived at all. The condition would have been detected if she'd sought care when she first felt sick.

"Next time," she promised.

"You won't be having any more babies," he told her.

She thought she'd enjoy her freedom, but she was never the same after that. There were no more modeling jobs. When the doctors cut out the baby, they'd botched the incision. More than one man lost her number after seeing it. She still did a little acting here and there, but nowhere enough to pay the bills. She was working at Target when they offered her money to pretend to be the girl's mama. She took it without a second thought. The way she saw it, it was the baby paying her back for everything it had stolen.

FAITH

Sixteen people attended the service at the Mattauk funeral home. Jo's family was there. Nessa's girls, Breanna and Jordan, took the train in for the day. The rest of the attendees were ladies from Nessa's Bible study group. Even with tears in their eyes, several of them had a hard time pulling their gaze away from Franklin as the pastor delivered the sermon. Only Harriett had skipped the service. There was work to do at the cemetery, she'd informed them.

Wearing the same black dress she'd worn when she'd buried her parents, Nessa sat in the first pew and stared numbly at the coffin. A closed casket had been the only option. One look at the corpse, and the mortician had informed her there would be no way to camouflage the discoloration. Still, Nessa had spent an entire day shopping for a new dress in the right shade of blue, and she'd requested the girl's makeup be done, though no one at the service would see it. Then she fixed the girl's hair herself. When she was finished, she'd looked up to see the girl's ghost watching her from the end of the mortician's table.

"I'm sorry, baby," she'd told the girl. She didn't know what else to say. The ghost was still standing there when she left. When Nessa got home later that night, her sofa was empty. The ghost had chosen to stay with her body.

For two days, Nessa had felt grief pressing at the dam she'd built to hold back the tears so she could get things done. As the pastor began the Lord's Prayer, the walls gave way and Nessa wept openly. The girl's mother should have been there to see her off, but Nessa hadn't been able to locate her. She'd failed her first test. Even her tears were proof that she didn't deserve the gift she'd been granted.

"Mama." Breanna slid her arm around Nessa and whispered in her ear. As always, she sensed the source of her mother's pain. "That girl knows you did everything that you could. I'm sure she's grateful."

Nessa couldn't find the breath to argue, so she shook her head. It didn't feel true. She cried so hard that Franklin had to guide her out the door after the service. She kept crying in the passenger seat of Franklin's car as they drove to the gravesite with her daughters sitting quietly in the back seat.

"Is it all right if I have a word with your mother?" Franklin asked the girls after he'd parked. "And if you don't mind, ask the others to wait a few minutes till we get there."

Blinded by tears, Nessa heard the doors open and shut. Then she felt Franklin take her hand. The fingers he wrapped around hers were warm.

"Hey," he said. "This isn't over."

"It is," Nessa sobbed. "Even her ghost is gone. She hasn't come back since I did her hair. She's given up on me, Franklin. She knows I can't help her."

Franklin didn't rush his response. He sat back and seemed to think it through.

"You did the girl's hair at the funeral home?" he asked.

"Of course I did!" Nessa had to stop to blow her nose. "I couldn't let her meet Jesus looking like some old white man did her hair."

"Did you ever consider maybe that was all the proof she needed?" Franklin asked. "I think it showed her how much you care. She trusts you to take it the rest of the way."

Nessa looked over to make sure he was serious, though she'd never known him to be anything but. She'd worked around sick people long enough to tell the difference between words intended to make you feel better—and words meant to convey the truth. Franklin wasn't just pumping sunshine. Whether he was right or not, he meant what he said. "You think?" she asked.

"I really do," he said.

Nessa sniffled. "But what am I going to do now that she's in the ground and the case is closed? How am I supposed to find the person who killed her?"

"Did you gather DNA at the funeral home like you said you would?" Franklin asked.

She shot him a wary glance before she answered. "Yes," she admitted. He hadn't approved when she'd mentioned her plan, but she'd taken a few strands of the girl's hair, anyway.

"And I suppose you've still got Laverne Green's coffee cup?"

She nodded. "In a plastic bag on my kitchen counter."

"Okay," Franklin said. "After the funeral, let's get the hair and the cup to a lab. The first thing we'll need to do is prove that the two women aren't related."

"Are you saying you believe me now?"

"Yes," Franklin said, letting the word drop as if he knew exactly how much it weighed. "I sent Laverne Green an invite to the funeral like you asked me to. I even offered to drive into the city to pick her up. I never heard back from her."

"That's because she was lying."

"If so, the test will confirm it."

"Are you going to get in trouble for doing all of this?" Nessa asked. "The case is supposed to be closed."

He could get in trouble—she saw it in his eyes. Franklin wasn't a renegade. He was patient, methodical, strictly by the book. He believed in process. He believed in the law. And yet she knew what he was about to say. He was going to throw all that out the window for her.

"You told me the girl was murdered, and that there are two other girls out there whose bodies haven't been discovered. I believe you, and I want to catch the man responsible before he kills anyone else. If that gets me in trouble, so be it."

It was exactly what she'd expected from him. Nessa looked down at their hands, still woven together.

"God gave you a gift, Nessa," Franklin said. "Now he's brought us together twice. I think it's pretty clear that I'm supposed to help you. I think that's what I was sent to do."

Franklin wiped a tear from her cheek with his free hand. Then he leaned over and kissed her. It wasn't hurried or anxious like the kiss Nessa had given him. Franklin wasn't conflicted. He knew what he wanted, and Nessa got the feeling he'd wanted it for a very long time.

"I'm sorry," he said, pulling back. "This is neither the time nor the place."

"I don't think you're sorry," Nessa told him.

Franklin smiled. "You're right. I'm not."

He leaned back in toward Nessa, and this time she met him halfway. She thought of the spark Harriett had said was inside her. She'd taken it for a metaphor, but now she wasn't so sure. Something inside her felt like it was burning bright.

The kiss lasted only a few seconds. Then Franklin was out of his seat and walking around the car to open her door. She slipped her hand through the crook of his arm. As they walked side by side across the graveyard, she was still glowing. Once, she might have felt guilty to feel so alive with the dead all around her. Now she knew she'd need that light for the darkness ahead.

HARRIETT HAD WANTED TO BURY the girl in her garden, but that would have broken a dozen laws and the morgue had refused to deliver the body to Woodland Drive. So she'd purchased space in a local graveyard instead. When she took Jo and Nessa to see the plot, they were surprised to find that Harriett had picked a barren corner on a hill overlooking the highway for the girl's final resting place.

"Are you sure this is the best spot?" Nessa had asked. There was no shade in sight and the grass beneath their feet was brown and brittle. "There are plots on the other side of the cemetery with flowers and trees."

"I bought three plots side by side," Harriett had told her. "That should be enough room for what I have in mind. Don't worry about grass. There will be plenty of that soon enough."

Now the brown grass was gone. In its place was a meadow filled with orange daylilies, purple ironweed, and white Queen Anne's lace. A path just wide enough for a coffin and pallbearers led to a clearing in the center of the flowers. A mound of dirt sat at the head of the open grave, and the mourners had gathered on either side. At the bottom of the hole, a biodegradable cardboard casket lay with a linen shroud on top of it. Harriett hadn't wanted a casket at all. Burial was meant to return a person to nature, she'd argued passionately. Wrapping the girl's body in a toxic cocoon of plastic and chemicals would defeat the purpose. The ecofriendly solution was the compromise they'd arrived at. Nessa had insisted on the linen covering, knowing her friends from church would take one look at a cardboard casket and assume she'd gone with the cheapest option.

Jo watched Nessa arrive on Franklin's arm, bearing her grief bravely. She, Art, and Lucy stood among the church ladies. Her own family, while proud of their heritage, had not been religious. Growing up, she'd been inside more churches than synagogues.

The rites and rituals of Christianity were familiar, but they weren't her own. As a little girl, she'd been fascinated by the Christian vision of heaven, with its white-robed God and plump little cherubs. A friend had told her heaven is where Methodists go if they've led a good life. Her mother had tutted when Jo repeated that.

"Anyone who needs a reward to be good isn't good. They just like rewards. Good people do the right thing because it's the right thing to do."

Those words had stuck in Jo's head for forty years—and they were still there, long after her mother had met her own reward. Jo remained skeptical of those who wore their religion on their sleeves. But she had no doubts where Nessa was concerned. If there was one person alive whose goodness could counter the world's evil, it was the woman who'd just come to bury a girl she'd never known.

Harriett was another story, Jo thought. She had purchased the plots. She had planted the flowers. For all Jo knew, Harriett might even have dug the hole. But she hadn't done it out of pure benevolence. Harriett's motivations weren't so easy to comprehend, but Jo was certain she had her eyes on a goal as well. As the pastor spoke, Jo let her gaze linger on the tall, regal woman with the mane of silver-blond hair. She wore a long, sleeveless dress of unbleached linen and though her feet were hidden, Jo knew they were bare.

Once the pastor had finished, Nessa and her daughters left ahead of the others so they could get home before their guests arrived at the funeral reception. Harriett didn't appear to be in a hurry to leave, and Lucy seemed keen to stay by Harriett's side.

"You worked wonders on the gravesite," Jo told Harriett. "It's lovely."

"Yes." Harriett no longer had time for false modesty. "But I'm not finished."

"Do you want a ride to Nessa's house?" Jo asked Harriett. "We're heading over there now."

"If you don't mind, I could use a hand before you leave." Harriett picked up the two shovels that lay atop the mound of dirt by the grave and held one out to the Levison family.

"You're kidding," Art Levison said with a nervous grin. His wife and daughter knew it wasn't a joke.

"I'll help!" Lucy offered eagerly.

"Great!" Harriett passed the second shovel to the little girl without a second thought. Lucy, dressed in her best shoes, hopped right into action.

Art looked over at his wife. "Is this okay with you?" he muttered.

Jo shrugged. "I know it's weird, but I guess it still counts as a mitzvah."

"I hope so," he said as they watched their eleven-year-old daughter shovel dirt into an open grave. "Isn't there someone at the cemetery who gets paid to do this?" Art asked Harriett.

"Yes, of course," Harriett replied. "But if you want something done right, you have to do it yourself. And find an eleven-year-old kid to help you. Am I right, Lucy?"

"Yeah!" Lucy said.

When the hole was almost filled and both Lucy and Harriett were covered with dirt, Harriett pulled a small burlap pouch out of her bag. "I'll do the rest of the shoveling. Take one of these and plant it when I'm done."

"What are they?" Jo asked.

"*Brugmansia insignis*. Angel's trumpet." Harriett opened the bag and pulled out a strange seed, which she placed in the palm of Lucy's hand. "Amazing, isn't it? One of these tiny seeds will grow into a twelve-foot-tall monster. Each of its flowers will be the size of a party hat, and every part of the plant will be chock full of poison."

"Wow." Lucy marveled as she studied the seed up close.

"You're planting a giant poisonous bush on this girl's grave." Jo didn't know what to say.

"Yes, because when the plant is in flower, it's impossible to ignore." Harriett pointed past the cemetery's fence at the highway that stretched from the city to the end of the island. "I want everyone passing by to look. I want whoever did this to know that the girl buried here hasn't been forgotten. I want him to see what we can do. And I want that motherfucker to worry."

"Woohoo!" Lucy cheered.

Jo felt her phone buzz in her pocket. When she pulled it out, she saw the call was coming from her gym, where she'd left her assistant manager in charge.

"I'm sorry to bother you." Heather was speaking so softly that Jo strained to hear. "But you need to come to the gym as soon as you can. The police are here."

"What? Why?" Jo asked.

"One of our clients passed away. They want access to her locker. I've told them I can't do anything without your permission."

Jo felt the energy flowing beneath her skin. Her body sensed where the conversation was going. The phone's connection briefly faltered. "Which client?" Jo asked.

"Rosamund Harding," Heather said.

A second surge made the line crackle. "Ask all the clients to leave. Tell them there's a plumbing emergency. I'll be at the gym in three minutes."

"Trouble at work?" Art asked when she hung up. Harriett had paused from her labors to hear what had happened.

"A client of mine died," Jo announced, her eyes trained on Harriett. "Rosamund Harding."

Harriett shook her head, disappointed. "I guess she didn't get to her husband first."

"I guess not," Jo confirmed. "Now the police want access to her gym locker."

"What a tragedy. Go do what you need to do," Art told his wife. "I'll hose off the kid and take over from here."

Harriett gave Jo a slight nod. She'd made Spencer Harding a promise, and she intended to keep it.

WHEN JO ARRIVED AT FURIOUS Fitness, Tony Perretta and his young partner were waiting for her at the front desk. The younger man held a pair of bolt cutters in his hands. They were going to get what they were after one way or another.

"It's been years since I've seen you in a dress." Tony gave Jo a once-over. "You look good as a girl."

"Dress or no dress, we both know I could take you out in ten seconds tops," Jo said.

"Is no dress an option?" Tony asked. They'd gone out a few times in high school, which Tony seemed to feel gave him license to say whatever he liked.

Jo gritted her teeth and let the comment slide. She needed something from him. "Listen, Tony, could I have a quick word with you in my office?" she asked.

She led the older cop around the corner and held a door open for him.

"That isn't an office," he said. "It's a supply closet."

"Wow," Jo marveled with big eyes. "Sherlock Holmes has nothing on you, Tony." Then she gestured toward the closet. "Let's have a chat and I won't make this too hard for you."

The cop grumbled under his breath and stepped inside.

"How did they kill her?" Jo asked as soon as the door was closed.

"What? Nobody killed Rosamund Harding," Tony told her. "She

crashed her car into a utility pole on Danskammer Beach Road this morning."

"Was she drugged?"

"I don't know what kind of drugs she'd been taking," Tony said. "The toxicology report isn't back yet. But that's one of the reasons I'm here. The husband said she has a history of opioid abuse. He thinks she may have drugs stashed in her locker."

"Rosamund hasn't been back to the gym since her husband's bodyguard chased her off. Even if she has drugs in her locker, they didn't have anything to do with her death."

Tony sighed. "Listen, Jo, I'm not here to chitchat. I just came to collect Mrs. Harding's things for her husband."

"Ah, so let me guess—this isn't really part of the investigation. You're just cleaning up any messes that may have been left behind. This mean you're taking odd jobs from the Culling Pointe set?"

She'd hit a nerve. Perretta reached for the door handle.

"I'm sorry, Tony," she said. "I shouldn't have said that."

"No shit," Perretta said, but he let his arm drop. "If you want to know the truth, Jo, I offered to come as a courtesy to you. Mr. Harding wanted to send his bodyguard to empty the locker, but I know you're not the guy's biggest fan. Now maybe you can quit being a giant bitch for one minute and let me do my goddamned job."

"Fine," Jo said. "But I want to see everything that comes out of her locker."

"I can't agree to that, Jo. There's no investigation. Her death was clearly an accident. So the stuff in her locker is private property. Rocca told me to sweep everything into a bag without even looking at it."

"Come on, Tony," Jo said. "Let me have a quick look. Otherwise, I'm going to have to insist that you leave my gym and bring me back a copy of the death certificate before I reveal which of the three hundred lockers in my establishment was rented by Rosamund Harding."

"You are such a pain in the ass," Tony said, not unappreciatively.

"Oh man, you have no idea," she said.

"I pity your poor husband."

Jo had to laugh at that one. "Really? I think he'd tell you he's got it pretty damn good. Now let's go. Get the bolt cutters and leave the kid at the desk. It's just you and me from here on out."

Jo peeked into the changing room to make sure it was empty. Then she guided Tony to locker 288, which was secured with a simple combination lock. A single snip of the bolt cutters and the lock fell to the ground at their feet. Jo stood back and watched as Tony retrieved a pair of sneakers, three sports bras, and a pliable purple item that resembled a small closed funnel.

"What the hell is this?" he asked, holding it up to the light.

"That, my Neanderthal friend, is a menstrual cup."

"You mean it's been—" With a grimace of disgust, he tossed the cup across the room into a garbage can.

"Probably should have worn gloves," Jo noted. "That it?"

Tony turned back around and ran his hand along the bottom of the locker. "Guess so."

"No drugs or stacks of cash or amateur porn. Still, can't say it was wasted time." Jo patted him on the back. "You learned a little something new today, didn't you, Sparky?"

She walked Tony back to the front desk, where he was reunited with his young partner, who seemed a bit miffed he'd missed out on the fun. Jo watched through the window as their cruiser drove away. Then her smile fell, and she turned to the young woman behind the desk. "Do me a favor, please. Print out a list of all the lockers that are rented by the month."

With the paper in hand—and a pack of Post-its—Jo returned

to the changing room. Around a third of the lockers were rented on a monthly basis. The rest were free to be used by anyone who supplied her own combination lock. It was against the rules to keep your stuff in a locker overnight unless it was rented, but Jo had never been one to strictly enforce the rules. Sometimes she even used the lockers to stow Hanukkah and birthday presents that she didn't want her nosy little girl detective to find.

Jo suspected that was why the police had been sent to clean out Rosamund's gym locker just a few short hours after she'd been declared dead. Her husband was worried that she'd stashed something in it. Jo wondered if he was hoping they would return with something specific—or if he'd be relieved when they didn't.

Jo went locker by locker. She opened the ones without locks—finding nothing more than an occasional tampon or pair of shower shoes. Whenever she came across a combination lock, she checked the locker number against the rental list. She'd brought the pad of Post-its with the idea of marking each locker that wasn't officially rented but was still being used. In the end, there were only two, and one of them held a pair of riding shoes she'd purchased as a surprise gift for Lucy, who'd soon be heading to summer sleepaway camp. The second locker was in an unpopular spot in the middle of a bottom row. The lock was a simple five-letter-combination sort that would be no match for a pair of bolt cutters. Jo pulled out her phone to text an employee to run out and pick up a pair at the hardware store. Then she stopped midsentence and put the phone down on a nearby bench. She squatted in front of the lock and dialed the letters until they read FAITH. Then she closed her eyes, gripped the base of the lock, and pulled downward. When the lock opened, Jo fell back on her ass in surprise.

Before she'd had time to fully recover, she was on her knees and inching forward. Jo peeked inside the locker and immediately slammed it shut again. Her fingers were trembling so violently that she could barely replace the lock. Then she grabbed her phone and fled to the opposite end of the changing room. She wanted to be as far as possible from what she'd just seen.

"Nessa," she said when her friend answered. "Get Harriett and come to the gym."

"I'm in the middle of—"

"Leave your daughters in charge of the reception," Jo said. "You need to get over here right away."

Then she hung up the phone and went outside to wait. Ten minutes later, she was still pacing back and forth when her friends pulled into the parking lot.

"Come with me," she told them.

Nessa caught Harriett's eye. She'd never seen Jo in such a state.

"Rosamund Harding died this morning," Jo said as she marched through the gym. "They say she crashed her car into a pole. Her husband had the police come collect her things from her locker. After the cops were gone, I started wondering if she might have been using another locker off the books." Jo pointed down at locker 165. "This one was never officially rented. There's no way to know whose stuff is inside. Except for one thing." She showed them the combination lock that read FAITH.

"Whoa," Harriett said.

"Exactly," Jo agreed. "There's more."

She pulled off the lock and took a step back.

Nessa hesitated. "Tell me there's not a severed head in there," she pleaded.

"Just look," Jo ordered.

Nessa stepped forward and opened the locker. Inside was a Polaroid of a naked girl. She stared blankly at the camera, her eyes wide with terror and her arms held out to the sides as if someone had ordered her not to cover herself. "Oh my God." Nessa dropped down onto a bench. "Is that her?"

Harriett, wearing a pair of latex gloves she'd found in the supply closet, was the one to pull the photo out. "It's her," she announced.

The girl in the picture was the one they'd just buried.

Nessa rubbed at her eyes as if trying to scrub away the image they'd seen. "Why would your client have a picture like that?"

"I think her husband took it," Jo said. "Rosamund must have found it and—"

"Jo?" Harriett interrupted. "Hold on for one second. Where did those flowers come from?"

All three heads swiveled toward the enormous vase of white lilies that stood on one corner of the changing room counter. They were identical to the ones Harriett had received at her house.

"I don't know." Jo felt the blood drain from her face. She hadn't noticed the flowers until that moment. She stuck her head out of the changing room door and called for Heather, who immediately rushed over. "Do you know where that bouquet came from?" Jo asked.

"No idea. When they arrived, I asked Art, but he said he hadn't sent them. So I put them in here. I can't believe they still look that good. They've lasted for over a week."

"What day did the delivery come?" Harriett asked.

"Memorial Day," Heather answered.

ROSAMUND HARDING
WASN'T HERSELF

Rosamund lay very still as the two women walked toward her across the beach. She wasn't convinced they were real. And if they weren't real, what the hell could they be? Her heart fluttered inside her chest. One of them looked like the lady from the gym. But that didn't make any sense. Why would she be here? And why did she keep getting closer?

Rosamund slid on her sunglasses and shut her eyes. The dark could be trusted. The dark was real.

She opened her eyes, and her heart hurled itself against her ribs. The women were only a few yards away, and Spencer wasn't home. There was no one around to say they were figments of her imagination. No one could tell her the sound of their footsteps was all in her head. For once, Rosamund had to figure it out for herself.

It was a sign, she decided. She'd put that picture inside the locker for safekeeping. Now the woman who ran the gym had shown up. She'd saved Rosamund once—she might be able to do it again.

Chertov came out of the house, and he looked angry. That meant he could see them, too. That meant they were real. She had one chance to get a message to the gym lady before the bodyguard caught her. So Rosamund plucked an apple out of the bowl on the table and carved the word that had been stuck in her head.

PEOPLE ALWAYS SAID THEY COULDN'T imagine what she had gone through. Rosamund knew they weren't being sincere. Of course they could fucking *imagine* it. What happened to her was their worst nightmare. You get right to the brink of glory and fame. The girl who takes your cash at the supermarket loses her shit when she realizes that's you on the cover of *People* magazine. Famous brands literally beg to sponsor you. Nike has a campaign just waiting to roll. You've got your own line of swimsuits and lingerie ready to launch right after the games. Then *poof!* One day you slip on a patch of ice and tear a ligament. Suddenly everything you've worked for your whole life is gone.

Of course people could imagine it. They just didn't want to. Because no one wants to admit their world is that fragile. No one wants to think that in less than a year, they could go from being America's sweetheart to a drug-addled drunk. But they could. Rosamund never bothered to point that out. She was content to sink into her own private abyss. She didn't crave anyone else's company.

She'd met Spencer at her worst. She got so drunk on their first date that she still couldn't understand why he'd ever asked for a second. It took a year to wean herself off the painkillers she'd kept taking long after her ankle had healed and the booze that wrapped her double-edged depression in a cloud of cotton wool. When the cravings were too bad to bear, she'd head for the gym. She'd been clean for six months when they married.

The anxiety was harder to shake. She found it difficult to socialize, but Spencer didn't seem to mind. He was always jetting off to meet a client in one exotic locale or another. There were a handful of events he needed her to attend every year. The rest of the time, Rosamund stayed at home with all the other beautiful things he'd collected.

She felt guilty that she wasn't yet well enough to be by his side.

"Rosamund, don't torture yourself," he told her. "I love you just as you are."

She adored Spencer. She honestly believed that he'd saved her. She tried so hard to be better for him.

SHE'D SPOTTED THE FLYER ON the bulletin board at Furious Fitness when they were in town to see what their decorator had done at the new house Spencer had bought on the Pointe. "PERSONAL ASSISTANT, CARETAKER, NANNY," read the headline. At the bottom of the page was a photo of a teenage girl who looked like Anne of Green Gables. Rosamund laughed. The girl was just what she needed. Someone to answer the fan mail that still came. Someone to make her the smoothies that would help her get into shape. Someone to hold her back from the edge. At the bottom of the page, the same telephone number had been typed a dozen times, and the paper was cut into a tear-away fringe. Rosamund ripped a number off and dialed it when she got to the car.

The girl's name was Mandy, and Rosamund's call took her by surprise. No one else had answered the ad. After she heard that, Rosamund offered her twice as much as she'd planned. She could sense how desperately the girl needed money, and it made her feel good to be able to give it. When she got off the phone, Rosamund felt more hopeful than she had in ages. Mandy was coming to see her that afternoon.

As evening approached, Rosamund waited and waited, but the girl never showed. She kept calling Mandy's number, and once she could have sworn she heard a phone ringing.

She told Spencer about it when he brought her a cup of tea. "Go to bed, darling," he advised. "You're upset and your mind's playing tricks on you. You'll feel better in the morning."

She didn't feel better, though. She felt groggy and sick.

After that night, she began seeing things—like the long, black hair on his robe. She heard strange sounds in the dark. Visitors seemed to arrive at strange hours of the night. Rosamund was acting crazy, her husband said. And Spencer was getting very worried.

Then she discovered the photos. There were three inside a portfolio case. At the bottom of one, someone had written *FAITH*. Rosamund stole an unlabeled photo and stuck it in a locker at the gym. Even then, she wasn't convinced that it was what it looked like. It had to be some kind of weird art instead. Then Chertov showed up at the gym, and she knew she'd found something real.

That was Rosamund's last truly lucid memory.

"Depressive psychosis," the doctor called it. He prescribed pills that arrived in an unlabeled bottle. He trained Spencer to administer a sedative in emergency situations.

SHE STOPPED TAKING HER PILLS after the woman from the gym showed up at the beach. When her head had cleared, she couldn't take her mind off the photo. The more she thought about it, the more terrified of her husband she grew. If the gym lady didn't come back soon, she'd ask Claude to help her escape from the Pointe.

INVASIVE SPECIES

Every few minutes or so, a client arrived at Furious Fitness in workout gear, gym bag slung over her shoulder.

"I'm sorry," Heather would say, handing each of them a gift certificate for the smoothie place down the street. "We're having plumbing problems, so we'll be closed for the next hour. Have a treat on us while you wait."

From her position right outside the changing room, Jo kept one eye on the entrance and the other on the crime scene. She watched anxiously as another client was sent away with a coupon. Thirty-two had already claimed one. "Any idea how much longer this will take?" she asked Franklin. "I'm not sure how many smoothies I can afford."

"Looks like they should be finishing up soon," Franklin said as the crime scene technician began packing his equipment. The combination lock had been bagged as evidence, as had the photo. The technician had dusted the inside and outside of the locker in question, but only two partial prints had been found. Jo, Nessa, and Harriett had all supplied fingerprints for comparison.

Jo heard the front door open once again. This time, Chief Rocca charged into the gym without so much as a glance at the young woman who'd held the door for him. He marched back toward the changing room, acknowledging Jo with a perfunctory nod as he passed.

She followed Rocca and watched him do a double take when he

spotted Nessa and Harriett sitting on a changing room bench a few feet from the locker in which the photo had been found.

"All three of them were here?" the chief of police addressed Franklin brusquely.

"Yes," Franklin responded.

"I'm sure you've made it clear to the ladies that everything they've seen and heard today must remain confidential for the sake of the case."

"That's going to be hard," Harriett said. "Everyone knows ladies can't resist the urge to gossip."

"Good afternoon, Mrs. Osborne," the chief acknowledged her coldly. "Taking some time off from your gardening?"

"I prefer *Ms.* Osborne," Harriett corrected him.

He replied with a lazy, lizardlike blink and returned his attention to Franklin. "This the locker where the photo was found?"

"Yes," Franklin confirmed, as Rocca squatted down in front of the locker. "Ms. Levison is the owner of the gym. She believes that the locker was being used by Rosamund Harding."

Rocca's head spun around to face Jo. "Do you have a record of Mrs. Harding renting the locker?"

"No," Jo said. "It was being used without a rental agreement."

"Were any of Mrs. Harding's belongings discovered inside the locker?"

"No," Franklin answered this time.

Rocca stood up. "Then how do we know that Rosamund Harding ever laid a finger on this locker?"

"The lock's combination was F-A-I-T-H," Jo said. "The only reason I was able to crack it was because Rosamund tossed an apple to Harriett and me with that word carved into it."

Chief Rocca responded with a snort. "I'm sorry, she *what*?"

"She—"

"No, no." Rocca cut her off, as though he had no time to spare and no interest in anything else she might say. "I heard you the first time—and once was more than enough. Let's just hope someone left some prints on that photo."

"But—"

"It's not that I don't believe you, Mrs. Levison," the chief said, making it perfectly clear that he didn't. "But I don't want to be the one who tells that story to the D.A. without some forensic evidence to back it up. Until we have fingerprints, I recommend you not breathe a word about any of this. Otherwise, you could have a very costly lawsuit on your hands. Some people are willing to do almost anything to protect their reputations."

"Yeah, the law does a great job of protecting rich criminals," Jo said. "What are you doing to protect the girls they kill?"

"The young woman in the photo was a prostitute who chose a high-risk lifestyle," Chief Rocca said. "She abused her body and died of a fentanyl overdose. The medical examiner declared that she alone was responsible for her untimely death, and we've found no proof to the contrary."

"You know what I find most remarkable?" Harriett chimed in. "How the girl wrapped her own body in a trash bag, tied the string in a neat little bow, and then disposed of herself in a patch of scrub. That takes real talent."

Chief Rocca turned his attention to the tall woman on the other side of the changing room. The gap-toothed smile that Harriett offered him seemed like a challenge. Whether he held his tongue out of contempt or decided it was best not to mess with her, the chief of police said nothing in return.

THE RESULTS CAME IN THE next afternoon. Nessa and Jo were in the middle of their workout routine when Franklin stopped by Furious Fitness with the news. The lab had found no fingerprints on the photo. The partial prints inside the locker didn't belong to Rosamund Harding. There was zero evidence she'd ever used the locker—aside from the bizarre story of the apple with the word *FAITH* whittled into its skin. There was also nothing, Franklin informed the three of them, to connect Spencer Harding to the girl in the photo. Even the lilies he'd sent couldn't be traced. The deliveries had been paid for in cash by an unidentified man the heavily tattooed florist could only describe as "painfully normal."

"Isn't it obvious what happened?" Jo demanded. "Rosamund found the photo and suspected her husband of murdering the girl. She hid the photo at the gym for safekeeping, but he knew she was onto him, so he killed her to keep her quiet."

Franklin was clearly pained to be the bearer of bad news. "While that's all very possible, there's not a single scrap of evidence to support it," he said. "We can bring Harding in for questioning, but unless he's in the mood to confess, there's no way we'll get anything out of him."

"So that's it?" Nessa looked crushed. "All these young women die and we have a good idea who killed them, but he gets to go free?"

"The law is reason free from passion," Franklin said. "Gut feelings don't get you very far with D.A.s or juries. We have to take our time and collect the evidence we'll need to get a conviction. Don't get discouraged. Justice may be slow, but she's also relentless."

He made a good point, Nessa thought. Then Jo made her case.

"In the time it takes to gather proof of what we already know is true, another girl could be murdered. Seems to me, the law does a good job of protecting the rights of the powerful and a pretty shitty job of taking care of the people who need its protection the most."

That was the truth, too, and Nessa knew it. Though most of the police officers she'd met did their jobs with the best of intentions, the system was designed to punish, not protect.

"Our legal system is far from perfect," Franklin said. "But it's all we've got. We throw it out, and we'll be left with nothing but chaos."

Jo felt every molecule vibrating with indignation. She liked Franklin, and she knew what he meant to Nessa, but his line of argument was ridiculous and she wasn't afraid to say it. "So we have to play by the rules while men like Spencer Harding do whatever they like. You know why he sent flowers to Harriett and me, don't you?"

"We haven't confirmed that he sent the flowers."

That statement floored Jo. "Does obeying the law mean abandoning your common sense? That's a four-hundred-dollar bouquet. Who the hell do you think bought it? Of *course* Harding sent the flowers. They were meant as a threat—what else could they mean?"

Franklin sighed. "I can't read minds, Jo, and I have to be honest with you, I doubt a grand jury would interpret flowers as a threat."

"Well, I'm telling you, if that motherfucker or any of his hired thugs set one foot inside my gym or my house, I will kill them all and enjoy doing it."

"Please don't take the law into your own hands," Franklin warned her. "You could be the one who winds up in jail."

"For defending myself?" Jo asked.

"There's no such thing as preemptive self-defense, Jo."

"So we know who the bad guy is, but there's nothing we can do. I guess that makes me, Harriett, Nessa, and every young woman in Mattauk sitting ducks."

Franklin looked over at Nessa and shuffled uncomfortably. Nessa knew there was truth in Jo's words, and so did he. "Jo, I swear to you, I'll do my very best to make sure this case keeps moving forward—and that the three of you remain safe."

He was so earnest. So dedicated. There was no doubt in Jo's mind that Franklin meant everything he said. She wished it could be enough. But it wasn't. Not even close.

FRANKLIN DROVE NESSA HOME, BUT Jo stayed behind. She asked Heather to look after the gym, then she climbed the stairs and claimed a treadmill by the second-floor windows. Running usually burned off her rage, but an hour passed and her hands were still balled up in fists. With every pump of her arms, she punched an invisible face. First it was Spencer Harding's, then Jackson Dunn's. Chief Rocca got his, and even Franklin wasn't spared. How could men get away with killing so many women? Why did the law stand between them and justice? How could anyone run the risk of another girl being killed? And with the energy coursing through her every muscle and vein, why was she still so powerless to do anything about it?

Fifteen miles later, Jo slowed to a walk and her surroundings began to come into focus once again. The woman on the treadmill to her right caught Jo's eye and gave her a wave. To her left, a petite brunette was running at an impressive pace. Something about the woman's posture made Jo do a double take. The large silver headphones she wore made it hard to identify her by her profile, but Jo could see enough of her face to be intrigued.

She hung out by the free weights until the treadmill stopped. When the woman stepped off, Jo headed her way. Seen from the front, the woman's delicate features were unmistakable.

"Claude?" Jo asked.

The woman lifted a finger and pulled off her headphones.

"I don't know if you remember me. My name is Jo Levison. We met at Jackson Dunn's Memorial Day party."

"Of course I remember you!" Claude's smile grew as she used

a towel to dab at the sweat dampening her hairline. "You're one of Leonard's whale-watching buddies. Your name is Jo and your friend is Harriett."

"That's right," Jo said. "And this is my gym. I haven't seen you here before. When did you become a member?"

"This is your gym? How amazing! I just joined this afternoon," Claude replied. "I don't usually run indoors, but, as I'm sure you've heard, we've been having some problems out on the Pointe that have made outside exercise a bit challenging."

"I haven't heard anything," Jo told her. "What's going on out there?"

"An invasive species of weed sprang up on the Dunn property and spread around the entire neighborhood. The flowers smell delicious and they're really quite pretty. The only problem is, they've attracted a rather large swarm of bees."

"*Bees*?" Jo barely got the word out.

"Yes. By the thousands, I'm afraid. Leonard won't do anything to harm them. I think he loves bees almost as much as he loves whales. I've got the best bee wranglers on the East Coast out on the Pointe trying to round them all up. But between the bees and the clouds of pollen, the plants have made outdoor exercise impractical for the last few days. So wait—does this mean you don't know about Jackson?"

Jo felt her stomach drop. She'd had a hunch where the story was heading the moment she heard the word *bees*. "No, what happened?"

"He's in intensive care in the city. Apparently, he was up on his roof deck yesterday when he was attacked by a swarm. He's deathly allergic, unfortunately. They're not sure he'll make it."

"Oh my God." When Harriett had tossed seeds off the roof of Jackson Dunn's home, she'd known exactly what she was doing. It hadn't been a prank. It was attempted murder.

"Between Jackson, the bees, and Rosamund Harding, this has been a difficult summer. I imagine you heard the tragic news about Rosamund?"

"I did. She was a client of mine."

"I remember," Claude said. "You spoke to her husband at the party. You and your friend seemed convinced that Rosamund wasn't safe with him. I think you were right, and I wish I'd done more to help her." Claude was hinting at something and Jo eagerly took the bait.

"What makes you think we were right?"

"Leonard can't stand Spencer. He's heard through the grapevine that Spencer launders money for some pretty bad men. Drug lords, dictators, oligarchs—you know the type."

"What? I thought Spencer Harding was an art dealer."

Claude sighed. "I was an art history major in college. I even managed my dad's collection for a while. I thought rich people bought paintings because they love great art. Maybe some do. But for many, the art world is a racket. Let's say you're looking to sell a ton of heroin or a bunch of illegal weapons. How are you going to get paid? You can't take cash and put it in a bank. The authorities would want to know where the money came from. So instead you buy an expensive work of art and then sell it to an anonymous buyer for an enormous profit. Now all that money can go right into your pocket, and no one looks at you funny. Leonard says deals like that are how Spencer got so rich so fast. Rumor has it, he also shares some unsavory habits with his clients."

"What kind of habits?"

"Drugs. Women—though I don't know if you'd call Spencer's type *women*. Apparently, he likes them young. That's one of the reasons Leonard despises him. He's made it clear that he wants Spencer to leave the Pointe. Maybe this latest turn of events will finally inspire Leonard to crack the whip. There's no doubt in my mind that Spencer Harding was responsible for his wife's death."

"How?" Jo asked. "I thought she drove into a utility pole."

Claude snorted. "You think Spencer doesn't know people who could hack into a car's computer system?" she asked. "But I'm not going to hold my breath waiting for the cops to figure it out. They'd never pin a murder on him, anyway. Men as rich as Spencer do whatever they like. Every time they get in trouble, they buy their way out. Spencer's got some of the best lawyers in the world on retainer."

"Justice will be served, one way or another," Jo assured her. "I promise you that."

Claude seemed to study Jo's face. "Harriett said there would be hell to pay if something happened to Rosamund. Do you really think she'll take action?"

Jo thought of the bees. "Spencer Harding has no idea what he's gotten himself into."

"Well, I, for one, am thrilled to hear it." Claude's dark eyes remained fixed on Jo's. "And I'll do anything I can to help. You guys ever feel like kicking some ass, just give me a call and I'll invite you out to the Pointe. You can get my phone number off my membership profile."

FURIOUS FITNESS WAS THREE MILES away from Harriett's house. Jo hoped that was far enough to burn off the energy that was still coursing through her. She ran at a brisk clip down the sidewalks in town. When she reached Woodland Drive, she stuck to the shoulder. There was more than enough room for cars to pass, yet a black SUV that took the turn onto Woodland after she did remained right behind her. Finally, she stopped and waited for the car to roll by.

Perverts always leered as they passed. Misogynists smirked, spat, or shouted insults. But it quickly became clear that the guy behind the wheel of the car belonged to neither group. He wore a polo shirt and sunglasses. His no-nonsense haircut was a style Jo had nicknamed "professional douche." Plenty of Jo's neighbors shared the same look, yet somehow, she sensed this man wasn't one of them.

Once the car was out of sight, Jo continued her jog up the hill toward Harriett's. The setting sun lit the sky a brilliant orange, and Harriett's jungle appeared in silhouette on the horizon. Jo stopped in the road and snapped a picture. When she got home, she'd show Art and ask if he saw it, too. The scene looked just like the old movie posters for *Apocalypse Now*.

As she neared the house, she could hear Harriett speaking to someone in the garden. Her voice was low, almost conspiratorial. Jo wasn't there to spy, and even if she had been, she couldn't have made out any words. She wasn't convinced Harriett was speaking in English.

"Hello?" Jo called out. "You there?"

The voice paused for a few seconds. Then Harriett replied, "Yes, in the garden, come on through."

Jo passed easily through the wall of vegetation that surrounded the property and found Harriett seated cross-legged in a patch of tall yellow flowers, her eyes closed and her hands cupped in her lap as though she were collecting some invisible substance raining down from above. Tendrils of silver hair snaked away from her scalp and a fine layer of dirt dusted her skin like bronzer. She appeared to be wearing a silk pillowcase, and she made it look good.

Jo scouted the garden for visitors. "Who were you talking to just now?" she asked.

Harriett's eyes slowly opened. Jo remembered them being hazel, but now they appeared brilliant green. "I was having a word with my silphium," she said, running a hand fondly over the flowers around her. "It was extinct until very recently, and it needs a little encouragement."

"It didn't sound like you were speaking in English," Jo noted.

"I wasn't," Harriett said. "These seeds were found in a grave that was over two thousand years old. Silphium only understands ancient Greek."

"You're telling me you know—" Jo started to ask. Then she stopped. "Never mind." She couldn't get distracted from her mission. "Harriett, what were those seeds you threw off the roof at Jackson Dunn's house?"

"A variety of Scotch broom," Harriett replied. "As a weed, it's very difficult to eradicate, but it does have lovely flowers."

"Scotch broom," Jo repeated. "Do bees like it?"

"Of course." Harriett rose out of the flowers like a cobra emerging from a snake charmer's basket. Even without shoes, she was at least four inches taller than Jo. "Is there something you're trying to ask me, Jo?"

Jo studied the witch looming over her. She'd never been frightened of Harriett, and she wasn't now. But she was wary of Harriett's power. Jo now realized Harriett needed to be handled with caution. There was something about her friend that wasn't quite human anymore.

"You knew Jackson Dunn was allergic to bees. And yet you spread seeds for a plant that would attract them."

"Yes."

"He's in the hospital," Jo said.

"You don't say?" Harriett replied with a hint of amusement but not a drop of concern.

"Were you trying to ?" Jo didn't want to say the words.

"Kill him?" Harriett shrugged as if the question were moot. "Not necessarily. No more than he was trying to ruin my career by excluding me from his rooftop gatherings. And no more than he was trying to traumatize me by grabbing my pussy."

Jo cringed at the phrase. "Yes, but—"

"But what, Jo?"

"I thought we were supposed to be the good guys."

"No," Harriett said, and Jo could see she was no longer joking. "Nessa is a good guy. I do what I believe to be necessary."

Jo felt the atoms inside her vibrating like mad and slamming into each other. "I'm the protector. I'm a good guy, too."

"Are you sure that's what you are?" Harriett asked her. "You'll have to decide soon. Do you want to follow the rules that have been laid out for us—or would you rather find the path that's meant for you?"

"I just want to make the world a safer place for my daughter," Jo said.

"Yes, but are you sure you're willing to do what it takes?" Harriett asked. "What if the world as it is will never be safe for her? What if you realize you have to burn it all down?"

They heard the sound of a car pulling up fast in the driveway. The engine switched off and a car door slammed. "Harriett!" Nessa shouted. "Where are you? Jo! Are you here?"

"We're in the garden," Harriett called. Her eyes remained focused on Jo. It was Jo's decision, she was saying, whether or not to tell Nessa about the bees.

Jo's lips stayed sealed as Nessa emerged from the brambles and charged toward the two of them, her phone in her hand.

"The lab just emailed the results of the DNA test that Franklin and I ordered." The words came gushing out before she'd reached Harriett and Jo, as though Nessa could no longer hold them in. "Laverne Green, the woman who claimed to be our girl's mother, is no relation of hers whatsoever. She was lying."

"Is there a chance she might have made a mistake?" Jo asked.

"Maybe she saw the missing person post and honestly thought the girl was her daughter."

"Nope." Nessa shook her head. "There's no way she made a mistake. Remember—she had an envelope filled with pictures. They were Polaroids, too, like the photo in the locker. She had to know that the person in those pictures wasn't her daughter."

"Has Franklin heard about all of this?" Jo asked.

"He found out this afternoon and tried to get in touch with Laverne Green. She's disappeared."

"If she isn't related to the girl, who is she?" Jo asked.

"I think she must be an actress, but Franklin isn't convinced. He says it would be extremely expensive to hire a good actress and forge a birth certificate and medical records for a make-believe child."

"The person responsible would have to be very connected and very rich," Jo said. "Like Spencer Harding."

"You think he's capable of arranging something like that?"

"Leonard Shaw's girlfriend, Claude, was in my gym today. Apparently, Spencer's a pretty bad guy. She's convinced he had Rosamund murdered, and she seems to think he knows people who can get just about anything done."

"Leonard Shaw's girlfriend was at Furious Fitness?" Nessa asked. "Why?"

Jo's eyes were on Harriett as she delivered her answer. "She said she needed somewhere to run. Apparently, they're having a problem with bees out on the Pointe."

"Bees?" Nessa asked. "How strange."

"Yes," Jo agreed, still staring at Harriett. "Very."

LATER THAT NIGHT, AFTER HER groceries had been delivered, Harriett didn't bother to dress. She left the house without a stitch on to walk among her plants in the moonlight. She pictured the confusion on Jo's face earlier that day when she'd shown no regret for what had happened to Jackson. Harriett wondered how long Jo would think in terms of good and evil. Her friend was an intelligent woman, and such simplistic concepts were beneath her. But some people, even smart people, relied on those labels to make sense of the world. They slapped them on everything without ever realizing the placement was arbitrary.

When Harriett was a girl, she'd been taught to live in fear of evil. Her grandparents, who'd raised her, had warned her that men would whisper lies in her ear and steal her purity the moment she let down her guard. She was told the urges she felt were sinful. The boys who would have satisfied them were filthy. The girls, unspeakable. After high school, Harriett had fled from the Midwest to New York. But even there, a thousand miles from home, wherever she looked, everything had been labeled.

That changed the day she discovered her husband was fucking the head of his production department. She'd known plenty of women who'd suspected their husbands were unfaithful. She'd listened to their Nancy Drew tales of marital espionage. Harriett hadn't spent months following Chase. She hadn't installed spyware on his phone. She'd assumed their relationship was mutually beneficial, and trusted him not to fuck it up. It had never occurred to her to question his whereabouts. Then his lover grew tired of playing second fiddle and sent a video to Harriett's phone.

She'd locked her office door and watched every second of it—from the moment the two had entered the frame, attached at the mouth and frantically fumbling to remove the clothing between them. She'd seen the woman get down on her hands and knees with Harriett's husband behind her. She heard the woman gasp as his penis slid inside her and listened to her husband pant as he pumped faster and faster. Harriett watched fifteen minutes of furious lovemaking followed by an hour and twenty-one minutes of stillness as the two slept, wrapped in each other's arms. It wasn't their first encounter. It wasn't even their tenth. They were comfortable with each other. Harriett knew they'd been doing what she was witnessing for a very long time.

When Harriett pressed play, her world had seemed solid, sturdy, dependable. By the time the video ended, she was surrounded by rubble. She wandered through the wreckage for months, distraught and disoriented. She no longer believed in anything.

Chase left for good in August. His girlfriend wanted a baby, he'd informed her during their final blowout. Two, if possible. Bianca was thirty-five, and her clock was ticking. The news shook Harriett almost as much as the video. She and Chase had agreed early on that they wouldn't have children. She'd always thought that was one of the things that bound them as a couple. Maybe Chase had meant it back then. Or perhaps, Harriett realized, he just hadn't been in a rush. After all, her body was the one on a schedule. He had all the time in the world. Now they were both forty-eight, and she saw in his eyes that he truly wanted a child. That was the moment she let him go.

Over the two months that followed, Harriett moved through the world by rote. She stuck to a schedule at first: wake, work, sleep, repeat. A few weeks passed, and the routine began to break down. She stopped sleeping, which meant no more waking. She took three weeks off work and watched her garden go to seed. The grass grew so high that she had to wade through it. Flowers that couldn't keep up perished from lack of sunlight. Colonies of iridescent scarab beetles flew from plant to plant, devouring their victims' leaves and leaving lacy skeletons behind. A hawk dropped the disemboweled carcass of a squirrel at her feet, and a coyote stopped to sniff at her late one night. By the time Harriett walked off the job on the thirtieth of October, the garden had almost completed its transformation.

On the morning of November first, she looked out her window and saw what it wanted to be. For the rest of the winter, she shut herself off from the world outside and began her own metamorphosis.

Harriett paused to stroke the leaves of a philodendron that had recently poisoned the neighbor's cat. It hadn't acted out of malice. There was no evil in the natural world. There was pleasure and pain and life and death. The plant had made the cat sick so it would nibble and piss somewhere else. It was an act of survival, nothing more. What she'd done to Jackson was no different. Maybe he would live. Maybe he wouldn't. Either way, he knew who was responsible. He'd fucked with the wrong female, and he'd think twice before he messed with a woman again.

Harriett's next pupil was parked across the street from her house. He'd been there for hours, waiting for Eric's car to pull out of her drive. Harding's bodyguard thought he was clever. He assumed no one had seen him. Harriett had been aware of his presence the entire time. As long as he kept his distance, Harriett didn't give a damn. He could watch all he wanted. She had nothing to hide. But she knew he wouldn't stay away, and so she'd been waiting for him to arrive.

A car door opened and closed softly. She heard shoes walking up her drive. The footsteps paused when the man reached the brambles and searched for a way through them. She watched from the shadows as he emerged in her garden. A thorn had scratched a long, red line across his thick neck, and a trickle of blood fed a growing stain on his collar. She enjoyed the way his eyes bulged as they took in his surroundings. He headed for the door of the house, which stood open. She didn't try to stop him from entering. She didn't waste time wondering what he would have done if he'd come across her inside.

Not long after, he stepped back through the doorway and into the garden. From behind him, Harriett reached out and gently brushed the side of his neck where the thorn had left a gash. His fingers instantly flew to the wound and came away covered with a thick green substance along with his own blood.

"Did you find what you were looking for in my house, Mr. Chertov?" Harriett asked.

He tried to go for the weapon hidden under his jacket, but his muscles were no longer obeying orders. Harriett took the gun and tossed it aside just before his knees buckled and he hit the ground.

She kneeled down beside the man. "Don't struggle. You've just received a large dose of conium. As it is, you don't have much time until the paralysis reaches your heart," she warned him. "Tell me why you're here, and I'll consider administering the antidote."

There wasn't an antidote, of course. But he didn't know that.

GOING ROGUE

Jo sat cross-legged on her bedroom floor, wearing nothing but a T-shirt and underwear. She'd turned the air-conditioning up to full blast and thrown an extra blanket over her sleeping husband. Her half of the bed was a swamp, and the sheets would need to be washed again in the morning. Her pillow, like so many before it, would likely end up stuffed in the trash.

Jo could feel the icy air swirling around her, but it offered little relief from the waves of heat. Before waking up drenched in sweat, she'd dreamed she was tied to a stake with flames lapping at her bare shins. She'd watched the hem of her white dress catch fire. Within seconds, her entire body was ablaze. Jo knew the dream well. For years, she'd lived in fear of it. Only in recent months had she begun to understand it. Now when the dream came, she let herself burn. Heat was energy, and energy, power. She wondered if she could learn to control it—to channel the fury and indignation that fueled it. She wanted to find out exactly what she could do.

With her eyes closed, Jo envisioned a brilliant blue orb of energy hovering above the palms she held cupped in her lap. She'd just set it spinning when a sound from another room broke her concentration—the faint whoosh of a window rising. Her eyes opened and the orb vanished. She was on her feet in an instant.

"Art." Jo shook her husband. He answered with a snore. "Art!"

"What?" he mumbled.

"Shhh! There's someone in the house. Call 911."

"Where are you going?" he asked, struggling to sit up.

Jo padded toward the door in her bare feet. "To get Lucy."

"Are you fucking crazy?" Art was fully awake. "Let me do it! Get back here!"

But Jo was already out the door and halfway down the hall. She peeked into the bathroom as she passed. It was empty, as was the guest bedroom. There was only one other room on the second floor—the one near the stairs at the end of the hall. The one with a poster of a K-pop boy band. The one where her eleven-year-old daughter was sleeping.

The door appeared closed, which told her she'd found the intruder. Lucy always slept with it open. But a sliver of space between the door and its jamb told Jo the latch hadn't caught. She readied her arm—elbow bent, palm facing out. Then she slammed her hand into one of the wooden panels. The door flew backward into the wall, where it stuck, its knob embedded in the house's thirty-year-old Sheetrock. Jo hurled herself over the threshold, expecting the element of surprise to work in her favor. In the split second in which the room was revealed, she saw her daughter on the bed, hands zip-tied, eyes bulging, the small stuffed pig she'd slept with since she was an infant crammed into her mouth. Jo's brain registered Lucy's hands frantically gesturing toward the left side of the door. Then Jo's world went dark.

She woke with the right side of her face pressed into carpet, her head throbbing, and her hands bound. A large body lay blocking her view of the room. She recognized the familiar hole in the back of Art's favorite Columbia T-shirt and wondered what the hell he was doing. Then the sound of duct tape being ripped from a roll brought her back to the bedroom, and Jo knew she didn't have long to act. A self-defense instructor who'd offered weekly classes at the gym always showed new students how to break out of zip ties. Jo thought of it as a parlor trick with little practical use, but the three simple steps had lodged in her brain: Tighten the zip tie with your teeth. Raise your arms over your head. Swing your arms down and apart with as much force as possible. Rage, fear, and frustration swirled inside her as she began to bring her hands to her mouth. Her body was burning and her arms were slick with sweat. She smelled hot plastic as she bent her neck toward her wrists. Before she could clench the loose end of the strap between her teeth, the band holding her wrists stretched like a piece of chewed gum and fell away.

The man was busy wrapping Lucy's ankles with a second strip of duct tape as Jo rose from the floor. She grabbed her daughter's new tennis racket and positioned herself behind him. "Get your fucking hands off my kid," she growled.

When he spun around, she caught him in the face with the edge of the racket. It wasn't enough to take him down, and he came back at her with a fist to her temple. Jo's knee rammed into his groin, and a kick to the abdomen sent him sailing into the bedroom wall. She was on him the second he hit the ground, with the handle of the tennis racket pressed against his throat. He was a large man, well over six feet, with a chest so broad she could barely straddle it. She took a good look at him, attempting to commit his appearance to memory. His most distinguishing feature seemed to be a lack of one. Even if she'd seen his face a thousand times, it wouldn't have left an impression.

"Who are you?" she demanded as his entire head turned purple. When he couldn't answer, she reluctantly lessened the pressure.

"Get the fuck off me." Blood sprayed from the man's mouth as he snarled, leaving a scarlet splatter pattern on Jo's white T-shirt.

Jo added a knee to his groin and crouched over him like an animal. "If you don't start talking now, I'm going to rip your head off." She was going to. She could feel it. She imagined the tendons popping one by one as she separated his head from his neck. She was going to make him suffer.

"Jo." It was Art's voice. He'd regained consciousness. "Don't kill him. Lucy needs you."

She could hear the wail of sirens in the distance.

Jo didn't need answers from the man. She knew everything. She could see it all, and felt it as keenly as though it had all come to pass. She knew who had sent him, and she knew why he was there. She lowered her face down toward the man's. "Do you feel this?" The heat flowed through her arms like molten lava. She put her hand on his face and heard his skin sizzle. "I'm marking you. Because when they let you out—and I know they will—I'm going to find you and kill you," Jo said. "And I want you to give Spencer Harding a message. I'm going to rip that motherfucker's intestines out and shove them into his eye sockets and out through his mouth. Make sure you tell him. And remind him that *I* know where *he* lives, too."

Then the police were inside. It took three of them to pull her off the man, whose face had been branded with a perfect print of her palm. Blisters would later form on the officers' hands where they'd made contact with Jo's skin.

JO SAT ON THE FRONT steps with her bare arms wrapped tightly around Lucy. Inside, the house was a whirlwind of activity, with cops, technicians, and photographers studying the scene. The neighbors had come out to gawk from their lawns. But all Jo could see was her eleven-year-old daughter lying bound and gagged on the rainbow sheets she'd loved since kindergarten.

"Nothing like this will ever happen again. Do you hear me?" Jo said, putting the universe on notice.

"I know, Mama," Lucy whispered. "I'll be okay."

Jo held her even closer. Though her child's life was no longer in immediate danger, lasting damage had been done. The three of them would live with the memory of that night for the rest of their lives. With luck, Lucy's recollections would grow hazier in time. But Jo knew she and Art would always be stalked by that image of their daughter—and the thought of what might have happened next. The men responsible would be punished. But Jo would never be able to forgive herself for leading Spencer Harding straight to her family.

Art appeared on the stairs with his old army surplus duffel in one hand and Lucy's suitcase in the other. His eyes were bleary with exhaustion.

"Where are we going?" Lucy asked.

"Dad's taking you somewhere safe," Jo said.

Lucy's eyes went wide and wild. "No, Mama! We can't leave you here by yourself! Dad, she has to come, too!"

Art looked off into the darkness. "Your mother says she has to stay."

For the first time in years, Lucy broke down sobbing, and Jo felt her heart breaking. It made no difference how strong Jo grew— Lucy would always be her kryptonite. That's why they'd gone for her. They knew Jo's child was her weak spot. If something happened to Lucy, it would destroy her. That had to be why superheroes never had children.

"Listen to me, sweetheart." Jo kept her voice calm. She'd cry when they were gone. "You and Dad are just going on a quick trip. As soon as everything's settled here, you'll come right back, I swear."

"But where are we going?"

"Somewhere fun," Jo promised. She and Art had decided to keep the destination a secret from everyone until he and Lucy were settled. They were heading to his brother's lake house in Vermont. It had always been Lucy's favorite place.

"Why won't you come with us?" Lucy cried.

Jo caught Art's eye. He didn't understand, either. "Because I need to stay here and make sure nothing like this will ever happen again."

"But how are you going to do that?"

"With the help of your aunts Nessa and Harriett," Jo said.

"Harriett's going to help you?" Lucy wiped her eyes. Suddenly anything seemed possible. Her daughter's fondness for Harriett had always struck Jo as unusual. Now she understood: they saw the world the same way. Harriett was feral, while eleven-year-old Lucy still lived by nature's laws.

"Yes, does that make you feel better?" Jo asked.

Lucy sniffled and nodded. Then she let her arms slip from her mother's waist and took her father's hand. Jo gave them both kisses and went inside.

She stood at her bedroom window and watched two police officers help Art pack the back of his SUV. Lucy looked up at the house before she crawled into the back seat, and Jo quickly stepped out of sight. She didn't want her daughter to see her bawling, and she was terrified of the fury brewing inside her. She didn't want to punish Spencer Harding—she wanted to destroy him. She planned to rip his bones apart at the joints, pound his skull into mush, and set fire to his flesh. She knew any reasonable psychiatrist given a glimpse of her daydreams would have had her committed.

"Mrs. Levison?"

Jo wiped her eyes before she turned around. "Yes?"

An officer who looked like he was fresh out of high school was standing there in the doorway. "Just wanted you to know that I drove by and checked on your friends. They're fine."

"You're sure? You saw Nessa James with your own eyes? You made sure she's okay?" Jo asked.

"Oh yeah," the kid said with an inappropriate grin. "She's *more* than okay, as a matter of fact. Mrs. James asked if you could please phone her when you have a chance."

"Thank you." Jo searched for her phone and found it right on the nightstand where she'd left it. She'd missed ten calls from Nessa in the past thirty minutes. She cleared her throat before she lifted the phone and dialed.

"Jo?" Nessa answered immediately, her voice breathless with worry. "What's going on?"

"A man broke into my house around three this morning. He was going to kidnap Lucy."

"Oh sweet Jesus," Nessa gasped. "Is she okay? Are you okay? And Art?"

"We're shaken but fine. The police are here and the guy is in custody. But I need you to call Franklin and have him meet us at your house. I'll pick up Harriett on the way."

"What's going on?"

"I can't say anything over the phone. I'll tell you when I see you. And be careful—I'm sure they know where you live, too."

"They?" Nessa asked.

"Spencer Harding's men," Jo said. "They're coming for us. I'll be there as soon as I can."

AFTER JO HUNG UP, NESSA stood by the side of the bed in her robe, staring at the phone. A warm hand slid from her shoulder blades to the small of her back, sending a tingle down her spine.

"I had another look around," Franklin said. "Everything should be locked up tight. But this evening I'm going to install a security system. You reach Jo? She doing okay?"

Nessa nodded. "I think so. She says the three of us need to talk to you. She's going to pick up Harriett and come over."

Franklin grabbed his button-down shirt off the floor and slid his arms into the sleeves. "Glad she gave us fair warning. I plan to be dressed the next time company comes calling."

Nessa winced. "You think that kid who came by is going to keep his mouth shut?"

"No," Franklin said bluntly. "I'm sure everyone in the department knows by now."

"Is that going to cause trouble for you?" she asked.

Franklin finished buttoning his shirt and leaned down to look her in the eye. "I couldn't care less," he said, and planted a kiss on her lips.

NESSA HAD SENT HER GIRLS back to school the morning after the girl in blue's funeral. As grateful as she'd been to have them there by her side, Mattauk was not a safe place for young women. She didn't put her worries into words. Breanna and Jordan were technically adults, but Nessa still did her best to shield them from the ugliness of the world.

When she dropped them off at the train, she'd made them promise to stay safe. Stick together, she told them. Trust your gut and don't take any chances. It was the same warning she always gave the twins, and given the grim ceremony they'd attended the day before, they seemed to take it a bit more seriously. But nowhere near as seriously as Nessa would have liked.

"We know why you're sending us away so quickly," Jordan said. "You want to spend some alone time with Franklin Rees."

"Excuse me?" Nessa feigned outrage and both her girls cracked up.

"Yeah, we saw him looking at you. Like a big dog drooling over a thick, juicy steak," Breanna teased.

Nessa felt her cheeks catch fire, and she fanned herself with her hand.

"He's smoking hot for an old man," Jordan said. "Good work, Mama."

"I don't know where y'all get your ideas," Nessa tutted. "Did you two ever stop to consider that *I* might be the dog and *he* might be the piece of meat?"

It was such a relief to hear her girls laughing. She'd worried about how Breanna and Jordan might feel when they learned there was a new man in her life. But the thought hadn't seemed to cause either daughter a moment's unease.

"I like him," Breanna told her mother. "I'm happy for you."

"Me too," Jordan said. "It's about time you got some action."

"I'll have you know I have *not* gotten *any* action." At that point, it was the truth. Even in Nessa's prim and proper world, two stolen kisses did not count as action.

"*Yet,*" said Jordan, and the two girls burst out laughing again.

"Look at her face!" Breanna cackled.

"You two been hanging out with Harriett?" Nessa demanded.

They put on their sweetest, most innocent expressions. "What makes you think that?" Breanna asked.

"But seriously, Mama, we're glad," Jordan said. "This is some scary business you've gotten yourself into. We're happy you've got someone to take care of you."

At the time, the phrase had annoyed her. Nessa had been on her own for almost ten years. She'd guided her children to adulthood and helped her parents pass on to the afterlife. She'd done it all by herself, and she'd done a damn good job of it. She didn't need anyone to take care of her. And yet that afternoon, when Franklin drove her home from Furious Fitness, she'd looked up at her house and realized she didn't want to be alone anymore.

There was plenty of food left over from the funeral, so after Nessa saw her girls off, she invited him in. It was almost midnight by the time they finally shared a dish of warmed-up mac and cheese.

Now Nessa watched Franklin as he sat on the bed and tied his shoes. His movements were measured, always perfectly precise. His shirt showed no sign of spending the night on the floor. The bows on his shoes could have set a new standard. It wasn't until he looked back and winked at her that she was able to believe this was the same man who'd been on top of her, or under her, or behind her all night. In the dark, she'd had nothing to distract her. The subject of babies never passed through her brain. She didn't once wonder if it might lead to marriage. What they'd done had felt natural, animal, elemental. Harriett was right: sex did get better with age.

In time, she'd confess everything to her friends. But after what had happened to Jo's little girl, today definitely wasn't the day.

JO PULLED HER CAR UP behind a black SUV parked across the street from Harriett's house. On the weekends, it wasn't uncommon to see cars parked along Woodland Drive, but they were almost always gone by Monday morning. Jo got out and looked through the windows. There was no one inside. Her senses tingling, she turned her eyes to Harriett's house, which sat still and silent on the opposite side of the road. A burst of panic sent her sprinting to the front door, which opened with a single twist of the knob.

"Morning." Harriett was at her workbench, scraping a plate full of bright red chunks into her blender.

"You're okay." Jo doubled over in relief.

"You sound surprised," Harriett said. "Smoothie?"

Jo shook her head over the sound of the blender. When the contents of the pitcher were a brilliant red, Harriett punched the off button.

"What's in that?" Jo asked.

"Beet juice," Harriett said, pouring herself a glass of the mixture. "Good and good for you."

"There's a strange SUV parked across the street," Jo informed her.

Harriett took a sip of her concoction. "Is there?" she asked without bothering to look. Her teeth were red when she smiled. "If it stays there too long, my nosy neighbors will have it towed. By the way, a baby police officer stopped by early this morning. He said you'd sent him. He wouldn't tell me why, but he said you were fine."

"No one bothered you last night?"

"Define *bother*," Harriett replied with an arched brow.

"Never mind." Jo wasn't in the mood for Harriett's sense of humor. "Someone broke into my house around three in the morning. He was there for Lucy. He tied her up and—" Her voice cracked. She stopped, pressed a finger to her lips, and willed herself not to cry. Then she finished the story.

"Lucy will be fine, Jo. You have my word." Harriett's voice had softened and her face appeared younger, as though she were channeling some long-ago version of herself. "When I was her age, I lived through something terrible, too. I survived, and so will she. Lucy has three things I didn't: good parents, a loving home, and me. You didn't kill the intruder, did you?"

"No," Jo replied. She'd wanted to. The urge had been almost impossible to resist. But she hadn't.

Harriett nodded. "That's okay. It's my job to make him suffer," she said. "But I assume you got a few good licks in?"

"Yeah. I hurt him."

"Badly?" Harriett sounded hopeful.

"Very," Jo said. "I don't think he'll be using his face for a while."

"How did it feel?"

Jo hesitated. "Better than sex."

"Excellent." Harriett flashed the gap between her teeth. "It's important that Harding gets the message."

"The message?" Jo asked.

"That we're not going to take his bullshit," Harriett said. "He knows we're onto him. There's a mole in the police department. Someone must have told him we found the photo."

"You figured that out quickly." Jo was impressed. It had taken her all morning to reach the same conclusion.

Harriett grinned. She'd extracted the information from Chertov in less than five minutes, but Jo didn't need to know that.

"But why send a guy to my house? Why not to yours—or to Nessa's?"

"I would imagine the detective's car parked in front of Nessa's house might have deterred them."

Jo's brow furrowed. "I'm talking about last night."

"So am I," said Harriett.

"Oh," said Jo, her eyes widening as she realized what that meant. "How do you—" She stopped. "Did you have something to do with that?"

Harriett shook her head and rolled her eyes. "You two seem to think I'm responsible for everything. All I do is stand back and let nature take its course."

THEY KNEW. THE SECOND SHE opened the door, Nessa could see there would be no need for a confession. Whether by gossip or witch-craft, Jo and Harriett already knew she'd slept with Franklin. Jo had too much on her mind to make any wisecracks, and didn't catch the wink Harriett gave Nessa as she breezed by.

"Can I get you guys some coffee?" Nessa offered awkwardly.

"No, thank you," Jo said before rounding on Franklin. They'd all known something bad would happen. She didn't know if he could have stopped it. What she did know for sure was that he hadn't tried. "Someone in your department tipped off Spencer Harding. He sent one of his thugs to my home last night. The man went straight to my daughter's room."

"What?" Nessa felt ill. She turned to Franklin. "You didn't tell me everything."

"We don't know for certain that Spencer Harding was behind the break-in," Franklin offered stoically.

"The man who broke into my house zip-tied Lucy's wrists and crammed a stuffed pig into her mouth. What do you think would have happened to her, Franklin? Rape? Torture? Would we have found her months from now in a trash bag by the side of the road?"

"Oh my dear Lord." Nessa's eyes filled with tears as Franklin shuffled uncomfortably.

"You don't want to think about it, do you? Well, that's too fucking bad, Franklin, because it's all I'm going to think about for the next thirty years."

"Now, Jo—"

Jo took a step toward him, and Franklin retreated slightly. She may have been the smaller of the two, but she had fury on her side.

"Don't," she warned him. Nessa could see her friend's body vibrating like a pressure cooker that was fixing to blow. "And don't tell me I don't know it was Spencer Harding, because I do. So does Nessa, so does Harriett, and so do you."

"I spoke with Chief Rocca before you arrived." Franklin's voice remained cool and calm. "The man who broke into your home is refusing to talk. But he'll crack eventually, and in the meantime, he's safely behind bars."

"Do you have any idea how many more men Spencer Harding can afford to hire? He's got hundreds of millions of dollars, Franklin. That's supervillain rich. He could pay people to come after each of us. He could send someone for Nessa's girls, too. I fucking *told* you we were all sitting ducks here. My eleven-year-old daughter could have ended up like the girl on the beach. Now you're asking me to wait for the system to work? The law won't protect us. We have to protect ourselves."

"You can't take matters into your own hands," Franklin said.

"Why not?" Jo demanded.

"Jo—" Nessa started.

Jo spun around to face her. "That's my job, is it not? Taking matters into my own hands? If the system functioned the way it should, I wouldn't be necessary. None of us would."

Harriett had laid herself down on the sofa where the girl in blue had once sat. Nessa looked to her for help, but received nothing but a grin in return.

"What exactly do you have in mind?" Franklin asked Jo.

"I'm starting to think I shouldn't tell you, Franklin. If you're just going to keep toeing the line, it's probably best that you leave. You don't want to take part in this conversation. And to be honest, I don't want what I'm about to say to be leaked back to Spencer Harding. Find the mole in your department, or my friends and I are going rogue."

"Jo, there's no need for that kind of talk," Nessa said.

"Isn't there? What would you say if a man had come after one of your daughters?" Jo stopped and shook her head. "No, you know what, it's your house, Nessa. So you decide. Either Franklin goes, or I do."

Nessa didn't like what she had to say, but she didn't hesitate for long. What happened to Lucy and the girls at Danskammer Beach could not happen again. She had a job to do, and in order to do it, she needed Jo. "Franklin, I'm sorry, but you have to go," she told him. "I promise I'll call you later."

"Nessa, tell me you're not serious," Franklin pleaded. "I'm supposed to help you, remember?"

"God sent Jo and Harriett to me first," she told him.

Franklin just nodded, as though he didn't trust himself with words, and headed straight out the front door. Nessa couldn't believe she was letting him go.

The instant he was gone, Jo wrapped her arms around Nessa. She knew the extent of her friend's sacrifice, and it broke her heart that she'd asked for it. "I'm so sorry," she said.

Nessa sniffled but refused to cry. "We gotta do what we've gotta do," she said. "I can't let my sex life get in the way."

"Was I right?" Harriett piped up from the sofa. "Was it what you needed?"

"Oh my God," Nessa said. "Looks like the best time might end up being the last time, but damn, was it worth it."

"It wasn't the last time," Harriett told her. "Not even close."

"You think Franklin's going to forgive me for what just happened? I just kicked him out of my house so the three of us could break the law."

"Franklin's a good guy," Jo said. "But we've wasted too much time letting the police take the lead. It's time to kick ass."

"Claude said we have an open invitation to the Pointe, is that right?" Harriett asked and Jo nodded. "Then why don't we rip the problem out at the root."

"What do you mean?" Nessa asked cautiously.

"You know what I mean. Let's kill Spencer Harding. What's the point in waiting any longer?"

Jo had expected those words to tumble out of Harriett's mouth eventually. The only thing that surprised her was how appealing they sounded. She glanced over at Nessa, whose face couldn't hide her own surprise. She didn't know about the bees. As far as Jo knew, Nessa had never seen this side of Harriett before.

"Are you serious?" Nessa asked.

"Still too soon?" Harriett shrugged casually, as if they all knew it would come to murder eventually. "All right. Then what shall we do now?"

"We should go public," Jo said. "Put some serious pressure on the authorities and tell people exactly what we know."

"What do we know?" Nessa said. "Franklin was right—we don't have much in the way of hard evidence."

"We know Spencer Harding's wife had a photo of a murdered girl in a locker at my gym. We know the photo was a Polaroid, just like the ones a woman who called herself Laverne Green showed you when she lied about being the girl's mother. We know Rosamund Harding is dead and Laverne Green is missing. Amber Welsh, whose daughter disappeared along Danskammer Beach Road, has vanished as well. We know that after I told the police how Rosamund Harding gave me the combination to that lock at my gym, a man broke into my house with the intention of kidnapping my daughter. I think anyone with a drop of common sense will agree that Spencer Harding has to be behind all of this, and that someone on the police force has been helping him."

"So you want to go to the media with our story?" Nessa couldn't quite wrap her head around it. "I suppose we could call the *Times*, or one of the local channels. Do you really think they'll listen?"

"Of course not." Harriett sighed, her first contribution to the conversation since proposing they execute Spencer Harding. "A story like ours would never make it past the fact-checkers. We'd be putting anyone who ran the story at the risk of a massive lawsuit."

"But maybe we could convince the media to start their own investigations," Jo said.

"The men who run the networks and newspapers all know Spencer Harding," Harriett said. "They sit next to him at fund-raisers. They trade witty banter at cocktail parties. They clink scotch glasses with him at Jackson Dunn's parties. And they buy their artwork from Harding's galleries. Even if we could convince a reporter to investigate, the story would never run. Their bosses would kill it. You two are still depending on a system that you both know doesn't work. Plan all you like; you're just delaying the inevitable."

Nessa bit her lip.

Then Jo perked up. "I know someone with a big audience and no corporate bosses. Someone who already wants to talk to us."

"You do?" Nessa asked hopefully. Harriett just smiled.

Jo pulled out her phone and brought up the page for the podcast *They Walk Among Us*.

"He'll listen," Jo said.

WHERE DO ALL THE GIRLS GO?

During her summer with her grandmother in South Carolina, Nessa had befriended a neighbor girl named Jeannie. Every morning before it got too hot to do much of anything, they'd walk two miles down the dusty dirt road into town. Nessa's parents sent her ten dollars a week for spending money, which amounted to a fortune back in those days. The girls would buy two bottles of Cheerwine and packets of BBQ Fritos, which they'd eat at a leisurely, ladylike pace while sitting outside the library on the town's best bench.

They were there late one morning when they spotted Miss Ella walking toward them, a stack of library books under her arm. She must have been around seventy-five years old and just under six feet in height. To twelve-year-old Nessa, she'd seemed impossibly old and improbably tall. She wore her silvery hair in a topknot, and her skirts swept the ground. A treasure chest's worth of necklaces dangled from her neck, none of them fashioned from gold. Instead, they were shells and berries and roots that grasped at her flesh as though they might be alive. They were jewels of nature rather than trinkets made by man.

Just as she reached the girls' bench, Miss Ella came to a stop. "You!" Her voice, sharp and clear, cut straight through the swampy air. The gnarled finger she'd raised was pointed at a car parked on the opposite side of the road. A man sat hunched down in the driver's seat, watching them, his hat positioned so it cast a shadow on his face. "I catch you with your pecker out again, and that nasty little worm's gonna shrivel up and fall off. You hear me?"

He must have. The ignition instantly turned over and the man peeled out of the parking space.

"You know that pervert?" Miss Ella asked the girls.

"Yes, ma'am," Jeannie said almost proudly. She seemed to relish the role of informant. "That's Earl Frady. He works down at the feed shop."

"Either of you see him again outside that feed shop, you come and tell me straightaway. You hear?"

"Yes, ma'am," Jeannie said with a wide grin on her face. As the woman walked away, Jeannie leaned over to Nessa. "She's gonna feed him to the gators like she did Mr. Cogdill."

"Who's Mr. Cogdill?" Nessa asked.

"Another old man who liked little girls," Jeannie told her.

Nessa was dying to ask about Mr. Cogdill, but she'd been warned not to talk outside the family about three things, if she could help it: the gift, dead girls, or Miss Ella.

"Did Miss Ella feed Mr. Cogdill to an alligator?" Nessa asked her grandmother as soon as she got home. She expected to be informed it was nothing but idle gossip.

"Jeannie tell you that?" her grandmother asked.

"Is it true?" Nessa asked.

"Yes," said her grandmother. "Though they'll never prove it."

It seemed that one day the previous summer, Carroll Cogdill, mortician, equestrian, and all-around pillar of the Low Country community, had gone missing while fishing in the swamp. The next morning, a giant gator had emerged from a water trap on the country club golf course and waddled across the green, pausing by the tenth hole to cough up a toupee. Everyone there that day knew it could only have belonged to the missing man. And when they cut open the gator, they found the rest of him. He'd been chopped into pieces, which the gator had subsequently swallowed.

Officially, Miss Ella had been cleared as a suspect. No one could offer any evidence that she'd ever met Carroll Cogdill, and she didn't appear to have a motive for killing him. Plus, as a woman in her seventies, it was assumed she lacked the upper-body strength that would have been necessary for the butchering. *Unofficially,* everyone in town was convinced it was her, but aside from Miss Ella, the only people who knew what had really happened were Nessa's grandmother and the mother of the two little girls Carroll Cogdill had raped.

"So she killed him." Nessa wanted to make sure.

"She did," her grandmother told her. "I'm not gonna lie to you."

"But the Bible says 'do not kill,'" Nessa reminded her grandmother.

"The Commandments only apply to humans," said the older woman. "Nobody goes to hell for killing a monster."

"YOU'VE BEEN AWFULLY QUIET," JO noted. She and Nessa were driving into town for an appointment with the host of *They Walk Among Us.* Josh Gibbon had responded to Jo's email immediately and proposed meeting at a café in town. "Something on your mind?"

Nessa wondered what Jo would say if she knew about Miss Ella. But in the thirty-five years that had passed since that conversation in her grandmother's kitchen, Nessa had never shared the story with a single soul. And that wasn't going to change. She figured she owed it to Miss Ella—a penniless old woman in South Carolina who'd risked everything to avenge the young and helpless. Miss Ella deserved discretion, even if she'd been dead for twenty long years. "Just thinking about all the bad men out there and what we should do with them."

Jo glanced over at her friend. "I'm sure Harriett was kidding about killing Spencer Harding." It was a lie. Harriett hadn't been joking—and the idea had been growing on Jo as well. She'd been fantasizing about it all morning.

Nessa responded with a smile. Jo was protecting her. It was sweet, in a way—and condescending in another. Somehow, Jo had discovered the truth about Harriett, and she was worried it would scare Nessa. But Nessa had been aware of Harriett's true nature all along. Women like Harriett and Miss Ella wouldn't exist if the world functioned as it was meant to. The way Nessa saw it, in these situations, you followed the rules first. You toed the line. You made sure to cross every t and dot every i. And when that didn't work, it was time to bring out the goddamned gators.

"You think Harriett was kidding?" Nessa asked pointedly.

"No," Jo admitted. "Not really."

"Me either," Nessa replied.

Just as the conversation was taking an interesting turn, Jo pulled into a parking space in front of the café, where a youngish man was sitting at a table by the front window.

"That's him." Jo turned the engine off.

"That hairy little frat boy?" Nessa scoffed. "Are you sure he's who we need to be talking to? He looks like he spent all night watching dirty movies and playing video games."

"That hairy little frat boy has thirty million listeners," Jo told her.

"Well then." Nessa was duly impressed. "Let's go spill some beans."

THOUGH HE'D BEEN EAGER TO meet, Josh clearly wasn't letting by-gones be bygones. He was going to make Jo pay for her rudeness. While she and Nessa tag-teamed the tale of finding the murdered girl and every strange thing that had happened since then, he sat back and listened, his face expressionless and his arms crossed over his chest.

"Wow. That's quite a story," he said when they finished. "Too bad no one's going to believe it."

"We have evidence," Jo argued. "There's a DNA test that proves the girl who died wasn't related to the woman who claimed to be her mother. We have pictures of the photo we found in the locker at my gym. And there's a man in jail right now for breaking into my house."

Josh Gibbon leaned forward. "Yes, and according to the story you just told me, you also have a friend who claims to be a psychic and another friend who seems to be the town witch, and the three of you are accusing one of the richest men in New York of being a serial killer."

"Sounds to me like a story millions of people would want to hear." Nessa tried to lure him with honey. "One that could turn a popular podcast into a cultural phenomenon."

"Really?" Josh turned to her. "'Cause to me, it sounds like a story that will get me sued straight into bankruptcy."

"Then let me ask you a question," Jo said. "Do *you* believe it?"

She simmered as Josh sat back, his fingers woven together pompously and resting on his ample paunch. In what screwed-up universe did this twentysomething Comic Book Guy get to cast judgment on her story? Jo wanted to pick up the table and hurl it across the room.

"Yeah," he finally said. "It's crazy as hell, but I believe it. Doesn't mean I'm going to put it on my show, though."

Jo closed her eyes. It was the only way she could resist leaping over the table and strangling him. Three girls were dead. Her daughter had almost been kidnapped. And this little shit wasn't interested. Fortunately, Nessa kept her cool.

"How many murdered women and girls have you featured on your podcast? How many who've been mangled and tortured and chopped into bits?" Nessa asked. "Hundreds?"

"At least," Josh admitted.

"A thousand or more?"

He nodded. "Probably."

"All those dead girls made you famous," Nessa said. "Don't you feel like you owe them? We just told you there's a monster on the loose. You going to help us stop him—or are you just out here looking to make a buck off those bodies?"

Josh stiffened. Nessa had clearly hit a sore spot. He didn't like having his motives questioned or his heroism called into doubt. "I started my podcast to shine a spotlight on killers who had gone undetected. I wanted to save lives, and I have."

"And I bet you've made a lot of money doing it," Jo said. "Now you're going to sit back and let a serial killer murder more girls because you're afraid of getting sued."

"I'm not *afraid*," Josh snapped. "But I can't go around making accusations if I don't have real evidence to back them up. Right now, there's only one body. One body is not proof that there's a serial killer at work in Mattauk." He looked at Nessa. "You say there are two other bodies in the water off Danskammer Beach. It's doubtful they would have lasted this long, but it could be worth having a look. Do you know where they'd be?"

Jo felt a flash of hope. He was starting to come around. He couldn't bear to have anyone question his white-knight credentials. Nessa was a genius.

"Yes, but the ocean floor is littered with lobster traps," Nessa said. "It's like a giant dump down there. That's probably why the killer chose the spot."

"Maybe the bodies are inside lobster traps."

Nessa had considered that, too. But it didn't make the situation any less hopeless. "There could be thousands of traps. We don't have the resources to pull them all up."

Josh's brow furrowed. "Why bring them up to the surface? Why can't someone go down and take a look?"

"You mean police divers?" Jo asked. "We can't go to the cops. We think someone on the force is tipping off Spencer Harding. And even if there isn't a mole, the police wouldn't send divers down just because Nessa says she sees dead people."

"Why does it have to be the police?" Josh had clearly experienced an epiphany. "We just need to find someone who's certified to scuba dive."

Jo fell back in her chair as a thought slammed into her. "I'm scuba certified." That's what she'd gotten from an employer one year in lieu of a promotion—scuba classes and gear. Refusing to acknowledge the insult, she'd learned how to dive. The skill came in handy every spring when her family visited Art's mother and stepfather in South Florida, allowing Jo to escape for few peaceful hours every day.

"Then I suppose all we need is the equipment," Josh said.

Jo hesitated for a moment before she added, "I have that, too. It's in my garage. I'd just need to clean it off and get tanks from the dive shop."

"You're really willing to go looking for dead bodies at the bottom of the ocean?" Josh suddenly seemed to be taking the whole enterprise more seriously. "Who the hell knows what else might be down there."

"If you're worried, you can come along and keep me company," Jo offered.

"Yeah, no thanks," Josh said. "But I'll happily throw in a GoPro."

WHEN THEY GOT BACK TO Harriett's, they found her stoned on the sofa, wearing headphones plugged into an iPhone.

"Did you know—" Harriett pulled off her headphones and took a toke. "That three hundred *thousand* women and girls were reported missing last year? Two hundred and forty thousand were girls under twenty-one. Half were women of color. Let's say ninety-nine percent made it back home safe and sound. That still leaves twenty-four hundred girls. Where are they? The FBI claims there are fifty serial killers active in the U.S. at any one time. So how many of those girls are everyone's favorite bogeymen taking? Five hundred? A thousand? What's happening to the others?"

"Where are you getting all these statistics?" Nessa asked.

"*They Walk Among Us,*" Harriett said. "Figured I ought to check it out. Josh Gibbon's a bit of a serial killer fanboy, isn't he?"

"What the hell, Harriett," Jo said, staring at the device in Harriett's lap. "We came all the way back here to tell you the news and you're lying there listening to a podcast? Since when do you have a phone?"

"Since always," Harriett said. "I own a leaf blower, too, but I seldom use that, either. How did your meeting go?"

"He's interested, but he wants proof. Do you think Celeste might be willing to take us out on her boat tomorrow morning?"

"Yeah. Her husband took the kids to his parents' house, so she and I are going to spend the night on the boat. We'll meet you at the dock at eight."

Jo shot Nessa a look. "You already arranged it?" she asked Harriett.

"Right after you left. I assumed your podcast friend would want to have a look for the bodies. A scoop like that would be too hard to resist."

"What did you tell Celeste we'll be doing?" Jo asked.

"I told her the truth," Harriett said. "I know we agreed to keep everything between the three of us, but Celeste is important to me and secrets are such a bore. Besides, she'll know soon enough as it is."

"And she's okay with it?" Nessa wasn't so sure.

"Finding evidence that two girls were murdered?" Harriett seemed perfectly at ease. "Yes, she's okay with it. She trusts me to know what I'm doing. And I trust her to tell me if I don't."

THAT NIGHT, JO TOSSED AND turned in Nessa's guest room. She couldn't stop thinking about what Harriett had said. At two in the morning, she texted Art and discovered he couldn't sleep, either. He called from the lake house, and over the next three hours, Jo told him everything. She didn't gloss over details or embellish ugly truths. Art stopped her here and there to ask questions, but when Jo was done, he sat quietly on the other end of the line. She could feel the pain in his silence, and she hated herself for hurting him.

"I'm so sorry, Art," she said through tears. "It's my fault that man broke into our house. I tried to do the right thing, but I put our family in danger. I'll never forgive myself for what happened to Lucy."

"Listen to me. You did not send that man after our eleven-year-old daughter, and I refuse to let you take responsibility for the actions of a psychopath like Spencer Harding," Art said, putting his foot down. "What I still don't understand, Jo, is why you didn't tell me any of this earlier. Were you worried I'd do something to mess things up?"

"No!" she cried, horrified by his interpretation. "I was just hell-bent on doing what I needed to do, and I was worried you'd try to stop me."

He cleared his throat. "What exactly *are* you trying to do?" he asked.

"Make the world a better place for girls like Lucy," she told him.

"But my efforts backfired. Now I have to deal with Spencer Harding or our family will never be safe again."

"Why would I stand in your way?" Art asked.

"To protect me," Jo said.

"You don't need protection. You think I don't know that? This newfound strength of yours—it isn't so new. You've always been strong, Jo. That's one of the things I admire most about you. But you have an Achilles' heel. You get frustrated and impatient when things don't get done the way you would do them. Then you take on the burdens all by yourself. And you'll just keep on taking them, one after another, until they finally crush you."

As much as she would have loved to argue, she couldn't ignore the truth in his words.

"What should I do?"

"Tell me everything from now on, and let me help you," he told her. "And let me do it my way. As strong as you are, we're stronger together. You may be the concrete, but I'm the rebar."

He'd tossed out the last sentence as a joke, but it lingered in Jo's mind until the sun came up. During the years she'd worked in Manhattan, Art had gotten up early each morning to make her coffee. And he'd greeted her with a drink every night when she got home. They may have been small things, but Jo could have listed a thousand such gestures. Maybe Art hadn't found success the way she had. Maybe he hadn't mastered the arts of housecleaning or lawn care. But throughout their marriage, he had given Jo the support she'd needed to grow. She knew that as strong as she was, she would have crumbled without him. If Jo was going to survive, she needed him back.

AT SEVEN IN THE MORNING, clutching steaming mugs of coffee, Jo and Nessa piled into the car. Before heading to the marina, they stopped by Jo's house to pick up the scuba gear. As Nessa pulled into the drive, Jo looked up at the dark upstairs windows facing the street. Two belonged to the room Lucy had slept in since she was a baby. Jo bit her lip hard to hold back the tears.

"You sure you're up for this?" Nessa asked. "We can find another diver."

"And tell them what?" Jo responded.

"I don't know. We'd come up with something."

"No," Jo said. "I finally know why I was chosen for all this. I know what I'm supposed to do."

"What's that?" Nessa asked.

"Whatever the fuck it takes."

JO SETS A BRIDGE ABLAZE

Three months after she was fired, Jo found herself standing in her bra in a bank bathroom, one pit of her blouse stretched over the nozzle of the hand drier. The wave of heat that had overwhelmed her in the waiting area had finally receded, leaving salty, lavender-scented tidal pools beneath her arms.

The beautifully bound copy of her business plan was perched precariously on the edge of the sink. Her phone lit up with the silent alarm she'd set. Only one pit was partially dry, but it was time to reclaim her seat in the waiting area. She slipped the blouse on, grimacing when the remaining wet patch clung to the skin beneath her left arm. Over the blouse went her best black jacket. She smoothed her wavy red hair, applied a layer of her lucky lipstick, and half-heartedly applauded herself for rolling with the punches.

She was about to take a seat on the waiting area couch when Jeremy Aversano emerged from one of the glass offices and made a beeline for her, one arm outstretched.

"How about that! I thought I recognized the name on my calendar! Lucy Levison's mom, am I right?"

Jo struggled to keep the smile on her face. Her photo graced several of the documents she'd sent in advance of the meeting. If the loan officer had bothered to read them, he wouldn't be surprised to see her. When Jo was doing her research, she'd immediately pegged Aversano as the father of one of Lucy's least favorite classmates. But she'd been more interested in the bank's lending history than the loan officer's procreative feats.

"Yes," she said. "I'm Lucy's mom. Among other things."

"Come on back! Must be something in the water these days," he said, glancing over his shoulder as he led her toward his office. "We've had a lot of grade-school moms in here lately. Once the kids start growing up, the ladies of Mattauk transform into entrepreneurs. And my wife's no exception. She's dying to set up a kids' cooking academy here in town."

Jo's heart sank a bit more. If he thought Jo was a stay-at-home mom, he definitely hadn't bothered to read her CV. She wanted to ask him if this was going to be a waste of her time. But she didn't. "I think a cooking academy is a wonderful idea," she said instead. "I'm always looking for after-school and holiday activities for Lucy. And she would love something like that."

"Well, I've told my wife to put together a business plan," he said with an indulgent chuckle. "We'll see what she manages to come up with."

Jo's smile froze in place. She'd met Aversano's wife at PTA meetings, and the woman had always struck Jo as rather intelligent. Was there something about her that Jo hadn't noticed—some mental infirmity that wasn't immediately obvious?

"So!" Aversano said, taking a seat behind his desk. "I know you didn't come here to chat about kiddie chefs. Let's talk about this business you'd like to start. A ladies' gym, is it?"

Thank God, Jo thought, as she pulled out a chair across from him. He *had* read something, after all. Jo relaxed a little, then opened the notebook she'd brought and twisted the silver Tiffany pen she'd been given in lieu of a bonus one year. There was a chance this could all work out. Her start-up costs would be high with all the equipment she'd need to purchase, but she had sized the market and lined up over two hundred prospective members. The gym's projected revenues were high, even in the first year. Her business proposal was solid. Aversano was a moron, but that wouldn't matter if she walked out with the money she needed. *Stay cool*, she pleaded with herself. *Just this once, play along*.

"A gym for women, yes," she replied, sounding as sunny as she could. "I've been a regular gym-goer for years, and during that time, I've noticed a significant gap in the market. Most of the gyms here on the island cater to a certain clientele. I call them the vanity crowd. Those of us who are more interested in fitness than cute workout gear have been forced to travel twenty miles or more out of the way—and make do with facilities that are hardly state-of-the-art."

Aversano's phone buzzed. He glanced down at it. His eyes lingered for a few seconds too long before they returned to Jo. "If you ask my wife, those cute workout outfits are the only reason to go to the gym."

"Did you really ask your wife about the idea?" Jo inquired, her curiosity piqued. She would have thought his wife would make a perfect recruit. A woman married to a condescending prick like Aversano had to have a decade or two of rage to burn off.

Aversano's head reared back and his chin disappeared as he chuckled. "Tilly and I don't talk shop."

"Well, I don't know Matilda well enough to say if she'd fit into Furious Fitness's target audience, but according to my market research, there are enough women like me on the island to support a sizable chain of gyms. If you'll turn to page eight—"

But he didn't. He sat back instead, leaving his fingers laced together on the desk. "I'm not so sure about the name. *Furious* Fitness. It sounds angry."

"Does it?" Her hands began to sweat. She could hear the pounding of her heart in her ears. *Say something!* she ordered herself. *And keep smiling.* "Maybe that's a good thing. There are a lot of angry ladies out there."

He rejected the idea with a shake of his head. "No, people go to the gym to look more attractive. There's nothing attractive about a bunch of angry women. What did your husband say when you told him what you were thinking of naming it?"

She felt the smile slip off her face. "My husband is not a female fitness lover. Nor is he an entrepreneur. We have discussed the name, because we're life partners, but he would be the first to tell you his opinion is irrelevant from a business standpoint."

"Irrelevant?" Aversano scoffed. "Seems like a lot of his money's gonna go into this little venture you're starting."

The pilot light inside Jo burst into full flame. The heat built beneath her sternum and radiated from her chest all the way down to her toes. Her hands were engulfed in fiery spheres.

"I am my family's primary breadwinner," Jo said. "The money is half his, but I was the one who earned it. My husband knows I'm an excellent businessperson and trusts me to make good decisions. Now, please, Mr. Aversano, would you mind if I took you through my business plan for Furious Fitness?"

"No need. I took a peek while you were in the waiting area. Next time you might consider getting an MBA to look at your documents. There are a lot of young guys out there who could help you polish things up."

The Tiffany pen clenched in her right hand seemed to go limp.

"I have an MBA," Jo informed him. "From Stern. It's on my CV."

Aversano flipped to the page. "So you do," he said, with one eyebrow raised. Then the eyebrow came down and all that was left on his face was the patronizing smile. "Very impressive."

"I also have twenty years of hands-on business experience."

"Running a hotel." He clearly thought that didn't count as business experience.

"It was the third-largest hotel in New York City. During my tenure, I brought down costs by twenty-five percent while increasing revenue by twenty. Employee turnover dropped by over sixty percent. And in case none of that sounds relevant, the hotel had a sizable gym and adjoining spa, which turned a healthy profit every year."

"And then you were let go, am I right?"

He'd been saving that for just the right moment. Her termination had never been public, and the *Times* articles hadn't used her real name. Aversano knew someone on the inside.

"Are you okay, Mrs. Levison?" he asked.

She knew the flush on her chest had climbed up her neck and perhaps even past her chin. A bead of sweat tickled as it rolled down her hairline.

"I'm fine," she told him. "The hotel and I both chose to part ways."

Aversano closed the folder and patted it with the palm of his hand. "Well, I think you've had a very interesting idea. Give us a few days to review and get back to you. Would you be able to find a cosigner for the loan?"

"Why would I need a cosigner?"

"We generally require cosigners in this sort of situation."

"What sort of situation?" Jo demanded, her every cell boiling. "I have an MBA from one of the best business schools in the country. I have two decades of experience. My credit score is 806. And if you'd bothered to do more than skim my documents, you would see I have every i dotted and t crossed."

"And I assure you, we'll take all of that into consideration."

They wouldn't. The decision had been made before she even stepped into Aversano's office. She wouldn't be getting the money. Once, Jo would have played nice, hoping Aversano might have a change of heart. *Don't burn bridges,* she'd always been told.

"The fuck you will. You can keep your goddamned loan." Jo stood up. When she opened her right hand to snatch her business plan off the desk, molten metal streamed out of her palm, forming a silver pool that ate into the surface of his sleek black desk. Miraculously, the rest of her now felt totally cool. The energy had been transferred.

"What the hell is that?" Aversano yelped. He pulled out a

Kleenex to wipe it up and immediately jerked his hand back in shock and pain. "It's hot!"

Jo stared down at the silvery pool, which was already starting to harden. It was all that remained of her Tiffany pen. That's when she started to laugh. It was all so ludicrous. If she could do shit like that, she didn't need Jeremy Aversano. And yet she'd been sitting there doing her best to suck up to a hack who couldn't melt a candy bar between his ass cheeks.

"Ma'am?" A security guard was at the door. Aversano must have pressed an alarm.

She couldn't stop laughing. "I'm leaving," she assured him between guffaws. He wouldn't have been much of a match for her, but she had no beef with a hardworking guard. "And don't worry," she told Aversano. "I'm going to make sure you are never, ever burdened by another grade-school mom."

Outside on the sidewalk, she pulled out her phone and called her financial advisor. "Liquidate my 401(k)," she ordered.

She'd never dared touch her savings before. It was very important that the money sit in an account where parasites like the man on the phone could feed on it.

"What?" He was horrified. *Completely*?"

"Every dime," she confirmed.

"There will be very serious tax penalties," he warned her. "How much do you need in cash? You should really consider leaving the rest invested."

"It will be well invested," Jo said. The path ahead seemed clearer than ever before. It was amazing how far ahead she could see now that she'd burned everything down.

As soon as she hung up, she scrolled through her PTA emails until she found Matilda Aversano's address.

I heard about your business idea today, she wrote the woman. *I think it's brilliant. I'd like to invest.*

WHATEVER IT TAKES

Jo and Nessa met Josh at the dock, and the three of them walked out to the boat where Celeste and Harriett stood waiting. Celeste had traded her nautical attire for a black T-shirt and leggings. Harriett looked fabulous in a sleeveless shift that appeared to have once been a sack of some sort.

"Oh my God," Josh muttered under his breath. "Who the hell is that?" The awe in his voice left little doubt that he was talking about Harriett.

"That's our friend Harriett. She was with us when we found the girl," Nessa said. "If you saw the news coverage of us, you must have seen her, too."

"If that's the woman who was with you guys, she's changed since then," Josh said.

"Has she?" Nessa squinted in the sunlight.

But Jo could see it now. The transformation had been so gradual that it had gone unnoticed, but the woman standing on the prow of the boat with one dirty bare foot propped up on the railing was not the same person who'd accompanied them to Danskammer Beach on that terrible day in May. Her skin was bronze and her hair had grown longer and wilder. Even from a distance, her eyes seemed golden. She was becoming something else, but the process hadn't yet reached completion. What would Harriett be, Jo wondered, when all was said and done?

"Hello," Harriett greeted their guest. "You must be Josh Gibbon.

I'm Harriett Osborne, and this is my friend Celeste Howard. I've been listening to your podcast."

"Thank you." Josh's smile was a study in faux humility. He seemed to wait for the praise he expected to follow. His smile dimmed as he realized there would be no kudos coming from Harriett.

After that, Jo noticed Josh never quite let his guard down or allowed his eye to wander away from Harriett for longer than a second or two. He seemed utterly captivated by her. She, on the other hand, appeared completely uninterested in him. While Celeste bustled about the boat like a woman embarking on a life-and-death mission, Harriett calmly watched the water. Jo got the sense that for Harriett, their plan was just one step toward a conclusion she'd long anticipated. How detailed was Harriett's foresight, Jo wondered? Did she know what would happen at each step of the way? Or had she simply picked up on a familiar pattern?

When they reached the right spot, Nessa asked Celeste to bring the boat to a stop. The vessel rocked on the waves as Jo lowered her mask. She tied the end of a rope to her waist while Josh handed her a GoPro mounted on a floating hand grip. She had her flippers on and a knife in a scabbard hung from her weight belt. She saw Nessa's mouth open to tell her she didn't need to do this. Before her friend could get the words out, Jo rolled backward into the water.

Her dive suit couldn't spare her the shock of the cold. She treaded water for a minute until she acclimated. Then she went under. Toward the surface, the water was a mossy green. It grew darker the deeper Jo dove, until she could see only what passed through the cone of light that issued from the tip of her flashlight. The water was filled with tiny specks that glowed like motes of dust in a sunlit room. She told herself not to imagine what might swim past. If the water was deep enough for a whale, there was no telling what could be lurking beneath her.

Jo descended farther into the depths, the only sound that of her own breathing. She checked her depth gauge and saw that she was already at forty feet. Even in Florida, she hadn't gone deeper than eighty. Never before had she felt so alone or so terrified. But she couldn't think of any other way to protect the child she loved more than anything else in the world. The little girl she'd put in danger. She remembered the look in Lucy's eyes as she lay bound and gagged in her striped pajamas. *Whatever it takes,* Jo reminded herself. As tears of fear and frustration rolled down her cheeks, her mask started to fog. Within seconds, she was blind. Then she felt herself being pulled farther down, as if by an unseen hand. The condensation inside her mask began to clear, and there, in the light of her flashlight, stood a mountain of lobster traps.

There had to be thousands of traps in all, some made of wood and others of wire, and all were clogged with seaweed. Even though most had been abandoned two decades earlier, they continued to catch and kill. Jo freed a crab and a fish before she felt a tug on the rope. Back on the boat, her friends were watching the feed from the GoPro, and now they were sending her a message: *Get moving.* She knew they were right. There wasn't enough time to liberate every trapped creature. She swam around the mountain of traps, aiming her flashlight beam into each one she passed. Then she spotted a trap lying on its side at the bottom, as though it had tumbled from the top of the pile. Only a few fronds of seaweed clung to its wires, but still she couldn't see into it. As she swam down for a closer look, she realized there was a black bag crammed inside.

Jo pulled out her knife and sliced open a small section of the plastic. A lock of long red hair floated up from the opening and undulated in the water like a flame. The skull to which it was still attached peeked out, as if the girl to whom it belonged was too shy to emerge. Her eyes were gone, as was her flesh. Jo hovered there, the GoPro held out in front of her. The girl remained perfectly still, looking back at Jo from two empty eye sockets as though patiently waiting for her picture to be taken.

Jo felt a hard yank on the rope attached to her belt, a signal for her to come up. But she kept on going. Now that she knew what to look for, it would be easier to locate the second girl. And it only took a few kicks of her flippers to find another trap, this one seemingly newer than the last, with a black plastic bag stuffed inside. Jo made an incision between two of the wires, revealing the bones of a hand with patches of flaking flesh still attached to it. Jo made sure the camera lingered for a moment on the long, pale fingers. Then she began her slow, careful ascent to the surface.

When she climbed up the swim ladder onto the boat, she was met with grim faces. She didn't need to tell the others what she'd found; they'd seen it all, too. She took off her mask and waited silently as her friends removed her flippers. As she turned to let them take off her air tanks, she spotted a slab of gray in the water nearby.

"It's the whale," she marveled. It was hard to believe she'd been so close to such a magnificent beast. "I didn't see her when I was coming up."

"She was right there the whole time," Nessa told Jo. "It's almost like she was sent here to watch out for you."

Jo glanced at Harriett, who claimed her innocence with a casual shrug.

THAT EVENING, THEY TURNED NESSA'S dining room into a podcasting studio, with three chairs around the circular table and a microphone carefully placed in front of each seat. Harriett watched them set up the equipment but turned down the chance to be interviewed on the podcast. Her part would come soon enough, she informed them. In the meantime, she had gardening to do, and her compost heap needed tending.

Before she left, she approached Josh. He was an average-size man with an average-size paunch. But standing before Harriett, he resembled a small, furry animal. When she reached out and placed a hand on his shoulder, he glanced down at it in awe. "In this war, there isn't a Switzerland," she told him. "There is no such thing as neutrality. You have to choose sides. You are very lucky, Mr. Gibbon. You have a chance to decide how you'll be remembered, and I'm now certain you will make the right choice."

As Harriett walked down the street on bare feet, her silver strands of hair sparkling in the moonlight, Josh watched from Nessa's front window. When she vanished around a curve in Woodland Drive, he drew in a deep breath as though a heavy weight had been lifted off his chest. He turned back to Jo and Nessa, who were waiting by their chairs at the table. His skin appeared waxy and white.

"She says shit like that all the time. You'll get used to it," Jo said.

"Shall we start?" Nessa asked politely.

They all took their seats at the table. Nessa and Jo waited while Josh, head bowed and brow furrowed, fiddled with the controls on his computer. When he looked up again, he'd become a different person. While the podcast was recording, he was in his element, and his cocky confidence returned.

"Hello, justice seekers. This is Josh Gibbon, and tonight we have a very special edition of *They Walk Among Us*. I'm recording the show live this evening, and for reasons that will soon become clear, it will be posted in its entirety, unedited, immediately after recording.

"I'm in Mattauk, New York—a place many of you will recognize as the beach town where a young woman's body was recently discovered wrapped in a black plastic trash bag. I'm joined by Nessa James and Jo Levison, two of the women who made that discovery, and tonight they have explosive new information to share with us.

Not only do they have proof that a serial killer has been at work here in this picturesque place, they believe they now know the killer's identity." He paused and shifted into earnest mode. "Honestly, folks, I thought by this point I'd seen and heard everything. I never imagined I could be shocked anymore. But these women's story, and the evidence they've provided, has shaken me to my very core.

"We'll start with you, Nessa. On the morning of May sixth, you made a gruesome discovery on Danskammer Beach."

"Yes." Nessa's voice came out as a whisper, and Josh gestured for her to speak louder. She cleared her throat nervously. "Yes," she repeated.

"What was it?"

"It was the body of a young girl wrapped up in a garbage bag. She looked to be around seventeen years old, and she was nude."

"How did you happen to come across the body?" Josh asked.

"My friends and I were walking down a trail from the road to the beach, and I spotted the bag in the scrub. I'm a nurse practitioner, and I used to work in a hospital. I'm familiar with the smell of death. I knew there was something terrible in that bag. And there was."

"The police claim the young woman was a prostitute who died of an overdose."

"They still can't tell us who she is, but they know she was a sex worker?" Her indignation came through clearly, though Nessa kept her tone polite. "What difference would it make if she was? Is it suddenly okay to kill sex workers?"

"Of course not." Josh looked taken aback. "I didn't mean to suggest that."

"If the police said she was a cashier at CVS, would you have brought that up, too?

"No. Probably not," Josh conceded.

"The police claim the girl died of an overdose while with a client, who panicked and got rid of the body. But that doesn't fit with what I saw. The bag hadn't been tossed out of a car. Someone had taken the time to wrap the girl up like a present and carry her down the trail. The bag's drawstrings were tied in a neat bow."

Josh lifted a finger to have Nessa pause for a moment.

"The pictures Nessa took of the bow are up on our website and will remain there until we're forced to take them down. Nessa, you and your friends called the police. But when they arrived, there was something you didn't share with them. Is that right?"

"Yes. I had a feeling there were other bodies nearby."

"Are you talking about ESP?"

They'd discussed how to handle the subject of Nessa's gift. Josh felt it was best to keep it vague.

"You can call it whatever you like. I'll call it women's intuition. Every lady listening right now knows exactly what I'm talking about. I had a feeling that I just couldn't shake. I mentioned it to my daughters that night when I got home, and they reminded me that a girl their age had disappeared along Danskammer Beach two years ago."

"A girl named Mandy Welsh."

"My friends Jo and Harriett met Mrs. Welsh. She told them she was convinced her daughter had been murdered. But two years later, police were still writing Mandy off as a runaway."

Josh turned to face the microphone. "We tried to reach Mandy Welsh's mother for this podcast, but we were unable to locate her."

"A few weeks back, Amber Welsh and her kids disappeared overnight," Nessa said.

"Overnight?"

"Literally," Nessa confirmed. "In less than twenty-four hours, a woman, three little boys, and an entire trailer disappeared without a trace. When we found out they were gone, Jo and I went right back to the police."

"And what did they say?"

"They said the disappearance wasn't surprising, considering the Welshes' background."

"Which was?"

"In a word? Poor."

"Nessa, what do you believe happened to Mandy Welsh?"

"I believe she was murdered by the same person who murdered the girl I found—and her body was dumped in the ocean off Danskammer Beach."

"When Nessa first came to me with her theory, I was skeptical. So this afternoon, with the help of a local scuba diver, I was able to take some video of the ocean floor off Danskammer Beach. That video has been posted to our website. The entire area is littered with hundreds of old lobster traps that were abandoned back in the nineties. Most of the traps are empty. Two are not. Inside those traps are heavy black plastic bags like the one in which the first girl was found. When the diver cut those bags open, we were able to see what we believe to be the remains of two girls inside. A link to the video has been sent to local law enforcement and the FBI. Do you know what this means, Nessa?"

"Yes," Nessa said. "It means there's a serial killer at work on the island."

"And you think you know who it is."

"Yes, we do," Nessa said.

"I'm going to turn now to Jo Levison, the owner of a popular gym here in Mattauk, and one of the two women who was with Nessa James the morning she discovered the body by the beach. Ms. Levison, news footage from that day showed you and your two friends down by the beach, is that correct?"

Jo slid forward in her seat and leaned toward the mic. "It is."

"In fact, that's how you and I first met, isn't it? I saw you on the news, and the next day I approached you about doing an interview."

"That's right."

"And you told me to go to hell."

"That's a nice way of putting it," Jo said.

"So why have you decided to speak to me now?"

"Because no one else will listen," Jo said. "We've gone to the police. We did all the right things, but we can't get the authorities to take any action. We don't want more young women to be killed."

"You recently discovered a clue that you believe could identify the murderer of the three girls."

"Yes. As you mentioned, I own a gym here in Mattauk. One of my clients was killed in a car crash on the sixth of June. Inside a locker I believe she'd been using was a nude Polaroid of the girl whose body Nessa discovered by Danskammer Beach."

"And do you know who the locker belonged to?"

"Yes. She hadn't officially rented it. But I know the locker belonged to my deceased client because she'd given me the combination to the lock. My client's name was Rosamund Harding."

"The Olympic diver?"

"Yes."

"And you say she gave you the combination?"

"She gave me an apple with the word *FAITH* carved into it. At the time, I had no idea that the letters were the combination to a lock."

"When did you figure out that's what it was?"

"After Rosamund died. The same day, the police came to empty out a locker she rented by the month. There was nothing in there but her gym clothes and supplies."

"Wait—the *police* came to clear out her locker?"

"Yeah, I thought that was unusual, too. Why would it be so important to empty her locker the same day she died? I wondered if they were looking for something specific. When they left, it occurred to me that Rosamund could have had something hidden in another locker—one of the day-use lockers that wasn't rented under her name. So I took a look, and sure enough, there was an unrented locker with a five-letter combination lock on it. I almost went out to buy a pair of bolt cutters until I remembered the apple. I tried the word *FAITH*, and the lock opened right away."

"And the Polaroid of the girl found at Danskammer Beach was the only item in the locker?"

"Yes. And in the picture, the girl was nude."

Josh stopped and cleared his throat. Jo realized they were about to pass the point of no return. Most people wouldn't have had the guts to keep going. But Josh did. "Just to be clear—you found this nude photo in a locker you believe was being used by Rosamund Harding, the recently deceased wife of Spencer Harding, the noted art dealer?"

"Yes. I'm convinced that Rosamund hid the photo at my gym to keep it safe. I think she was afraid of her husband and the men who worked for him."

"Do you believe Spencer Harding may have had something to do with the death of the girl whose body was found on Danskammer Beach?"

"I can't think of any other reason for Rosamund to have the picture."

"Did you call the police when you found the photo?"

"Of course," Jo said. "They say there's not enough evidence to look into Spencer Harding."

"Have they questioned him?"

"Not to my knowledge," Jo said.

"Why wouldn't they question him?"

"I don't know," Jo said. "What I do know is that after I found the photo, a man broke into my house in the middle of the night. I caught him in my daughter's room. He'd—" She stopped to wipe away tears. "She was bound and gagged when I found her. Now the man responsible is sitting in the Mattauk jail, refusing to say a word."

"Why do you think he broke into your house?"

"I'm convinced Spencer Harding sent him there to kidnap my daughter. I believe he wanted to scare me and my friends away from looking into the death of the girl at Danskammer Beach."

"Is your daughter safe now?"

It was a simple question, but it hit Jo hard. Nessa reached over and took her hand as Jo choked back a sob.

"For now. The only way to keep her safe for good is to send Spencer Harding's evil ass to jail, and I'm not going to rest until it happens."

"Neither will I," Josh Gibbon told her. "And I won't rest until the girls at Danskammer Beach have names. To all of you out there, thanks for listening. There's obviously much more to this story, and we'll be putting it all together in the days to come."

THE FIRST AND LAST
TIME MANDY WELSH
BROKE A PROMISE

Mandy had never seen a Maybach before. As far as she knew, it was just another nice car with dark windows. When it pulled up beside her on the road that ran along Danskammer Beach, she took a step away toward the scrub. A half mile back, she'd spotted a trail that snaked through the trees to the water and an old man fishing where the waves met the shore. Mandy had always been a fast runner. If she kicked off her shoes, she could make it back there in minutes.

Then the window lowered. "You must be Mandy." The man behind the wheel was handsome. Mandy's mother had warned her not to trust handsome men.

She said nothing in return. She already had a heel halfway out of one shoe.

"You're on your way to see my wife." The man said it slowly, as if she might be stupid. She didn't want him to think she was dumb, so she cleared her throat.

"What's her name?" She didn't sound nearly as tough as she wanted to.

"Rosamund Harding. She's very excited to meet you. I'm Mr. Harding," he told her. "I'm heading home. Hop in and I'll give you a ride. It's cold and you're limping."

The cold hadn't bothered her, but her feet ached from walking three miles in her funeral shoes. Still, she demurred. "That's okay," Mandy told him politely. "I could use the exercise."

The man sighed. "Here," he said, opening his wallet and pulling out his license. She bent forward without moving her feet. The name on the card was Spencer Harding. "My address is Eighteen Culling Pointe Road."

That was the address she'd been given. Still, she stayed put.

"Don't get me in trouble," Spencer pleaded. "Rosamund will murder me if she finds out I let you walk the rest of the way."

Mandy remembered the kind voice on the other end of the line. Mrs. Harding did seem like the sort of person who'd be upset by such things. And it was very cold, now that he mentioned it. And the back of her heels were worn raw.

"Okay," Mandy agreed, trying to smile as she reached for the door handle. "Thank you."

"My pleasure," he assured her.

WHEN, AT LAST, SHE REALIZED what was happening, Mandy cried for her mom, who was always so sad. Whenever Amber got drunk, she'd make Mandy promise to always be extra careful. She worried bad luck might have rubbed off on her girl.

Mandy refused to ever let her mom know that it had. So she opted to play it safe and not fight. And when it was over, she thought, she'd keep it all to herself.

In the end, it wasn't a decision she got to make.

MAYDAY

Jo woke to the sound of the doorbell. She shoved back the du-
vet that a kind soul had draped over her after she'd passed out
from exhaustion. Looking around the tidy living room, she
concluded that she was on Nessa's couch. She hadn't even made it
to the guest room the previous night. She'd dreamed of a mountain
of bodies at the bottom of the ocean, all of them girls. One by one,
she'd carried them up to the surface. The last one had been her
own daughter, her limbs tied and a stuffed pig crammed into her
mouth. Jo felt more tired than she had when she'd laid her head
down.

According to her phone, it was just short of nine o'clock in the
morning. Jo stood up and stared at the front door, wondering if she
should chance a look out the peephole. Then a knock at the window behind her made Jo leap to her feet. The curtains were open a
crack, and Jo could see a woman through the gap. She stood with
her hands cupped around her eyes, peering in through the glass.

Sorry! she mouthed, and gestured for Jo to open the window.

Jo grabbed her phone and began to dial 911.

The woman rapped again. When Jo looked up, she was pinning a
copy of the *New York Post* to the window with one hand. A photo
of the same woman accompanied an article's byline. She was a reporter.

Jo walked to the window, but didn't unlock it. "What do you
want?" she demanded.

The woman glanced over her shoulder as though she didn't want to be overheard. Instead of answering, she fiddled with her phone, then placed the screen against the window. A news broadcast was playing, and the chyron at the bottom was crystal clear. It read *Spencer Harding Presumed Dead*.

Jo unlocked the window and lifted it. "What happened?"

"Spencer Harding's helicopter crashed into New York Harbor late last night. It's believed he was the only one on board. Would you care to comment?"

Jo had no comment. Only questions. Had his death been painful enough? Had he known the kind of fear she and her daughter had felt? "Me? Why?"

"Given the seriousness of the allegations you made against him yesterday, it's hard to believe his death and your story aren't related in some way."

Jo resisted the urge to let out a whoop of joy. "Holy shit," she marveled instead.

"Is it okay if I quote you?" the reporter asked.

"No," Jo said, trying to remember the response she always heard people give on TV. "I have no comment at this time."

She slid the window shut, locked it, and pulled the curtains. Then she raced upstairs to Nessa's bedroom. She rapped once on the door but didn't wait for an answer.

"Wake up!"

Nessa sat bolt upright. She was still wearing the outfit she'd worn out on the boat. Apparently, she hadn't found the energy to change into her nightclothes. "What is it?" she said. "Is everyone okay? What's happened?"

"Spencer Harding is dead," Jo said.

"Jesus." Nessa flopped back down on the bed. "You almost gave me a heart attack."

"Someone just rang the doorbell, and when I got up, there was a reporter at the window. She said Spencer Harding is dead and people think it might have something to do with the podcast."

"There's a reporter outside?" Her curiosity piqued, Nessa hauled herself out of bed and went to the window. She let out a snort when she peeked out the blinds. "You said there was *one* reporter outside?"

Jo joined her. The street in front of Nessa's house was jammed with television vans. "They're going to ruin my damn yard," Nessa said.

"If it makes you feel any better, I'm sure Harriett can fix it. You mind if I turn on the news?" Jo asked.

Nessa sighed. "I'd say that's probably a good idea."

THE LOCAL NEWS WAS FILMING live in front of Nessa's house. When they pulled up the blinds and peered straight down from Nessa's bedroom window, they could see the blond reporter standing in the middle of the lawn.

"These folks got a lot of nerve," Nessa grumbled as Jo turned up the sound on the television.

". . . the stunning allegations made against Harding have sent local police scrambling. Divers are currently scouring the ocean floor off Danskammer Beach in search of the two bodies filmed by Josh Gibbon, host of the true crime podcast *They Walk Among Us*. Detective Franklin Rees, the lead detective on the Jane Doe case, says that despite the compelling story told by Ms. James and Ms. Levison, it is still too early to draw conclusions."

The program switched over to an interview that had been taped at Danskammer Beach while the sun was still rising in the east. Franklin stood in front of the camera with bags under his eyes and a coffee cup in his hand.

"From the beginning, the Mattauk PD has been diligently searching for evidence that will lead us to the truth about what happened
here in Mattauk this spring. While we take Ms. James and Ms. Levison's allegations seriously, they wouldn't stand up in a court of
law. We must have proof to back them up before we can take action.
We are looking for that proof as we speak."

The camera returned to the reporter in Nessa's front yard. "That
interview was filmed early this morning, and it now appears as if
the proof they've been searching for has at last been found. I'm
going to hand it over to my colleague, Frances McDaniel, who's
reporting live from Danskammer Beach."

"Thank you, Madeline. What you're seeing behind me are two
lobster traps being raised from the ocean floor. They appear to be
the same traps we saw in the video posted last night by Josh Gibbon of *They Walk Among Us*, which quickly went viral. According
to the podcast, the traps contain the bodies of two more girls—and
may be evidence that a serial killer has been at work here on the
island. The lead suspect at this moment is Spencer Harding, whose
Culling Pointe mansion can be seen in the distance. Late last night,
in the hours after the latest episode of *They Walk Among Us* was
released, Mr. Harding's helicopter plunged into New York Harbor.
Authorities do not think the crash was due to a mechanical failure.
Harding announced a mayday situation shortly before the aircraft
went down, and it's believed he may have experienced a medical
emergency while piloting the craft."

The show switched to footage of the crash that had been filmed
by a passenger on the Staten Island Ferry. A tiny red light in the sky
grew larger and brighter until the aircraft materialized out of the
night sky and plunged into the water a few hundred yards away.
The videographer must have been knocked over as waves rocked
the ferry. Once they were back on their feet, the only signs of the
helicopter were the bubbles rising to the surface.

Jo felt Nessa's arm slip around her. "It's over," Nessa told her. "You found the bodies when the rest of us couldn't. You got our story out. Who knows how many lives you may have saved? You're a hero, Jo Levison. You've done Lucy proud."

Jo threw her arms around Nessa and buried her face in her friend's shoulder. For two days, she'd been fighting back the tears. Now they came flowing out all at once. Never before had she felt so terrified. But with Spencer Harding dead, her family could come home. There was nothing on earth that she wanted more—but the things she'd been willing to do to bring them back had surprised even her.

"Hey," Nessa nudged her. "Looks like Harriett just showed up."

"Harriett?" Jo wiped her eyes on her sleeve and glanced out the window. A barefoot woman in a burlap sack was walking down Woodland Drive toward Nessa's house. The crowd parted for her as she made her way to the front door, the reporters struck dumb by the sight.

Downstairs, the doorbell rang, and Nessa hurried to answer it with Jo on her heels.

"It's a little early for a lawn party, don't you think?" Harriett said when Nessa opened the door.

"Come in, come in," Nessa quickly ushered Harriett through the door as cameras flashed behind her. "Did you hear? Spencer Harding is dead. It's over."

"Spencer may be dead," Harriett said, "but it's far from over."

Jo felt her heart sink. "What do you mean?"

"You think Spencer Harding put the girls in those lobster traps and rowed them out to sea? There had to be other people involved."

Jo must have looked crushed.

"I didn't mean to upset you." Harriett sounded serious and sober for once. "No one's going to tip their hand by coming after us right now. We're safe for the moment. You can bring darling Lucy home."

"What should we do about the others?"

"Those who deserve punishment will receive it," Harriett assured her.

"I'm getting pretty sick of waiting for justice," Jo said.

"Justice may be relentless, as Franklin says, but she's also hobbled by rules," Harriett noted. "That's why I choose vengeance. She's the only mistress I serve."

AT THE BEGINNING OF JULY, they buried Mandy Welsh. The Hereford County medical examiner had not been able to determine her cause of death. Mandy's father was the only family police had been able to locate, and he gave Nessa permission to arrange the service and to have his daughter interred beside the girl in blue. With two years left on his sentence at Sing Sing, he wouldn't be allowed to attend the funeral. Since the Welshes hadn't gone to church, Nessa held the service at hers. Over a thousand people attended. She'd asked for all seats to be reserved for members of the community, but to her consternation, there appeared to be reporters in the pews.

As soon as the pastor finished his prayers, Nessa rose from her seat between her two daughters and made her way down the aisle. She'd attended her share of funerals over the years, but she had never given a eulogy before. When Jonathan died, she'd been too grief-stricken to speak. When her parents passed, Breanna and Jordan had spoken for the family. At the girl in blue's funeral, she'd felt it wasn't her place to say anything. But now she knew she'd been wrong. This time, she planned to stand before the whole town and speak for Mandy Welsh, whose family wasn't there to see her off.

When Nessa looked out over the podium, her fear vanished. Not only was it gone, she couldn't imagine how it had ever weighed her down. Nessa adjusted the microphone, which the pastor had positioned too high. Then she scanned the somber crowd, cleared her throat, and began.

"Let me make something clear," she told those sitting in the pews and clustered in the aisles. "We have *not* gathered here to talk about the man who killed Mandy Welsh. You will *not* hear me say his name today, and I ask that you all avoid his name, too. We are here to talk about Mandy. I've spoken with dozens of people who knew her—you'll hear from some of them later—and they all told me the same thing. This was a *good* girl. The kind of girl who started taking care of her brothers when she was barely more than a baby herself. A girl who, despite having nothing, always had love and kindness to share. Mandy may have been sweet and soft-spoken, but this girl was strong—so strong. Mandy crammed more work into each of her days than most of us could bear in a week. The afternoon she was abducted, she was walking *five miles* out to Culling Pointe to interview for a job that could help her family make ends meet. Mandy had just turned sixteen, but she was already supporting three little kids.

"And yet when this girl, this best of *all* girls, went missing, no one but her mama went looking for her. They said, with no reason to support it, that Mandy must have run away from home. Now we know, two years later, that she'd been stolen and abused. After that, she was murdered and tossed into the sea. If she'd been rich, they would have sent out a search party. If she'd lived in one of the mansions on Culling Pointe, they would have had every officer on the island knocking on doors. But Mandy was poor, and her dad was in jail, and to them, that meant she wasn't worth their time."

Nessa paused to wipe her tears with a handkerchief. "There is nothing we can do for Mandy now. The damage has already been done. But there are two ways we can honor her memory. We can identify the other girls found near Danskammer Beach, and we can make absolutely certain that this never happens again—to any girl, no matter who she is or where she comes from."

As she was walking back to her pew, her eyes panned the crowd. Lucy waved to her and Jo gave her a proud thumbs-up. Art had taken his glasses off to dab his eyes and missed the exchange. It wasn't until Breanna and Jordan jumped up to greet her with hugs that Nessa spotted the person she'd been seeking. Franklin stood by the church doors, tall and stoic. She hadn't spoken to him since the day she'd asked him to leave her house. He met her gaze and held it until she turned to sit. When the service was over, she looked for him again, but he'd already gone.

THE ANGEL'S TRUMPET HARRIETT HAD planted on the girl in blue's grave had grown to a height of six feet and burst into bloom. Its enormous flame-colored flowers could be seen from the highway below. It had become known in town as the burning bush. After Mandy's coffin had been lowered into the ground and the other mourners began making their way to their cars, Harriett and Lucy filled in the grave and planted another angel's trumpet on top of it.

"It's going to look like the whole hill is on fire," Lucy noted.

"That's the idea," said Harriett. "Let it serve as a warning."

Jo stood silently, holding her husband's hand as their daughter finished burying Mandy Welsh. One story may have ended, but her own family's remained far from resolved. The man who'd broken into their house had managed to retain one of the best criminal defense lawyers in Manhattan and post a two-million-dollar bail. He was currently under house arrest, with an ankle monitor that kept track of his movements. Worried what Jo might do, Art had begged her not to make any housecalls.

Though the man continued to keep his silence, there was no doubt now about what had happened to girls who were kidnapped for Spencer Harding. When the police searched Harding's beach house, they'd found a safe filled with Polaroids. The photos showed, in lurid detail, the crimes he'd committed. Jo and Art knew their daughter might have narrowly avoided the same fate. And they'd both agreed to let Harriett punish those involved in whatever way she saw fit.

THE THIRD VICTIM REMAINED IN the Mattauk morgue, waiting for someone to claim her. With Nessa's guidance, a forensic artist had created a digital portrait of the girl, and Nessa swore it was her spitting image. She'd been a stunning girl with features experts thought might suggest Chinese ancestry. The media coverage had remained intense for weeks. The story had made every major website, magazine, and newspaper. But no one stepped forward to claim the girl as their own. It was as if she had fallen right out of the sky.

NEWSNIGHT

The evening after Mandy's funeral, *Newsnight* aired a special episode devoted to the Danskammer Beach murders. For a week, sensational promos had teased exclusive details and never-seen-before evidence. At showtime, Jo, Nessa, and Harriett gathered in front of Jo's giant television. The police had been uncharacteristically tight-lipped since Spencer Harding's death. The investigation was still ongoing, they said, whenever the media asked. Now they'd granted *Newsnight* access to their case files. At least that was what Jo, Harriett, and Nessa assumed. No one from the show had contacted the three of them. Even Josh Gibbon, who'd been busting his ass to keep investigating the case, had no idea what the revelations would be.

The show started with a picture pulled from a magazine. It showed Spencer Harding standing in his art gallery. Hanging on the walls were paintings worth millions, but Harding seemed oblivious to their presence. His suit screamed power, as did his stance. He glared at the camera with his arms crossed, as if warning it to keep its distance.

This evening on *Newsnight*: Spencer Harding was the undisputed king of the New York art world. Over the course of two decades, he rose from obscurity to become the most powerful and influential dealer in Manhattan—some might even say the world. Brilliant,

handsome, and phenomenally wealthy, he counted the
world's richest men as his friends and clients.
Those who worked with Spencer say he was gifted with
impeccable taste and an uncanny eye for talent. None
of his colleagues or clients ever suspected Spencer
Harding was hiding a sinister secret—or that the
beachside mansion where he threw glamorous parties
also doubled as a slaughterhouse, to which he lured
innocent young women before robbing them of their
lives.

"Jesus Christ. They're making him sound like a James Bond villain," Jo groaned as the show's title sequence rolled. "Do we really have to watch this shit?"

Nessa paused the television and turned to Jo. "Yes," she said. "We do."

"Here." Harriett passed her joint to Jo. "This will help."

Jo took the joint. Art would recognize the smell when he got home from the movies with Lucy, but under the circumstances, she knew he wouldn't hold it against her.

Jo inhaled deeply as the show's host appeared on the screen. The wind tousled his silvery hair as behind him waves crashed onto Danskammer Beach.

Spencer Harding's downfall began on a sunny morning
in the final days of spring. That's when three local
women stopped here on this lonesome road that runs
along Danskammer Beach, just outside the picture-
perfect town of Mattauk, New York. They told police
they were out for a walk by the shore. What they

discovered, just off a narrow trail that snakes down to the water, would shake two communities to their core. By the end of the summer, both Spencer Harding and his wife, famed diver Rosamund Stillgoe Harding, would be dead. The bodies of three young women would be lying in the county morgue. And headlines would be fixated on the man who's become known around the world as the Collector.

"What?" The pot hadn't done much to mellow Jo's mood. "The only paper that called him the Collector was the fucking *New York Post*." Other media hadn't dared follow suit. Jo, Harriett, and Nessa had made it clear from the beginning that they would only grant interviews to outlets that agreed to a set of conditions Jo had typed up. Condition number one: No comic book nicknames.

"I'd prepare myself for a few more unpleasant surprises, if I were you," Harriett told her.

"Why?" Jo demanded. "What do you know?"

"I know how the world works," Harriett responded.

Jo rolled her eyes. "Fine. Don't tell me." A picture appeared on the screen—an average-looking child who showed no signs of growing into a man as conventionally handsome as Spencer Harding had been. "Oh, great, here comes the supervillain's origin story."

"Shhh!" Nessa shushed her.

Spencer Harding was born John Anderson, the only child of a Manhattan orthodontist. He spent the first fifteen years of his life in this middle-class building on the Upper West Side. At three bedrooms,

the family's apartment was spacious by New York
standards, but hardly ostentatious. Classmates
from P.S. 333 remember young John as a studious,
sensitive child with a passion for art. He's said to
have started his own collection at the age of ten,
purchasing a work that would one day be valued at
over six million dollars.

But John Anderson's idyllic childhood wasn't to
last. Shortly after his sixteenth birthday, his
parents were murdered in a tragic home invasion.
The killers were never captured. John received a
small fortune in life insurance, which was placed in
a trust he could claim when he turned eighteen. He
lived with a classmate's family until he graduated
from high school. Then, John Anderson disappeared.

"How about that?" Jo sneered. "His parents were murdered.
He's fucking Batman."

"If he'd been fucking Batman, this would be much more interesting," Harriett said, and they both cracked up.

"You two obviously aren't listening," Nessa said. "Good old
Spencer must have murdered his parents."

"You think?" Jo asked.

"Pretty sure," Nessa said.

"Yeah, sounds about right," Harriett said. "No one gets rich that
fast without having blood on his hands."

No one seems to have seen or spoken to John for
the next ten years—until the day he reappeared in

Manhattan. Now, however, he was calling himself
Spencer Harding. And thanks to extensive plastic
surgery, he was virtually unrecognizable. He'd
created a new identity for himself—one he fiercely
protected.

In 2001, a new gallery opened in Chelsea. Its
handsome young owner seemed to have an inexhaustible
source of private funding. Soon his client list
rivaled those of far more established dealers. Their
curiosity piqued, a few of his competitors hired
private investigators. But no one could ever find out
much about the mysterious Spencer Harding. Though
often photographed out on the town with models
and actresses, he avoided publicity and never gave
interviews. Those who knew him say he rarely spoke
about himself or his background. The little clues
he dropped never added up to much. One of Spencer's
clients was certain he'd been raised in L.A. Another
had been told he was English by birth. But DNA
evidence has now confirmed that Spencer Harding was
indeed John Anderson, the orphaned teen from the
Upper West Side.

By 2005, Spencer Harding had become one of the
wealthiest men in the country and the handsome bad
boy of New York society. But many Americans first
heard his name four years ago, when he married
the Olympic athlete Rosamund Stillgoe. It was, by
all accounts, a whirlwind romance. Depressed after
a torn ligament kept her from competing in the
Olympics, Rosamund was swept off her feet by the
dashing multimillionaire, whose penthouse apartment

famously featured its own helipad. Little did she
know that her Prince Charming would turn out to be a
monster—or that the helicopter in which he'd whisked
her away would one day serve as his coffin.

"Who writes this shit?" Jo asked. "Is there some kind of style guide you can buy if you're hired to write for the Dead Woman Industrial Complex?"

"I find the music quite captivating," Harriett said. "That lonesome guitar twang really speaks to the unfolding tragedy."

"Ladies," Nessa chided them. "Focus?"

Later on Newsnight: Rosamund Harding cut off contact
with her family and disappeared from public view.
Was her disappearance by choice? Or was she being
held captive by her husband?

Jo sobered instantly at the sight of the Hardings' wedding portrait. "Poor Rosamund," she muttered. "If only we'd known what she was trying to tell us with that apple. We could have rescued her from the Pointe on Memorial Day."

"I wish we had," Harriett agreed. "I underestimated her husband. I didn't think he'd kill her. I can't make the same mistake again."

"So you *don't* know what's going to happen?" Jo said, just to confirm.

"I see the war, not the battles," Harriett replied.

"What the hell is that supposed to mean?" Jo asked.

"Stop!" Nessa once again brought them to order. The show had begun again with news footage taken the day Nessa had discovered the girl in blue.

On May sixth, three local women stopped along
Danskammer Beach. They took a little-used path that
led from the road to the water. Along the way, they
discovered a nude corpse in a thick black trash bag,
its drawstring tied in an elaborate bow. The body
belonged to a young Black female, whom authorities
estimated to be between the ages of seventeen and
nineteen. There were signs of intercourse, but no
wounds or bruising on the body.

Chief John Rocca of the Mattauk Police Department
says the medical examiner had no trouble determining
the cause of death.

Jo recoiled at the sight of the police chief in his formal uniform, sitting across from the show's host. Square-jawed, laconic, and handsome, Rocca was the type of man that movies and television had trained her to trust. She knew millions of *Newsnight* viewers would take what he said as the gospel truth.

"How did the girl die, Chief Rocca?"
"She died of a fentanyl overdose."
"Given the cause of death, did you have any
theories about what might have happened?"
"Yes, sir. We initially believed the body belonged

to a sex worker who had likely overdosed in the
company of a client. We thought the man must have
panicked and disposed of the body off Danskammer
Beach Road. That theory seemed to be proven when
a woman came forward and claimed the girl was her
daughter."

"Was the girl her daughter?"

"No. The moment I met the woman, there was
something about her story that didn't quite click
with me. DNA tests later confirmed that she was not
related to our Jane Doe in any way."

"Then who was the mystery woman?"

"An actress paid to impersonate the girl's mother."

That's when the case, which had seemed so clear-
cut, suddenly began to look much more complicated.

"You located the woman and brought her in for
questioning?"

"We did," said Rocca.

"And what did she tell you?"

"That she'd been employed by a man named Danill
Chertov."

Jo paused the program on an image of Chertov. "Spencer Harding's bodyguard!" Jo exclaimed. "I fucking knew it!"

"Yeah, but there's something wrong with all of this." Nessa
looked spooked. "The police are claiming they did DNA tests. But
Franklin and I were the ones who had the tests done. The department refused."

Harriett snorted.

"What?" Jo demanded.

"Nothing," Harriett said.

"No, seriously." Nessa had grown used to her friend's bizarre sense of humor, but this time Harriett had gone too far. "What do you think is funny about all of this?"

"You'll see," Harriett said. "Continue, please."

"Was the Mattauk Police Department already familiar with Mr. Chertov at the time?"

"Yes, sir. Our department had had at least one prior run-in with Mr. Chertov. We knew he worked as a bodyguard for Spencer Harding."

"Did you think that Mr. Chertov was acting on his employer's orders in this case?"

"We did. When the actress came forward to identify the body, she brought documents that would have been difficult to forge. A birth certificate. An immunization schedule. It was not a cheap operation. Someone with deep pockets had to be footing the bill."

"Spencer Harding?"

"Yes, sir."

"Why would a wealthy, well-known art dealer pay an actress to impersonate a dead girl's mother?"

"To convince my department to close the case."

"Why would he want the case closed?"

"That was the question we wanted to answer."

"At what point did Harding become a person of interest in the Danskammer Beach case?"

"The day the actress identified Mr. Chertov as her employer we placed Mr. Chertov and Mr. Harding under surveillance."

Nessa pressed pause. "What the hell?" she said. "That can't be true."

"Is he claiming he suspected Spencer Harding all the way back at the beginning of June?" Jo asked.

Harriett sniggered. The snigger turned into a chuckle and the chuckle into a howl. "I saw that plot twist coming a mile away! Keep going!" she urged. "Press play!"

"What are you laughing about?" Jo demanded. "This isn't god-damned funny."

"She's stoned," Nessa grumbled.

"Yes, and yet I'm the only one who knows what's going on."

June sixth, exactly one month after the body was discovered on Danskammer Beach, a deliveryman on his way to Culling Pointe came across an accident on Danskammer Beach Road. When police arrived at the scene, Rosamund Harding was discovered in the driver's seat, dead from what the medical examiner would later determine was a head injury. She appeared to have been alone at the time of the accident.

"Chief Rocca, was there anything about the accident that struck you as strange?"

"To start with, it was an unusual location for an accident. Danskammer Beach Road is straight and flat. We don't see many crashes out there, and when we do, they're alcohol related. We did not believe Mrs. Harding was intoxicated at the time of the crash. But it wasn't until we discovered that the vehicle's internal computer network had been hacked that we suspected Ms. Harding had been the victim of foul play."

"So someone remotely hacked into the car and caused the fatal crash?"

"The accident took place at four fifteen A.M. The car's black box showed that in the moments before the crash, the vehicle had been steadily accelerating until it was traveling at well over one hundred miles per hour. Three seconds prior to the collision, the headlights were cut. Sunrise that morning was at five forty-six A.M. There are no streetlights along Danskammer Beach Road, and it was a moonless night. Mrs. Harding would have been driving blind."

"You would have to be a pretty good hacker to orchestrate something like that."

"Yes."

"Good hackers don't come cheap, do they?"

"No, sir, they do not. On the dark web, prices for a murder of this sort tend to start in the low to mid six figures."

"A fortune to most, but a pittance to a man like Spencer Harding."

"That is correct."

"When you informed Mr. Harding of his wife's death, what was his response?"

"He received the news with very little emotion. The officer who placed the call referred to him as 'robotic.'"

Knowing that Spencer Harding would do his best to thwart any investigation into his wife's death, police began by looking into Rosamund Harding's life. Their inquiries took them to a women-only gym in downtown Mattauk—the same place where officers had first encountered Danill Chertov. One afternoon, while

Rosamund Harding was working out on a treadmill,
Chertov had barged into the gym in search of her.
After an altercation with the establishment's owner,
the police were called. Chief Rocca had a hunch that
the gym might hold a clue to Rosamund Harding's fate.

"And what did you find?"

"In the locker she rented? Gym clothes. A pair of
sneakers. But my gut told me there had to be more.
I had my men execute a search of a locker that
hadn't been rented to Mrs. Harding but was locked
nonetheless. That's where I found the photo."

"You're aware that the owner of the gym claims *she*
was the one who discovered the photo in Rosamund
Harding's locker?"

"She let me and my men into the locker room."

"And that's it?"

"That was the extent of her involvement at the
time."

"Are you fucking kidding me?" Jo wasn't sure she'd heard that
right.

"Did he just make that all up?" Nessa asked, one hand clenching
Jo's arm.

A professional lawman's hunch led to a smoking gun—a
Polaroid of a naked girl. The moment Chief Rocca
saw it, he knew it was the same girl they'd found
dead by Danskammer Beach weeks earlier. On the upper
right corner, forensic technicians found a partial
thumbprint.

"Who did the thumbprint belong to?"

"It belonged to Mr. Chertov."

"How do you think the picture ended up in the locker?"

"We believe Mrs. Harding discovered it among her husband's belongings at home and placed it there for safekeeping. Unfortunately, that discovery likely led to her untimely death."

"What did you do after you identified the owner of the fingerprint?"

"We immediately sought to bring Mr. Chertov in for questioning. But we wanted to do so without tipping off his employer, whom we knew to be a flight risk."

"You were worried that Spencer Harding would get wind of the plan and fly away."

"Yes, literally."

Jo turned down the volume as the show transitioned into another commercial break. "Have I stepped into an alternate universe?" she asked. "In my world, none of this happened. Am I right?"

"You are indeed," Harriett said.

"Franklin said there were no fingerprints on the photo—just two partial prints inside the locker that couldn't be identified," Nessa pointed out.

"Clearly someone was lying," Harriett said. "I'm fairly certain it wasn't Franklin."

"But this is the chief of police. How could he make something like that up?" Nessa marveled.

"Who's going to call him a liar? The case is closed," Harriett said.

"We could!" Jo argued.

"He hasn't mentioned our names once," Nessa muttered. "It's like we don't even exist."

"He's rewriting the story," Harriett explained in a tone that suggested she shouldn't have to. "You guys have been around the block a few times. Don't you know this is what they do? By the end of this, we'll have a whole new set of heroes and villains." She pointed at the television. "Go ahead, turn it back up."

Unfortunately, Danill Chertov proved elusive. It wasn't until the evening of June eighth that he was pulled over by a Mattauk police officer stationed along Danskammer Beach Road. Over the next twenty-four hours Chertov would make a confession that would chill even a seasoned law enforcement officer like Chief Rocca to the bone.

"He told us Rosamund Harding had been killed because she discovered evidence of her husband's secret fetish."

"Fetish?"

"Spencer Harding had a sexual fixation. He liked very young women."

"You mean girls?"

"Some of them were underage, yes."

"But that wasn't where his deviance ended, was it?"

"No. Harding liked the girls to be unconscious when he abused them."

"As though they were dead?"

"Yes."

According to Chertov, Harding had people who would supply him with young women between the ages of fifteen and nineteen. Some were sex workers. Other

girls were abducted from their own neighborhoods.
They would be drugged and sexually assaulted in the
beachfront mansion while Harding's wife was away. On
the occasions when his wife was inconveniently at
home, she would be drugged as well.

"How many girls were there?"

"According to Chertov? Too many to count."

"What happened to all of them?"

"Most were driven home while still groggy, with
several hundred dollars stuffed into their pockets
and no memory of what had happened to them."

"But some never made it home."

"No."

At least three of the girls died of overdoses at
Harding's beach house. When that happened, Chertov
would place the body inside two heavy-duty lawn
bags and drive it to the forgotten trail off desolate
Danskammer Beach. The same night, under the cover
of darkness, a local fisherman named Randall Duffy
would land his boat on Danskammer Beach, pick up
the bag, and cram it into an old metal lobster trap.
Then he would toss the trap and its contents onto an
underwater heap of abandoned lobster traps.

"How many traps are down there?"

"Thousands. After all the lobsters died in ninety-
nine, that's where the local fishermen sank their
traps."

"So when he dumped a body, Randall Duffy knew the
odds were pretty good that no one would ever find
it."

"It was a needle in a haystack."

Unfortunately, the perfect plan depended on a less-

than-perfect man. Randall Duffy used the money he
made from dumping bodies to fund a heroin addiction.
Police believe he died of an overdose just hours
before he was scheduled to make his last pickup from
Danskammer Beach. According to Danill Chertov, he
had no idea that the body he'd left in the scrub was
still there, just waiting to be found.

Jo stopped the video on an image of Randall Duffy standing on
the fishing boat he'd used to dump the bodies, wearing only a pair
of swim trunks. He looked to be in his mid-fifties, with a perfectly
round, hairless head and a perfectly round, hairless belly to match.
Nessa squinted at the screen. "I've never seen that guy before."
"Me either," Jo agreed.

By the evening of Tuesday, June ninth, Chief Rocca
had heard more than enough from Danill Chertov.
An arrest warrant was issued for Spencer Harding.
But by the time the billionaires on Culling Pointe
were woken up by the sound of sirens outside their
windows, the man who had raped countless young
women and murdered at least four people was gone,
his helicopter en route to Manhattan. At ten to
midnight, it would make a fatal plunge into the
harbor, less than a mile from the famed Statue of
Liberty.
   "What happened? How did he get away?"
   "He was tipped off," Rocca said.
   "By someone inside of your department?"
   "No, sir. By a podcast."

Nessa gasped. "That lying motherfucker."

That very same night, the popular podcast *They Walk Among Us* released what it called a "special episode." It featured an interview with two of the women who had discovered the first body. They claimed to also know the location of two additional bodies at the bottom of the ocean off Danskammer Beach. The host of the podcast, Josh Gibbon, sent a scuba diver down to check out their claim. The video footage was posted online the same night as the podcast. It clearly showed the remains of two bodies crammed into lobster traps.

"How did these women know where to look for the bodies Danill Chertov had paid Randall Duffy to dump in the ocean?"

"I'm sad to report that they were tipped off by a detective on the case. He was apparently involved with one of the women."

"Detective Franklin Rees."

"That is correct."

"And what happened to this detective?"

"He has since been relieved of his duties."

And for good reason. Thanks to that leak, Spencer Harding was able to flee Culling Pointe before authorities arrived to arrest him. Until Harding's body is recovered from New York Harbor, we have no way of knowing what brought down his helicopter. For now, all we know is that the man who brought suffering and heartache to so many will forever go unpunished.

Nessa was sobbing.

"I can't watch any more of this," Jo said.

"You must," Harriett insisted. She was no longer laughing. In fact, she'd never sounded so serious. "You have to see what they're willing to do."

After Harding's death, two bodies were recovered from the water off Danskammer Beach. One belonged to a local girl, Mandy Welsh. The second body has yet to be identified. Spencer Harding's house was also searched, and thanks to information gathered from Danill Chertov, a hidden room was uncovered.

"It's been called a sex dungeon."

"I would say that's an apt description."

"What did you find?"

"A safe filled with pictures. Thousands of Polaroids of girls lying lifeless on the bed in the sex dungeon."

"Pictures like the one Rosamund Harding had hidden in her locker."

"Yes, sir.

"Why Polaroids?"

"No digital files means you can't be hacked. As long as you can keep the physical photos under lock and key, you don't have to worry about anyone seeing them."

"But it sounds like Rosamund Harding found one."

"Yes. It seems one of the photos never made it into Harding's safe. His wife may have stumbled across it."

"That must have been extremely disturbing for her."

"I'm sure it was. Some of the photos we retrieved from that house will probably haunt me for the rest of my life."

"Why did Rosamund Harding hide the photo in a gym locker? Why didn't she go straight to the police?"

"We believe she lived in fear of her husband. This was a brilliant, powerful man with more money than he could possibly spend. We know from her browsing history that she was desperate to escape. But no one came to her rescue, and in the end, the man she married took her life."

"How do you think Harding got away with it for so long?"

"No one would have ever guessed that a man like Spencer Harding would commit the kind of crimes he committed. He was a monster with a perfect mask."

"And Danill Chertov? What happened to him?"

"Mr. Chertov disappeared the same night Spencer Harding died. He left on a flight to Belarus the next morning."

"So the two men responsible for these horrible crimes both escaped justice."

"In *this* world, maybe. I believe they'll be paying for their crimes in the next."

"Well," Harriett said after Nessa turned off the television in disgust. "Now we have proof Rocca's one of the bad guys."

"We know he's a liar, for sure," Nessa said.

"No, it's more than that. He was involved in the murders somehow."

"How do you know he wasn't lying so he wouldn't look completely incompetent?" Jo asked.

"Because Rocca said he arrested Danill Chertov on the night of June eighth. He claims they kept him in custody until Chertov informed on his boss. Rocca said he used Chertov's intel to get an arrest warrant for Harding. But I know for a fact that none of that ever happened."

"How?" Nessa asked.

Harriett grinned. "Chertov broke into my house on June seventh. He's been in my compost pile ever since."

The room fell silent.

"So we're fucked," Jo finally said.

"Why?" Nessa asked.

"Don't you see? We can't prove Rocca lied without revealing that Harriett killed someone."

"Do *you two* believe that Rocca was involved?" Harriett asked her friends.

"Of course," Jo said.

"Then who else do we need to convince?"

WOLVES IN SHEEP'S CLOTHING

There were no more requests for interviews. After Chief Rocca's appearance on *Newsnight,* the episode of *They Walk Among Us* featuring Nessa and Jo was pulled from the podcast's website and replaced with an apology from Josh Gibbon. He refused to explain his actions to Jo over the phone, worried the conversation might be recorded. Later that day, Nessa spotted him pumping gas at a station in town, wearing a ridiculously unkempt beard and dark glasses. When confronted, Josh admitted that while he knew everything she and Jo had said to be true, he couldn't afford to stand by them. His credibility had taken a serious hit. He'd lost sponsors and received hate mail from thousands of listeners. He pleaded with her to leave him alone.

"Just take my number." She scribbled it down on a scrap of paper when he showed no sign of pulling out his own phone. "If you hear anything new or receive any tips, please let me know."

"Why?" he asked. "Spencer Harding is dead. He's not going to hurt anyone. Didn't the three of you get what you wanted?"

Not yet, Nessa thought as she watched Josh drive away. Harriett seemed confident that Rocca would be punished, but Nessa couldn't figure out how. If Harriett had a plan, she hadn't shared it. *I'll do my job,* she'd told Nessa. *You focus on yours.* Nessa's job was to identify Spencer Harding's victims, and two of the three girls still remained nameless.

That truth was tormenting Nessa several days later as she pushed a cart through the Stop & Shop aisles, her arm reaching out to grab the usual items as though it had a mind of its own. She was so lost in her thoughts that she got all the way from produce to canned goods before she finally sensed someone was following her. She spun around, hoping to catch the lurker off guard. Behind her was a woman Nessa recalled seeing in the parking lot who'd done a double take as Nessa passed her.

"You're Ms. James?" the woman asked shyly.

"I am," Nessa said, steeling herself for what might come next.

"My name is Mary Collins, and I've heard you have the sight," she half whispered. "My girl disappeared a year ago. We're from Queens, but she was out on the island visiting a friend when she vanished."

The woman pulled a photo, creased and dog-eared, from her wallet. When she held it out, Nessa took it, though she could hardly bear to look. Smiling back at her was a teenage girl with braids and braces.

"She's beautiful." Nessa stroked the face in the photo with her thumb and ordered herself to stay strong. "What's her name?"

"Lena. They told me she ran away from home—like that girl Mandy Welsh. I never believed them, but what could I do? Have you seen Lena, Ms. James? Can you tell me what happened to her?"

"I'm so sorry." It broke Nessa's heart to say the words. "I haven't seen your girl. But I'll be sure to keep an eye out for her. I promise I will."

The girl's mother looked so crestfallen as she tucked the photo back into her wallet that Nessa stepped forward and wrapped her arms around the woman.

"I miss her so much," Mrs. Collins whispered into Nessa's shoulder. "This whole time I haven't had any peace."

They stood there in the canned vegetable aisle, Nessa holding a woman she'd only just met as they both cried.

Later that afternoon, Nessa lay on Harriett's sofa, her brain thumping. The migraines were becoming a regular occurrence. Harriett made a tonic that helped relieve the pain, but the headaches usually returned by the next day. This one, though—it was worse than the others.

"The pain is telling you something," Harriett said. "It will go away once you get the message."

"For God's sake, what is it?" Nessa croaked. She had a hunch, but she didn't want to confront it.

"I don't know," Harriett responded. "It's not meant for me."

That conversation ended with a knock at Harriett's door.

"Pardon me for a moment," Harriett said. "That must be my next client."

FOR THE PAST FEW WEEKS, there had always seemed to be someone knocking on Harriett Osborne's door. Annette Moore kept track of the visitors. She'd lived in one of the houses across the street from 256 Woodland Drive ever since she returned home from her rained-out Hawaiian honeymoon two decades earlier. In all the years that she and Harriett Osborne had been neighbors, the two women had exchanged exactly sixty-two words. But the mental dossier Annette kept on Harriett was nothing short of exhaustive. She liked to think of herself as the eyes and ears of Woodland Drive, and the truth was, Harriett Osborne was the only resident worth watching. Throughout the months of July and August, Annette had noticed a steady stream of visitors to the Osborne house. The women—they were always women—would park their vehicles several blocks down the street and travel the rest of the way on foot. They clearly didn't want their cars to be spotted outside the witch house, as it had become known throughout Mattauk. They'd stand on the porch, one toe tapping nervously as they checked over their shoulders to make sure no one was watching, and wait for the front door to open. There were *always* people watching, of course. It wasn't just Annette. And a few of the visitors would have set tongues wagging. Among them, Annette recognized the mayor's trashy daughter-in-law and prissy Juliet Rocca, the chief of police's wife. But after what happened to the head of the homeowners association, Annette kept her mouth shut. Brendon Baker still showed up once a month to weep on the witch's front steps. Everyone in Mattauk knew all about it—and no one dared mess with Harriett Osborne.

According to Annette's observations, Harriett's guests usually stayed for twenty minutes. A few would disappear into her jungle for hours. But when the women emerged, they invariably carried a little brown baggie. As they speed-walked back to their cars, clutching the bag as though it were the most precious object, they all seemed a little more at ease in the world.

"You know, I think Harriett Osborne is selling marijuana out of her house," Annette said as she peeked between the blinds.

"Naw, Eric sells the pot. Shrooms, too," her teenage daughter replied absentmindedly as she shot aliens on the TV.

"Who's Eric?"

"You know, the hottie from the grocery store." No more explanation was needed. Mother and daughter both managed to be near the front window whenever Eric delivered Harriett's groceries.

"How do *you* know he's the one who sells drugs?" Annette demanded.

Her daughter rolled her bloodshot eyes. "Everyone knows," she said. "His prices are crazy good."

"I don't know who told you that," Annette snipped, "but you're not allowed to hang out with them anymore." She swiveled back toward the window just in time to see another woman rap on Harriett Osborne's front door. Annette gasped and pressed her forehead to the glass. "Oh my God, I think that woman works for your dad."

She remembered the woman from the Halloween party at her husband's dental practice. He'd forced his oral hygienists to dress as the backup singers from "Addicted to Love," a video which none of them were old enough to remember.

"Is it the lady with the great boobs or the one with the sweet ass?" the daughter inquired.

"Excuse me?" Annette glanced over her shoulder and saw an alien's head explode on the screen. "We don't talk about other women like that."

"Really? Then tell your revolting husband. That's how he refers to his 'girls' when his friends are around."

Annette felt nauseous. Truth was, she'd been nauseous for years. "My revolting husband happens to be your father."

"Yeah, don't remind me," said the girl.

Annette watched Harriett greet the hygienist, whose ass, even in scrubs, did appear to be sweet.

"If Harriett Osborne's not selling drugs, what are all of these ladies buying?"

Her daughter snickered. "Payback," she said.

Annette's daughter had never shown a gift for prophesy—or for anything, other than alien massacres. But in that one word, Annette suddenly saw her whole future. She let the blinds fall back into place and didn't say anything else.

The next night, Annette was lying in bed when her husband came home late from work. She remained silent and still as he headed straight for the bathroom as he always did. He liked to wash up before coming to bed. These little things she'd always blithely accepted—the late hours, the showers—had taken on new meaning. When he emerged a half hour later, Annette switched on the bedside lamp, ready to confront him. But her eyes were immediately drawn to a flaming red rash peeking out from the waistband of her husband's tighty-whities and inching its way up his belly.

"What is that?" she gasped in horror.

Her husband snatched a shirt out of a drawer and pulled it on, hiding the rash. "What does it look like?" he snapped. "You bought the wrong soap again."

He'd always been good at that—convincing her she hadn't seen what she'd seen. But Annette suspected the rash was Harriett's handiwork. Perhaps it was the payback the hygienist had been seeking. What could he have done to the woman to deserve such a punishment?

"No." Annette wasn't going to let it happen this time. "You didn't get that from soap. You got it from something *else* that you shouldn't have touched."

She slept in the guest room that night—and all the nights after that.

By the end of the week, the rash had conquered her husband's chest and scaled his neck past the collar of his shirt. Annette walked in on him in the bathroom as he was about to climb into an oatmeal bath and saw that it had consumed his entire body, all the way down to his ankles. She woke up that night to the sound of her husband tiptoeing past the guest room, down the stairs, and out the front door. Intrigued, she assumed her favorite position at the living room window. She saw him on his knees on Harriett Osborne's porch, his rash-covered fingers woven together as he begged. Harriett didn't appear to be listening. Her eyes had found Annette in the window across the street.

The next morning, after her husband went to work, Annette threw his clothes on the lawn and called an attorney. When the doorbell rang that afternoon, Annette opened the door to find Eric standing on her front porch. The sight of him in a tight T-shirt and jeans would have been gift enough. But he flashed his movie-star smile and held out a small brown paper bag.

Annette took it and looked inside. At the bottom were a few shriveled mushrooms.

"Harriett says these will help your depression."

"How does she know I'm depressed?" Annette wondered.

"If you weren't, you would have kicked that asshole to the curb a long time ago." Eric smiled again. "Those are her words, not mine."

"Let me get my purse," Annette said.

"No need," Eric told her. "They're a gift. And if you want some company, Harriett says feel free to stop by after business hours any time this week."

AFTER THE *NEWSNIGHT* DEBACLE, TRAFFIC briefly dipped at Furious Fitness. A handful of women canceled their memberships and a few were noticeably chillier. But most of Jo's clients came and went as they always had. Some even made a point of stopping to tell her she had their support. The first time it had happened, Jo had sprinted straight to a shower stall and turned the water on cold. Then she stepped under the frigid spray in her workout gear and sneakers. Steam had risen from her skin as she cried.

Lucy had proven remarkably resilient, just as Harriett had predicted. The two of them had begun spending hours together each week. Jo didn't know what they discussed, and when she asked, Lucy would find a way to dodge the question. But she seemed stronger and more self-assured every time she came home covered in dirt from Harriett's garden. It was Jo who couldn't forget what had happened. She ran ten miles every morning and worked out for hours after Lucy went to bed. Nothing she did seemed to help. The man they'd been after had escaped from justice. And most of Mattauk thought she was to blame.

The smug, satisfied face of Chief Rocca haunted her. It was his face she destroyed when she hit the punching bag. It was his face she pummeled with her fists when she ran. Not only was he a lying sack of shit and an accomplice to murder, he'd used the *Newsnight* interview to brazenly take credit for everything she, Nessa, and Harriett had done. None of them had expected to receive any praise. But to see their work ignored and their names besmirched—it was too much to take. Jo thought she'd left all that behind when she finally escaped the corporate world. But it didn't seem to matter where a woman was—there was always someone waiting to shove her out of the spotlight and into a steaming pile of shit.

She spent less time at the gym now, and more time with Lucy. After the break-in at their home, Jo hardly let the girl out of her sight. Every morning, Art found them both asleep in Lucy's twin bed. Jo had installed a security system, and new locks had been put on all the windows and doors. The house was a veritable fortress, but Jo never felt safe. Art understood, but she could see he was worried. At some point, Jo's need to protect their daughter would do more harm than good. Unable to send Lucy away, she'd already canceled her sleepaway camp.

"It's okay," she overheard Lucy telling Art. "Mom needs me to be here right now."

That night, Jo had spent hours on the Spin bike she'd had installed in the basement. She could have ridden to the moon and back—it wouldn't have made any difference. There was no way to burn off her rage or the terror that fueled it.

ON THE LAST DAY OF August, Jo got Lucy out of bed early. Art was headed to a meeting in Manhattan, so Jo took their daughter with her to open the gym. They were at the front door, with the key in the lock, when Jo spotted the reflection of someone coming up behind them.

Before Jo could react, Lucy wheeled around like a miniature ninja, her fists clenched and her arms poised to punch.

"Hey there," said a woman in black leggings and a windbreaker. She held out a hand to Lucy. "I'm Claude." There was nothing patronizing about the gesture.

"Lucy," the girl replied, unclenching a fist to shake the woman's hand.

"You've got quite a bodyguard," Claude told Jo. "I wouldn't want to mess with her."

"She's pretty tough." Jo hugged her daughter proudly, then gave Claude a once-over. "You look like you're raring to go this morning. We don't usually open for another hour or so. The bees still bothering you out on the Pointe?"

"They haven't been quite as bad since Jackson's been in the hospital," Claude said.

Jo grimaced. "Oh God. He's still in there?"

"Leonard told me he's being released soon. I know this will sound horrible, but it's been much more pleasant on the Pointe without him. This has been my first harassment-free summer in ages."

"Morning!" Heather, Jo's assistant manager, joined them, and Jo stepped aside so she could open the doors. "Well, hello there, Miss Lucy. I could use some help getting things ready. If we get our work done fast enough, I can buy you a smoothie before we open."

"Yes!" Lucy raced inside to get started.

"You are a saint for offering, but you do not have to babysit," Jo told Heather.

"Babysit?" Heather scoffed. "Lucy's one of the best workers around—and she's definitely the cheapest."

"Okay then," Jo said. "But the second you need some kid-free time, you just let me know." She held the door as Heather passed through and waited for Claude to come inside as well.

"Actually, I'm not here to work out," Claude admitted. Her tone had changed, and some of her confidence seemed to have slipped away. "I was wondering if you might have a few minutes. I have a question I'd like to ask you."

"Okay," Jo said. "What is it?"

"Come across the street for a quick cup of coffee?" Claude asked.

"Sure," Jo said. "I can spare a few minutes." She opened the gym door and peeked her head inside. Heather and Lucy were unwrapping the previous day's laundry. "I'll be back in a sec."

"No worries," Heather said. "Lucy and I got this. Take your time."

The café had only opened a few minutes earlier, and they were the first and only customers. Claude bought a coffee while Jo grabbed a juice. Then they chose a table near the front window.

The morning light was unforgiving. Claude appeared pale and on the verge of tears. "First of all, I just want to tell you how sorry I am."

"For what?" Jo asked.

"For what happened to your beautiful daughter—" Claude paused to wipe her eyes and gain control of herself. "And to all those other girls. I knew Spencer was rotten. I knew he had something to do with Rosamund's death. But I had no idea he was capable of such atrocities. And to think it was happening right under my nose! I haven't been able to sleep in weeks."

"I think there have been a lot of people going without sleep lately," Jo told her, hoping they could move on to a different subject.

"Well, I want to do something," Claude said. "I want to make sure nothing like this ever happens again."

The words struck a familiar chord. Jo had told Lucy the very same thing. "Do you have something in mind?"

"No, but I bet we could come up with something together. Something big."

"Something big?" Jo smiled, wondering where this was all going. "Okay."

"Leonard says he'll fund it. He feels terrible, too."

Jo's smile faded. Claude was serious.

"Between you and me, I've never touched a dime of his cash," Claude said. "But this is important to me. No one teaches girls how to take care of themselves. We train them to be pretty and kind and polite right before we set them loose in a world filled with wolves. Then we act surprised and horrified when some of them get eaten. After my father died, I came very close to being one of those girls. The only thing that saved me back then was luck."

Jo thought of her own upbringing. Her good, solid, middle-class mother had tried so hard to iron out her rough edges—and blamed herself when she realized she hadn't succeeded. Those rough edges had rubbed quite a few people the wrong way. Somehow Jo had always sensed those weren't the kind of people she wanted around her. And as she grew older, she saw that those who wanted girls to be docile and disciplined were often the same people who took advantage of them.

"What if we created a program for girls that combines assertiveness training, self-defense, and martial arts?" Jo suggested. It was something she'd daydreamed about countless times in the past. "So the next time some asshole snatches someone's kid off the street, he gets a lot more than he bargained for."

"Yes! I love it!" Claude exclaimed. "We can do a pilot here in Mattauk. And then we'll use Leonard's money to take it national. Maybe even global."

It was moving too fast and sounding too good to be true. "That's pretty ambitious," Jo said. "And expensive."

"Leonard said he'll give us twenty million if we come up with something good."

That couldn't be right. "Twenty million *dollars*?"

"He gives hundreds of millions to charity every year. Twenty million is just a drop in the bucket. Plus, he has an ulterior motive. He needs to wash some of the taint off Culling Pointe."

"Oh my God, Claude."

"We can get more if we show we're successful. We could start an organization devoted to preparing girls for the world. You could be the CEO."

"Me?" Jo repeated. Her head was spinning.

"Why not? You're a successful businessperson. You know the world of fitness, and you kick serious butt. Plus, you have a girl of your own. I know this all sounds crazy, but if Leonard says yes, would you be interested?"

Jo figured it wouldn't look terribly professional if she leaped from the table and jumped up and down. "I'll need to discuss it with my husband."

"Of course!" Claude agreed. "Maybe we could do a little market research just to prove to ourselves and our gentlemen friends that the idea could work. Do you think we could use your social media accounts to send out an invite for a free self-defense class for girls? We could see how many young people come—and how many of their moms sign up for Furious Fitness memberships before they leave."

"Sure. I'll get on it right away," Jo told her.

It wasn't the CEO title that appealed to her most—or the millions they'd be able to spend. The program itself could be just what she needed—a way to teach Lucy how to fight for herself. The solution seemed so simple now. The relief it brought Jo was intoxicating, and the gratitude she felt was beyond expression.

"Wonderful! I suppose I should let you get back to work now," Claude said as she gathered her things. "By the way, would you mind asking your friend Harriett to reach out to me? We're still having a terrible time with those flowering bushes that have taken over the Pointe. I'm hoping she'll know how to help."

Jo felt her brow furrow. "I'd be happy to."

ART ARRIVED HOME WITH HIS own good news. His latest play had found a backer. Casting would begin at the end of the month. The money was surprisingly good, but Jo's delight had nothing to do with the family finances. Art finally felt like her partner again. That evening, Jo cooked everyone's favorite lasagna, Art made strawberry shortcake, and the Levisons enjoyed their best family dinner in years.

After the dishes were washed, Jo picked up Nessa and the two of them drove to Harriett's. They found her on her hands and knees in the garden, harvesting seeds from the spiky pods of a large, tropical-looking plant. When she saw them, she sat back on her haunches.

"You have news." Harriett stood up and eyed Jo closely. "Does it call for champagne? Chase left a stash in the cellar."

"Wouldn't hurt." Jo hadn't been able to stop smiling all day.

"I'll grab a bottle." Harriett passed her basket to Nessa.

"What are these?" Nessa ran her fingers through the reddish-brown seeds. "They're pretty."

"Castor beans," Harriett told her.

"For castor oil?" Nessa asked. Her grandmother had rubbed a little on her skin every night before bed and taken a tablespoon every morning by mouth to help keep her regular.

"Mmmhmm." Harriett hurried toward the house. "Wait here."

Nessa watched until she was sure Harriett was out of earshot. "She seem a bit off to you?" she asked Jo.

Jo laughed. "Are you kidding? Harriett's never been *on*."

"You ever wonder what she knows that we don't?" Nessa asked.

"Every day," Jo said. "I almost want to give her a call when I wake up in the morning and ask her if I should bother getting out of bed."

Harriett soon reappeared in the garden with a bottle of champagne in one hand, three flutes in the other, and two more bottles tucked under her arms. Nessa rushed over to help her.

"Geez, Harriett. Do you figure we have enough champagne?" Jo asked.

"We'll see," Harriett said. "There's more where that came from. Have a seat. I'll start a fire."

Jo and Nessa sat side by side on a wooden bench that faced a fire pit Harriett had built in her garden. The late-August day had been blistering hot, but the evening breeze that came in off the ocean was cool and sweet. Soon a fire was dancing inside the circle of rocks, which resembled a miniature pagan henge.

"Now," Harriett said once they all had full glasses in their hands. "Tell me."

"You sure you're ready?" Jo joked. "You don't want to make some pigs in a blanket or knit us all flute cozies?"

"I'm ready." Harriett seemed to have lost her sense of humor.

"Okay then." Jo shot a quick glance at Nessa, who was gazing at her champagne with thirsty eyes.

As Jo recounted the events of the morning, Harriett listened closely. She didn't ask any questions. She drank in the information like soil absorbing the rain.

"I know what this means after what happened to Lucy," Harriett said when Jo had finished. For a moment she seemed more human than usual—like the woman Jo had met in a parking lot years before. "Here's to both of you." She lifted her glass and drained its contents in a single gulp.

It was an oddly somber toast.

"Wow," Jo said.

"Yes, here's to Jo." Nessa lifted her champagne glass and put on a cheerful smile.

"*Skål.*" Harriett guzzled her second glass of champagne, then humorlessly poured herself a third and downed that one, too.

"Thanks, guys." Jo wondered if her announcement had conjured bad memories for Harriett. Perhaps she should have been more sensitive. She knew Harriett's advertising career had ended abruptly. But it was hard to believe that anything as mundane as a job could remain a sore spot for the woman Harriett had become.

While Jo and Nessa chatted, Harriett couldn't seem to sit still. She had quickly drained most of the first bottle of champagne by herself, but she didn't appear to be drunk. She walked among the plants in her garden like a general inspecting her troops, stopping to sniff at a leaf here, judge the plumpness of a berry there. The silver in her hair had overtaken the blond, and it reflected the moon's shimmering light.

"So what does Art think?" Nessa asked Jo. "He must be proud."

"Oh, definitely." Jo beamed. "Doesn't hurt that he got some good news of his own today. His latest play is being produced! He met with the investors this morning."

"That's wonderful! I'm so glad things are turning around for you. I was starting to wonder if we'd all been cursed." Nessa's good cheer faded as she reached up to massage her temples. She was sure her brain was about to burst out of her skull.

"How are the migraines?" Jo asked quietly.

Nessa wished she could report that they were improving. But the truth was, she'd spent most of the day in her darkened bedroom. She'd been leaving Harriett's potions unconsumed, hoping she'd finally understand the message that the headaches were trying to send her. The pain felt like a writhing ball of chaos, static composed of unintelligible voices. Sometimes, when she listened closely, it would seem as if a single word or thought might break through. But then, just as quickly, it would sink back under and be lost in the din.

Nessa looked up to see Harriett looming over her. She handed Nessa a tiny bottle of green gunk. "Drink it," she ordered, and watched as her command was obeyed. Then she took a seat at the fire and turned her attention to Jo. The unearthly golden glow had returned to Harriett's eyes.

"Did she mention the weeds?" Harriett directed the question at Jo.

"Sorry?" Jo responded.

"Claude," Harriett said. "Did she mention the Scotch broom?"

"As a matter of fact, she did," Jo told her. "Apparently, the plants have taken over the Pointe. Claude asked if you might be willing to help with the problem. I'd be really grateful if you did, Harriett. I know you hate the people out there, but I'd consider it a personal favor."

"Are you able to contact her?" Harriett asked.

"Sure," Jo said. She'd copied the phone number from Claude's membership file into her contacts.

"Tell her to have someone meet me on Jackson Dunn's dock at eight tomorrow morning."

THE DAY HARRIETT FINALLY
OPENED HER EYES

Harriett lay on her back in the garden, gazing up at the chaste tree. She'd watched it grow from a seedling, and earlier in the year, it had achieved a glorious adulthood. Only a few months before, it had worn a corona of lavender blossoms. Now those blooms had withered, fallen off, and returned to the soil. The berries had been harvested, and the tree had disrobed for the winter.

The air was warm for October, but a frost had settled over the garden the previous night, and the ground beneath her still held a chill. Her robe was close at hand, tossed over a nearby bush, but she never reached for it. Harriett liked nothing between her skin and the earth. That summer, she'd discovered that a different world lay beneath her. One busier than the city at rush hour, yet as tranquil and dark as the shore just before dawn. She could feel mycelium weaving a net just below the surface, the roots of the plants pushing ever deeper, and earthworms slipping like silk through the soil.

She'd purchased marijuana for the first time three weeks earlier. She'd smoked it with Chase many times in the past, but had never liked the way it slowed her down. Back then, she had enjoyed pot like a forced vacation—begrudgingly, one eye on the clock. But for the first time in decades, Harriett had nowhere to go and no one to meet. And all she wanted, more than anything, was to bring the world to a halt.

Harriett had pushed herself after Chase left in August. She figured she'd leaped higher hurdles than him in the past. She intended to throw herself into her work and make Max recognize her as the partner she'd long been. Then, before she could settle on the perfect words, the announcement was made. Max's dream partner would soon be joining the agency. After months of pleading, he'd finally persuaded Chris Whitman to relocate to New York from London.

Harriett had tried digging a hole for her disappointment as she had in the past, but this time, it refused to stay buried. Instead, it grew tendrils that wrapped around her and squeezed. By the beginning of October, she had found herself barely able to function. That's when the pharmacy called to tell Harriett that her birth control prescription was ready for pickup—and she realized she hadn't had a period in more than four months.

Already injured, Harriett found herself floored by the insult. She'd avoided pregnancy her entire life. For reasons she hadn't shared with a soul, she'd never once contemplated procreating. Now Harriett's husband was busy trying to knock up another woman—and her own traitorous body was ordering her to close up shop. It wasn't as if she wanted her period back—and she still had no desire for children. But she wanted the fucking option, and now, in an epic act of cruelty, the universe had denied her even that.

The day after Max's big announcement, Harriett bought two ounces of pot and declared she was taking a few weeks off. She had every intention of driving down to the Carolinas, where the beaches would be warm. Then she'd popped out to the garden to smoke a joint, and everything around her had come to a stop. Three weeks later, she still hadn't left.

After she fired the landscapers in September, Harriett let the garden grow wild. Chase had always kept it clipped and pruned within an inch of its life. Now that Harriett was free, she figured the garden should be, too. The vegetation ran riot in no time, and she found she loved nothing more than to sit back and watch. No longer restrained, the dainty rosebushes around the perimeter revealed their true natures, redirecting their energy away from blooms and into extending their stems and taunting trespassers with their thorns. The pretty little perennials engineered to delight the human eye found their flower beds pillaged by hardier species to whom the earth truly belonged. Stoned, Harriett existed on the timescale of the plant world. Her companions were slow, but now she could see they were sentient, intelligent, and very much alive.

Once the sidewalk in front of the house had disappeared from view, she often heard passersby talking about her. Even when she was out of sight, she seemed to be very much on her neighbors' minds.

"Has anyone checked on her lately?" she overheard a woman say.

"She's lost her damn mind," someone else diagnosed.

"Brendon Baker will get her all sorted out," a man told a companion.

"Milo told me she's gonna get eaten by cats," a child weighed in another day.

Lying on a bed of soil, Harriett listened and wondered if they might be right. She wasn't behaving as a woman in her late forties should. She'd maintained a steady high since that first joint in the garden, and put a serious dent in her dilettante ex's collection of wine. Once morning glory vines had sewn up the last few gaps in the wall of foliage that surrounded the house, she'd taken to spreading out on a lawn chair in her underwear. Then those few strips of cloth disappeared, followed shortly by the lawn chair. *This isn't normal*, Harriett often told herself. Then her eyes would latch onto a butterfly and follow it as it lazily looped across the sky.

For the first time in ages, she'd found a place that welcomed her—one where she felt she truly belonged. So much of the human world seemed designed to exclude her. There, men valued women for their youth and fertility. Those who could no longer procreate were cast aside. But now Harriett knew nature wasn't prone to mistakes. Her grandparents had looked to the Bible for God's word, never realizing it was written on the world all around them. That scripture was telling Harriett she was still around for a reason— and would be for decades. If she was going to spend those years in her garden, Harriett wanted to know more about it.

Deliveries arrived from rare bookstores across the country. Every evening, she'd bring in the boxes stacked in towering piles on her doorstep and rip them apart in a frenzy. She'd lost all interest in everything beyond her garden. There was so much to learn about the things she'd discovered within. She bought books to identify the new plants that had commandeered the flower beds and books that might hold the cure for the unusual rash on her leg. She ordered books on entomology and biochemistry to find out why the bugs never nibbled the mint and why thyme drove the bees wild. After a hawk dropped the corpse of a squirrel at her feet, she devoured a nineteenth-century tome on the ancient art of augury. She found a suggested dosage for jimsonweed seeds in the diary of a colonial-era cunning woman, then spent an entire night tracking the constellations as they sailed across the sky. She devoured the private journals of Catherine Monvoisin, the infamous poisoner, and chased them down with biographies of Agrippina the Younger and Lucrezia Borgia. She developed a recipe for a magnificent pesto.

She was reading up on rootwork one evening when the doorbell rang. Without pulling her eyes from the book, she'd opened the door.

"Well, hello there!" The handsome deliveryman was standing on the other side of the threshold with three stuffed grocery bags in his arms and a shit-eating grin on his face.

A week had passed since his last visit, and during that time, Harriett had given up clothes. "So sorry!" She'd reached for a bag and used it to cover her shame, certain he could see through her skin to her shriveled, old ovaries.

"No apologies necessary," he assured her. "I'm Eric, by the way."

She'd come to think of herself as a hideous crone. But Eric certainly hadn't seemed scarred by the sight. Maybe, she thought, she'd been mistaken. Maybe that wasn't how it all really worked.

IT WAS THE LAST DAY of her three-week vacation, and Harriett was basking in the sunshine when she heard a car pull into her drive. The sound of the doorbell didn't rouse her, and she managed to ignore the persistent knocking that followed.

"Harriett Osborne!" a man finally called out. "Are you back there? Can you hear me?"

The man's brusque intrusion into her thoughts jolted Harriett upright. He'd given up at the front door. Now she could hear him prodding at the vegetation surrounding the garden, looking for a way past her defenses. She snatched up her robe and held it to her chest. "Who are you?" she demanded.

"It's Colin Clarke!" A long pause followed as Harriett racked her brain for a clue to the man's role in her life. "I'm the lawyer representing you in your divorce." He sounded concerned, as though she'd forgotten the president's name. The man was important. She should have known who he was.

"Of course!" Harriett jumped to her feet and wrapped the robe tightly around her, but somehow couldn't figure out what her next step should be.

"My office has been trying to reach you for days," he called through the plants.

"Oh no, I'm so sorry!" She had no idea where she'd last seen her phone. She didn't know an explanation was required, so she didn't bother to give one.

"Mrs. Osborne—" he started again, clearly worried.

"*Ms.*" She didn't really say it. The word just slipped out.

There was a pause. "*Ms.* Osborne, may I come inside? Your husband and his attorney have an offer they'd like me to present."

"Inside?" The house could use a good cleaning, and it reeked of pot.

"Is that a problem?" he asked, his voice now teetering on the line between concerned and frustrated. "*Ms.* Osborne, is everything all right?"

"I'll meet you at the front door," she said, though she was sure she'd regret it.

When she opened the door, she realized she'd screwed up. She'd met the man on her doorstep exactly three times, and each time she'd been in tears when they parted. She'd known Colin Clarke by reputation long before she hired him. Everyone said he was the best divorce attorney in Mattauk. He specialized in representing well-off women whose husbands had retained Manhattan heavy hitters. Clarke was famously cold and formal. He made it clear to his clients that they would never be friends. The questions he asked would at times seem brutal. He might need to know things they wouldn't want to share. But if they were honest and forthright, he'd ensure they left their marriages with every cent they deserved. Now he was standing in Harriett's doorway in a lovely Italian suit—and an expression that made it clear that he was not at all pleased with her.

It had been weeks since Harriett had cared much about her appearance. There were likely leaves in her hair and fur on her legs. Having walked around naked for days, the robe felt like a sober-minded nod to convention. But Mr. Clarke clearly did not agree. His eyebrows lifted as his head reared back. For a moment, she wondered if she might smell terrible, too.

"Are you sure this isn't a bad time?" he asked.

"Yes," she told him. "Please, come in."

As he walked past her, she read his reaction in his stiffened spine. When she turned back toward her living room, she realized why. Almost every inch of flat surface was claimed by pots, each holding a plant of a unique size, color, and shape. Only the coffee table had been put to a different use. It held the remains of Harriett's last meal, as well as a large cannister that had once been filled with marijuana. Beside it lay empty rolling paper packets.

"I've taken up gardening," Harriett said.

"So it seems," Clarke replied in a soothing voice, as though she might be dimwitted or dangerous.

"The south-facing windows make the living room an ideal greenhouse." For some reason she couldn't quite fathom, she needed him to understand.

"Do you know what all of these plants are?"

The question threw her. It was something one might ask a child. "Of course," Harriett replied self-consciously. "I bought or gathered the seeds myself. By April, the plants will be ready for the garden."

"Ah yes, the *garden*," he said with a sigh. "I drive past on my way to work every day."

"It's much more interesting on the inside. I'll show you around, and then we can chat," Harriett offered. "The garden really is wonderful this time of year."

The idea didn't appear to appeal to him. "Are you certain we'll have a place to sit?"

It was another strange question. "Of course," she said.

BEFORE THE ATTORNEY HAD ARRIVED, she'd been lying on a patch of bare dirt in the center of the garden. She'd cleared the ground herself the previous day. Soon, she'd build a compost heap on that spot. The imprint of her naked body remained in the dirt. Around it, a fairy circle of thirteen white mushrooms had sprung up.

"Look at these beauties!" Harriett squatted down as if to greet old friends face-to-face. "So that's what I felt growing beneath me. *Chlorophyllum molybdites.* Highly poisonous. My mother was an avid mushroom hunter. She used to call it 'the vomiter.'"

"Careful," said the attorney, reaching out as though to drag her back.

"Why?" Harriett laughed and looked up. "I don't plan to eat them."

Her gaiety drained away as she watched the man's eyes roam her garden. What he saw was wild and dangerous. She rose to her feet and guided him to two chairs that stood facing each other on the garden's last remaining slab of concrete. As she sat down across from the lawyer, she caught a glimpse of her dirty feet and hair-covered legs and wished she could tuck them beneath her. When she spoke, she did her best to sound sane.

"So, Mr. Clarke. What does my ex want from me now?"

Clarke opened his briefcase and pulled out a document. "Your husband is offering to purchase this house and the land on which it stands. Given the current state of the property, I'd say his offer is quite generous."

Harriett shook her head. The suggestion was silly. "This is my house," she said. "I gave Chase first choice of the properties. His lady friend decided she wanted the apartment in Brooklyn. So I took the house. It was all decided months ago. As far as I'm concerned, the arrangement has worked out beautifully."

"Apparently he's received a few phone calls from concerned neighbors. I've witnessed the evolution of your garden myself, and I'm afraid I've also heard the chatter about town. Everyone in Mattauk is talking about the weeds."

"What weeds?" Harriett asked.

Temporarily speechless, Clarke sat back in his chair. Then he pulled in a deep breath, apparently determined to see his mission through. "I don't ordinarily make recommendations of this sort, Ms. Osborne, but in this case, I feel the need to. You are clearly struggling to take care of your property. And when I tried to reach you at work, I was informed that you've been taking some time off. Take the money your husband has offered, Ms. Osborne. It's a substantial sum. Buy yourself an apartment and hire someone to help you. You'll be able to live comfortably for the rest of your life."

Harriett had seen the look on his face before. After her parents died, her grandparents had worn it as well. She scared him—the way she'd once frightened them. Without uttering a single word on the subject, they'd made it clear that something about her wasn't right. It seemed Mr. Clarke dealt with fear the same way her grandparents had—by turning it into disgust.

"I don't understand," she said, attempting to adopt a logical tone. "What makes you think the property isn't exactly the way I want it?"

"For heaven's sake, look around you, Ms. Osborne!" he cried, as though making one last-ditch appeal to what little of her sanity was left. He rose from his seat and cupped a bunch of purple berries that dripped off the end of a scarlet stem. "I don't know what these are, but my wife spends half her time uprooting plants just like this from our yard. You're letting them grow into giants."

"That's pokeweed, and I planted it. The berries are generally written off as poisonous to humans, but there are healers who swear they can treat skin diseases and various forms of inflammation. I thought I'd investigate."

What she'd been convinced was a perfectly reasonable response was greeted with thinly veiled scorn. "You thought *you'd* investigate? Do you have a medical degree?"

"No," Harriett countered, without much confidence. "But I have read a fair amount on the subject, and as you pointed out, I do have time on my hands."

Clarke gaped at her like she'd announced she was building a spaceship to travel to Mars, then glanced down. "What's this?" With the tip of his shoe, he nudged a tangled clump of green spilling over the sides of a planter she and Chase had purchased on their honeymoon in Provence.

"It's red clover."

"Isn't clover considered a weed?"

"By people who don't know any better. This summer, I harvested the flowers to make tea."

His eyes widened comically. "Did you *drink* it?"

Harriett's throat was tight and tears had sprung to her eyes. If she'd known why she was under attack, she might have fought back. The fact that Clarke's cruelty was unprovoked made it smart all the more. What was the point of this, she wondered? Why had this man she barely knew—this man she was *paying*—come to her house to berate and humiliate her?

"Women have been drinking clover tea for hundreds, maybe even thousands, of years. It helps regulate our hormones during perimenopause."

Clarke squirmed with discomfort and promptly changed the subject. "And this lovely thicket?" He swiped his hand across a patch of plants whose formerly bright yellow parasols were now turning brown. "What purpose do these plants serve?"

Harriett winced. "That's wild parsnip. It really doesn't like to be touched." The plant contained a powerful phototoxin. She would need to give him a salve to soothe the rash that would cover his hand by the end of the day.

"So you're telling me you *purposely* grew all the weeds in this garden."

"I didn't say that." He was putting words in her mouth.

She pulled her gaze away from him and let her eyes roam the garden. There wasn't a leaf she didn't recognize or a seed she didn't know how to use. Once colder weather arrived in mid-November, the vegetation would die and the neighbors could rejoice. But next spring, when the plants from her living room joined the garden, Harriett's magnificent vision would be realized. This was *her* land they were standing on, she reminded herself, and yet this man was insisting she view the garden through *his* eyes. Where she saw promise and possibility, he saw proof of a broken mind. Harriett knew she would never convince him of her sanity, so she found herself faced with a choice. She could either believe her own eyes—or she could see what the man told her to see.

It wouldn't have been such a leap, truth be told. She'd been seeing things through men's eyes for years. Her entire career, men had informed her what was good and what wasn't. And she'd always assumed they were right. Even if an ad was meant to speak to women like her, a male creative director would decide if it was worthy of airtime. They'd listen to her opinion, but the final call was theirs. After a decision was made, you either drank the Kool-Aid—or you found yourself another job.

What made them so confident in their vision, Harriett wondered? And what had kept her from insisting on her own? She'd always hated Chase's design for the garden. Every spring, she'd ask if they could try something different. And every fucking year, Chase's vision would prevail.

"I introduced half of the plants to this garden," Harriett said. "The other half showed up on their own."

"That's an odd way to grow a garden, don't you think? No wonder it's out of control."

"It's nature," Harriett said.

"It's hideous," Clarke countered.

Harriett smiled and cocked her head. Suddenly, everything seemed clear. "Mr. Clarke, do you find my garden offensive because you can't control it?"

"Gardens are where nature is trained and domesticated. You've let it run rampant. Do you want your neighbors to consider your property an eyesore?"

Harriett nodded. At last she understood why he'd come. He didn't want to look at her garden; therefore, it shouldn't exist. He'd landed on a solution he believed would suit everyone. Chase would have his house. The town would have its monument to good taste. And Harriett and her garden would be back under control.

"Tell me, Mr. Clarke—is there a reason I should care what you think?"

"Excuse me?"

"I'm genuinely curious." She crossed one leg over the other so he could get a good look at how furry it was. "Can you give me one good reason?"

"I'm not the only one who's concerned, Harriett."

"Ms. Osborne."

"Ms. Osborne. Most of your neighbors share my view."

"Perhaps, but I'm an adult, and this is my house. I can grow what I like in my garden. Wear what I choose. What difference does it make what you or anyone else thinks is normal? Why the fuck should I care if you approve?"

"I'm merely concerned—"

Harriett stopped him. Her smile spread like sunshine across her face. She hadn't felt this good in ages. "You're *concerned*? How sweet of you. Are we related in some way? Are we friends? Have I been over to your house for dinner? Are any of your children named after me?"

"No," he admitted. "But you are my client."

"Yes, and I believe you've been well compensated, am I right? Have I failed to pay any of your bills?"

"No."

"Then I'm not sure what your cause for concern might be. Do your male clients receive this level of service?"

"I'm afraid you've misunderstood—"

"No," Harriett snapped, cutting him off. "I haven't. You came here to run me out of the neighborhood. I've been paying you by the hour to settle my divorce, and now you're here wasting both my time and my money. You've been feeding on me a little too long, Mr. Clarke. The house is mine. As soon as you leave, I'll find a new attorney. And don't you dare send me a bill for this visit."

"Ms. Osborne—" Clarke stopped and reached up to the skin on the left side of his neck, where there was a sizable black nub just above his collar. Moments earlier, it had been a mere speck. She could see it growing, its body ballooning with blood as the lawyer's faced turned white. "Oh my God, it's a tick!"

She'd been thinking about parasites right before it appeared. Had she conjured it? If so, what else could she do? The tick was the size of a dime now, much bigger than any she'd ever seen. Its head remained buried in the lawyer's flesh, and despite his frantic efforts to remove it, the parasite refused to let go. How much bigger could it get? Harriett wondered. She licked her lips and waited to see.

"I know what it is, Mr. Clarke," Harriett said. "I'm perfectly capable of recognizing a bloodsucker when I see one. Perhaps you should follow my example and remove yours before it bleeds you dry."

LATER THAT DAY, AFTER THE sun had set, there was a knock at the door. Harriett flung it open at once, fully prepared to confront the next challenge. On the other side of the door was the handsome deliveryman, her grocery bags cradled in his arms. They stood there, face-to-face. Eric didn't remind her of Chase, and he bore so little resemblance to Clarke that it was hard to imagine they shared the same species.

"May I ask you a question?" Harriett inquired.

"Sure," he said.

"What do you think of my living room?" She stepped to the side so he could see it clearly. She watched his eyes tour her indoor garden.

"Yeah, I've been meaning to ask you about that," he replied cautiously.

"Really?" Harriett steeled herself for disappointment. Maybe all men were the same after all.

"Looks like you've got a real green thumb."

The grin returned. "I guess you could say that."

"Well, I've been having some trouble with rot in my grow room, and I was wondering if you might be interested in taking a look. I don't have much money, but I could pay you in product."

Harriett beamed. "Please. Come inside," she said.

He was still asleep in her bed the next morning when she pulled on a Tom Ford–era Gucci skirt and took the train into Manhattan for what, she half knew, would be her last day of work.

WHALES

ndrew Howard had taken the kids to visit his parents, and Harriett and Celeste had spent the night in the cabin of Celeste's boat. Enveloped in a fog of intoxicating smoke, their skin sticky with sweat and salt, they'd explored every last inch of each other's skin. The sex in Celeste's previous relationships had settled into a predictable pattern after two or three months. She'd always assumed that once you found something you enjoyed, you should do your best to repeat it. Four months had passed since that first afternoon with Harriett, and new discoveries kept being made. Celeste never knew how Harriett would decide to take her—and she never anticipated how she would respond. It was a quest with no destination. An adventure without a map. Celeste realized she'd never really known her own body. Without inhibitions or anxieties to limit her, there was nowhere she wouldn't go. She didn't look to the future, and she no longer dwelled on the past. Falling for Harriett had freed her from all that.

At sunrise, Harriett had risen from bed. That wasn't unusual. Harriett never seemed to need sleep. But when an hour had passed and she hadn't returned, Celeste went up top to find her. There was no one on deck, but she didn't panic. Then she'd heard a faint splashing in the distance. Using binoculars, she scanned the horizon. There was Harriett, buck naked, doing the breaststroke. A whale breached in the distance, then disappeared beneath the waves.

Now Harriett stood on the bow of the boat as it neared the

Pointe, a white dress pinned to her form by the wind. Her long, sun-stained limbs could have been carved from oak, and a silver-streaked nimbus of hair framed her head. Celeste brought the boat alongside Jackson Dunn's dock, where Leonard Shaw was waiting to greet his guest.

When Harriett gave Celeste a kiss, she seemed unusually tense. "Meet me back here at ten, please," she said. Then she stepped down onto the dock.

Standing at the boat's wheel, Celeste suddenly recalled the story of how Culling Pointe had gotten its name. Maybe she was still a bit stoned, she thought. She could see the deer being herded into the water and drowned—all because they'd dared to walk on their hind legs. On a rock outcropping above the beach, a woman in a black dress swung from the gallows. The men who'd strung her up watched as her body's death spasms subsided. She hadn't been a witch, of course. Just a woman who'd been taught how to bring life into the world and trained to know which herbs could postpone death.

Now, four hundred years later, a real witch had come to Culling Pointe. Celeste smiled at the thought. They had no clue what they were in for.

LEONARD HELD OUT A HAND from the dock and Harriett took it. His flesh was warm and as smooth as a wax poppet. As soon as she was on land, he pulled his hand away as though he'd touched something unpleasant. A year ago, she might have found him charming, this fifty-five-year-old billionaire dressed in All Stars and paint-splattered khakis. She would have read volumes into the rumpled hair, intelligent eyes, and approachable grin. Such things had meant a great deal to her once. Now they meant nothing at all.

"Hello," he greeted her. "I'm so grateful you've come."

"Thank you for meeting me," Harriett said just as the whale appeared a few hundred yards away. "I brought someone to see you."

Leonard smiled. "She does seem to follow you around," he jested.

"I met her last summer," Harriett told him. "The day after my husband left me, I went to sit by the water, and she appeared. We've been friends ever since."

"I assume you're joking, but female humpbacks are quite social," Leonard said. "They often form long-term friendships with other females."

Harriett beamed as she shook her head. "I wasn't joking at all."

Leonard smiled back at her. He wasn't easily thrown. Harriett found him intriguing, and she wasn't sure why. That was one of the reasons she'd come. There were others, of course. Some of them were still taking form in her mind.

"Do you know much about whales?" he asked casually.

"I know that they're out there," Harriett told him. "I think it's hard for most people to wrap their heads around the idea that there are enormous creatures below the surface that they're unable to see. They'd rather sit on the beach and admire the sunrise and pretend there's nothing lurking under the waves."

"But you know."

"I do. And once you know what's out there, you never forget," Harriett said.

"I hear them sometimes in the summer," Leonard said. "The males sing. No one knows why the females don't."

"Because they're listening," Harriett told him. "And remembering. By the time they're my age, they know all the songs and they know all the singers."

Leonard laughed. "I can see why Claude likes you. She claims to know all the songs, too."

"I bet she does," Harriett replied. "Where is she, by the way?"

"Back at the house. I'll take you for a short tour of the Pointe and we'll meet her back there for breakfast, if that works for you."

"Certainly," Harriett said. "My friend is picking me up at ten."

"Which friend—the lady or the whale?"

Harriett lifted an eyebrow. "Whoever gets here first, I'd imagine."

The dock ended in a wooden walkway that led up to a set of stairs and then continued over the dunes. Half a mile down the beach to their left sat Spencer Harding's house, which remained empty, its lawn overgrown and flower beds gone. Jackson Dunn's glass house was off to the right. A child and a dog frolicked in the sand, while the boy's mother watched from the porch, a steaming cup of coffee in her hand. In her wide-legged white sailor pants and navy boatneck shirt, she radiated old Hollywood glamour. Harriett had once envied such women— so perfectly turned out. In her youth, she'd imagined birds and woodland creatures doting on them, Cinderella-style, each morning. As she got older, she realized the secret wasn't magic. It was underpaid servants.

"That's Jackson's daughter and grandson," Leonard said. His head tilted back and Harriett followed suit. Someone standing at the roof deck railing quickly took a step back.

"Oh dear, I think Jackson may be avoiding me," Harriett said.

"On the contrary," Leonard replied. "He was the one who recommended you as a horticulturalist. He's probably on his way down to say hello."

And there was Jackson when they rounded the corner, waiting for them in the yard, dressed in the clothes of a larger man. During his weeks in the hospital, he seemed to have shriveled. His skin, once as brown and taut as a sausage, looked loose and faded. Behind him, several giant bushes erupted out of the soil, their branches ablaze with bright yellow blooms.

"Hello, Harriett," he said, tipping his cowboy hat from a careful distance. "You're looking—uh—anyways, it's good to see you."

"Jackson," she replied as her eyes feasted on what little was left of him. "I hear you spent some time in the hospital. How nice to see that you're on the mend."

"Yes, it was a close call, but I'm feeling much better, thank you. And thanks so much for coming out to the Pointe today." His voice quivered as he spoke. He was terrified of her now, and she relished it. Creatures like Jackson only understood power and fear. She'd finally gotten through to him. "I know Leonard's told you about our Scotch broom infestation." He presented the bushes beside him like a television spokesmodel. "I'm sorry to say that it may have started right here on my property. I feel terrible about it, and I'm willing to spend whatever it takes to deal with the problem."

Harriett suspected his checkbook was in his back pocket. "That's awfully kind of you, Jackson, but I'll charge you the same fees I'd charge anyone else."

Jackson smiled with relief, and a thought seemed to pop into his head. "Oh, and you'll be glad to know that next Memorial Day, we're gonna open up the roof deck to all our guests. Make it less of a pecker party up there."

"After all these years, you've finally decided to break with tradition?" Harriett asked.

"Yes, it's about time," Jackson replied.

"Well, it's certainly very optimistic of you," Harriett said. "To assume that there will be a next year."

A faint buzzing could be heard from the bushes, and Jackson glanced nervously over his shoulder. A pair of bees emerged and circled lazily overhead.

"If y'all will excuse me, I really should get back indoors."

"Thank you, Jackson," Leonard said. "I'll be in touch about the fees later."

"I enjoyed that encounter far more than I expected," Harriett announced cheerfully as they headed for the sidewalk.

"You obviously can't stand him," Leonard noted. "May I ask why?"

"I used to loathe Jackson," Harriett said. "Now I know such feelings are pointless. I don't hate anyone anymore, Mr. Shaw. I simply think Jackson Dunn is a blight on humanity."

As they reached the sidewalk, Harriett came to a stop and took a moment to admire the view. On Memorial Day, every lawn on the Pointe had been a smooth patch of green. Now there were at least four bright yellow bushes growing on every lot.

"The Scotch broom certainly has taken root," Harriett said.

"As I'm sure you know, it's an invasive species, and it spreads incredibly fast. I don't remember a single bush on the Pointe this spring. Now look. The gardeners spend half their day uprooting plants, and the next morning, there are more. No one wanted to use herbicides with so many children out here this summer, so the Scotch broom got its way for the season."

"It's quite lovely." Harriett walked across the road to the nearest bush and reached out to stroke one of its flower-laden branches. "Eradicating Scotch broom isn't easy. The bees will move on eventually—perhaps you should consider learning to live with it?"

Leonard shrugged. "Personally, I'm not opposed to the idea, but apparently many of my neighbors consider the plant a bit garish."

"Garish?" Harriett laughed.

"I know, I know." Leonard grimaced with embarrassment. "Rich people are nuts. If you'd come to me back when I was growing up in Brooklyn and told me I'd be spending all my time with these fancy assholes, I'd have headed straight to Coney Island and jumped off the Wonder Wheel. But in this case, they happen to be right. The Scotch broom has to go. It may be pretty, but it's also a fire hazard. This stuff lights up like kindling, and as you can imagine, we're very safety conscious these days. After everything that's happened this summer, all the mothers out here are popping more Xanax than ever."

"If I were them, I'd want to keep my eyes open and my wits about me," Harriett said. "I've heard Xanax can lead to dementia, but here at the Pointe, it appears to make people go blind."

Leonard gave her a funny look. Harriett's sense of humor didn't always translate.

"The families will all clear out next week after Labor Day, am I right?" she asked.

"Yes," Leonard confirmed. "The gentlemen sometimes fly in for weekends during the off-season, but the kids and the moms will be gone. School starts on Wednesday in the city. By Tuesday, they'll have all shipped out."

"Then next week sounds like an excellent time to get rid of the pests. Can you ensure the Pointe will be empty? My process is proprietary, and I don't want to show up with a stack of NDAs for your neighbors to sign."

"I'll make sure it's just the three of us. So you think you can do it?" Leonard asked.

Harriett scanned her surroundings, taking careful note of the bright yellow bushes in each yard. "Oh yes, I'm positive," she assured him. "In fact, I think I'm going to enjoy the challenge."

"Wonderful!" Leonard said. "Now, how about breakfast?"

They hopped in a golf cart parked at the curb, and Leonard drove in the direction of a tall white wall at the easternmost tip of the Pointe. None of the other estates appeared to have fences, much less a fortresslike wall.

"Someone likes their privacy," Harriett noted.

"This is my compound," Leonard admitted. "I put up the wall in the nineties when my house was the only one here. Back then, the wall was all the security we had on the Pointe. I suppose it's no longer necessary, but it does a good job of deterring unexpected guests. I'm afraid I'm a bit of an introvert," he added, almost bashfully.

"And yet you've surrounded yourself with people."

"Occupational hazard," he said. "Business is all about networking."

A gate in the wall opened as they approached, and Leonard steered the golf cart down a long drive. His house was positioned on the eastern tip of the Pointe, with his nearest neighbors half a mile away in either direction.

"So, this is all yours?" Harriett asked. The grounds seemed as vast as those at Versailles. The tall white wall hadn't spared them from the Scotch broom; Harriett noted that the bushes were as plentiful here as they were on the rest of the Pointe.

"One of the benefits of being a pioneer," Leonard explained. "I got here first, so I chose the best land for myself. Then I leased the other lots."

"The lots are leased?" Harriet was astounded. "There's not a mansion here that's worth under ten million dollars. And you're telling me the people who built them don't own the land underneath them?"

"Nope. The lots are leased for five-year terms, and the community association decides which leases will be renewed. I wanted to be able to rid the community of undesirables if I needed to. Until now, it hasn't been necessary. I try to choose my neighbors very carefully. Everyone here was thoroughly vetted. That's why it's so upsetting that someone like Spencer Harding slipped through the cracks. Claude was furious with me when she found out about him."

He brought the cart to a stop in front of a lovely stone manor, where Claude was waiting for them. Ever the hostess, she greeted Harriett like an old friend, and while Leonard futzed with something in the back of the cart, she guided her guest through the house's first floor toward an oceanfront deck. The interior was decorated with exceptional taste. Brilliant blue tiles formed a dizzying pattern on the floor, and a chandelier dripped from the exposed wooden beams on the ceiling. Harriett kept her eyes open, but she didn't see any servants.

"The two of you live here alone?" she asked.

"Yes," Claude said. "When we don't have guests."

"I imagine a place this size might feel lonely without other people."

"The house once belonged to my father. To me, it's always felt like home."

Harriett's neck stiffened, as though she were a dog picking up a scent. "I was under the impression Leonard built this house in the nineties."

"He *bought* it in the nineties, a few years after my father died. He had it shipped, stone by stone, from Brittany. I'd almost given him the boot, and it was his way of saying sorry. He offered it to me as a gift, but I couldn't even begin to pay the taxes on an estate like this, so Leonard keeps it in his name."

The breakfast table overlooked the ocean. The places were set with bone china, and a silver coffeepot sat in the center of the table.

"Would you like a cup?" Claude asked as they took their seats.

"No thanks." Harriett pulled a joint out of her pocket. "Do you mind?"

"Nope." Claude seemed amused. "As long as you're willing to share."

Harriett lit the joint, took a toke, and passed it to Claude.

"I noticed those lovely flowers in front of the Harding house are all gone."

"Yeah, the place is a mess." Claude sidestepped the question as she inhaled. "Did you see Jackson Dunn on the way in?" she asked, exhaling a cloud of silvery smoke.

"I did," Harriett confirmed. "I assume you were behind his up-coming break with tradition?"

Claude laughed at the idea. "Are you kidding? He would never listen to me. I just told Leonard that he might want to make sure there was no bad blood between you and Jackson. He knows Jackson's got some unfortunate proclivities."

"It's ironic," Harriett observed. "Leonard told me he had every-one out here vetted. You'd think a penchant for sexual harassment would be one of the first things you'd find during that process."

"Leonard does his best, but the truth is, a few good lawyers and a filing cabinet full of NDAs can work wonders. It's amazing how much dirty laundry a few hundred million dollars is able to hide," Claude said. "By the way, it's funny you mention sexual harass-ment. Did Jackson ever grab your crotch, by any chance?"

"As a matter of fact, he did," Harriett confirmed.

"Yeah, he tried that with me once, too, when he was really drunk. Leonard made sure he never stepped out of line again. Men like that need to be trained like dogs."

"Why bother to train them?" Harriett asked. "It would be bet-ter to just put them to sleep, don't you think?"

Leonard emerged from the house at that moment, a tray laden with food balanced on one hand. When he reached the table, he served fruit, croissants, and soft-boiled eggs in pretty blue cups, and did it without so much as a wobble.

"You're good at that," Harriett noted.

"I'm not fancy like Claude," Leonard said. "I worked my way through college as a waiter."

"Leonard is the personification of the American dream." Claude gave him a playful pat on the ass. "Janitor's kid goes to Harvard on a scholarship and works his way up to the top."

"Impressive. What was the secret to your success?" Harriett asked.

"A penis," Leonard deadpanned, and Claude burst out laughing.

"That, and an almost supernatural ability to sense what others are after," Claude added. "Leonard can peer into people's hearts and minds."

"Yes, I've noticed," Harriett said. "You two seem to have honed in on my friend Jo's deepest desires."

Claude blanched. "I was horrified by what happened to Lucy. I wanted to do something to help."

"Lucy will be fine," Harriett assured her. "I'll see to that. But the self-defense program is just what Jo needed."

"That butt-kicking academy is stroke of genius." Leonard beamed with pride.

"Jo deserves all the credit," Claude said. "It was her idea. The next time a man like Spencer Harding goes after a girl, he may be in for a surprise."

"Instead of training every girl in the country, why not just get rid of the handful of men like Spencer Harding?" Harriett suggested.

"Why not do both?" Claude asked.

"She's so ambitious," Leonard joked. "Speaking of ambition, didn't you have a successful career in advertising before you left it all for the world of plants?"

"It could have been a success," Harriett said. "But it turned out I was missing something very important."

"Which was?" Leonard asked.

"A penis," Harriett said, and they all laughed loudly.

"Well, we're certainly glad you've turned to horticulture," Claude said. "If you can get rid of the weeds on the Pointe, you can name your price. Leonard will ensure Jackson pays it."

Harriett took a toke on her joint. She hadn't touched any of the food. She plucked a pomegranate aril from her fruit salad and squeezed it until its red juice stained her fingertips. "Money matters very little to me. I charge what I believe is fair—no more and no less," she said. "I suppose that's why I'll never be rich enough for a house on the Pointe."

"Oh, I don't know about that," Leonard said. "I never expected to be wealthy, either. I just happened to stumble into a lucrative field."

"You're in finance, are you not? Hard field to stumble into."

"I retired from finance ten years ago," he reminded her. "Now I'm just an ordinary retiree."

"An ordinary retiree with the clout to make a man like Jackson Dunn shake in his boots."

Leonard laughed. "He's worried I won't renew his lease. After what happened with Harding, I've been cracking down. This is a family community. I don't want any more trouble."

Harriett turned her eyes to a flock of seagulls pecking the sand. As she took another toke, three of them lifted off and flew directly toward a pair of French doors that Leonard had left open. The sound of glass breaking soon followed.

"Shit." Leonard jumped up. "There's food out on the counters."

Claude groaned. "Will you excuse us for a moment?"

"Of course," Harriett told him. "Do you mind if I have a quick stroll around the grounds?"

"Not at all," Leonard said. "Just keep an eye out for our seabeach amaranth. We have one of the biggest patches on the Eastern Seaboard."

Harriett nodded, her attention already focused on a small older woman who'd appeared in the spot where the flock of gulls had been. The visitor walked to the edge of the scrub that separated the brilliant green grass from the beach and waved. She wore the somber gray dress of a domestic worker, and her hair was hidden beneath a kerchief of the same colorless fabric. She was twenty years older than Harriett, and she wore her age like a badge of honor.

Harriett trekked across the lawn to where the woman stood. "Hello," she said. "Are you looking for me?"

"Yes, I've been waiting. When I saw the weeds and the bees, I knew you would be coming," the woman responded.

"And now I am here. My name is Harriett."

"Isabel." The woman kept an eye on the house, but she didn't seem afraid.

"What do you do on the Pointe, Isabel?" Harriett asked.

"I tend to the houseplants, and I take care of the workers. I know how to cure fevers and heal wounds, and protect the weakest among us from harm."

Harriett was delighted. "You are like me. I knew the second I saw you."

"Yes, women like us recognize each other."

"Do you know why I've come?"

"The same reason I have. Girls are dead," Isabel said. "You are here to avenge them. Spencer Harding is gone, but the scales are not balanced yet."

"No," Harriett agreed. "They certainly are not."

"The people who work here on the Pointe over the summer see everything. But when the families go home, the workers leave as well. During the winter, when no one is watching, terrible things happen here. When people come back in May, it's like the soil has turned poisonous. I can feel it now, seeping into my shoes. Mr. Harding was a bad man, but he was not the only one."

"Who else is bad?" Harriett asked.

"Mr. Dunn. Two summers ago, a young woman named Rosalia came here with her mother to work on the Pointe. I did not know her, but I've seen pictures. She was a beautiful girl. One night, there was a party at Mr. Dunn's house, and Rosalia was asked to serve drinks to the men. The next morning, the girl was gone. The police said she had run away. But there was nowhere for her to run.

The guards would have seen her if she'd gone through the main gate. The only other way to leave the Pointe was by water, and Rosalia didn't know how to swim."

"Where is her mother now?"

"She was not allowed to stay. She's back in Mexico. That's where we met. She is the one who asked me to come here. She blames Mr. Dunn for what happened to her daughter."

"That seems reasonable. Anyone else you think I should know about?"

"Yes, the police officer on *Newsnight*. He visits Mr. Dunn all the time. I watched the show, and I heard him say he didn't get to the Pointe in time to arrest Mr. Harding. But that isn't true. One of the cleaners was working next door to Mr. Harding's house that night. She said the police officer was with Mr. Harding before the helicopter left."

"Is there any way to prove it?" Harriett said.

"There will be video," Isabel said. "Mr. Shaw records everything." Her gaze shifted to a point somewhere behind Harriett. Leonard and Claude had returned to the table. Leonard bit into a croissant and gave them a friendly wave.

"Did you take care of the plants at the Harding house?" Harriett asked.

"Yes, I did," Isabel told her.

"Do you know what happened to the pale-yellow flowers that were growing out front?"

"The wolfsbane?" Isabel knew exactly what Harriett was asking. "After Mr. Harding died, Ms. Marchand asked one of the gardeners to tear it all out."

"Why do you suppose she would do that?" Harriett asked.

"Maybe so no one would see that some of the plants had been uprooted the night before."

"That's what I thought." Harriett held out a hand. "Thank you,

Isabel. When you're ready to leave the Pointe, just head to town and ask for the witch. Any person in Mattauk will know where to find me. If you can stay an extra week or two, I'd love to have you as my guest. I suspect I can learn a great deal from you."

Isabel closed her eyes and nodded happily. "It would be my pleasure," she said.

As Harriett walked back across the lawn to the house, she thought of the video. It wasn't the right time to ask. The knowledge of its existence was enough for the moment.

THE OTHERS

Nessa sat in her car across the street from an old beachfront cottage. From the outside, the house looked cozy. Its blue-trimmed windows with their overflowing flower boxes were a perfect contrast to the weathered gray shingles. Nessa had never been inside, but she'd driven past on several occasions over the previous weeks. No matter what time of day she went by, there was always a silver SUV in the drive. So far, she'd resisted the urge to pull in behind it.

Nessa kept her hands on the wheel and left the car idling. She was scared. Not of the man who lived in the cottage, but of what he would say to her when she knocked on the door. She knew this was one of those moments when things were decided. If he sent her away, there would be no coming back. If he invited her in, she'd be there to stay.

Nessa had already turned the wheel toward the driveway and her foot was making the transition from the brake to the gas when the front door of the cottage opened and Franklin stepped out-side. Whatever happened, she knew she would always be grateful for the few moments that followed. Dressed in an old T-shirt and jeans, Franklin walked barefoot down the crushed-shell drive and crossed the road to her where her car sat on the shoulder. Then he leaned in, his forearms resting on the edge of her window.

"Is this a stakeout?" he asked.

In that instant, Nessa knew everything would be okay.

"I've missed you," she told him.

"You didn't need to," he said. "I've been here the whole time. I've seen you drive by. I'm glad you finally decided to stop."

After she pulled her car into the drive, Franklin guided her down a little path that circled around the house to the back porch. It was nothing more than a wooden platform with two Adirondack chairs and a table between them. The dunes started right at the edge, and beyond them lay the sea.

"There aren't many places like this anymore," Nessa noted. When she was a girl, there had been hundreds of similar cottages along this stretch of shore, all owned by Black families who arrived every summer. Nessa's great-grandfather had learned how to swim on the island. Her parents had met on a beach nearby. Now the families like hers were long gone and only a few cottages remained. The rest had been razed to make way for mansions and oceanfront condominiums.

"The house belonged to my great-uncle," Franklin said. "He was a cop, too. When things got too much in the city, he'd come out here by himself to fish. Over the years, developers offered him a fortune for the land, but he said you couldn't put a price on solitude."

"You feel the same way?" Nessa asked.

Franklin laughed. "I like the house. Solitude is overrated. Have a seat. You want a beer?"

"Sure," Nessa said, settling down into one of the wooden chairs and trying to remember the last time she'd had a beer.

She listened to Franklin bustling about in the kitchen, opening the fridge and popping the tops off bottles, and realized she felt at home. She'd expected it all to be awkward, but it hadn't been. It was like easing into a warm bath on a frigid day.

Franklin appeared on the deck with two bottles in hand. He passed one to Nessa before taking a seat beside her. For a few minutes, they sat in silence, sipping their beers and watching the waves.

"I'm sorry about how we left things," Nessa said.

"You're sorry you did what you had to do?" Franklin asked. "If you guys had taken my advice, Spencer Harding would still be murdering girls. And Jo had every right to be furious after what happened to her daughter. I should be the one apologizing to the three of you."

"I'm sorry Chief Rocca lied and said you were the source for the podcast. I know you lost your job because of it."

Franklin looked over at her. "Do you honestly think I wanted to keep it after everything that happened? You and your friends were right. The system is broken. If you're looking for justice these days, you have to find it by other means. That's what you did. Then they went and blamed Harding's escape on you. What they did to me was bad. But that was damned *low*."

"Can I ask you—was anything the chief said on *Newsnight* true? Was Danill Chertov really an informant?"

She wished she could be more direct, but unless she wanted to see Harriett arrested, she couldn't let on that Chertov was dead.

"Not to my knowledge," Franklin said. "I was the lead detective on the case. If they brought Chertov in for questioning before Harding's death, they must have hidden him pretty well, because *I* didn't see him. Half of what the chief said on *Newsnight* was meant to cover up his incompetence. I just haven't found a way to prove it."

"He wasn't covering up incompetence," Nessa said. "He and Harding were working together. Harriett went out to the Pointe this morning and spoke to a woman who works there. The lady said Rocca was at Harding's house before the helicopter took off that night."

"Doing what?" Franklin asked, his curiosity clearly piqued.

Nessa shrugged and took a drink. "No idea. But it means the chief lied when he said Harding escaped after he was tipped off by the podcast. Rocca was at Harding's house. He could have arrested Spencer at any point, but he didn't. There should be security tapes that can prove it. We're going to see if we can get our hands on them."

"I'm impressed," Franklin said. "You guys are turning out to be better detectives than I am."

Nessa stared out at the water. "We're still missing most of the story. I can feel it. The gift has limits, and this sure isn't how my grandmother taught me to use it. I think you were right, Franklin— the two of us are meant to work as a team. I shouldn't have pushed you aside like I did. We need your help. *I* need your help."

"You really mean that?" Franklin asked.

Nessa nodded. "I do," she said.

"Then come on," he said, rising out of his chair.

"Really?" she asked. "Now?"

Franklin laughed. "Look who's got a dirty mind."

Nessa felt her cheeks burst into flame. "I've been spending too much time with Harriett."

"Sounds to me like Ms. Osborne is an excellent influence," Franklin said, holding out a hand to help Nessa up. "We'll get to that later, after I cook you dinner. There's something I want to show you first."

He led her through the sliding doors and into a tasteful living room decorated in shades of blue. It opened onto an old-fashioned kitchen with white cabinets and appliances that had to be as old as the house. There wasn't a crumb on the counters or a dish in the sink.

"You're awfully tidy for a man," Nessa said, though Jonathan had been tidy, too. "I drop by unannounced, and your house is spick-and-span."

"That's what ten years in the military will do to you. For your information, I'm a whiz with an iron, too." He shot her a wink over his shoulder and Nessa clapped a hand to her heart as though ready to swoon.

Down a short hall from the living room were the cottage's two bedrooms. The door to one was open, and Nessa could see a perfectly made bed with a nightstand beside it. Franklin opened the second door, and the smile slipped off Nessa's face. The walls were plastered with pictures of girls. White girls and brown girls—they all looked like babies to Nessa. File boxes sat stacked against the walls, and three computer monitors cluttered an old desk.

"What is all of this?" Nessa asked.

"After your *They Walk Among Us* interview aired, I knew my days on the force were numbered. So I went straight to headquarters and started making copies of files I thought could prove useful," he said.

"Who are these girls?"

"Missing persons cases going back a couple of decades," Franklin said. "All were last seen on the island. Most lived here, but some were just visiting. All between the ages of thirteen and eighteen."

"How many are there altogether?"

"I started with hundreds," Franklin said. "I've managed to narrow it down to a couple dozen girls who might be connected. About two-thirds vanished in the last couple of years."

Could they all be Spencer Harding's victims? Nessa shuddered at the thought. "A woman came up to me in the store the other day. She said her daughter disappeared a year ago when she was visiting the island from Queens. Her name was Lena." Nessa tapped her temple trying to dislodge the girl's last name from her brain.

Franklin already had it. "You must mean Lena Collins." He walked across the room to a picture pinned to the far wall. Nessa stepped forward and recognized the girl from the photo her mother had pulled from her wallet. "Seventeen years old. Captain of her school's soccer team. Came out with a friend whose grandparents have a house not too far from here. It was two weeks before her high school graduation. File says she ran away, but there was nothing to suggest that this girl wasn't happy at home."

"And Harriett mentioned a girl who worked on Culling Pointe a couple of years ago. She disappeared after serving drinks at a party thrown by a man named Jackson Dunn."

"Rosalia Cortez." He took a few steps and tapped a picture of a stunning young woman with wild black hair and sweet eyes. "Also seventeen. She and her mother came here on H-2B visas to work on the Pointe. She was saving money to attend a nursing college in Guadalajara. Her school records were in the file. The girl was smart as hell—not the kind of person who'd be easily duped."

"You know them all," Nessa marveled.

"Of course," Franklin said. "If you're looking for someone, it helps to know who they are."

"It sounds like no one really looked before."

"No," Franklin said. "Girls this age are often assumed to be runaways. But girls don't run away if they're saving for nursing school. And they don't run away if they're two weeks from their high school graduation."

"And you think all these disappearances could all be connected to Spencer Harding?"

"Not all of them," Franklin said. "But maybe a few. And if so, their families deserve to know."

"Could any of them be the two girls we found who haven't been identified yet?" Their ghosts may have moved on, but the girl in blue and the girl in the red hoodie hadn't left Nessa's memory. Their faces were on her mind every morning when she woke. They were with Nessa each night that guilt and frustration kept her awake.

Franklin shook his head. "That's one of the strangest things about this whole case. I haven't found a single clue when it comes to those girls. But don't worry—I'm going to keep looking till I do."

Nessa turned to him. "So this is what you've been doing since you lost your job?"

"All day, every day," he said. "I figured when I had some conclusions, I'd come share them with you."

"I can't believe you did all of this," Nessa said.

"The eulogy you gave at Mandy Welsh's funeral inspired me. I wanted to do something to deserve you." He put an arm around Nessa's shoulders and gently guided her out of the room. "Now, if it's possible, let's pick this up in the morning. I have a few important questions to ask you about this team we're forming."

Franklin closed the door to the office behind them. They walked back through the house to the deck and its gorgeous view. Nessa came to a stop. The migraine that had been her constant companion was gone. For the first time in weeks, her mind felt clear.

"What do you want to know?" Nessa asked.

"You like steak?" Franklin asked.

Nessa remembered the joke her daughters had made. She stepped up to Franklin and put her arms around his neck.

"I love it," she said.

They didn't eat their steak until midnight.

"SO HOW WAS THE SECOND time?" Jo asked the next day as they did squats in front of a mirror at Furious Fitness. "Better than the first?"

Nessa glanced around to make sure no one was eavesdropping. "It felt like a religious experience," she whispered. She'd never shared such private thoughts with another woman before.

Jo laughed so hard she nearly dropped her ten-pound barbells. "You mean like angels singing and harps playing?"

"To be honest?" Nessa stopped and smiled at the memory. "Yeah. I don't know what it is about that man. He just knows exactly what to do."

"Well, whatever he did, you definitely needed it. You looked like a whole new woman when you walked through the door this afternoon."

"That's because my headache went away," Nessa said.

"I bet," Jo joked.

"No, it wasn't the sex." Nessa was suddenly serious. "My migraine disappeared after Franklin showed me all the work he's been doing. I think there are more dead girls around here who need to be found, and they've been yelling at me all at once. They're frustrated that no one's been looking."

Jo set down her barbells. "Shit," she sighed, her fears confirmed. "Remember that morning we drove out to Danskammer Beach to look for the first body? I thought that was going to be the worst day of my life. Now we're in the middle of a fucking conspiracy. You're saying there are more dead girls out there, and we know the chief of police and Jackson Dunn are involved somehow. God knows who else is. And somehow we're supposed to bring them all to justice."

"I know, but what are we going to do?" Nessa asked. "We obviously can't go to the police. And after that *Newsnight* special, no one in the media's going to talk to us."

"As soon as we're done with our workout, let's reach out to Josh Gibbon and see if he wants to rehabilitate his reputation. Bet he'll be interested in that surveillance footage from the Pointe, if we can get our hands on it."

"I guess we could give it a shot, but what do you want to bet he's got our numbers blocked?" Nessa asked.

"If he does, then we'll just have to hunt the little bastard down, won't we?"

"Jo?" The door to the weight room opened. It was Heather, who'd been promoted to manager just that morning. "You asked me to remind you about the young women's self-defense class?"

Jo had posted an invite on social media the day before. Nervous that turnout wouldn't be enough to impress her benefactors, she'd done her best to put it out of her mind.

"Is it five already?" Jo asked, glancing down at her smartwatch, which told her they were still fifteen minutes short of the hour.

"No," Heather said, "but I thought you might want to come out a bit early. Your friend Claude just arrived, and we've got quite a few people out front."

"Really?" Jo felt a jolt of excitement. She set her barbells aside and jogged out of the weight room, with Nessa right behind her. From the stairs to the first floor, she could see a crowd of girls and their mothers crammed into the gym's reception area. A line to get inside stretched into the parking lot.

"Oh wow," Nessa gasped. "You've really started something."

Claude was practically bouncing with glee when she greeted the two of them at the bottom of the stairs. "Oh my God, Jo, I think every mother in Mattauk is here with her daughters!"

"I had no idea it would be so popular," Jo said. "Heather, would you mind calling Art and asking him to bring Lucy over?"

For the first time, Jo could envision a day when Lucy would walk to the gym on her own. The fear that had been Jo's constant companion since her daughter was born no longer felt like an invincible foe. For years, it had lurked inside her, springing out the moment Jo lost sight of Lucy in the grocery store—or Lucy took too long walking home from a friend's. Within seconds, the fear could grow into something monstrous. Jo scanned the crowd of mothers who'd come to Furious Fitness with their daughters. Jo could tell they all knew that same terror. Like her, they'd battled it daily. Now it was starting to feel like their war might have an end.

"I knew." Claude reached out a hand to Nessa. "Hi, I'm Claude."

"Shit, sorry," Jo said. "This is my best friend Nessa James. Nessa, this is Claude."

"What a wonderful thing you guys are doing for these girls," Nessa told Claude. "I'm so proud of Jo. I think she's really found her calling."

"Maybe, but I don't know if I'm prepared to deal with this many girls on a regular basis," Jo admitted, her confidence a bit shaken. "There have to be two hundred girls here, and it's not even five."

"Leave the logistics to me," Claude said. "I'm used to handling Leonard's charity events."

"What kind of stuff does Leonard's charity do?" Nessa asked.

"Right now, we're focused on building schools in developing nations. Earlier this year, we were in the Caribbean. Before that, we spent a month in Nepal. We had four hundred kids show up for opening day there. So I have a lot of experience with crowds this big."

"Great. So where should we take these girls?" Jo asked. "There are too many to fit inside the gym. I guess the park's a few blocks away. Why don't I lead them all over there, and we can have one giant class?"

"See? You're already getting the hang of it!" Claude cheered her on. "While you're teaching them how to kick butt, I'll go around and group the girls by age and assign them to classes. I'm thinking six classes in total, and each girl comes once a week."

Jo gazed out over the crowd, which had continued to grow while she, Claude, and Nessa were chatting. There were giddy little girls wearing shirts emblazoned with glittery unicorns and surly teens rocking red lip gloss and eyeliner. Every variety of girl was represented. Rich girls, poor girls, good girls, badasses. It was the makings of a formidable army. She would teach them everything. She would make them invincible. This was the generation that would finally turn the tables. Maybe when their own daughters were born, they wouldn't need to spend their days fighting fear.

Jo looked over at Nessa. "Looks like I may have my hands full for the rest of the day. You want to get in touch with Josh Gibbon like we talked about?"

"The podcast guy?" Claude asked. "Aren't you done with him after that *Newsnight* debacle?"

"I'd love to be done with him," Jo said. "But he's still the only person in the media who's likely to return our calls."

"I'll reach out to him," Nessa said. "You two go have fun."

"Thanks, babe." Jo gave Nessa a hug and hurried outside to meet her army. "You ladies ready to kick some butt?" she shouted out at the crowd, and a cheer went up from the girls and their mothers. "Then let's go take over the town!"

As Jo led her army to the park, cars slowed and drivers stared. Jo hoped they all got a good look. *Consider yourselves warned, motherfuckers,* she thought.

NESSA CALLED JOSH GIBBON RIGHT away, but he didn't answer the phone and his voice mail was full. She made five more attempts that evening from Franklin's house. Josh wasn't responding to Nessa's urgent texts or emails, either. Please! her last text to him read. I have news!

The next morning, Nessa sipped coffee while she watched the sunrise from Franklin's deck. With her hopes in check, she opened her messages. There were six from Jo, two from her daughters, and one from Josh Gibbon.

I'm in town. I have news too. Are you at home?

Nessa's squeal of excitement brought Franklin out to the deck in his boxers. "Lemme guess. You heard from Gibbon?"

"Mmmhmm." Nessa was already typing. When can we meet?

"It's six fifteen in the morning," Franklin noted, settling into a chair beside her with a cup of coffee in his hand. "Gibbon strikes me as the kind of guy who doesn't get up before noon."

Nessa had just set the phone aside when a chime proved Franklin wrong.

About to head back to Brooklyn. Stop by your house before I go?

Just give me fifteen. Nessa wrote back.

"I gotta get dressed and get home!" Nessa launched herself out of the lounge chair and toward the sliding glass doors. "Josh is coming over before he heads back to the city."

"He's here in town?" Franklin asked. "I thought he didn't want anything to do with Mattauk anymore."

"I don't know what he's doing here, but he says he's got news."

Franklin started to rise from his seat. "I'll come with you."

"No, stay here and enjoy your coffee," Nessa told him. "The kid's skittish enough as it is. I show up with a posse, he might not talk at all."

"I still don't understand. Why's he want to see you? Why not Jo?"

It was a fair question, but Nessa felt annoyed by the unspoken assumption that seemed to accompany it. "'Cause I'm the one who's been texting him—and Jo is scary." Nessa scrunched up her face. "You think I can't handle this on my own?"

"I think you can handle just about anything," Franklin assured her. "But I'm trained to be cautious. You'll let me know what he tells you?"

She bent over his chair and planted a kiss on his forehead. "You kidding? As soon as I'm finished with Josh, I'm coming right back here. You're going to have a very tough time getting rid of me again."

Nessa made it out of the house in record time, but paused once her key was in the ignition and fished her phone out of her pocketbook. Was it strange that Josh wanted to come by first thing in the morning? She scrolled through the messages she'd exchanged with him until she reached her first. She'd sent it to Josh, along with the second, third, and fourth. There was no doubt the responses had come from him.

She turned over the engine, then sat for a few seconds more, staring out at the dunes. Something was off. Franklin had sensed it, and now she felt it, too. Back in her hospital days, Nessa had learned to rely on her intuition. It always seemed to know when a tale wasn't true. It informed her if a black eye came from a fist, not a fall. It whispered a warning if a visitor wished a patient harm. From time to time, it would insist that she double-check a prescribed medication—even if the doctor who'd ordered it was standing beside her. Nessa's intuition may have injured a few egos among the medical staff, but it had also saved lives.

Now it was telling her to proceed with caution. But it wasn't telling her to go back and get Franklin—or to stop by Jo's house on the way. Whatever it was, Nessa was sure she could handle it. She put the car in reverse and backed out onto the street.

When she reached her pretty white house, Nessa stopped across the street and left the engine idling. There were no cars in the drive. Her visitor had yet to arrive. The windows were dark and everything looked just as she'd left it. But something told her the house wasn't empty. There was someone waiting for her inside. The text was a trap, her gut warned her. Josh hadn't sent it. Whoever was inside had lured her here.

Then a silhouette appeared in the dim living room. As it moved toward the window, it acquired color and dimension. A familiar face took form—pasty white skin, bushy beard, and unkempt hair. Purple bags drooped beneath the eyes. Nessa sat back with her hand over her pounding heart, relieved to see she'd been wrong. It was Josh after all.

Nessa almost raised a hand to wave. Then she remembered. There was no one at home to let Josh in. Her foot slammed on the gas and she sped away. When she reached a safe distance, she dialed Franklin.

"There's someone in my house," she told him. "The text was a trick."

"I'll be right over."

"I won't be there," she said. "There's a key hidden behind a loose brick on the first step."

"I don't understand," Franklin said. "Where are you going?"

"Brooklyn," she said. "I'll call you as soon as I get there."

She looked up the address of Josh's studio and plugged it into her GPS. The hour-long drive into the city was agony. When she finally reached the address in Greenpoint, Nessa saw nothing but a dingy industrial building. She parked the car and approached the entrance slowly, giving her gut time to warn her if necessary. But nothing seemed out of the ordinary, and now that it was almost eight o'clock, the sidewalks and streets were busy. Nessa looked for a bell, but found only an old red button.

She pushed it, expecting nothing, but a kid in his early twenties appeared almost instantly. Behind him, Nessa could see a sun-washed loft space filled with modern furniture. And thanks to Harriett, she was able to quickly identify the stench wafting through the doorway. A few months earlier, she would have sworn it was a skunk.

"I'm sorry, is this Josh Gibbon's studio?" she asked.

"Oh my God, it's you!" the kid squealed with excitement.

Nessa took a nervous step back. "You know me?"

"Of course I know you!" he said, looking like he might give her a hug. "I'm Chet. I help Josh with the show's website. I posted all the pictures you took at Danskammer Beach and the footage that was shot after you found the first body. Nessa James, am I right?"

"Yes," Nessa said. "So this *is* his studio?"

"It used to be Josh's house *and* his studio. But the biz just moved to better quarters down the street. That's where he's at, if you're looking for him. He was there all night. The construction crew is there during the day, so Josh works the graveyard shift."

"You're saying Josh is right here in Brooklyn—at a studio down the street?" Nessa confirmed. "Right now?"

"Should be. Unless he popped out for something to eat. You know, it's so funny you're here. Before Josh left for work last night, he gave me a package to send to you."

"To *me*?" Nessa asked. *Something bad is going down,* she thought. *Really bad.*

Chet held up a finger. "Wait here," he said, before disappearing into the house for a moment. When he returned, he had a padded manila envelope in one hand.

Chet's bloodshot eyes opened wide as he held up the envelope for his guest to see. Nessa's address was scrawled on the front in black Sharpie. "Creeeeepy! But you must be used to this kind of thing, with your ESP and all."

Nessa reached out, took the package and felt through the padding. It seemed to be empty aside from a small, rectangular object.

"What time did Josh leave for work last night?"

Chet shrugged. "Dunno. Maybe eight?"

"Have you heard from him since?"

"No, but I wasn't expecting to," Chet said. "He hasn't been using his phone for the past few days. He thinks it's been hacked. He's gotten too paranoid, if you ask me. I mean, I love Josh to death, but you gotta admit, he's not the poster boy for mental health. I think all this serial killer shit has really damaged his brain."

"Who does he think hacked his phone?" Nessa asked.

Chet shrugged again and shook his head. "You gotta ask him. He won't tell me anything. Like I said—totally paranoid."

A bad, bad feeling was pressing Nessa to act. "I need to talk to Josh right away. What's the address of the new studio?"

Chet pointed down the street to an old brick factory at the end of the block. "Entrance is around the corner," he said. "Not sure if the buzzers are working yet. There's still a lot of construction going on."

Nessa felt nauseous. "Thank you," she told the kid.

"Sure thing," he responded. "Keep up the good work!" He called out cheerfully as she hurried away.

Right before the intersection, Nessa passed a newly painted sign for Gibbon Media on the factory wall, just above a faded ad for a long-defunct funeral home. When she turned the corner, Nessa spotted a young man in dirty shorts and a baseball cap with an untrimmed beard sitting on the short set of steps that led up to the front door.

"Josh!" she shouted, and he rose. He paused for a moment at the top of the stairs as if waiting for her to catch up. Then he walked straight through the glass door and into the foyer.

"Oh Jesus," Nessa whispered as it became clear what that meant. She'd suspected as much when she'd seen Josh in her living room, but she'd prayed all the way to Brooklyn that her suspicions were wrong.

At the top of the stairs, Nessa tried the handle and found the door unlocked. Inside the building, construction equipment clogged the entrance. She squeezed between it and hurried up the stairs to the second floor, reaching the landing just in time to see Josh vanish through a wooden door with a sign that read *Studio*.

This door was locked. Surprising herself, Nessa raised a foot and kicked at it. It took four tries before the wood splintered and the door flew open.

The studio was a white room with no furniture aside from a table and six chairs. Sound-absorbing panels lined the walls and a six-headed microphone crouched like a spider in the center of the table. Exposed industrial pipes crisscrossed the ceiling. Hanging from one of them, an electrical cord looped around his neck, was Josh Gibbon.

"No," Nessa groaned.

She scrambled on top of the table to check for signs of life. There was no pulse and his flesh was cold. Josh had clearly been dead for hours. His ghost stood in the studio's doorway, gazing up at the corpse as if captivated by its swollen head and blue face. Then it looked straight at the package Nessa had stuck in her purse, and she knew that was why she'd had to come to New York. She climbed down from the table and ripped it open. Inside was an unlabeled microcassette. When she looked up, the ghost was gone, and there was only one Josh left in the room.

Nessa grabbed her phone and dialed 911. As soon as the police were on the way, she started snapping pictures. She wasn't going to let anyone rewrite history again.

As she held the camera up, a new text arrived from Josh's phone. *Sorry I missed you*, it said. *I'll catch up with you later.*

The threat was clear.

NESSA GOT BACK TO MATTAUK at a quarter past midnight. Harriett, Jo, and Franklin were waiting for her outside her house, Jo pacing the sidewalk and Harriett sitting on the lawn smoking a joint and sipping a Chateau Lafite Rothschild. The second the car came to a stop, Jo pulled open the door and wrapped her arms around Nessa. When Jo finally let go, Harriett stepped forward and handed Nessa an empty glass, which she filled to the brim with wine.

"I'm so sorry," Jo said. "I should never have asked you to talk to Josh on your own."

"It's okay." Nessa stopped speaking to guzzle the wine. "I think I managed to take care of myself pretty well."

"Yeah," Jo agreed. "Speaking of which, you and Harriett are

really starting to give me a complex. If you're both so good at protecting yourselves, what the hell am I here for?"

"You'll find out soon enough," Harriett said.

Jo spun toward her. "Is that supposed to be a joke? If not, what does it mean? If you know something, Harriett, you better tell me!"

"What I know and what you discover may not be the same thing," Harriett said.

"Would you stop speaking in riddles? You're an advertising executive, not a fucking Zen master."

Nessa left them to argue and went to greet Franklin, who was waiting for her by the front door. As soon as she was within reach, he pulled her close.

"You okay?" he asked.

"I am," she said. "Poor Josh. His ghost was here this morning. He came to warn me. I don't know what would have happened to me if he hadn't."

"I couldn't see any evidence that someone broke into the house, but I need you to have a look for yourself. You ready now or do you need a few minutes?"

"Let's do it now," Nessa said.

She toured her own house, carefully noting the position of every object and examining every scuff and mark. Nothing seemed out of place until she reached the living room. There, sitting on the coffee table, was her grandmother's scrapbook, filled not with family memories but of newspaper clippings and sketches of all the women she'd found. The message was clear. Whoever had been in her house knew about her gift.

JO HAD SPENT ALL AFTERNOON searching through boxes in the gym's basement storeroom, looking for the microcassette player she'd purchased back in the nineties when such devices were cutting-edge tech. She found it in a box, along with a collection of tiny tapes that she'd used to practice her responses to job interview questions.

Nessa, Franklin, Harriett, and Jo gathered around Nessa's dining-room table with the cassette player in the center. Then Jo leaned forward and pressed the play button.

"Okay, we're recording." It was Josh Gibbon's voice.

"What is that thing?" asked a female voice. She sounded young and nervous.

"This? It's a microcassette recorder," Josh said.

"Like from the Middle Ages?"

"Like from the days before people could hack into your phone. So let's get started. I'm standing in a broom closet at Brooklyn Flea with a young woman and her mother who just came up and introduced themselves to me. Would you mind repeating everything you just told me, starting from the top?"

"All right. Umm. My name is—"

"Okay, stop," Josh said. "Don't use your real name. Who's your favorite celebrity?"

"Beyoncé?"

"Great. We'll call you Beyoncé."

"All right," the girl said, as though she suspected he might be insane. "My name is Beyoncé. I'm fourteen years old, and I live here in Brooklyn."

"I just want to cut in for a moment to say that Beyoncé's mother is here with us. Right, Mom?"

"Yes, that's right," said an older woman.

"Okay, Beyoncé. One more time."

"Yeah, so I'm a big fan of your podcast. I listen to *They Walk Among Us* every week, and my mom and me went to see you live at the Bell House last year. Like I told you, I'm fascinated by serial killers, and something happened to me that I thought you'd want to hear about."

"Tell me your story."

"Yeah, so I was out on the island at the beginning of July visiting my friend—" She paused. ". . . Kim Kardashian."

"Good job," Josh praised her. "No real names."

"So Kim and I stayed late at the beach talking to some kids. Before we went home, she stopped to pee in the public restroom, and I waited outside in the parking lot. It was just getting dark when this man pulled up beside me."

"What kind of car was he driving?"

"I dunno much about cars," the girl said. "But it was black and nice. Anyways, he gets out and tells me he's a police officer. He said someone had reported me for keying one of the cars in the lot. He told me I had to come with him to the station so the witness could ID me."

"What did you say?"

"I figured he was full of it, so I said I wanted to see his ID. Mom told me that when a cop's out of uniform, they have to show you their ID. But the guy wouldn't do it. So I told him to go to hell."

"And what did he do when you said that?"

"He grabbed my arm and tried to drag me to his car."

"How'd you get away?"

"I kneed him in the nads just like Mom taught me. Then I ran into the restroom and banged on the door. My friend let me inside and we called her parents to come get us."

The conversation was interrupted by a knock on the door.

"Just a minute!" Josh Gibbon called out. "Did you recognize the man?" he asked the girl.

"Not when it happened. But the next day, I was watching TV and I saw him on an ad for *Newsnight*. He was the cop talking about the Danskammer Beach murders."

"Hey!" someone shouted in the background. "You aren't supposed to be in there!"

"Okay!" Josh shouted back. "Are you positive?" he asked the girl.

"Oh yeah. A hundred percent."

"Thank you, Beyoncé. I have your number. I'll call you this evening, and we'll set up a studio date to record this for real."

After that, the recording came to an end. Jo leaned forward and pressed the stop button.

"That girl would be dead if she hadn't fought back. How many teenage girls would kick a cop in the balls? Every girl in America should be able to do what she did."

"Now we know how Rocca was involved," Harriett said. "He was using his job to kidnap teenagers."

"The girl on the tape said Rocca approached her the beginning of July, the day before the *Newsnight* episode," Jo said. "That's three whole weeks *after* Spencer Harding's helicopter went down.

"What does it mean?" Nessa asked.

"It means that not only was Rocca involved—he didn't stop after Spencer died," Franklin said.

DEFILED

J o." Art was gently shaking her.

"What!" She sat up so quickly that she almost bumped heads with him. "Is Lucy okay?"

"She's totally fine," he told her. "I didn't mean to scare you."

The sun was streaming through the bedroom windows. For the first time in ages, she'd missed sunrise. "Oh my God," she said, her hand reaching for her phone on the nightstand. "What time is it?"

"Eight thirty. I knew you got home late, so I let you sleep in. Lucy's been fed and she's keeping herself entertained. But I gotta hop in the car. I have a meeting in Manhattan at eleven."

"Isn't it Saturday?"

"Every day is a workday for the foreseeable future," Art said. "That's showbiz."

"Okay, no problem." Jo yawned and planted a kiss on his chin before scooting around him to the edge of the bed. "Go make good art. I got it from here."

She grabbed a pair of leggings off the top of the hamper and pulled them on.

"Hey, before you run off, there's something I wanted to talk about."

"Sure," she said as she searched for a top to put on over the sports bra she'd worn to bed. "What is it?"

"I'm going to have a lot more meetings on my calendar going forward. There will be times when I need to spend the whole day in the city. After a while, I'll need to be there all night, too."

If he hadn't been half out the door, she would have climbed right on top of him. This was the Art she'd fallen for—the one who could go for days without sleep when he was in the zone on a project. The one who always had three projects lined up. That Art had been gone for so long that Jo had started to wonder if he'd been a figment of her imagination. And yet here he was, sitting on the side of her bed. He even looked years younger than the man she'd been married to a few weeks earlier. If she hadn't known better, she would have wondered if the man in her room was a time traveler.

"We have plenty of money for a pied-à-terre," Jo told him. "Why don't you look for a small place in Manhattan or Brooklyn?"

"Jo," he said in his serious voice.

"What?"

"I don't think it's a good idea for the family to be apart. It's gotten too dangerous. For God's sake, Josh Gibbon was murdered yesterday."

Unpleasant memories from the previous day flooded back into her mind. "In Brooklyn," Jo pointed out half-heartedly. She knew where Art was headed, and she knew he was right.

"He was murdered because of what happened here in Mattauk," Art replied. "You've been telling me that the story is bigger than anyone knows—that there are other people involved in what happened at the Harding house. And you know what? You are totally right. One of them just murdered a podcast host. Do you honestly think our family is safe if we stay here?"

Jo felt like the floor was dissolving under her feet. "So you're saying you want to leave Mattauk. What about Furious Fitness? What about my career?"

"What about Lucy, Jo?" he demanded.

"Don't go there," Jo warned her husband darkly. He'd hit her weak spot. "You know I always put Lucy first."

Art nodded. "You're right, and I'm sorry. Look, you don't need to close down the gym for good. Let's rent a place in the city for a few months while I work on the play. Put your self-defense club on hold and let Heather run Furious Fitness in the meantime. You can pop in and check on her whenever you like. But I'd feel a lot better if you and Lucy were in the city with me."

"What would I do all day while you're at work?" Jo asked.

"Same thing I've been doing for the past couple of years," Art told her.

Jo tried her best to hide how much the idea horrified her.

Two hours later, she was pounding a treadmill, fleeing from a gaping void that was opening underneath her. Lucy sat in one of the windows that lined the street-facing side of Furious Fitness's second floor, reading a battered copy of *Carrie*. Several concerned citizens had already informed Jo that the content of the book wasn't suitable for an eleven-year-old. But Jo went by the rule her father had imposed when she was a child of Lucy's age. If you're old enough to understand all the words, he always said, you're old enough to read it. The rule had driven her mother completely insane, and yet she'd never once challenged it.

As Jo recalled, her parents' relationship had been a Venn diagram with a thin sliver of overlap. Each had their own distinct spheres of influence. Her father ruled the family finances, the kids' education, the television schedule, and the yard. Her mother, meanwhile, was the undisputed queen of all social events, children's attire, meals, and manners. In the house they'd shared for fifty years, her parents' only common ground had been the dining-room table and the master bed. In her younger years, Jo had found the arrangement old-fashioned and inflexible. She had sworn her marriage would be different. But it hadn't been. Not really. Now Art was asking to swap spheres for a while. It was a reasonable request. Sensible. Logical. The truth was, she just didn't want to.

She was running from the thought when she saw Lucy wave to someone who'd just walked up the stairs. Then Claude's frantic face appeared beside her, and Jo pulled out her headphones.

"Jo! You almost gave me a heart attack!" Claude cried. "People are dropping like flies around here! It's not a good time to stop answering your phone!"

"Sorry." Jo hit the cooldown button, and the treadmill slowed to a crawl. As soon as she'd gotten to the gym, she'd shoved her phone into one of the drawers at the front desk. She knew Art would be texting about his plan, and she wasn't ready to talk. "You heard about Josh Gibbon?"

"It's all over the news! They say your friend found him—the lady I met here the other day?"

"Nessa."

"Such a terrible tragedy. And what an awful thing for your friend to see. Didn't Nessa find the girl down by Danskammer Beach, too?" Claude asked. "Does she have some kind of secret power for finding dead bodies or something?"

"It was my fault that Nessa found Josh," Jo said, sidestepping the question. "I was the one who asked her to go talk to him."

"I know. I was there when you asked," Claude said. "I still don't understand it. Didn't he throw you under the bus when he apologized for having you guys on the show?"

"Yeah, but we discovered something new about the murders and we couldn't go to the cops or the newspapers with it. We were hoping Josh could help."

"Oh my God. What did you find?"

Jo didn't hesitate. "Remember Chief Rocca—the cop they interviewed on *Newsnight*?" she asked, and Claude nodded. "He claimed Spencer took off in his helicopter before the police had a chance to arrest him. But Rocca was at the Harding house right before Spencer fled."

"I've met Rocca," Claude said. "He's been at a few parties on the Pointe. You really think he let Spencer escape?"

"That's exactly what I think. He should have arrested Spencer, but he didn't—probably because he's involved in it all. And we know Rocca has a thing for young girls. He tried to drag a teenager into his car in July."

"In *July*?" Claude seemed shocked. "But Spencer died in June."

"Yep, which means Rocca is still at it."

"How did you find out about all of this?"

"Reliable sources," Jo said. "Do you think there might be security footage from the Pointe that shows Rocca at Harding's house?"

"Of course," Claude said. "The entire neighborhood is covered by cameras. And the guys at the front gate keep a log of everyone who visits and the time they arrive. So yeah, if Rocca was there that night, we can definitely prove it. I'll be happy to gather the evidence."

"That would be great," Jo said. "'Cause until we round up all the bad guys, there's a chance I could end up dead. There's no doubt in my mind that Rocca was responsible for Josh Gibbon's death."

"Then let's take the bastard down," Claude said. "I'm not going to stand by and let him murder anyone else. If he touches a hair on your head, I'll kill him myself."

"My husband would prefer that I avoid getting murdered in the first place. This whole thing has got him really worried," Jo admitted. "Art's doing some work in the city, and he wants Lucy and me to move there for a while. I know it's a lot to ask, but maybe we could pause our self-defense program until things get under control?"

"You can't go to Manhattan," Claude announced with her arms crossed and her mind clearly made up.

"I can't?" Jo felt her heart sink.

"Of course not. Brooklyn is a much better place to live these days. Leonard owns a building downtown. The ground floor would make a great location for the first New York City branch of Furious Fitness. If we started a club there, we'd get girls from every possible background, which is exactly what we want. And I happen to know that there's a great three-bedroom apartment available on the tenth floor. We could throw that in as part of the bargain."

"You're serious?" Jo asked.

"Completely," Claude said.

"Why would you do something like that for me?"

Claude's nose wrinkled as if the conversation had gone bad. "*That* is a question no man would ever ask. I'm not your fairy godmother, if that's what you're thinking," she told Jo. "I'm doing it because I'll never be able to find a partner who's as good as you."

FIVE MINUTES AFTER FRANKLIN GOT up to make breakfast, Nessa opened her eyes to see Breanna and Jordan standing at the end of her bed in front of the window. The sunlight streamed around them, forming heavenly coronas around their bodies. Nessa sat straight up and shrieked at the sight.

"We're alive, Mama," Jordan said, reaching out an arm for Nessa to pinch.

"Don't do that to me again," Nessa ordered. She could still hear her pounding heart in her ears. "What are you doing here? Why aren't you two at school?"

"Don't you know the rule?" Breanna asked. "You get a day off whenever your mom finds a dead body."

Jordan sat down on the side of the bed. "The police say Josh Gibbon committed suicide," she said. "Did he?"

"No," Nessa set them straight.

"Who do you think got to him?"

Nessa shook her head. "I don't want you two getting involved in all of this. You shouldn't even be here. This town isn't safe."

"You think we aren't involved already?" Breanna asked.

"You think the city's any safer than the island right now?" Jordan added. "The same man's been parked across the street from our dorm for the last two nights."

Nessa's face must have shown her horror because Breanna jumped in. "Don't worry, Mama. We know what we're doing. We saw the man, but we made sure he didn't see us."

"We figured it would be best if we all stuck together for a little bit until things settle down."

"It's gonna get worse before it gets any better," Nessa told her two girls. She could feel it deep down in her bones.

"We know," Jordan said, just as the doorbell rang.

A few moments later, they heard Franklin coming up the stairs. "Nessa?" He kept his voice low. "There's a lady at the door. She needs to talk to you about a sensitive subject. She says her name is Annette."

Jordan and Breanna ran to the window.

"You sure have made some weird friends since we've been gone," Breanna said.

Nessa threw on a robe and went downstairs. Before she opened the door, she peeked through the peephole. Waiting on her front porch was an unfamiliar white woman wearing a dressing gown identical to her own.

"Hello?" Nessa said.

"Oh, hi there." The woman smiled nervously. "You don't know me. My name is Annette Moore and I live across the street from Harriett Osborne. I saw you both on the news a while back, and I know you visit her house a lot, so I thought maybe you two were good friends."

"We are," Nessa confirmed cautiously, wondering what Harriett might have done to the nosy neighbor lady's yard—and mildly annoyed that the woman had no trouble locating the house where Harriett's Black friend lived.

"Well, I was making myself a cup of tea about an hour ago when I heard sirens coming up the street. They didn't pass by, so I peeped out my blinds, and there were three cop cars parked in front of Harriett's house."

Nessa closed her eyes and rubbed them with the heels of her hands. "Damn it," she groaned.

"Harriett opened the door and let the cops in. I thought maybe she'd called them for some reason. Then about fifteen minutes ago, two of them dragged her out and shoved her in the back of a police car. There are still three police officers in her garden. Since pot is legal now, they must be looking for the shrooms."

"You're talking about psilocybin? They won't find any," Nessa said. "Harriett doesn't grow mushrooms like that in her garden."

"I know. Eric grows them for her," Annette said. "She gave me a baggie the other day. Harriett and I took some together to celebrate my divorce. It changed my life."

"Harriett." Nessa groaned again. "Thanks for letting me know, Ms. Moore. I'll get dressed and go get her."

"Wait." The woman reached out and grasped Nessa's arm. "There's one more thing. If there's bail to be paid, it's on me. I'm afraid I have to insist."

"Why?" Nessa asked.

"I owe her." The lady didn't choose to explain further, but Nessa could see that she took it very seriously. "Women like us need to stick together."

"All right then." Nessa wasn't going to argue. "I'll make sure you get the bill."

Nessa closed the door and turned around to find her family had been eavesdropping. They stared at Nessa, waiting for her to make the first move.

"You heard what she said. I gotta get some clothes on."

"I'll go keep an eye on the officers in Harriett's garden." Franklin was already pulling on the sneakers he'd left in the entryway. "Make sure they don't find anything that wasn't already there."

"I'm going with you!" Jordan followed Franklin out the door.

"I'll toast you a bagel for the road," Breanna told Nessa. "You can't kick ass unless you've had breakfast."

After they'd all rushed off, Nessa stood in the foyer for a moment and listened. Just a few months earlier, her life had been quiet. Suddenly, it was full once again. But the sound of the waves was louder than ever. A storm was on its way.

———

NESSA MARCHED ACROSS THE MATTAUK Police Department parking lot like a woman on a mission. Though she'd never thought of herself as a pushover, she'd always preferred playing nice when she could. But not today. Today she'd be taking no prisoners.

She barged through the door of the police department and was met by a stench that brought her to a stop. The building reeked like an ancient grave, with a sharp top note of mildew and a base of black mold. A young officer named Jones was manning the desk with his undershirt pulled up over his nose, which Nessa was one hundred percent certain violated uniform regulations.

She went up to the desk, slammed her purse down on top, and made a show of searching the room with her eyes. "My friend Harriett Osborne was arrested this afternoon. Where is she? I'd like to know what she's been charged with."

"I'll have to check," came the muffled response.

"My ass, you'll have to check. I'd bet you anything she's the only woman here. What's she in for? Don't make me repeat myself."

"Possession of a Schedule I substance," Jones responded.

"I can't understand you," Nessa said, though she could. He reluctantly pulled the shirt down from over his nose.

"Possession of a Schedule I substance."

"You mean *shrooms*?" She scoffed. "How much?"

"Twenty milligrams."

"*Twenty milligrams?* That's a class A misdemeanor," Nessa announced with conviction. She'd perused New York's penalties for drug possession before she got out of the car. "And it's only a matter of time before psilocybin possession is decriminalized in this state. You can't hold her for something like that."

"We can and we will," said a voice behind her. She spun around—Chief Rocca had just entered the building. "A search of Ms. Osborne's home is currently under way. If we find over six hundred twenty-five milligrams, your friend could be looking at life in prison."

If he expected Nessa to be intimidated, he had another thing coming. It was hard to look at the man without punching him in the face. She might have tried if she'd thought she had a chance of doing some damage. "You think I don't know the law? I was married to a cop for fifteen years. Until you find something, you have no right to keep her locked up. And if you think you're going to plant something there, I'll have you know there will be witnesses. Where is she?"

"In a holding cell, Ms. James." He stopped and sniffed at the air. "What is that smell?" he asked the desk officer.

"I believe it's mold, sir," Jones wheezed. "It's been like that for an hour or so."

"Chief Rocca, are you going to tell me you've got Harriett Osborne locked up for possession of a few measly mushrooms in a building with a serious mold problem? Look at that!" Nessa pointed her index finger at the ceiling, where a patch of furry black mold had snuck past a door at the back of the room and was now creeping across the ceiling tiles. "You know black mold is toxic, right?"

As if on cue, the door to the holding cells opened and another young officer appeared. "Sir?" The boy's face was unnaturally pale, and he clutched at his throat with one of his hands. "Sir, I think we have a problem back in the holding cells."

"Then deal with it!" Chief Rocca barked.

The young cop stood there for a moment, mouth open and chest heaving. Then he fell to the ground with a heavy thud.

"Get him out to the parking lot!" Nessa ordered. When Jones and Rocca stood frozen in shock, she knew it was time to bellow, "Do what I say, damn it! I'm a nurse!"

The two men rushed to the collapsed officer. Each took an arm, and together they dragged her patient out the front door.

"You," she ordered Jones once they were all outside, "hold the kid for me. We need to keep him upright. Chief Rocca, you call an ambulance."

While Rocca made the call, Nessa quickly frisked her patient. Just as she'd expected, there was an albuterol inhaler in his pants pocket. The kid was asthmatic. She shook the inhaler and opened his mouth, making sure his tongue wasn't blocking his airway. Then she held his nose, inserted the inhaler into his mouth, and sprayed.

"Inhale slowly and hold, honey," she told the barely conscious boy. As he began to cough, she counted to sixty. "One more time, okay?"

After the second squeeze, the boy's breathing remained labored, but at least he was getting air into his lungs. Nessa could hear an ambulance in the distance. She left the kid with Jones and marched up to Rocca.

"If you keep my friend locked up back there in some mold-infested cell, I will sell everything I own to fund the biggest motherfucking lawsuit this county has ever seen."

"Bring her out," Rocca ordered Jones.

"Are you kidding?" Nessa scoffed. "That boy is not going anywhere. He's gotta keep the patient in an upright position until the EMTs get here. If you're too chickenshit to go back in the station, just give me the damn keys already."

Keys in hand, she stomped back into the building, following the path of the thick black mold on the ceiling to the door that led to the holding cells. When she opened the door, a stench unlike any she'd ever known washed over her. Peering inside, she wondered if she might have opened a portal to outer space. Everything beyond the threshold was a pure, inky black. She took a tentative step forward and felt the mold squish beneath her feet like a sodden shag carpet. Slowly, her eyes began to differentiate between the wall to her right, the floor beneath her, and a jail cell to her left. Fearing the worst, she frantically wiped the mold from the cell's bars until she located the keyhole. When she opened the cell door, she saw what she'd been dreading. A human shape sitting upright on a bench, every inch of it covered in mold. It seemed to have been overcome almost instantly, like a figure buried by ash at Pompeii. The body was rigid and the mouth stretched wide-open in one last scream.

"Oh Jesus," Nessa sobbed. "Harriett."

"I'm pretty sure that's not Jesus, and it's definitely not me," announced a voice from the cell next door.

Nessa rode a wave of relief out of the cell and down the aisle. Harriett was sitting cross-legged on the floor in the center of a perfectly mold-free circle, her eyes closed. Until that moment, Nessa had only seen the benevolent side of Harriett's powers. The flowers that lured you in with seductive fragrances. The elixirs that cured headaches and hangovers. Now, at last, Nessa had witnessed Harriett's dark side firsthand. She'd always known it was there. But she'd clearly underestimated what it could do.

"What the hell, Harriett? You scared the crap out of me!" She pointed back the way she had come. "Did you do that on purpose?"

"Do what?" Harriett's eyes slowly opened. In the dim light of the holding cell, her irises seemed flecked with glistening gold.

"Kill the man in the first cell," Nessa whispered.

"I had to. I promised Lucy."

"Lucy?" Nessa was confused.

"Do you know who he was?" Harriett asked. "That was the man who broke into Jo's house."

"I thought he was under house arrest awaiting his trial," Nessa said. "Why did they bring him back in?"

"Perhaps because they knew I would soon be in an adjoining cell?" Harriett offered. "Who knows what Rocca had in mind, but the man and I had an interesting chat before he died. I offered him a chance to confess his sins. I probably could have helped him survive the mold, but after I heard his sins, I didn't feel so inclined. He was hired to scare the three of us out of Mattauk. He thought killing Lucy might do the trick."

"He told you that?"

"People get chatty when death's at the door. He also informed me he was getting paid very well to stay silent."

"Who was paying him?"

"He didn't know. He said he'd never met his employer, and he claimed he'd never heard of Spencer Harding." When Harriett rose to her feet, she seemed to be a few inches taller than she had been before. "So do you think I did the wrong thing?" she asked.

The question felt like a test, Nessa thought. But she knew the right answer, and she had no problem giving it.

"No," Nessa said. "The man was a monster."

"The mold ate him alive," Harriett informed her. "He died in terrible agony."

"He was going to kill Jo's baby. I'm sure he killed others. He got what he deserved."

Harriett nodded. "I'm so glad we see eye to eye on this subject."

Nessa watched Harriett walk out of the cell and through the police station, her bare feet leaving a trail of jet-black prints. Something important had just been decided. Nessa wasn't entirely sure what it was. But she knew things would be different going forward.

Outside in the parking lot, the young officer Nessa had saved was being loaded into the back of an ambulance. The chief of police was waiting to ambush Nessa and Harriett when they emerged.

"What have you done to my station?" he snarled at Harriett.

"Excuse me?" Nessa shot back. "A mold problem you've left untreated just killed a man. If I were you, I'd be very careful what you say right now. We're contemplating a hefty lawsuit."

Rocca ignored Nessa and focused on Harriett. "I just got off the phone with the hospital. The officers who were executing the search of your garden have all been admitted for treatment. Two of them were attacked by ants, and one brushed up against something that left him in so much pain that he had to be sedated."

"Oh dear," Harriett droned. "I did warn them to be careful around my plants, particularly the *mala mujer*. I know it's pretty, but it will fight back if you fondle it. Sounds like one of your men didn't listen. Did they happen to find any of the mushrooms they were after?"

Rocca's face had turned an unsettling shade of red. "I swear to God, I'm going to be all over you from now on. You may have gotten lucky this time, but you won't the next."

Harriett gave him a grin. "I'm no lawyer, but that certainly sounds like harassment. Does that sound like harassment to you, Nessa?"

"It does, Harriett," Nessa agreed. "As does locking you up for possessing a few mushrooms and making you wait in a moldy cell.

I'm sure your lawyer would love to know what probable cause led to the search of your home in the first place."

"Her husband, Chase Osborne, informed me that she was selling drugs out of their yard."

Nessa's jaw dropped at the betrayal, but Harriett took it all in stride.

"Chase is not my husband, and the yard to which he referred is mine. He hasn't lived in the house for almost a year now. As for my business, all I sell is peace of mind to women who have to deal with sad little men like you and Chase. Since you and my ex-husband seem to be in regular contact, perhaps you can ask him what your future might hold. He's had a taste of what I can do."

"Are you threatening me, you fucking witch?" Rocca snarled.

"*Fucking witch*. You say that as if it's an insult," Harriett replied. "For your information, I don't plan to ever see you again."

They walked around him to Nessa's car and climbed inside.

"You've become quite a badass, my dear," Harriett noted as Nessa peeled out of the parking lot. "Feels nice, doesn't it?" Harriett reached into her thicket of hair and pulled out a fat joint.

"Harriett, you snuck a joint into jail?" Nessa marveled. "And when the hell did you and Eric start growing shrooms?"

"When I learned they can help treat depression," Harriett said. "Why obey laws that are in no one's best interests?"

Nessa wasn't going to argue. "Well, I don't know where you hid your stash, but we both know you were lucky as hell they didn't find it."

"Yes," Harriett agreed. "Which means it's time to celebrate."

"Put that away until I get you home!" Nessa ordered.

"Only if you agree to give it a try," Harriett said. "If you like it, I'll send you off with a thank-you gift. A few puffs before sex, and I swear you'll see God."

Nessa glanced over at her. "Fine," she said, and Harriett cackled in triumph. But when she pulled up in front of Harriett's house a few minutes later, they found a familiar Mercedes parked in the driveway. Chase Osborne leaned against the trunk, looking pasty and hungover.

"Ugh," Harriett grumbled at the sight of her guest. "I had a feeling he'd show up. His conscience always briefly kicks in after he does something shitty."

"Are you going to kill him?" Nessa asked.

"No," Harriett replied, as though the result wouldn't be worth the effort. "If I killed people for being morons, I would have murdered Chase years ago." She opened the door and slid out. "But I'll give you a shout if I need any help with a body."

AFTER NESSA DROVE OFF, HARRIETT greeted Chase with all the enthusiasm she would have shown a chin hair. When they'd first met in their twenties, he'd seemed like such a fascinating mystery. Unfortunately, it hadn't taken long to solve it. By the time they were married, Harriett had realized that everything he did was completely predictable. He valued money, sex, status, and food—in that order. Chase was a very simple creature.

"What in the hell is going on here?" he asked her. "When I pulled up about thirty minutes ago, there were policemen in the garden, and all of them were screaming. Then ambulances arrived and rushed them away."

"Did any of them go near the compost heap?" Harriett asked.

"Not that I know of," Chase said.

"Then I forgive you. Go home."

"I don't understand. Are you saying this is all my fault somehow?"

"I know you narced on me, Chase. That's pretty despicable, even by your standards."

Either he'd invested in acting lessons or Chase was genuinely shocked by the accusation. "What are you talking about?" he asked.

"I've spent the last couple of hours in a cell at the Mattauk police station. The chief of police told me that you personally informed him I was selling mushrooms out of my home."

"What? I didn't—" He went pale. "That guy was the chief of police?"

"How did that fact escape you?" Harriett asked.

"He wasn't in uniform!" Chase said. "He was wearing shorts and a polo shirt! I wouldn't turn you in to the police. Do you think I'm that stupid?"

"Yes," she said honestly.

"I was drunk, and I was talking to Jackson—"

"Jackson Dunn?" Of course. It was starting to make perfect sense.

"He's the reason I'm out here on the island. He invited me to stay for Labor Day weekend. Last night, he had a small party. Just a few of the boys. I was talking to Jackson and another guy when your name came up—and the weed problem on the Pointe. Jackson said you had a way with plants, and I may have made a joke about you growing crazy shit in your garden. I never thought anyone there would use the information against you. It's not like Jackson and his friends are upstanding citizens. In fact—" He paused, looking terrified.

"Tell me," Harriett ordered.

"That's why I came to see you. Last night Jackson asked if I'd be interested in a girl for tonight."

"A girl?"

Chase had suddenly gone pale. "I was drunk," he said. "But I got the sense that he was talking about something sketchy."

"What did you say?" Harriett asked.

"I said okay."

"You said *okay*?"

"I was drunk, and he's the man who pays my fucking bills, Harriett. I have a baby on the way, I can't—" He stopped.

"Congratulations," Harriett said, surprised that she felt nothing. It seemed that wound had healed nicely. "You've successfully passed your DNA to a new generation."

"I'm sorry. That's not how I meant to tell you."

"I figured it was only a matter of time. Let's get back to the girl you were offered."

"Jackson didn't say anything about the girl's age or anything, but I just got this sense that . . ." Chase looked truly ill. "I left first thing this morning. I'm going back to Brooklyn right after this. I don't give a damn if I lose the account anymore. I don't give a damn if I lose my job. I feel like I just had a brush with something evil. I know you have something to do with all of that stuff that happened with Spencer Harding, and I thought I should tell you. I think Jackson might be some kind of pervert, too."

It was as close to a selfless act as Chase Osborne would ever muster. The species wasn't entirely corrupt, Harriett observed. Once in a while, one of them would surprise you. Such actions never redeemed them completely, of course, but it did make Harriett wonder if they really deserved to be wiped off the planet.

"Thank you, Chase."

"Do you think Jackson might do something to me? A lot of weird shit has been happening lately."

"No," Harriett assured him. "You have my word. Jackson can't do anything to you."

Chase's phone dinged and its screen lit up. He glanced down, then his head jerked back up. "Jackson's dead. Did you do that, Harriett?"

"Go home," she told him. "And don't come back to the island for a while. It might not be safe for you here."

ÉMINENCE GRISE

Jo's phone pinged just as she set it down on the front desk at Furious Fitness. A text message had arrived from Claude.

Got the surveillance video of the Harding house. I just pulled up outside the gym. Can we talk?

Jo glanced out the window. Sure enough, Claude was sitting in a car across the street, holding up what looked like a thumb drive. Jo eagerly waved her over.

"You okay?" Jo asked as Claude pushed through the door. She barely resembled the woman Jo had come to know. Her skin was sallow and her eyes swollen.

"I didn't sleep last night," Claude said. "You were right. Rocca was at the Harding house a few hours before Spencer crashed. Have a look at file number one."

Jo immediately inserted the drive into her computer. It contained two video files labeled "ONE" and "TWO." When she clicked on file ONE, she saw black-and-white footage of the street-facing side of the Harding house. Three kids sped by on bikes and a woman in a gray uniform walked through the frame in the direction of the nearest neighbor's house. A time stamp in the lower right corner read *JUNE 9 19:00*.

"The files are twelve hours long. Spencer Harding's helicopter went down just before midnight on June ninth, am I right?"

"Yes," Jo confirmed.

"So you're looking at seven o'clock. Fast-forward to 21:38."

Jo slid the cursor to the right point and pressed play. A man in a polo shirt and shorts appeared on the sidewalk and turned down Harding's drive.

"That's Rocca, isn't it?" Claude asked, tapping the screen.

Jo moved the cursor back a few seconds and paused on a frame where the man's face was visible. If she'd passed him on the sidewalk, dressed casually and out of context as he was, she might not have recognized him. But the gait definitely belonged to Chief Rocca.

"So he was at Harding's house three hours before the helicopter crash."

"He was," Claude said. "And did you notice which direction he came from?"

Jo studied the still image. "It looks like he was coming from the direction of Jackson Dunn's house."

"That's what I thought, too," Claude said. "So I had a look at a few other files. Open the one labeled 'TWO.'"

Jo clicked on the second file. This time, the camera was facing the Dunn home. At 21:32, Chief Rocca exited the house. He walked briskly and with purpose. Even from a distance, the scowl on his face was unmistakable.

"Do you know what happened forty-eight minutes before Rocca decided to pay Harding a visit?" Claude asked Jo. Jo thought for a moment, then shook her head. "A forty-three-minute-long special episode of the podcast *They Walk Among Us* was released—the same episode in which you and your friend accused Spencer Harding of murder."

"So Rocca was with Jackson Dunn that night. As soon as the podcast was over, he headed to Spencer Harding's house. Three hours later, Harding's helicopter crashed in New York Harbor. An hour after that, the Mattauk police officially arrived on the Pointe."

"Yes," Claude said. "And now you have proof that Rocca let Spencer escape."

"And some pretty compelling evidence that Jackson Dunn was involved, too."

"Yes, but it's too late to make Jackson pay for his crimes. It hasn't made the news yet, but he died yesterday."

"Bees?" Jo asked.

Claude nodded. "He was on his roof deck when it happened. One of the staff members witnessed the whole thing. She told me that a swarm swooped down out of nowhere. Jackson was stung hundreds of times, but she wasn't touched. The poor woman was so traumatized that I had to give her the rest of the weekend off. She said Jackson suffered horribly."

Jo was quiet for a moment. "Good," she said.

"There's something else I need to show you," Claude said. Her hand was visibly shaking as she leaned over and replayed the second clip. Once again, Chief Rocca exited the Dunn home. Just as he reached the sidewalk, Claude hit pause. "See?" She pointed to the glass windows. A pair of silhouettes could be seen on the drawn curtains. "There are still two men inside."

Jo leaned in. Claude was right. There were two figures standing in Dunn's living room. A noticeable paunch identified Jackson. The second man appeared leaner.

"That can't be Spencer," Claude said. "And we just saw Rocca leave for the Harding house."

"Who do you think it could be?" Jo turned to find Claude crying. "Oh my God, what's wrong?" she asked, pulling Claude into a hug.

"I think it might be Leonard."

"Leonard?" Jo asked as Claude sobbed. That seemed ridiculous. When Claude finally pulled back, Jo handed her a tissue. "Did the footage show Leonard entering Jackson's house?"

"I watched hours of footage, and there was nothing on it,"

Claude said, using the tissue to wipe her eyes. "But Leonard went whale watching that night. I walked down to the dock with him and left him there when it got boring. He could have entered Jackson's house from the beach. The footage from the camera covering that entrance is missing."

"Do you have any reason to suspect Leonard might be involved?"

"No," Claude said. "But it wouldn't be the first time a man hid the truth from me. If it turns out Leonard lied, after all that I've been through, I'm going to kill him, Jo. I'm serious. I will beat the man to death with my own two hands."

There was no doubt she meant it. "Want to find out?" Jo asked.

Claude balled up her tissue and nodded. "Yeah."

Just then, Heather burst through the door of Furious Fitness. "OMG, you beat me to work again! Don't you ever sleep?" It wasn't easy impressing a boss who worked as hard as Jo.

"The place is all yours," Jo told her. "I was just about to go out for a jog. You coming?" she asked Claude.

"Right behind you," Claude said as Jo took off.

By the time Claude caught up, Jo was already halfway down the block, her arms pumping like pistons as the rage inside her propelled her forward. "Where are we going?" Claude asked.

"The police station," Jo told her.

"To see Rocca?" Claude asked. "Do you really think he'll tell the truth?"

"He will if I beat it out of him," Jo said. But when they reached the station, the parking lot was barricaded by sawhorses and the front door was cordoned off with yellow caution tape. The warning seemed rather unnecessary, considering the building itself was covered in furry black mold.

"Shit, I forgot about this," Jo said. "I should have known the station would be closed."

"What happened?" Claude panted.

"The cops fucked with the wrong bitch," Jo said. "Come on, let's jog down to Grass Beach."

"Grass Beach?" Claude asked, her eyes still fixed on the mold.

"It's a beautiful run," Jo replied. "And all the police officers live down that way."

ON THE OUTSKIRTS OF MATTAUK, a bridge carried the road over a sea of tall grass that grew in the swampy land separating the town from the beach. It was a peaceful stretch of highway where one was unlikely to encounter another human so early in the morning. The air hadn't yet lost its nighttime chill, and the breeze off the ocean sent ripples across the grass. Jo's eyes landed on a patch in the center of the marsh that appeared to be moving against the wind. Something was out there among the reeds. Suddenly, it took a sharp turn to the left, followed by another, until it was heading back the way it had come.

Jo stopped to watch. Claude raced past her, then slowed and doubled back.

"Probably a dog," she said.

"Maybe." Jo had to be sure. "Hello?" she called, sending a flock of birds shooting into the sky. "Someone out there?"

"Help!" a frantic girl cried in response. "I'm lost! I can't find my way out!"

"Don't panic!" Jo shouted back at her. "Just walk straight for a moment so I know which way you're facing." She watched carefully as the grass moved. "Okay, stop! Now turn to your five o'clock. Then start walking forward from there."

The grass bent in another direction. "Am I doing this right?" the girl shouted. "I can't see a thing!"

"You're headed in the right direction! Keep going, you've got a few hundred yards till you reach the edge of the marsh."

Soon a girl with a tear-slicked face emerged from the grass, her pretty gray running shorts and tank stained green and black. Her skin appeared to be speckled with moles, until Jo realized they were moving. The girl shrieked when she noticed the ticks and frantically brushed them away with both hands.

"Breanna?" Jo rushed to greet her. "Oh my God, are you okay?"

"It's you." The girl began sobbing.

"Why were you out there?" Jo turned her around and swept the ticks off her back. "What the hell happened?"

"Jordan and I usually run together, but she and Mama slept late this morning. I always come this way when I'm alone. It's supposed to be safe because all the police live down here by the water. I was crossing the bridge when a cop car pulled up beside me. He said something had happened to my mom, and he'd give me a ride back to the house."

"No, no, no." Jo didn't want to imagine what might have happened to Nessa's girl if she'd gotten into the car.

"Then I realized it was that cop from *Newsnight*—the one who lied about you and Mama. I told him I'd run back to the house myself, and he started to get out of the vehicle. I figured I wouldn't be able to get away if he pulled his gun, so I jumped off the bridge and hid in the grass. I stayed down there until I heard him drive away. But after he was gone, I couldn't find my way out."

The story sounded all too familiar. "Was there anything unique about his patrol car that would identify it if we saw it parked in a driveway?" Jo asked.

"Yeah," Breanna said. "It had a big number one painted on the hood."

Jo took her phone out.

"What are you going to do?" Claude asked.

"I'm going to get Breanna's mom out of bed."

NESSA WAS ALREADY AWAKE AND at her computer. While she'd been sleeping, an email had arrived. The author had written "The Girl in Blue" in the subject line. A few days after she found the body by Danskammer Beach, Nessa had posted portraits of the girl on every major missing persons site. A few responses had trickled in at the beginning of the summer, but this was the first email she'd received in weeks.

To Whom It May Concern:

I am certain the Girl in Blue is my niece. Her name is Faith Reid, born March 29, 2004.

I have enclosed a photo. Please contact me at your earliest convenience.

Dana Reid
Montego Bay, Jamaica

Faith. The name couldn't be a coincidence. Her heart pounding, Nessa opened the picture Dana Reid had attached and found herself face-to-face with the girl she'd found at Danskammer Beach. She was leaning in for a closer look at the pendant Faith wore around her neck when the call came in from Jo.

NESSA LEFT THE CAR RUNNING and the driver's-side door standing open. Barefoot and still dressed in her nightgown, she grabbed Breanna and held her against her chest. Jordan, who'd hopped in the passenger seat before Nessa could back out of the drive, stood with her arms wrapped around her mother and her twin. The tears running down Nessa's face felt scalding hot. She'd never contemplated killing another human being before. Now it was all she could think about. For the first time, she understood exactly how Jo had felt the night a man had come for Lucy.

"Jordan, drive Breanna to your aunt Harriett's house," she ordered. "Tell her what's happened, and ask her to get all the ticks off your sister and make sure she's okay."

"You're not coming with us, Mama?" Jordan asked.

"Not now," Nessa told her.

"Your mother and I have someone we need to visit." Jo shifted from foot to foot. She was having a hard time standing still. The energy racing through her system couldn't be contained much longer. It needed to be released before it blew her to pieces.

"The chief of police?" Jordan scoffed. "You've got to be joking. What are the two of you going to do? The guy's a dirty cop. He could shoot you."

"Don't worry. I'm going with them," Claude said. "I'll make sure I get everything on camera. Rocca won't try anything stupid as long as I'm there."

That didn't seem to do much to convince Jordan. She kept her eyes on her mother. "How's she going to protect you? Rich white ladies generating their own force fields these days?"

"Go," her mother ordered. "*Now*, Jordan."

"I'm not ready to be an orphan," Jordan snapped.

"Now!" Nessa roared.

Jordan glowered but kept her lips sealed. Then she climbed into the driver's side of Nessa's car and slammed the door. Jo put an arm around Nessa as they watched the girls drive away.

"Something very bad is about to happen," Nessa said. "I can feel it."

Jo squeezed her friend's shoulder. "I know," she replied. "You ready?"

"Let's go," Nessa said.

THEY FOUND THE COP CAR with a number one on its hood parked beneath a massive house that sat atop stilts and hovered over the dunes. There was no way to reach the front door. A locked gate blocked the stairs that led up to the porch. The place was a fortress.

"Follow me." Jo stomped around the house and climbed atop a grass-covered dune that faced the house's deck. The sliding doors that led into the house were standing open, and their curtains fluttered in the wind. Rocca was sitting at a table with a cup of coffee in front of him.

"Morning, motherfucker!" Jo bellowed with her hands cupped around her mouth. "You ready for us to tell everyone in Mattauk what you really do for a living?"

Nessa climbed up on the dune beside Jo. Down on the beach, two joggers paused to see what would come next. The next-door neighbor appeared on his porch wearing nothing but boxer shorts.

"Chief Rocca sure has a very nice house, doesn't he? You ever wonder how he can afford to live this way on a small-town cop's salary?" Jo called out to their audience. "I can tell you! He pays the bills by pulling little girls into his cop car and selling them to perverts like Spencer Harding."

"It's the truth!" Nessa shouted. "And ten minutes ago, he tried to kidnap my girl. He went and messed with the wrong mama this time."

Rocca yawned in response. "What are you talking about? And why are you bothering me on my day off? Get the hell off my property before I have you both arrested."

"Go ahead and have us arrested," Jo told him. "It'll give us a chance to show your colleagues the security footage from the Pointe. It's pretty clear from the videos that you were with Spencer Harding for three hours before he fled the Pointe in his helicopter."

"Honey?" A petite woman appeared on the deck with a plate, which she set down in front of Rocca. She'd been pretty once—and might be again if she got help for her sickly complexion and thinning hair. "What's going on out here?"

"A couple of crazy women are claiming to have something that doesn't exist, and they're about to get their butts thrown in jail." Rocca picked up the piece of coffee cake his wife had just brought him and took a large, leisurely bite.

"They have the security footage from the Pointe. I gave it to them." Claude stepped into view and Rocca's face instantly fell.

"What the hell are you doing here?" he demanded.

"They know what you, Dunn, and Harding were doing at the Pointe. Kidnapping girls and killing them. Was Leonard involved, too? That's what I want to know." The force of Claude's fury took even Jo by surprise. She was out for blood.

"Is this some kind of joke?" Rocca snarled.

"John," Rocca's wife broke in. "What is she talking about?"

He coughed and cleared his throat. "Go back inside, Juliet," he ordered. "None of this concerns you."

"Does it have anything to do with the fifteen-year-old girl you assaulted on your boat?"

"What—" Rocca looked up at his wife, but he couldn't seem to finish the thought. His hand rose to his throat and his mouth stretched open as he desperately struggled to breathe.

"Have some more coffee cake, sweetheart," the woman said, cramming the remainder of Rocca's breakfast into his wide, gaping mouth. "I made it from scratch just for you."

JULIET ROCCA'S LAST DISH

Juliet Rocca began baking every day when her three boys were little. Even back then, their father worked long hours and late nights, and the sun often rose before he strolled through the door. While they were dating, John had informed Juliet that he intended to become Mattauk's chief of police. At the time, becoming engaged to a future pillar of the community felt like a glorious destiny. Juliet had developed mood boards for every room of her future house back in fifth grade. She already knew the names of her unborn children. She was thrilled to discover that John was a planner, too. It just never occurred to her that he would work toward his goal with such single-minded persistence.

When John wasn't out on patrol, he donated his time to the local high school's softball team. Appearances were everything, he told her. The town needed to see their future chief giving back. Saturday was game day. Sunday after church, John took his boat out on the sound to decompress. Juliet despised softball, but she and the boys attended every game. John said it was important for the community to know the whole family was watching. But that wasn't why Juliet sacrificed her Saturdays. Outside of church, softball games were the only way her boys could see their father for three consecutive hours each week.

To compensate for John's absence, Juliet poured her love for her boys into every pie, cake, and cookie she baked. Only she could detect the bitter aftertaste of her guilt. She watched over them as they grew, relieved that none of the boys seemed scarred by their father's neglect. They may have inherited John's height, heft, and good looks. But on the inside, they were her children, stuffed plump by their mother and filled with sweetness and affection.

The baking became more than a hobby the year after the boat burned. The girl who'd set it on fire was in jail. Her accusations had been completely discredited—John's fellow officers had seen to that. Once, Juliet had asked John if there might be any truth to it all. He'd glared at her with utter contempt and told her he couldn't be married to anyone whose head was filled with such ugly thoughts. Ashamed, Juliet begged for forgiveness. Divorce had never featured in any of her daydreams. She had no idea what might happen to her and the boys if their family ever broke up.

John spent more time at home the following year and threw all his energy into making the Rocca world appear perfect. The boys had never been cleaner. The lawn had never been lusher. The Christmas decorations had never been cheerier. Juliet's sphere was reduced to the kitchen, and for twelve months, she never stopped baking. Each brownie was a brick in the wall she built to shield her children from their father's disdain. She countered John's insults with banana bread. She snuck them shortcake after spankings. By the time summer rolled around once again, the punishments for squirming in church or coming home with grass stains on their jeans had become so draconian that no baked goods could compensate. Juliet and the children lived in fear. They were all so relieved when a fancy new boat appeared in the driveway that Juliet never dared ask her husband where he had found the money.

But she couldn't slow down the production line. She kept baking, day and night. She made chocolate croissants for Sunday school and cupcakes for the PTA, and almost single-handedly supplied every bake sale in town. Everyone told John he'd married the perfect homemaker. He took a tray of his wife's baked goods to work every morning. His softball players munched cannoli in the dugout. She made sure each Mattauk police officer got a custom-baked birthday cake. Her giant sons and their friends gorged on mountains of muffins and miles of strudel.

When the last Rocca boy left for college, the pastries and desserts began to pile up. Unable to bear seeing her work go to waste, Juliet started consuming her own creations. John let her put on five pounds before he informed her she was getting too fat. But Juliet couldn't stop eating. She was left with no other choice than to start throwing it up.

That worked for a while. Then Juliet's hair began falling out in clumps. Her skin reeked of onions and sores formed on her gums and her lips. Their family doctor was John's fishing buddy. She couldn't take her troubles to him. Fortunately, she found help in the ladies' room at church. That's where she heard Rosa and Sofia Mancino whispering about the witch on Woodland Drive.

"Harriett Osborne can fix that, no problem," Rosa assured Juliet when she showed the sisters the growing bald patch on her scalp. "She'll probably even do it for free. When I went to see her, she wouldn't take any payment."

So, the next day, Juliet took the witch a Snickers cake instead.

"My name is Juliet," she informed the wild-looking woman who answered the door. "I need your help."

"I know who you are. I've been hoping you'd come." Harriett stuck a finger into the center of the cake and then popped it into her mouth. "Tastes like distraction with a side of denial," she said. Then she carried the cake to the backyard and unceremoniously dumped it on top of the compost heap.

"You keep eating shit like that and you'll die," the witch told her. "Is that what you want?"

"No." Juliet began to sob. "But I can't seem to stop."

"You're filling your face because there's something you're trying hard not to see," the witch told her. "If you want to get better, the first thing you need to do is look. For the next three days, you will drink nothing but water and consume nothing but air. You will spend eight hours every day staring out at the ocean. At the end of that time, everything should be clear."

"And that will end it?"

"No," Harriett said bluntly. "This will." She passed Juliet a little brown bag.

Juliet opened it and looked. Inside were what appeared to be three small white carrots and two index cards. Written on one was a single URL. The other contained a set of instructions. The first line read "Purchase a pair of neoprene gloves."

Juliet looked up. "Is this a spell?" she asked. "I don't know if I'm up for something like that. I'm not like you."

"Think of it as a recipe for the last thing you'll ever need to bake," Harriett told her. "But the truth is, Ms. Rocca—and I suspect deep down, you already know this—every recipe is a spell. And all cooks are witches."

LOOKING OUT AT THE OCEAN, Juliet found her thoughts lingering on her husband's first boat. She remembered the girl who had set it on fire. And by the time the sun went down on the third day of her fast, she'd seen what she'd been blind to for all those years. That girl had no reason to lie. Amber Welsh had been telling the truth.

Juliet went inside and opened the little brown bag the witch had given her. She typed the URL into her phone. Three pencil-drawn portraits appeared on her screen. One was the girl they'd found down by Danskammer Beach. The second was Amber Welsh's daughter, who'd gone missing. When she realized she knew the third girl—the one who remained unidentified—Juliet vomited one last time. Then she went to the store and bought a pair of neoprene gloves.

PART THREE

On Labor Day morning, a bloated body wearing the tattered remains of a twelve-thousand-dollar suit washed ashore on Governors Island, where it was spotted by a group of picnicking tourists. Two teenage brothers from Akron, assuming the figure was a mannequin and the smell was just eau de New York, posted pictures on social media. The photos were yanked off the site as soon as it became apparent that their subject was, in fact, a decaying corpse. By that time, however, Jo had a screenshot of one of the posts saved on her phone.

She picked up Nessa and drove along Woodland Drive to Harriett's house. A woman neither of them had seen before opened the door.

"Hello, Jo and Nessa," she greeted them. "I am Isabel. Harriett is waiting for you both in the garden."

They found Harriett snipping golden pods from a beanlike vine into a basket. Each gracefully curved pod was the length of a finger and covered in velvety golden hairs.

"Cowhage," Isabel warned when Nessa went for a closer look. "Don't touch."

Harriett appeared to be in an excellent mood. "I see you've all met," she said. "Isabel used to work on the Pointe, but she left a bit early this year. She'll be staying here as my guest and holding down the fort tomorrow."

"You're going somewhere?" Jo asked.

"Celeste and I are taking the boat out. I have an appointment on Culling Pointe."

Harriett set her basket aside and took a seat in a chair by the firepit. "So what's the latest?" she asked. "Spencer Harding crashed into the Hudson. John Rocca had a heart attack while chowing down on coffee cake. Jackson Dunn was killed by a swarm of bees. And I can tell just by the look on your faces that the two of you have brought more news."

Nessa glanced at Isabel nervously.

"Isabel is one of us," Harriett said. "She knows everything. As a matter of fact, she was at Jackson's house, watering his plants, when he died."

"I was traumatized," Isabel deadpanned.

"So," Harriett said, "what do you ladies have to tell me?"

"The girl in blue's name is Faith Reid," Nessa said. "Her aunt emailed me from Jamaica."

"Jamaica? How interesting," Harriett said. "You're getting closer."

"And Spencer Harding's body washed up in New York City this morning." Jo took out her phone and pulled up the screenshot before passing the device to Harriett.

"Oh dear. It seems as though something's been eating his face." Harriett looked up with a grin. "A fitting end, wouldn't you agree?"

"Harding, Dunn, and Rocca are all dead. Is it over?" Nessa asked cautiously.

"You tell me," Harriett said. "How's your headache?"

"It's still there," Nessa admitted. "It eased up for a while, but now it's bad as ever."

"Hmmm. There's your answer, I suppose," Harriett replied matter-of-factly.

"This is the one who sees the dead?" Isabel asked Harriett, who nodded. It was clear they had been discussing Nessa before her arrival.

"Come here, child," Isabel told Nessa. "And sit down beside me."

Nessa obeyed, and the older woman took her hand. Isabel closed her eyes, as if listening to the rhythm of blood pumping through Nessa's veins. "I feel you being called, and I feel you resisting. That is the source of your pain," she told Nessa. "There's something you need to see, and you're frightened."

"What is it?" Nessa whispered.

"I don't know, and neither do they." Isabel gestured to Jo and Harriett. "That is why your skills are more important than any of ours. You are able to see what has been done. Without that knowledge, we don't know who to punish—or who to protect—and the crimes against our kind go unaddressed. Now we need you to stop resisting and guide us where we need to go."

"How do I do that?" Nessa asked.

"Accept that what you find may be worse than you ever thought possible. And believe that you possess the strength to see it."

"But I'm not sure that I do," Nessa confessed.

Isabel squeezed Nessa's hand. "This is what you were made for," she told her. "Why do you think women are designed to outlive men? Why do we keep going for thirty years after our bodies can no longer reproduce? Do you think nature meant for those years to be useless? No, of course not. Our lives our designed to have three parts. The first is education. The second, creation. And in part three, we put our experience to use and protect those who are weaker. This third stage, which you have entered, can be one of incredible power."

"Can be?"

"There have always been those who want to deny women power. And there are also women who refuse to accept it. Some, who've mastered the games men play, choose to betray their own kind.

These women are our most dangerous enemies. But many women are simply too frightened to see things as they really are—or to accept that the world men have made must be destroyed."

"Destroyed?" Jo had been listening closely.

"The day is coming," Isabel said. "When I was a girl, bad men didn't need to hide what they did to women. Now they must keep it behind closed doors. There are more of us than ever. For every woman of my generation, there are three of you."

"Yes, but are we really supposed to destroy the world?" Jo asked.

"Not *the* world—*their* world," Isabel said. "The world men built to suit their needs and desires. As soon as it's in ashes, we can build a better world to replace it."

"That's right," Harriett chimed in. "And our work won't be over until that happens." Her head turned toward the sound of a car pulling up the drive. "That's Celeste," she said, rising from her seat. "Isabel, would you like me to introduce you?"

"It would be a pleasure," Isabel said.

"I'll see you ladies tomorrow," Harriett told Jo and Nessa. "Get a good night's sleep."

Jo waited until they'd disappeared into the house, leaving her alone with Nessa. "What the hell was all of that?"

"I don't know," Nessa admitted. "But I think we're gonna find out soon enough."

THE NEXT DAY, THE TUESDAY after Labor Day, was Lucy's first day of seventh grade. Jo dropped her off at her new middle school. The kids swarming the entrance ranged in size from munchkin to monster. Lucy fell right in between.

Lucy planted a quick kiss on her mom's cheek. "Don't pick me up after school," she said. "I'll walk home."

"Only if you walk with a friend," Jo insisted. "And if Dad's not there when you get home, make sure all the doors are locked and don't open them for anyone. Do you know what to do if there's a fire or the toilet overflows?"

"Mom." Lucy opened the door. "Relax. I got this."

Jo had no choice but to let her go.

When she arrived at the gym, Jo planned to head straight for the treadmills, but Heather called out to her as she passed the front desk. "Jo? There's a woman on the phone who wants to speak to you."

"Take a name and number for me, please," Jo said. "I gotta get rid of some energy."

"She doesn't want to give me her name," Heather replied. "Should I tell her you're not in?"

Jo stopped on the stairs. "No, I'll talk to her," she said.

When she reached the front desk, Heather passed her the phone. "This is Jo," she said.

"Is he really dead!" a woman asked. The voice was oddly familiar.

"Excuse me?"

"That piece of shit Rocca. He was the one who convinced everyone Mandy ran away."

Jo felt her knees wobble. It was Amber Welsh. "Yes," she confirmed. "He died of a heart attack when my friends and I confronted him about his involvement with Spencer Harding."

"Did he help that evil bastard kill Mandy?"

"It's likely, but we don't know for sure," Jo answered honestly.

Amber set the phone down, and Jo could hear her sobbing in the background. "I'm sorry," Amber said when she picked up the phone again. "I should have known he was in on it, after what he did to me."

"To you?" Jo asked.

"Yeah, to me and at least one other girl before me. That's how long Rocca's been at it. I swear to God, I would be putting a bullet in that pervert right now if he wasn't already dead."

Jo spoke to her softly. "I don't know if you heard, Amber, but we found Mandy's body."

"Yes, I did. Thank you," Amber said. "You and your friend made good on your promise. I'm sorry I called her a witch."

"Harriett wasn't offended. We've been worried about you. Your family left town so abruptly. Are you and the boys okay? You're not in trouble, are you?"

"No, no. In fact, I've stayed clean all summer, and my boys have a real house for the first time in their lives. The only thing missing is Mandy. But at least now I got some closure. I just hope my baby found peace."

"We buried her in a beautiful spot, Amber. I'll take you to see her whenever you like."

"I can't come back," Amber told her through tears. "Not ever. That was part of the deal."

"What deal?" Jo blurted out.

"The charity wants me to make a clean start. No looking back. And now that my luck's changed, I'm not gonna screw things up."

"The charity?" Jo repeated. "What charity?"

"Thank you, Ms. Levison," Amber said. "I'll always be grateful for what you've done."

"Wait!"

Then the line went dead.

Jo bolted out the front door of Furious Fitness. It wasn't until she was halfway to Nessa's house that she realized she still had the gym's phone in her hand.

NESSA MET HER AT THE front door. "Did you read my mind?" she demanded.

Jo doubled over to catch her breath. "No," she managed to say.

"I've been emailing with Dana Reid—the woman down in

Jamaica. Dana said her niece, Faith, was living in Montego Bay when she disappeared. She has no idea how she got to the States. Faith didn't even have a passport. But every time I start thinking that the name could be a coincidence, I go back and look at the picture she sent, and there's no doubt it's the girl in blue. She's even wearing a gold necklace with a snake pendant. Ms. Reid says it was a family heirloom."

"It actually makes perfect sense," Jo said. "That's why she was never identified. No one here knew her. She didn't live in America."

Nessa didn't seem convinced. "You okay?" she asked. "You look like you're about to have a stroke."

Jo sat down and held up the cordless phone clenched in her fist. "I brought the wrong phone. Can I borrow yours for a sec?"

Nessa punched in her passcode and handed Jo her phone. Jo typed a query into a search box and began to scroll through the image results.

"What are you looking for?" Nessa asked.

Jo stopped suddenly on a group shot. She enlarged it, checking each face one by one. Then she gasped. Her face was bone white when she passed the phone back to Nessa. "Do you recognize anyone in this picture?"

Nessa scanned the picture on the screen. "I see Leonard Shaw," she said. "Is this a photo from one of his charity events?"

"Yes," Jo said. "In Jamaica. This is him with local volunteers. Look closer. Is there anyone else in the picture you recognize?"

Nessa scanned the faces again. This time, she stopped on a face in the second row. It belonged to a girl of sixteen or seventeen, with big black eyes, rosy cheeks, and dimples. Nessa recognized Faith.

"Claude wondered if Leonard might be involved. That's why we were on our way to Rocca's house that morning—to ask him about it. But so much happened, and it seemed so unlikely—" Jo stopped. "I should have taken her hunch more seriously."

Nessa's headache, previously a dull throbbing pain, had suddenly flared into a full-blown assault on her brain. "Harriett's on her way out to the Pointe right now. We need to get her away from there. My head's about to explode. You okay to drive?" she asked Jo.

"Yeah," Jo said.

"Mama, where are you going?" Breanna called out from inside the house.

"Out to the Pointe. Your aunt Harriett might be in trouble."

THE VOICES

Nessa's skull felt like a room crowded with people, some demanding her attention, the rest screaming for it. Whenever she tried to focus on one voice, it would be drowned out by another. They kept growing louder, as though each had a frantic message to deliver.

"You sure you can do this?" Jo asked as she drove along Danskammer Beach. She could see the agony etched into Nessa's face, and she knew her usually stoic friend was suffering horribly.

"I have to." It was all Nessa could muster, but the message was clear. Harriett might already be at the Pointe. They couldn't leave her there on her own. Jo scooped up Nessa's hand and held it until she pulled up to the gate at Culling Pointe.

"That's strange," Jo muttered. The gate was locked, and there were no guards to be seen. She released Nessa's hand and pulled out her phone to call Claude.

"Jo?" Claude answered.

"I'm trying to find Harriett. There's an emergency. Is she with you?"

"No, not yet," Claude said. "Leonard's down at the dock whale watching. He'll bring her to the house when she arrives. I hope everything's all right. Is there anything I can do?"

"Yes. Ness and I are at the Culling Pointe gate. Can you come let us in?"

"Sure," Claude said. "Just give me a sec."

Jo parked her car along the shoulder of Danskammer Beach

Road. She climbed out and met Nessa on the other side of the vehicle. The warm sun shone down on them and waves lazily lapped at the nearby shore as they walked to the gate.

Nessa stopped a few feet from it. "I don't like this place," she announced, staring down at the pavement ahead of her as though it were flaming brimstone.

"You look like you're going to vomit," Jo whispered back. "Why don't you wait in the car?"

The screaming inside her head was so deafening that Nessa couldn't hear herself think, and words she hadn't been able to process rolled out of her mouth.

"They've been waiting for me," she said. "I should have come a long time ago."

Nessa heard an engine drawing closer. Then a golf cart appeared with Claude behind the wheel. The gate opened and Nessa stepped over the property line. The voices fell silent. They knew she'd arrived.

"What's going on?" Claude asked. "Everything okay?"

"Everything's fine. Harriett never carries a phone and we need to find her so she can deal with a family matter," Jo said. "Why are there no guards at the gate?"

"The season is over. Everyone's gone home," Claude said. "Harriett didn't want anyone around when she got to work on the plants, so we gave the staff a holiday. Jump in and we'll drive down to the dock and see if she's gotten here yet."

Jo climbed into the front seat of the cart beside Claude, while Nessa took the back.

"*Harriett* wanted the Pointe to be empty today?" Jo asked.

"Yeah." Claude stepped on the gas and steered the golf cart back the way she'd come. "She said her methods were proprietary, and she didn't want anyone snooping around."

They rounded a turn and the Pointe unfurled before them. What had once been a patchwork of perfectly landscaped lawns was now a sea of yellow. At least three bushes grew in every yard.

"Wow," Jo said.

"The Scotch broom has taken over," Claude said. "I have no idea how Harriett plans to get rid of it, but you can see why she wouldn't want anyone around to get in the way."

Nessa leaned forward over the front seat and clutched Jo's arm. "Jesus, they're everywhere," she croaked.

"Yeah," said Claude. "It's a real invasion."

Nessa fell back against her seat. "Stop the cart," she ordered. "I'm going to be sick."

"Right here?" While Claude glanced up at the rearview mirror, Jo laid a hand on the dashboard. A plume of black smoke rose up to the heavens, and the vehicle rolled to a stop.

"What the hell?" Claude stared at the steering wheel.

Nessa scrambled out of the golf cart and vomited on the nearest yard.

"We'll be right back," Jo told Claude. She waited until Nessa's stomach had emptied and then guided her friend to the shade of one of the yellow-flower-covered bushes. "Are you okay? What did you see?" she asked quietly.

Nessa shook her head. There was no way to describe all the girls who'd come to stand around her. None of them appeared to be more than seventeen years old. Every shade of skin, every color of hair, every shape of body—they were all represented. Nessa recognized some of the faces from the walls of Franklin's office. Lena Collins was there, standing a head taller than most of the others. She spotted petite Rosalia Cortez nearby. On the surface, they seemed to have nothing in common, aside from their youth. But Nessa knew there was another trait they all shared. These were all girls the world felt free to ignore. They were girls whose families weren't rich enough to demand attention. They were girls who were chosen because people with everything thought their lives were worth nothing.

They'd been here the whole time, just a few miles away from her. And Nessa had never known. While she'd pottered around her pretty house with its white picket fence, girls almost the same age as her daughters had been stolen from their mothers. Young women had been sacrificed to beasts whose presence she'd never suspected.

"How many are there?" Jo asked.

"More than a dozen," Nessa told her. "They're all dead."

"*A dozen*? How?" How could so many girls have been killed in a place where cameras were always watching? Then the truth hit Jo all at once. She knew what the men on Culling Pointe did when their families were gone. It wasn't just a few bad apples. They were *all* part of it. They had to be. Every last one of them. These men who ran the world could only be satisfied by what they weren't supposed to have.

"Guys?" Claude was coming toward them, a look of concern on her face. "What's going on?"

Jo stood up. She didn't see any reason to lie. They'd need Claude's help going forward. "There were more girls murdered here than we knew about. Nessa can see them."

The blood drained from Claude's face, but she didn't appear to doubt Jo's claim. "*Murdered?* How many?" she asked.

"Nessa says at least twelve," Jo said.

Claude put her hand to her heart as though trying to keep it from bursting out of her chest. Then she cleared her throat. "Do you know who killed them?"

Jo didn't want to tell her like this, on the side of the road next to a pile of vomit, but she hadn't been left any choice. "Claude, I'm so sorry. You were right about Leonard. I should have taken your hunch more seriously," Jo told her. "That's why we drove out to the

Pointe. We found evidence that implicated him and we're worried that Harriett might be in danger."

"Leonard?" Claude repeated the name as though she didn't quite recognize it, but the accusation didn't seem to surprise her. "Are you sure he was involved with their deaths?"

Jo glanced over at Nessa, who nodded. "Yes," she said.

Claude bit her lower lip when it began to tremble. Her eyes lifted away from Jo's face and focused on a patch of ocean visible between two of the mansions. She stayed silent long enough to make Jo anxious. Then she said, "He fucking lied to me."

Jo could hear the grief in those four simple words. They sounded heavy and hopeless. They came from a woman who was giving up. A woman who'd bet everything and lost. Who'd tried everything she could think of and failed anyway.

"I'm so sorry." Jo took a step toward her, but Claude took a step back.

"He said he wouldn't let me down again," she said flatly. "He promised. I trusted him."

"Claude," Jo started, but her friend turned away.

"Just a sec," Claude said.

She walked back to the broken-down golf cart and pulled a nine iron out of a bag. Then she left Jo and Nessa and marched off down the street.

"Where are you going?" Jo called.

"To find him," Claude answered.

Jo held out a hand to Nessa. "I don't think we want to miss this. Do you think you can get up and walk?"

They made it to Jackson Dunn's deck overlooking the beach just in time to see Claude reach the dock below, the nine iron resting against her shoulder. Leonard stood at the end of the dock peering out across the waves with his binoculars. He turned at the sound of her footsteps, but he never looked up. He was unaware they were being observed.

"There were more than three," Claude said. "How many girls died here?"

"What are you talking about?" Leonard let the binoculars drop to his side. His face still wore the remains of a smile, as though there was still a chance it was all just a joke.

"How many girls did you let these rich assholes kill?" Claude demanded. "Tell me the truth."

Leonard took in a breath. Jo and Nessa waited to hear the denial he appeared to be concocting.

"I don't know," he finally said. "Rocca took care of it all. Don't worry. There won't be any more surprises. Spencer was a sick fuck. He wanted to put his where he was able to see them. But the other bodies are gone. They won't be found."

"Neither will yours." Claude brought the nine iron down from her shoulder.

"Oh, c'mon, Claude," Leonard cooed, reaching out an arm.

The nine iron caught the morning sun as it swung through the air. A thwack and a scream followed. The binoculars fell to the dock as Leonard stumbled backward with his injured arm pressed to his chest.

"Oh *shit*," Nessa gasped.

"Whoa," Jo said with an amused snort. "She did it." The violence hadn't disturbed her at all. She could feel the cells of her body tingling.

"After everything I did for you." Claude stepped toward him.

"Oh, you did it for *me*?" Leonard sneered through the pain. "So the money had nothing to do with it? Anything happens to me, and you won't see a cent. Everything I have will go to the whales."

"I loved you," Claude said just before the nine iron made contact with the side of his head. A spray of blood painted her outfit.

"Me?" Leonard sputtered. "Or Daddy?"

She swung again and caught him in the stomach. He barely had time to double over before Claude nailed him in the crotch. He fell to his knees, and she struck him in the back of the neck. And when he was flat on the ground, she kept swinging, bringing the nine iron up over her head and smashing it down against his motionless corpse.

She finally stopped when her legs wore a candy-apple coating of Leonard's blood. Then she looked down at the club and hurled it into the sound.

Nessa clapped a hand over her mouth. "Oh my sweet Lord," she whispered.

"That asshole helped kill all those girls," Jo said. "He deserved what he got."

But it wasn't the gore that had gotten to Nessa. As Claude walked back down the dock and up the stairs from the beach, she wasn't alone. Nessa could see the ghost of a pretty girl in a blue dress following closely behind her.

WHEN FAITH REID'S SERPENT
HELD ITS TONGUE

Her mother gave her the necklace for her thirteenth birthday. A coiled snake that dangled from a thin gold chain, it had nestled against her mother's sternum for twenty-five years. From the time she was little, Faith had been told that the pendant had been passed down through her family, and that the necklace came with a story. One day, both of them would be hers. This was that day.

"You know the story of the Garden of Eden," her mother said.

"Of course." Faith and her mother went to church every Sunday.

"The version you've heard is all wrong." Her mother reached out and lifted the serpent pendant from her daughter's skin. "They say the serpent came and tempted Eve to eat an apple from the tree of knowledge, and because of Eve's sin, mankind was banished from Eden. But that's not what happened at all."

"It's in the Bible," Faith argued. "It's God's word."

"God may have dictated the Bible, but it was put down on paper by men. And over the years, men have changed things that don't make them look good. In the original story, Eve was the hero, and this snake was her friend."

She let the serpent fall back to its new home on Faith's chest.

"You want to know what really happened?"

"Yes," Faith said. She did. More than anything.

"Well, they say God made man before woman. That part is true. But when he was done making Adam, he figured he could do a lot better, so he gave it another go. The second creation was superior to the first in every way but strength. She wasn't much of a match for all the lions and bears. So God decided to keep them both."

"I thought all the animals in Eden were tame," Faith argued.

Her mother lifted an eyebrow. "Don't kid yourself, girl. No animal is ever totally tame," she said. "They're either too lazy to eat you or waiting for just the right moment."

"Yeah? What about the snake?"

Her mother waved away the suggestion. "The snake lived in the tree of knowledge," her mother said. "It had all the juicy red apples it wanted."

Faith laughed. She loved her mother's strange stories.

"So one day, when Eve was taking a nap under that very same tree, the snake slithered down to her. It had waited till Adam wandered off so it could have a word with her alone."

"Where did Adam go?" Faith asked.

"Doesn't matter," her mother replied. "Eve's the hero of this story. And that's the first thing the snake told her. 'You are the best of God's creations,' he said. 'First came the animals, then Adam, then you. God kept getting better as he went along. He would have made you stronger, too. But he ran out of material. So you're just gonna have to stay on your toes.'"

"To fight off all those hungry animals?" Faith asked. What other dangers could a garden hold?

"No," her mother said. "The most dangerous beast in Eden was Adam."

"Adam?"

"He was God's first try at humans, remember? And from the outside, he was magnificent. Tall and sexy, with glistening skin and firm buttocks and—"

"Okay, Mama," Faith laughed.

"What I'm saying is, Adam was fine. But there was something wrong with him—the thing that had convinced God to try again. He'd just come off making the animals when he went to work on Adam, and he forgot to change one little thing. Like the animals, Adam was driven by bodily needs. When Adam wanted to rut, all the reason God gave him went right out the window. With animals, sex is natural. What made Adam so dangerous was his desire to dominate."

Faith stared at her mother in horror.

"I know, I know," her mother said. "You don't want to hear this. Believe me, Eve didn't either! But she listened, because she knew the snake was trying to help, and she asked it if there was anything she could do. 'Eat from the tree of knowledge,' it advised her. 'If you're ever going to make it out of Eden in one piece, you're gonna need to use your head.'"

"So she ate the apple and God kicked her and Adam out of Eden."

"Nope." Her mother's hoop earrings swayed as she shook her head. "When Eve ate the apple, she realized there was a whole world beyond Eden. The snake told her she could spend her life in a garden taking care of some man's insatiable needs—or she could see what else was out there. So she put on some clothes and went out to explore. What would you do if you were wearing her shoes?"

Faith didn't even need a moment to ponder the question. "Listen to the snake," she said.

"Good." Her mother was serious now. "Because from now on, it's going to talk to you. It's the voice in your head that whispers to you when you're in danger. Promise me that you'll always listen."

"I promise," Faith said.

"You're gonna meet lots of men in your life, and most of them will be harmless. Some will even be good. But stay far away from those who seem driven by their desires. Don't be one of the women who think they can feed those men. Those that do meet one of two fates. They either end up getting eaten—or they turn into monsters."

FAITH'S BELOVED MOTHER DIED THE following year, and the fourteen-year-old went to the other side of the island to live with her aunt. This was the side that the tourists flocked to, and there were twice as many men to look out for. Over the next three years, the snake kept Faith safe. It always knew which ones were bad news. Sometimes its warnings surprised her, but she always listened. When it told her to stay away from the friendly middle-aged man who ran the charity, she'd kept her distance.

Then one afternoon, a woman came to the restaurant where Faith worked and sat down at a table looking out over the Caribbean. She was delicate and pretty, but her voice was strong and her smile wide. Over the course of the meal Faith served her, they chatted about Faith's hopes and dreams. She was impressed that Faith worked all day and studied all night.

"Why don't you come back with me to the States?" she said. "I know an empty apartment you can have in Brooklyn, and I've got connections at all the best schools."

This time, the serpent stayed silent.

THE MONSTER

Claude rounded the corner and stopped. Someone had beat her to the swimming pool. A naked girl lounged on a float with her eyes closed, one arm tucked under her head, her other hand lazily dipped in the water. For a moment, Claude marveled at the girl's beauty. In New York, such physical perfection could be a bonanza for a decade or more. Here in south Florida, a young woman's expiration date arrived sooner. Everything ripened and rotted much faster down south.

"Hello?" Claude called out. She and Leonard had flown in less than an hour ago. One of the workers clearly hadn't gotten the news. She didn't mind, but she thought Leonard might. The staff at his New York townhouse was trained to remain unseen.

The girl lurched upright at the sound of Claude's voice, and the float almost capsized. When her eyes landed on Claude, she slid off into the water and held the float against her breasts.

"Sorry!" Claude did her best not to laugh. "I didn't mean to startle you. I thought you'd like to know that the owner is coming. I don't want you to get into trouble."

The braces on the girl's teeth glinted. She was younger than Claude had first thought. Fifteen. Maybe sixteen. Just old enough for a work permit. This was probably her very first job. "Are you his wife?" the girl asked.

Claude had to laugh. "No," she said. "I'm here to help renovate the property." She and Leonard had discussed marriage, but everything felt wonderful just as it was. She didn't want to mess with the magic. Claude walked down to the edge of the pool and held out the towel she'd brought with her. "Who are you?"

The girl hesitated, then she swam to the edge of the water and accepted the towel. "I'm Clio," she said.

"What do you do here?" Claude asked.

"What?" Clio's eyes went wide for a moment. "Oh no, I don't work here. I live in town."

Claude stopped smiling. Town was ten miles away. "Does your mom know you're out here?"

"She dropped me off," Clio replied.

"How did you get on the property? Who let you in?"

"Leonard gave me the pass code the last time he was here," Clio said.

"*Leonard*," Claude repeated.

"Oh no," Clio groaned. "You're his girlfriend, aren't you?"

"How old are you, Clio?" Claude asked.

SHE HADN'T *TRUSTED* HIM. TRUST hadn't been necessary. Leonard had saved her. Since the day they met, he had denied her nothing. He gave her his fortune, his time, and his heart. Leonard fell asleep every night with his arms wrapped around her. He woke up early each morning to make her coffee. If he went away for more than a day, he always brought something back for her. He had a knack for choosing just what she'd want.

Everything she had, Claude realized, Leonard had given her. Happiness, freedom, respect. She'd rebuilt her whole world on the foundation he'd offered. Now that ground was heaving beneath her. She felt fissures forming and concrete cracking. A yawning abyss opened up in front of her, and she teetered, her toes over the edge.

CLAUDE GRABBED A CROQUET BALL off the grass as she made her way from the pool to the house. Her mascara was running and her vision was blurred when she threw the ball at Leonard's head. Otherwise, she wouldn't have missed.

"What the hell?" he asked, captivated by the hole the croquet ball had left in the wall.

"I met Clio," she snarled.

That scared him. Leonard held up his hands. "Claude—"

"I'm calling the police, you fucking monster. That girl is sixteen years old." She never would have guessed he'd be one of those men. Not in a million years.

"Sixteen is the age of consent in many states."

"Not here."

Leonard nodded. He kept his cool. "If you think you should call the police, you should do it," he said. "But it will be the end of your career."

"Are you threatening me?" Claude shrieked.

"No, no," Leonard assured her. "I would never do that. I swear, whatever you decide, I'll accept it. I won't take any action against you. But everyone you work with has something to hide. I'm not the only man with a taste for young women. They'll all praise you for your bravery, but they'll never invite you into their homes again. You'll be right back where you were after your father died."

That hadn't occurred to her. "I don't care. I can't let you victimize little girls."

"Victimize?" Leonard scoffed. "Did Clio seem unhappy to you? The money I give her keeps her off the street. Hell, Clio's mother pays one of our cleaning staff to tell her when I'm coming to town. Then she drops her daughter off at my house. Everyone's getting what they want right now. Do you have any idea what could happen to that girl if you go to the cops?"

What *would* happen? Clio would be stuck with a mother who wasn't going to win any awards for her parenting. Leonard would hire the best lawyers and get off with a slap on the wrist at most. Clio would be broke, and so would Claude. Whatever justice they received would come at a hefty price.

"This is how things work, Claude. That girl is lucky. There are far worse men in the world than me."

"Like who?" she wanted to know.

"You really want me to tell you?"

"Yes, I do. But first, write me a check," Claude ordered.

"For how much?" Leonard asked, as if it were nothing to him.

"Enough money so Clio never has to come back here."

"Sure," Leonard said with a shrug. It made no difference to him.

"And then sit down and make me a list."

"A list of what?" he asked.

"All the men you know who are worse than you."

LEONARD SWORE HE'D NEVER LIE again. He promised complete transparency. He bought her father's mansion on the Brittany coast and secretly had it reassembled, stone by stone, on land he'd purchased off the coast of New York, on a peninsula that jutted out into the sea. It was such a beautiful present. Maybe, Claude thought, they could make it all work.

THE RULES OF THE CULLING Pointe community were as follows: Summers were family time. Girls were only allowed off-season. No girls under sixteen were permitted, and nothing rough was allowed. No girl would be brought to the Pointe more than once. Each girl would be paid enough so she never felt the need to come back. Every man on the Pointe would contribute five million dollars to

Leonard's charities each year. Claude would oversee how the money was spent.

The girls she chose had to meet three criteria: They had to need the money. Their parents needed to be distracted, on drugs, or dead. And the girls needed to be innocent—the element of surprise had to work in Claude's favor. Wherever she traveled, she would look for girls. And wherever she went, she would find them. Most of them were smart enough to avoid middle-aged men. None of them ever questioned Claude's motives.

She had a pep talk she would give the girls who cried afterward. What you just received was a shot in the arm, she would tell them. A little dose of ugliness. A glimpse of the way things really work in this world. You survived, and now you're not only immune— you're stronger than you were before. Take the money you've made and the wisdom you've earned and put them both to good use. That's what I've done, she'd say. Claude had said it so many times that she'd come to mean it.

She had a different chat with the few who seemed inclined to take their stories to the police. Do you know what would happen to you? she'd ask. We have the country's best lawyers on retainer. If there were ever a trial, you would certainly lose. After that, every time anyone searched for your name online, they'd know you were a prostitute. We would ensure that the stories never went away. We would sue you for defamation of character and take every dime you ever earn. We would haunt you for the rest of your life. Claude only had to say that a handful of times. But she believed that speech, too.

It all worked like a charm. The arrangement couldn't have been more ideal. Claude had found a way to make sure everyone got what they wanted.

Until Spencer Harding arrived.

She'd never wanted him on the Pointe. She'd heard whispers

about his lifestyle during her art world days. Back then, interns at his gallery were forced to sign lengthy NDAs, and few stayed for long. Spencer had never married, and he had no family. Even in middle age, his reputation was far from pristine. Claude told Leonard they didn't have enough leverage to keep him under control. There was no guarantee he'd obey the Pointe's rules.

She was supposed to have the final word on such things, and that word was no. Then Spencer got married. He promised twice the yearly fee. Her answer remained no.

"I think we should be a little more flexible," Leonard said. Claude later learned that he'd already signed off on Spencer's lease.

After Rosamund told her about the girl who never showed up, Claude spoke to the police herself. Chief Rocca assured Claude that the girl came from a bad family and had likely run away. But he drove out to the Pointe to speak to the Hardings nonetheless. The girl was never located, but Rocca stuck around.

For the men of the Pointe, Rocca's presence was emboldening. He refused to look directly at Claude—or speak to her with any hint of respect. It had been easy to keep the other men in line. She had files on each of them, should she ever need the leverage. But she had nothing on Rocca. Claude, whose favor everyone on the Pointe had once curried, was now spoken about as a nuisance.

Then she found Faith. The girl had caught Leonard's eye in Jamaica but refused to give him the time of day. Claude brought her back to deliver a message: only she could have wrangled the headstrong beauty. She took the Polaroids for Leonard. Faith was a special gift, and it seemed fitting to let him choose the wrapping. But Leonard was worried the girl would fight. He told Claude to give Faith to Spencer instead.

"A little gift to win him over," he'd said.

The next morning, the girl was missing.

"Where's Faith?" Claude demanded. "Did you kill her? Where's the body?"

"It's been taken care of," Spencer said. "That's why we need Rocca. No woman has the stomach to do what he does."

Claude knew it wouldn't stop there, and it didn't. Spencer had Rosamund killed. Two dead girls were found at the bottom of the ocean. The disease was spreading.

So Claude googled aconite. Then she pulled up a few of the plants Harriett Osborne had mentioned and tossed them into her juicer. It was easy to replace the fluid used to sanitize Spencer's helicopter— and she made sure the cleaning person wore a new set of gloves.

BURN IT DOWN

Between the flowering bushes that had overtaken Jackson Dunn's yard, Jo and Nessa waited for Claude to come up the stairs from the beach. Blood splatter decorated her shorts and white shirt, and a bright red smear stretched from one temple to the other where she'd wiped her eyes with the back of her hand.

"He knew," she muttered, as though the fact still astounded her.

"You did what you had to do," Jo assured Claude. "Nessa and I will help you dispose of the body."

"Oh no, we won't," Nessa announced. She saw what Jo couldn't. Her eyes were locked on the ghost of Faith Reid, who'd followed Claude up the stairs.

Nessa thought of the Polaroids of Faith posed in front of a mirror. Before she died, the girl had been dressed for something important. Someone took those photos. Someone wanted to make sure she chose just the right outfit.

"No?" Jo asked as Claude came to a stop in front of them, Faith beside her. "Why not?"

"Claude took the picture you found in the locker." They stood silently, surrounded by the bright blast and heady scent of the flowers around them. Claude's lips stayed sealed.

"How do you know?" Jo asked.

"Faith is telling me," Nessa said. "Claude brought her here. Faith wouldn't have trusted a man, but she went along with you, didn't she, Claude?"

Claude's face was grim. "I never expected Spencer to kill her," she said.

The confession hit Jo like a blow to the gut. "Oh my God," she gasped. "What *did* you expect?"

"I expected her to leave the Pointe with enough money to build a bright future. That's how it was supposed to work."

"How it was supposed to work?" Jo repeated.

"But instead, she was murdered," Nessa said. "Like Mandy Welsh and a dozen other girls who were brought here."

"I didn't know anyone other than Faith had died. There were rules the men here were supposed to follow. They ignored me."

"So you were in charge?" Jo felt rage building inside her.

"She supplied girls," Nessa said. "They trusted her because she's a woman. She betrayed them."

"I made sure the girls I brought here weren't harmed," Claude argued. "Rocca was the one who changed all of that."

"Let me get this straight—you were okay with the girls being raped, but you drew the line at murder?" Jo asked.

"They needed money, and they got it! I even made the men donate to charities that build schools for girls around the world. I got Leonard to hand over millions of dollars to train young women in self-defense."

"So they could protect themselves from people like you?"

Nessa crossed her arms over her chest. "While girls were being raped and killed, this bitch was living like a queen. And the perverts got to call themselves philanthropists."

"Nothing's going to stop them from doing what they want to do," Claude argued. "These are some of the richest men in the country. For God's sake, they had the chief of police bringing them girls. The only thing I could do was make sure some good came out of it all. For fuck's sake, Jo. Their money is helping us teach girls how to protect themselves from predators! Some of their money funded your husband's new play!"

Jo could feel the fire shooting through her veins and waves of energy traveling down her limbs. She saw heat ripples radiating from her skin and smelled the grass singeing beneath her feet. She'd tried her best to control it. Now Jo closed her eyes and let go. Nothing had ever felt so good.

She knew then what she was meant to do. She knew why Nessa had found her. Nessa was the light in the darkness. Harriett was the punishment that fit the crime. She was the rage that would burn it all to the ground.

"You know what's going to happen, right?" she asked Nessa.

"Yes," Nessa told her. "I do now."

"Jo," Claude begged, "think of all the good you can do!"

"Oh, I am," Jo assured her.

When Jo opened her eyes again, they fell on one of the yellow bushes. She reached out and grasped the tip of a flower-covered branch between two of her fingers. A thin wisp of smoke wafted up from between them. When Jo let go, a tiny flame was glowing at the tip of the branch. She leaned over and blew gently, and the entire bush burst into flame. The flames leaped to a nearby bush and soon it, too, was ablaze.

Jo began to laugh. It started with a snicker, but then she just couldn't stop. Several more bushes were already burning.

"Can you believe we were worried about Harriett?" Jo could barely get the words out. "She planted these fucking bushes. She's known what would happen since Memorial Day."

That's when Claude bolted, zigzagging between the burning bushes and disappearing in the direction of the mansion her father had bought after he'd stolen his first fortune. The house her partner had shipped across the ocean and rebuilt to say he was sorry. The estate she'd shared with the man she'd just killed.

"Should I chase her down?" Jo asked.

Nessa looked over at Faith, who was already fading. The girl smiled as she shook her head.

"Naw, let her go," Nessa answered. "Harriett had this all planned out. Claude isn't going to last very long."

Then the two women walked arm in arm through the burning bushes, then down the road toward the Culling Pointe gate.

HARRIETT STOOD ON THE DECK of the boat, eating an apple as she watched the smoke rise from the Pointe. One by one, the mansions along the south beach burst into flames.

"The fire is traveling fast." Celeste was watching through binoculars. "I'm surprised none of the houses have sprinkler systems."

"They do. Isabel dealt with them the last time she watered the plants," Harriett said. "May I borrow the binoculars? There's a painting I'd like to see go up in flames."

With the binoculars to her eyes, she watched with great satisfaction as the Richard Prince nurse was put out of her misery. A slight turn to the right, and she could see Jackson Dunn's roof deck being consumed by the blaze.

"It's time." Harriett pulled Celeste to her and kissed her. "Meet me at Danskammer Beach?"

"See you there," Celeste said.

Harriett pulled off her dress, grabbed an empty backpack off the deck, and dove into the water.

WHEN HARRIETT WAS TWELVE YEARS old, she watched her father push her mother down the stairs. She listened to him lie through his teeth when the police arrived. And she knew his friends on the police force would never question a word her God-fearing father said.

No one in a uniform bothered to ask Harriett what had happened. She sat with her mother's corpse until the men from the morgue finally came to collect it.

The night after her mother's funeral, Harriett cooked dinner for herself and her father. Steak, potatoes, and a side dish of mushrooms that she'd picked in the yard. She ate just enough of the mushrooms to spend the night vomiting. Her father was dead within hours.

Only Harriett knew for sure what had happened to her mother, but everyone in town must have suspected the truth. Men like her father couldn't hide their real natures from everyone. So the actions she'd taken made perfect sense to her. Her father should have been punished. He'd cheated his way out of it, and she'd made things all fair and square.

The problem was, no one else felt that way. Not Harriett's grandparents, who escorted her to church twice a week. Not the other churchgoers, who refused to share the same pew. It was her Sunday school classmates who gave her the nickname that stuck with her through high school. Even after she'd learned to keep her head down and play by the rules, they continued to call her the Bad Seed.

After graduation, she'd moved a thousand miles to escape the taunts, but thirty years after she'd gone east, she could still hear them. She'd even avoided having children, terrified of what she might bequeath to them. Then one day, at forty-eight, Harriett found herself all alone in her garden. Everywhere she looked, she saw the fight for survival. Bugs spraying birds with foul-smelling chemicals. Plants that fought fungi with their own brand of poison. And then her eyes landed on a cluster of death cap mushrooms growing near one of the trees. She remembered what she'd been thinking the day she picked some just like them: that her father had to be stopped or someone else would be next. Who knew how many lives had been spared by her act of destruction? How much misery would that one man have spread? Maybe other women would have been able to steer clear of him, but Harriett knew one thing for certain: she wouldn't have survived if she hadn't done what she did.

Other women brought life into the world. Harriett realized at that moment what her gift would be.

CLAUDE MADE IT OUT OF the mansion with mere seconds to spare. When she heard the roof give way, she didn't look back. She knew the sight would destroy her.

There was enough data on her computer to ensure she wouldn't suffer. Names, photos, and videos—each worth a fortune. She'd been collecting for years. In the back of her mind, she must have known this day would come. She'd even kept the laptop in a waterproof case.

Claude set the case down in the dinghy they kept where the tide couldn't reach it. Then she dragged the boat to the water's edge. She felt a wave of heat hit her back, and she knew the beach grass had caught fire.

The sound of a splash startled her, and she turned to see a woman rising out of the surf wearing only a backpack. Naked and larger than life, Harriett grinned.

"I told you I'd get rid of the bushes," she said.

Claude knew why Harriett had come. "Let me leave," she begged. "I swear, I'll give you anything."

"Thanks!" Harriett reached into the boat and took the case. "This should do." She unzipped it and cracked open the laptop. "Password?"

"You'll really let me go?"

"I always keep my promises," Harriett said. "The boat is yours."

"A-M-six-seven-nine-eight."

"Your father's initials and the day he died. How poignant." Harriett typed in the password and nodded. "Thank you!"

She returned the laptop to its case and slipped it into her back-pack. Then she turned and walked back into the water. Within seconds, she'd vanished beneath the waves.

Claude dragged the boat to the water and climbed inside. As she rowed away from shore, she was forced to confront the burning house. She saw Leonard's beloved grill explode, and she watched the propane tank fly through the sky.

Harriett surfaced at a safe distance from the destruction—just close enough to enjoy Claude Marchand's final scream as the pro-pane tank hurtled straight toward her boat.

FRANKLIN WAS SPEEDING DOWN DANSKAMMER Beach Road when he saw Nessa and Jo walking toward town, the fire on Culling Pointe raging behind them. He threw the car into park and left it idling with the driver's-side door standing open as he ran to Nessa and threw his arms around her.

"Are you all right?"

"I'm fine," Nessa told him. *Better than fine*, she thought.

"The girls told me you were out here. Why didn't you call me?" he asked.

"It was just supposed to be me and Jo out there today," Nessa said. Like Jo, she now knew it to be true. Harriett had planned it all. "Your part's going to come soon enough. There are a dozen girls out there who need their names back."

"Look!" Jo pointed across the water. Someone was swimming toward them.

They walked through the scrub to the beach, where a woman was emerging from the surf, naked but for a backpack. Her body shone like bronze under the sun.

"That was fun, wasn't it?" Harriett asked.

EPILOGUE

Jo watched her twelve-year-old daughter bound toward the car, dressed in the chic black uniform she'd worn to self-defense class. Thanks to generous funding from the Leonard Shaw estate, every girl in Jo's ever-expanding program had received one.

"There were only three papers left!" Lucy climbed into the SUV. "Everyone in Mattauk is reading the review of Dad's play!"

Jo glanced over at the stack of *New York Times* on her daughter's lap. "JOHN WILLIS, BILLIONAIRE PHILANTHROPIST, DEAD AT 59." The photo beneath the headline showed the famously bespectacled titan of industry standing on the terrace, forty-nine floors above the streets of Manhattan, where his body had been discovered. Security footage had captured the middle-aged mogul's bizarre death. Ornithologists could only cite one other example of a human being mobbed and killed by a flock of seagulls. From what Jo had gleaned from the gossip going around, it was true that animals did indeed go first for the lips, nose, and anus.

"It's a good day to have a review in the *Times,* that's for sure," Jo said. And an even better day to have the theater critic refer to your first Off-Broadway production as a "triumph." "Text Dad and tell him to pick up seven more copies before he drives home from the city."

She turned off Mattauk's Main Street and onto a road that would bypass town and take them straight to the beach. Lucy's head was still bent toward her phone when Jo brought the car to a sudden stop. "Holy shit," Jo said. "It's true." One of her clients had told her, but she hadn't quite believed it.

"What?" Lucy lifted her head and let out a cackle. The monstrous weeds around Brendon Baker's old house had vanished— and the For Sale sign in the front yard now exclaimed *Sold!* "It's like it never even happened. Where did he move?"

"Back to the city," Jo said. "I heard he told the agent he wanted to be surrounded by asphalt."

Lucy tittered. "Dumbass," she said. "Doesn't he know that won't stop Harriett?"

"I think Harriett's too busy for a man like Brendon Baker these days."

"But she'll be at lunch, right?" Lucy looked worried. She was bringing a tart she'd learned how to make at Mattauk's popular new cooking academy for kids. The dewberries had come from Harriett's own garden.

"She promised, didn't she?" Jo asked. "Harriett always keeps her promises."

NESSA AND FRANKLIN SAT SIDE by side on the sand at Danskammer Beach. Though they'd both retired, a lifetime of discipline had left them both early risers. Every morning, as soon as there was enough sunlight to see, they'd set off on a stroll. It wasn't unusual for them to return home in the afternoon. This morning, they'd walked east from the cottage, following the shoreline past the public beaches, Grass Beach, and the Mattauk marina. When they were halfway along Danskammer Beach, Nessa had stopped.

"You want to head back?" Franklin asked. The girls were coming out for the weekend, and Nessa had invited Jo and Harriett for lunch.

"Why don't we rest here for a second," Nessa said. She often drove out to sit in the same spot. The dead girls were gone now, their spirits at rest. Faith's and Mandy's families knew what had happened. But the third girl had no one else to mourn her, so Nessa did.

Her name, they'd discovered, was Mei Jones. A fifteen-year-old girl who'd lost her parents in a car accident, she'd come to Mattauk to live with the chief of police and his wife as a foster child. According to Juliet Rocca, the girl had disappeared the night after she arrived. It wasn't uncommon, she was told, for foster children to run away before settling into a new home. Juliet had insisted her husband open a missing persons file, but no leads ever came in. After Mei's disappearance, Juliet spent months trying to hunt down any family members. She later learned no report had ever been filed.

The medical examiner couldn't say for sure how they'd murdered her. But there was no doubt Mei had died on Culling Pointe. Nessa raked her eyes down the charred peninsula. Nothing had survived the fire. And nothing would ever be built there again. Leonard had left the land to a whale conservation group. They had already confirmed that Culling Pointe would forever remain undeveloped and barren.

"You good?" Franklin took Nessa's hand. The wedding ring she'd worn for so long now hung from a chain around her neck.

Nessa looked over at him and smiled. "Yeah, I'm good," she told him.

HARRIETT GLANCED UP AT THE sun. Every minute she had to spend with Lucy was precious, and she didn't want to be late for lunch. If they got to the boat soon, she and Celeste could be back to Mattauk by noon.

The garden they'd come to visit was lovely—perhaps the prettiest in all of East Hampton. In late spring, it opened to the public for two days. Harriett could see it was tired of putting on a show. It wanted to be free of shears and mowers. And the man who spent his summers in the nearby mansion didn't deserve to enjoy its blooms or its fragrances.

She'd met the man once, years before. He was the CEO of the holding company that owned a third of the ad agencies in Manhattan, including the company that had just dumped Max—and the one that still employed Chase and his second wife, who'd soon give birth to the couple's first child. The CEO's name had leaped out to Harriett when she'd gone through Claude's files. She'd assumed always he was just a garden-variety dick like her old boss and her ex-husband. Instead, she learned he'd been a frequent guest at Culling Pointe.

"Beautiful," Harriett said. They'd arrived at a rustic wooden arbor with a bench half hidden by wisteria vines.

"The article in *Gardens Illustrated* said he comes here to think," Celeste told her.

"Perfect," Harriett said. "Let's give him something to think about."

She pulled a glass tube from her pocket. Celeste took a step back as Harriett kneeled on the grass and unscrewed the metal cap, in which she'd drilled several small holes. "Here you go, ladies." She placed the tube on the ground and watched with pleasure as its three eight-legged occupants scuttled straight for the bench.

ACKNOWLEDGMENTS

So many women helped bring this book to life.

My mother, Katherine Miller, who relished nothing more than a righteous fight.

My childhood best friend, Erica Waldrop, the model for every delinquent with a heart of gold in my books.

Patricia Berne and Fitzallen Eldridge, who inspired and encouraged a weird little girl.

All the women of Barnard, but especially Joan Rivers.

Lilian Schein, whose kindness and generosity made it possible for me to stay in New York.

Susan Roy and Leeanne Leahy, the brilliant strategists who gave me my first jobs in advertising.

Suzanne Gluck, my firecracker agent, whose advice I've relied on for fifteen years.

Andrea Blatt at WME, who made this book so much better than it was.

Sanjana Seelam and MK Goss at WME, who acted as its tireless champions.

Rachel Kahan at William Morrow, who I knew was my editor the moment I met her.

Manpreet Grewal at HQ Fiction, whose enthusiasm is wonderfully infectious.

And the women at Made Up Stories, who are currently working some magic of their own.